VANISHING BY DEGREES

VANISHING BY DEGREES

A Novel

David Orsini

VANISHING BY DEGREES

First Edition Quaternity™ Books 2019

Quaternity™ Books

ISBN 978-1-943691-13-5
Cover Design by James Buchanan

Other Books by David Orsini

The Woman Who Loved Too Well
The Ghost Lovers
The Subtleties of Seduction
Bitterness / Seven Stories

Forthcoming Books
Schemes, Disguises, & Traps
The Weaver of Plots

CONTENTS

1	Arrival	9
2	Hiding and Vanishing	31
3	Preliminary Rules	41
4	Ari Bachman	57
5	The Night of the Dance	73
6	Boyd's Girlfriend	87
7	Brenda Flynn	101
8	Kurt Drexler's Plot	129
9	Three Deaths	163
10	Boyd Henderson	183
11	Confessions, Doubts, and Promises	201
12	Verdicts	221
13	The First Test	243
14	The Second Test	265
15	The Third Test	289
	Study Guide	323

CHAPTER ONE
ARRIVAL

The lift-off comes when we are least expecting it. We ascend as if our bodies are space capsules hurling through an endless void beyond the rims of earth. We've been told to be ready at all times. So familiar are the days that precede it, though, so apparently safe from malevolent harm or from murderous enemies, that we are no longer anticipating the rapid fire of a rifle or the barrage of bullets tearing through our flesh and hurling us across the long corridors. Those corridors, spattered with our blood and cluttered with our crumpled or sprawling bodies, go on gleaming with polished surfaces and with the afternoon light of the June sun that streams incandescent rivulets through the panoramic windows. But the sunlight cannot retain the tranquil glow that, only minutes earlier, it brought to the southwest wing of our school in Green Hills, Maine. The glow has turned eerie, touching as it does our fallen and disfigured bodies.

There has been no Code Red warning. There has been only our split-second awareness that a killer is in our midst and firing bullets from his AR-15.

Even my ability to predict the future has failed me. My devious ways have clouded my foresight. I have not anticipated this terrifying moment when a killer is rushing upon us.

"It's Henderson!" Dion Williams shouts, his deep, usually assured voice tightening with fear. The jagged sounds of the shooting cause all of us to turn and to pause, though only for a moment. A tall figure at the opposite end of the hall is heading toward us. He is wearing a helmet, a camouflage combat uniform, a flak vest, and army boots. His large, rough hands are grasping the AR-15 that he has just fired. He *is* Henderson. He's often posted photos of himself on Facebook and on Instagram wearing that same uniform and wielding the same rifle. With swift strides he is moving toward us, past the sprawled and bleeding body of Ms. Patel, our biology teacher, and past the bullet-battered body of Mr. Marchand, our Advanced French teacher and our JROTC instructor.

"He's shooting at us!" Dion yells, still not quite believing what he sees.

Henderson keeps firing his rifle, moving with methodical steps toward us.

The eleven of us, close friends ever since we bonded in the first grade, have been walking at a brisk pace. We left our biology class only minutes earlier and are making our way at the end of the crowd of other juniors and seniors that, like ourselves, are hurrying on to their next classes in the southwest wing. Now, without another word, we eleven friends and the twenty other students who are there turn from Boyd Henderson and race across the corridor, weighed down though we are by our backpacks and impeded by our scrambling and jostling. Some of us bump against one another. Some of us push forward the hastening figures in front of us. A few of us scream with terror.

A bullet flies into Alessandro Bianchi, who has been running beside me. His forehead blows open, and brain tissue scatters on the air and on my left shoulder in the same instant that his long, muscular body keels over, rests momentarily on his knees, and then falls face down.

I keep running, pushing my way with zigzagging trajectory beyond Jayden McDonald, Dion Williams, Shiloh Jackson, and Ari Bachman as bullets mow them down.

I race past our computer wiz Jason Teng, beautiful Chloe Bradbury, and good-natured Brenda Flynn as they fall away behind me. The rat-tat-tat of Henderson's rifle is singeing the air with the velocity and heat of its bullets.

I run faster, always zigzagging through the long corridor ahead of me. I feel flushed. I hear my ragged breathing.

I trip over the fallen body of Sonia Janowski, the sheen of her amber blonde flowing hair covered in blood and with bits of her flesh.

Then, suddenly, our school's champion swimmer Abigail Emerson and I are the only ones running.

I am only vaguely aware that she is falling.

In those final moments, there flashes through my mind the full realization that I am not going to reach the emergency exit door that stands a hundred feet ahead of me. I, Cassandra Winslow, having lived for a mere eighteen years, am being thrown out of life.

"It isn't fair!" my mind protests and then protests once more. "It isn't fair!"

I wince at the burning sensation of the bullets entering my back and the sight of the blood gushing out of my chest. I hear, though only for an instant, the thud-thud-thud of the bullets just before they cut their way into my neck and blow massive holes into my brain.

I die in that very moment, the world that I had known so briefly scattering away into explosive flashes of darkness and coiling back into its own brightness that I can no longer fathom.

This is the moment of my liftoff. My Spirit springs free of my earthbound body. My whole being glows as though it is a ghostly spacecraft in search of a mystical orbit. All at once I am a Shadow, traveling on a beam of light into a supernatural reality.

I go out of ordinary time and enter the world not of the dead. I have left my dead self far behind me, back there, within Earth that is time-trapped and temporary. Sojourn, the new world that I enter, is also time-bound. But it is tethered to a more quickened, supernatural time that precedes the journey into the Eternal. Spirits, Shadows, and Shades live here. It is a vast world that never seems crowded. Apparitions, Phantoms, and Specters also reside here. Capacious rooms and long, wide halls and corridors fan out with sinuous velocity. Space keeps winding and curving and meandering even as it spreads its voluminous dimensions into still wider rooms, corridors, fields, plains, avenues, and whole cities.

Eventually, in varying episodes here in Sojourn and back on Earth, I shall be a Shadow, an Apparition, and a Phantom. During the first months of my training in the Afterlife, I shall acquire the appropriate powers of each kind of ghost. Right now, my being is entirely a Spirit only at times. For the first months after my death and all through my training in ghostliness, I shall appear to be full-bodied, even though my body of flesh and blood, yoked as it is to the Spirit-Life informing it, is vanishing by nearly imperceptible degrees. Gradually, I shall be a fully radiant Spirit.

So Mr. Steerforth explains, shortly after our arrival here. Our orientation packet of information tells us that his first name is

Robert. He is answering Dion's question about why our bodies sometimes glow so brightly that the light appears to consume or conceal them or, possibly, makes them disappear.

"The light here has a way of doing that," Mr. Steerforth calmly answers him. "For now, Spirit-light will take hold of you every once in a while. It wants you to get used to it. It wants you to be comfortable. So don't you or your classmates or your teachers worry about losing your bodies and turning into Spirits. Each of you has always been a Spirit. Now you need to learn how to be a Spirit without a body."

My earliest experience of the supernatural world is this meeting with Mr. Steerforth. He is a manager of things here, though he is not the commanding officer. Call him a meticulous advisor, if you like. He is one of the leaders who will decide what is going to happen to our group now that we are dead to our earthly lives. But I'll tell you more about that later.

First, I want to tell you more about Sojourn. It is a natural satellite of Earth that is located in a transitional space between our homes in Green Hills, Maine, and the First Heaven. It is a haven and a temporary place for those of us who are waiting to make the journey to The First Heaven. Sojourn is invisible to even the largest telescopes, the swiftest spacecraft, and the most advanced NASA instruments. We, the earthly dead who have recently arrived here only to discover that we are not dead in Sojourn, have not lost our memories of Earth or our yearning to return to the places that knew us well and the people that gave us their unconditional love. Perhaps, we shall never lose that memory or that yearning. But we are millions of miles away from Earth, which is The Second Heaven and the one that most human beings never recognize as a treasure beyond price and as a world filled with miracle workers and beneficent Spirits.

"Some folks do manage to see Earth for what it is, though," Mr. Steerforth tells the thirteen of us during the first day of our orientation. "A few philosophers, maybe, and a poet or two. Surgeons, nurses, schoolteachers, scientists, and caring parents—the ones who value life and who always work to make things better."

As he speaks, his lanky body sometimes glows. Its amber sheen moves in and out of brightness that on this first day leaves us awed in an altogether different way. I wonder whether he is a god or some holy messenger. Whenever the brightness covering him becomes dim, we see Mr. Steerforth as the man he must have been in the moment that he died. His oblong face, with its forehead, cheekbones, and jawline similar in size; his slightly tousled dark hair; and his well-groomed beard give him the look of a college professor who may be in his mid-thirties or even forty.

Jayden McDonald has the same idea.

"Were you a college professor?" he asks.

"I was a vice-president of a steel corporation in Pennsylvania."

"Did you like it?"

"I had a great life. I enjoyed every minute of it."

"You must miss it very much."

"In the beginning I did. But I've learned to accept who I am now. All of you will, too, eventually."

"How?" Sonia Janowski, with her scientific interests, asks him. "How did you die?"

"A brain aneurysm. It was a quick death."

"When?"

"Sixty-two years ago."

"Where did it happen?" Jason Teng, our high school's computer wiz, inquires.

"I was involved in a symposium of global business leaders. It was a lovely summer day in Brazil. I'd been speaking to ninety-nine other corporate leaders about the importance of diversifying our products and our markets. I believed that what I was saying was meaningful and helpful. I felt that everyone who was in that room appreciated what I was saying. I remember thinking that I was living through one of my happiest days. That was my last thought before I keeled over and fell away from the speaker's podium. That was the moment I died, without a warning and without a chance to say goodbye to my wife, our two sons, and our daughter."

Ari Bachman quietly studies him. He begins to regard him now as one like all of us.

"You know then," he says. "You know the pain that doesn't leave you. You know how it feels to be cut off from earthly life when there are so many years that you haven't lived."

"Yes," Mr. Steerforth answers him. "I know. It's true that I lived twenty-five years more than most of you lived. But I wasn't supposed to die at the age of forty-two. My father lived for ninety-six years. My doctor thought I was going to live to be a hundred. Only a week before I died, he told me that I was in fine shape. But that's how life is. Sometimes, it plays tricks on us."

His brown eyes look straight at us with interest and even enthusiasm. Death has not deprived him of his keen-eyed glance or of his easy-going manner, anchored as it is to a gentleman's reserve. Right away, we know where we stand with him. There will be no pretense between us. There will be no hedging of truth or casual lies meant to keep us from dealing with the tragedy that has enfolded us.

"You'll get used to the way things are now," he tells us, nudging us toward a hope that now seems impossible for us to attain. "You'll stop feeling sorry for yourselves."

He pauses, observing the effect of his words upon us, here in the conference room where we are seated at a long table suitable for a symposium that invites questions and answers and an exchange of ideas. The thought enters my mind that such a table, with its mahogany sheen and its solid structure, might also be suitable in a Hall of Justice, where prosecutors and judges oversee grueling interrogations. But, with the wiliness that has often served me well, I push that dark thought down into the deeper corner of my awareness. I want to believe that Mr. Steerforth is really on our side. My intuition tells me that he will always be on the level with us. But he will also call a spade a spade. When he evaluates the ways that we conducted ourselves while we were alive on Earth, he may not be as friendly as he appears to be. My insight tells me about the easygoing man he used to be. My knack for interpreting the future sends ominous flares about his more recently acquired hardheartedness as a Spirit who is both hunter and prosecutor.

I suppress my apprehension. I concentrate on this specific moment.

Now all of us are listening with the concentration that his words merit. In this hour at least, he understands our sorrow and our longing to go back to the life that has finished with us too soon. Even when Ari cries out angrily, his voice stifling deep sobs, Mr. Steerforth understands.

"I want to go back," Ari says, his words rising out of his angry whisper and finding the deeper notes of a plea. "I want to be with my mother and my father. I want to see my brother and my sister. I want to ask them to forgive me."

The room falls silent, though only for a moment. Ari has dared to reveal his emotions. He has broken the silent pact that has always existed between each of us separately and with all the others we have called our friends and acquaintances.

Now Ari's anguished crying pierces through the silence. The cries that he tries to suppress rack his muscular frame and leave him breathless and despairing. He is not used to crying. He was a cross-country champion, a goalkeeper for the soccer team, and a first-rate boxer. His manly self-image has never before permitted crying. His face is flushed, and tears roll down his cheeks. If we were back at school on the Earth that has abandoned us, some of us girls and a couple of his soccer teammates might hurry to comfort him, once we had gone past our awkward hesitation. But Ari's cries are filled with such profound grief, and his body is so contorted by the pain of even deeper sobbing that we do not move from our chairs. Instead, straining to maintain control, yet failing, all of my classmates burst into angry tears and bitter moaning. Even Ms. Patel begins to weep, discreetly covering her face with her hands while our wailing unsettles the precise orderliness of the conference room. Only Mr. Marchand refuses to weep. War-hardened and fatalistic, he and Death are no strangers. On many battlefields in Afghanistan, he has seen his friends die, and he has killed enemies. Now Death has overtaken him. It was in the cards. It was his fate. Weeping won't change things.

Instantly, three women who are Mr. Steerforth's assistants leave their places at the table and hurry to comfort those of us who are crying or, at least, to help us tamp down our fears. They bring us rallying words and soothing water from Sojourn's magical springs. Here, in this supernatural region, we require no other food or drink.

One of these women is big-bodied, tough-minded, and unsentimental. The other two are very slim and immaculately groomed. Later, we shall learn that the two women who come forward to greet us first of all are sisters and that they spent their earthly lives in Boston, Massachusetts. Today, they appear to be separated by a generation, though our group will learn in the days to come that they were born within a year of one another. They died a few years after they entered their nineties. The older, big-bodied sister, who appears to be nearly forty, is Mrs. Howard Adams. The other Spirits sometimes address her as Maggie. She is the first to come forward to greet us. When she was alive on earth, she was a registered nurse who assisted her husband in his practice of internal medicine. She and her husband were the same age. But he died when he was thirty-eight, shot down with their three children by a teen-age serial killer at a ski resort in Aspen, Colorado.

The second woman coming forward to greet us is Mrs. Adams' sister, Miss Melanie Dickinson. Today, she appears to be a blue-eyed blonde woman of twenty-two. The man that she loved saw her on Earth for the last time when she was that age. That was the year when her fiancé, Captain Randall Johnson, was killed in the Second World War. Always, during the many years she lived on earth without him, she worried that in the Afterlife her fiancé would not recognize her because she had grown old.

Shortly after her arrival in Sojourn, though, she was elated to learn that she could choose to be the age she was when her fiancé last saw her on Earth.

She is going to tell us all these things and more during the days of our training.

While she was alive on Earth, Miss Dickinson enjoyed platonic friendships with many eligible men. But she never accepted their proposals of marriage.

"I'm already married," she used to tell them. "I'm married to the Spirit of a brave man who died fighting for your freedom and mine."

My foresight, even with its limited powers here in Sojourn, tells me that we are going to meet her fiancé very soon.

Miss Dickinson is a self-assured woman. She owned a successful dress shop in Boston. She also designed an impressive line of dresses and gowns that became a national brand.

These sisters do not try to cheer us. They know that such a response to our grief is inappropriate. Instead, they choose words that nudge us toward the probability of hope and the possibility of rescue.

The third woman is no less encouraging, though far more artificial. She is Mrs. Robert Steerforth. My classmates, teachers, and I have learned that her first name is Amelia, though we never address her by that name. She is a well-groomed, sophisticated woman who had hosted many grand parties for her husband's business associates and their wives. She also led fund drives for the poor and the disabled and for high school graduates in need of college scholarships. Those are impressive credentials that convince most of the group that she is on our side. But I recognize her type. Beneath the decorum, there exists a cynical view of human beings and an unforgiving nature. For this meeting, she chooses to appear as a woman of forty, though she died when she was ninety-two. Her auburn hair is pulled back to make a neat coil at the nape of her neck. If you saw her, you would probably say that her oval face, her hazel eyes and upturned nose, and her sculpted cheekbones make her a lovely woman. But my classmates and two of our teachers, who are sitting at the conference table, uncertain of our surroundings and traumatized by the loss of our earthly lives, regard Mrs. Steerforth's kind manner and her heartening words as more important than her attractive appearance.

Only I see through her. She will be giving all of us a hard time.

"Everything will be all right," she tells us, as she offers the spring water to Ari, Chloe, Brenda, and me. "You'll see."

"It's only natural that you feel this way," Mrs. Adams explains, the equally contrived calm of her demeanor and encouraging voice working their solace upon Sonia, Abigail, and Shiloh. "You've just begun your journey."

She offers the same show of compassionate solace to Alessandro, Ms. Patel and Mr. Marchand.

Miss Dickinson echoes similar sentiments. But her words are heartfelt and sincere. She stirs my trust.

"Be patient," she advises Jason, Dion, and Jayden, "and don't worry. You'll be happy again. I promise."

The spring water helps us. So do the kind words. But only when Mr. Steerforth, with a prayerful gesture, clasps his hands does our crying cease. All this while he has been observing us with apparently sympathetic eyes as he stands by his chair at the head of the table. It is in this instant that I realize his prayerful hands contain supernatural powers. He could have offered those powers minutes earlier. But he prefers that we cry ourselves out. He respects our anguish. He believes that in this hour at least we should not suppress it. He knows that it is impossible for us and for anyone else to deny the tragedy that has happened to us. He understands that, anchored as we are to this natural satellite of Earth, we carry with us our memories of the lives that we had never stopped wanting to live, even during those times when we confronted disappointment or worked our way through uncertainty and through our own fallible individuality.

"You've had your cry," Mr. Steerforth says, his manner fatherly yet matter-of-fact and emotionally detached. "There will be other times when you will cry again, because you're thinking of home. As Mrs. Adams told you, crying is a natural response to everything that has happened to you."

Mr. Steerforth's words give us pause. I need to know his answer to Ari's plea about going back to his parents and his friends. My classmates and our teachers want to know, too. I raise my hand and wait for Mr. Steerforth to peer my way and, with a nod of his head, signal me to say what I have a mind to ask him.

"Will we ever be allowed to go back?"

With no hesitation, he answers me.

"Eventually. For a day, a week, a month, or even a year. But only as benevolent Spirits or unrelenting Phantoms or wily Shape-shifters. Unless the Evaluation Committee decides that you should have the chance to relive your last week or month or year on Earth. You will know the answer to that after some of you have reviewed your lives with the Evaluation Committee and with your group."

I tense up. The prospect of talking about myself with a committee of strangers and with my classmates and teachers does not appeal to me.

Resentful and impatient, I ask another question, fragmented though it is.

"Evaluation Committee?"

Mr. Steerforth notices my displeasure and smiles in the face of it.

"We are a committee of five. Captain Johnson heads the committee. Mrs. Steerforth, Mrs. Adams, Miss Dickinson, and I assist him."

I probe further.

"What do you do? What is it you are looking for?"

"We want you to tell us the truth about yourselves. We already know everything about your earthly lives that has been important. We know about the good that you have accomplished. We also know the mistakes that have blemished some of you. Nevertheless, we want to find out whether those among you who have done wrong can be honest with yourselves and with us. We want you to tell us about the most grievous wrong that you have committed."

He pauses. He studies our reactions to his words. Only after that does he tell us more.

"Those of you whom the committee calls will become involved in an important conversation with the Five Spirits and with some of your classmates and your two teachers. You will need to explain the dangerous wrongdoing or grievous crimes that your earthly lives concealed and for which you have not paid the full penalties. I've already mentioned that we know the lives that you have led. We are calling you to account for your behavior."

"How long will that take?"

"That depends on how long it takes for each errant person among you to tell the truth. There is much for them to tell. There is something that all of you can learn. Afterwards, there will be even more to do."

Hearing this brief exchange of words, my classmates and my two teachers become uneasy. I can imagine what they are thinking. Being accused of wrongdoing that they have probably taught themselves to forget will make death an even more lacerating experience. Being compelled to review the lives that they no longer possess will intensify the anguish that is burning through their souls.

I feel the same way. Anger is rousing the rebellious part of me. That part is no stranger to me. I can't help myself. With a voice both sullen and grating, I lodge a protest.

"It will be too painful!" I exclaim. "Reliving our mistakes is a bitter kind of punishment."

Mrs. Steerforth comes into it now. Her confident voice, with its steely edges, never wavers. She is nudging me forward—and not only me, but also everyone else in our group.

"All of you can bear up to it, if you try," she says. "Admitting your most grievous wrongdoing will set you free. You can begin a clean slate after that, here on Sojourn, before you make your journey to the First Heaven."

Miss Dickinson coaxes us now. Her voice is more soothing than Mrs. Steerforth's, but no less insistent.

"Make a good beginning here," she says, "if the Evaluation Committee calls on you. Tell us what we already know. Tell it to the group. Own up to it. Stare it down, if you must. But tell it as it really happened, no matter how painful it is for you to recall it."

Murmurs of uncertainty rise from my classmates and me. Once again, I guess what they are thinking. Jayden McDonald speaks out now for all of us. Tall and good-looking with brown hair and blue eyes, he was the captain of our tennis team and an equally first-rate soccer player. He was also known for his good humor and his friendly disposition. Here, in this Sojourn moment, his words sound as troubled as they are melancholic.

"Each of us made so many mistakes while we were living on Earth," he says, his gravelly voice searching for answers. "How do we choose? How can we know which of our mistakes harmed others or ourselves most of all?"

"You will know," Mrs. Adams answers him. "When you recall your life back there on Earth, you will understand, possibly for the first time, what you did well and what you did badly or failed to do. Your memory of it will be like a dream that unspools itself while you are awake."

"Or like a nightmare," Mrs. Steerforth says, unwilling to deny the anguish that yokes itself to the memory of our most grievous mistakes.

Once more, I raise my voice in protest.

"It's not right!" I declare. "It can never be right. There are no killers among us. You should be going after Henderson. He is the killer. He is the monster who killed all of us."

Mr. Steerforth comes back into it.

"Yes," he agrees. "Boyd Henderson is everything you say he is. He is a killer. He is a monster. His actions are unforgivable."

I push forward.

"He's the one who should confess his sins. He's the one who should call himself a foul murderer."

"Henderson has already been dealt with," he says. "Two days after you died, a state trooper from Roanoke, Virginia, killed him in a shootout that took place on a mountain trail there, in the midst of giant redwoods, white pines, and Siberian elms and in sight of a magnificent park and lake."

Nobody speaks. Our breathing comes faster. Mr. Steerforth's words weigh heavily upon us. After these conflicted seconds, Shiloh Jackson breaks through the silence and speaks his mind. He is a Native American. His wiry physique and tawny skin enhance his good looks. While he was alive, he made many friends and excelled at hockey and boxing. He acquired an enviable reputation for his rigorous discipline and his realistic appraisal of things.

"Henderson deserved what he got," he says, his voice raspy and bitter. "It's too bad he couldn't be shot over and over again. Always."

No one in our group disagrees. We merely listen and cloak our consent inside the new layers of stillness.

Mr. Steerforth has more to tell us.

"Shooting Henderson again and again won't be possible," he explains. "He will be brought before The Spirits and prosecuted for his crimes. If the First Spirit condemns him, Henderson's body will vanish for all time. Even his Spirit will disappear for all eternity."

Once more, a hush falls upon all of us. To vanish so completely, to disappear forever—the mere thought disconcerts and appalls us. That is a dying different from our own. That is death made unremitting and irrevocable.

My body trembles before the bleakness of that thought.

As though she means to solace all of us, Miss Dickinson softens her voice while she offers more information to the entire group about our public confessions.

"Tomorrow, our committee will begin hearing the testimonies of those among you who are being called to explain your lives," she says. "Tell the committee why your life on Earth counted for something. Tell us about one of the good things that you accomplished. Tell us about one of the things that you did not do and should have done. Tell us, also, about the mistake you made that hurt someone who trusted you."

Again I lodge a protest.

"Isn't it enough that we have been murdered? We've been cut off from our lives when we had hardly begun them. What good will come from our reliving what we've lost? What's the good of our humiliating ourselves by confessing our sins in public?"

"Good will come from it," Miss Dickinson says. "You'll see."

Mr. Steerforth tells us more.

"Once again I must remind you. We already know about your lives," he says. "If those of you whom the committee calls declare the truth of who you are, the committee may change the fact of your dying and the dying of every other member in your group."

His words astonish us. It is hard to fathom what we are hearing.

Mr. Marchand, who had withdrawn to the privacies of his own anguish, makes contact with the group once again. Excited, he begins speaking in French.

"Cela peut-il être vrai? Pouvons-nous vraiment récupérer nos vies sur Terre?"

The Steerforths and Miss Dickinson have no trouble understanding him, even though he speaks at a fast clip. Neither Ms. Patel, nor my classmates have any difficulty understanding him. Nevertheless, Mr. Marchand repeats his questions in English.

"Can it be true? Can we really reclaim our lives on Earth?"

"Sometimes," Mr. Steerforth says. "Once in a while, the committee finds reasons to push the clock back, so that those persons who have recently died can return to Earth and replay the scenes of their deaths. On special occasions, some of those persons who have died escape death in the new scenario."

Now Alessandro, one of Green Hills High School's excellent boxers and swimmers, asks the question that is goading the uneasiness of all our classmates.

"Does that happen very often?"

"No," Mr. Steerforth answers him. "Only in rare cases."

Mrs. Steerforth offers us a further clarification. She reminds us that even in Sojourn nothing comes free.

"On the other hand," she explains, "there have been instances when all but one of the dead are given back their lives on Earth. But a situation like that occurs only when one person in the group is willing to sacrifice herself or himself, so that the others may reclaim their lives."

"Will that happen to us?" Ms. Patel asks. "Will one of us be asked to sacrifice his or her life, so that all the others may go on living on Earth?"

"Maybe," Mr. Steerforth says. "Maybe not. Let's find out what happens."

"That is why the testimonies that some of you give tomorrow are so important," Mrs. Adams warns us. "The committee will be judging you as individuals and as a group. Follow Ms. Dickinson's advice. Be brief. Be honest. Your fates depend upon what you tell us about yourselves."

Mr. Steerforth says more. He wants to set us straight. He prefers that we understand the journey that we are about to navigate.

"Even if the committee allows your group to relive your last day or even your last year on Earth, that will not happen until we hear the testimonies of those whom we call to tell about their lives and after we determine whether your going back will really make a difference."

This news does not dismay us. In fact, it pleases and surprises everyone in the group. It gives us time to hope that we might, after all, go back to our lives on Earth. The news surprises us in other ways, too. The thought of going back not only exhilarates us. It leaves us with a vague apprehension. Which of us will reclaim our lives? Which of us will die again?

Instantly, I begin searching my past life. I ferret out incidents when I did not behave well. I recall the times that I betrayed my friends, mistreated anyone who challenged or competed with me, and lied to my parents. I explore the ruthless part of my nature. I sift out the malice and the envy. Then I back away. The memory of the imperfect being that I was becomes a bruised and scalding awareness. I do not care to revisit those scenes.

I panic. I try to remember all the times when I did the right things. I search for clues. Frantic, I cannot recall the scenes that validate my kindness, generosity, and empathy. If they are there, they have been lost inside the welter of other scenes that brand me self-centered, deceitful, and untrustworthy. I cannot bear to remember them. I cringe at the thought that, on the following morning, I shall have to confront the committee who already knows the tarnished facts of my life on Earth.

I try to devise a plausible narrative that will excuse my wrongdoing and that will enhance the good that I have accomplished. In my imaginary narrative, I equivocate. I use language ambiguously so that what I call my good intentions will deflect the disappointment and hurt that my erring conduct has wrought upon others. But I cannot go on with it. I wonder what I will say to the committee and how they will judge me. They are hunting me down, and I am unable to hide from them.

I hide me from myself.

CHAPTER TWO

HIDING AND VANISHING

On the following morning, while all of us are seated at a round table in the orientation room that is reserved for our group and our advisors, I stay low-keyed and polite as I ask Mr. Steerforth a careful question and devise, as well, two equally cautious remarks.

"Is it really necessary for us to answer questions about our lives? You already know everything about us. Our group knows all that we need to know about one another."

Mr. Steerforth answers me with his well-bred patience.

"Yes, the committee does know a great deal about your lives," he says, as he directs his words not only to me, but also to everyone else in our group. "But we are interested in what each of you is willing to tell us in your brief biography and what you prefer to conceal."

Mrs. Adams joins in. She does not surprise me. She shows an interest in us that is more business-like than warmhearted. Today, her manner is too precise and a bit militant. She has a job to do, and she wants to do it well. Always "on task," she begins coaching us about the way that we should conduct ourselves when the Evaluation Committee questions us in the uneasy days to come.

"Don't conceal anything when the committee interviews you about your lives. Don't lie. Don't offer half-truths or fake information about yourselves. Tell the whole truth, as harsh or bitter as it may be."

Before Mr. Steerforth closes this phase of our orientation, he directs new words to the group. He tells us that everything that we do and say here in Sojourn is being instantly recorded on a panoramic video wall that always surrounds us. What my group says and does here will remain for others to see and hear for all time and into eternity. With a wave of their hands, the Five Spirits can call forth the scenes that are now unfolding around us. Not only the newly dead in Sojourn will see and hear all that happens to us during this trial. Some persons who are alive on Earth will also see and hear us while the committee of Spirits prods us to speak the truth about ourselves and about our involvement in the tragedy that has overtaken us.

You, my reader, are one of those persons.

Mr. Steerforth knows who you are. He knows what you look like. He knows where you live. He knows when you were born. He knows how much joy you will experience and how much sorrow. He also knows when you will make the journey to Sojourn.

I know you, too.

The Spirit life that has already begun to imbue my being with new radiance has touched my eyes with extraordinary powers. I see you, though I can no longer see all of the future. Already, I confide in you. Maybe I'll set you straight about a few things that matter.

Don't expect me to use the jargon or slang or catchwords that are currently in fashion with some high school seniors. I've never mimicked the speech patterns of peers who crave group acceptance even at the cost of their individuality. I can be matter-of-fact, diplomatic, abrasive, or even empathetic. I can be devious, courteous, and helpful and all at the same time. But the language that I own belongs to me and to nobody else. I want to set you straight about what you can expect. I am not the stereotypical teenager. Nor are the classmates who have figured importantly in my life stereotypical. We are not carbon copies of anyone else. We are ourselves, distinct and problematic on our own terms.

Whenever I tell you what happened before and on the day of the school shooting, I'll give you information about the thirteen of us, eleven students and two teachers, who arrived in Sojourn at the same time. You already know some of the story. We died within minutes of each other after Boyd Henderson, a disaffected classmate who was filled with heartbreak and bitterness, shot us down in one of the long, polished corridors within the southwest wing of our high school. I'll keep reminding you of that school massacre. Otherwise, you may begin to feel that everyone in our group is still alive, the way we used to be when we were making our way through our time on Earth. You may feel that way because our Spirit-lives have begun to take complete possession of us even as our bodies keep slowly vanishing, here on the natural satellite that is always orbiting millions of miles away from our first home. We are alive in this Spirit world. Yet, despite our full-bodied appearance that is vanishing by imperceptible degrees and that will be consumed more and more by a luminous ghostliness, we have died to our lives in Green Hills, Maine, dispossessed by random chance or by the contrivances of the Fates of the lives we represented while we were on Earth.

You need to know more about us. Only then will you understand with accurate clarity everything that happened to us before we died. You may then perceive with keener insight all that is happening to us right now, while we are here in this interim space that is located halfway between Earth and The First Heaven, between the temporal and the eternal. At times, I'll tell you how old we are. I'll describe our looks and our personalities. I'll mention our achievements and our problems. I'll place us on the social scale. Many of us come from upper middle class and affluent backgrounds. I'll mention the ethnic groups from which we derive. Knowing all these details about each of us may increase your awareness about the tensions we experienced, the conflicts we confronted, and the privileges we enjoyed or were denied while we lived on Earth.

Here we are, all thirteen of us. "A baker's dozen," you might say, if you were in a lighter mood. Or "unlucky thirteen," if you believed in the messages hidden within certain numbers. After all, we are the thirteen who were murdered on the thirteenth of June. Our killer, Boyd Henderson, began firing his AR15 rifle at thirteen minutes after one o'clock, the thirteenth hour on that sun-drenched afternoon. It took him thirteen minutes to kill all of us. The work of Random Chance? The relentless Fates? Your guess is as good as mine. The guessing goads our conscience without leading us to a clarifying answer.

At any rate, we are here, within the natural satellite that orbits halfway between Earth and The First Heaven. We are keeping our bodies until they slowly vanish away. When that happens, we shall become fully radiant Spirits. Sometimes, we shall reclaim our bodies for special assignments here in Sojourn and for the occasional missions that will bring us back to Earth. So Mr. Steerforth has been explaining to us during these days of our orientation.

During one of our afternoon sessions with Mr. Steerforth, I ask the questions that are troubling all thirteen of us.

"As our bodies vanish, will our memories of who we were on Earth fade as well? How much of the selves that we are now will we eventually lose?"

"Try to be patient," he says. "You will find out soon enough. That is part of the adventure you are about to begin."

I wonder whether his answer is merely an evasion. Possibly, he believes that telling us the truth of our situation too quickly might leave us melancholic or apprehensive or despairing.

I'll tough it out, I tell myself. I'll keep reminding myself who I was while I lived on Earth and what I did while I was there. Right now, I am still that person. Whatever changes overtake me will do so gradually and even imperceptibly.

In the meantime, my classmates and I are learning how to be ghosts. Our ghost training begins a few days later, after we have grown familiar with our new living quarters. We are drilled in the art of teleporting. We draw upon our will power. We tell our Spirit/bodies that we want to be in a different location. We concentrate on that space and tell ourselves that we are there. And so we are. At any rate, we are there during those times when our minds take control of this new skill of ghost-flight.

The practice sessions limit our transporting to spaces within the grounds of this barracks-like orientation center. On some days, we sit in one of the conference rooms within the voluminous hangar where we ghost recruits ready ourselves for flying. We listen to Mr. Steerforth's instructions about clever ways to disappear and reappear. Then we make various attempts to do so. But rarely are our airlifts successful. We rely too much upon our bodies. We have not yet learned to trust our ghostliness or to negotiate with its Spirit powers. Our hesitation keeps us grounded when we should be flying.

"It's all a matter of concentration," Mr. Steerforth says. "Once you have the hang of it, you will vanish in an instant. Right now, of course, you are learning to vanish by degrees. You are maintaining a bond with the body that you will never completely relinquish. Keeping that bond is important."

Bitter and morose, Ari challenges the remark. He raises his hand, and with a nod Mr. Steerforth signals him to speak.

"Why should our bodies be important to us?" Ari asks. "We are dead. Everyone who counted in our lives will never see us again. Why should it matter whether we keep our bodies? They will only remind us of who we have been and are no longer."

Mr. Steerforth observes Ari with concern that simulates fatherliness. He has grown used to nudging Ari toward an acceptance of his situation and toward a belief in his future.

"You will always be the person you have been," he explains. "Even after your body vanishes. But there will be times when it will become necessary for you to return to your body. Your journeying back to Earth or back here to Sojourn may sometimes require you to appear as your full-bodied self. That is why my body is now visible. The First Spirit has sent me from The First Heaven to help you adjust to your new lives after your earthly death. He believes you will be more comfortable if you see me in the body that identified me when I lived on Earth."

Ari listens, without surrendering his brooding expression. But his brown eyes reveal a keener interest in Mr. Steerforth's next words.

"In your new lives as ghosts, you may have to make your body visible. Possibly, you will be allowed to visit the family and friends you have left behind. The success of your visits will depend upon your knowing how to vanish and how to reappear in an instant."

Now it's my turn to ask a question. I raise my hand, and Mr. Steerforth nods his permission.

"How long will it take before I do that? How many attempts must I make before I learn how to vanish, and how do I make myself reappear?"

Mr. Steerforth calls forth words that he has often summoned during these training sessions.

"You concentrate. You allow your will to overtake your hesitation. You focus on whatever needs to be done. Remember that here, on Sojourn, you're breathing a different atmosphere. Your body is taking on new capacities. When you learn how to be a proper ghost, you will find it very easy to travel back to Earth and to return to Sojourn and The First Heaven."

Dion Williams gets excited. He smiles and then breaks into laughter.

"That means we can go back."

Every one of my classmates and I find pleasure in seeing and hearing Dion laugh. Our recollection of all the other times that we shared his laughter while we were alive on Earth touches this new, unexpected laughter with melancholy. But the melancholy does not steal away the quickened happiness of this moment. Dion and happiness were always loyal partners, whether he was using his six foot-six inch African American frame to win basketball games or driving with savvy awareness his 2010 Ferrari or conferring with his father about pursuing a similar career path as a research scientist for a pharmaceutical corporation.

"That means we can go back," Dion exclaims once more. "We can reenter our lives on Earth."

Silence takes hold of all of us. I, for one, am positively elated.

"We can go back!" I cry out, echoing Dion's elation and his laughter. "We can go back!"

All the others there—Jason, Ari, Alessandro, Brenda, and Chloe, as well as Sonia, Jayden, Abigail, Shiloh, and our two teachers—are genuinely astonished. But no laughter hurries out of them. Instead, they become very still. The possibility of returning to Earth awes them.

Quickly, Mr. Steerforth sets us straight.

"You will be allowed to return to Earth only when there is an important reason for your doing so."

Now Miss Patel speaks up.

"Who will decide whether our going back is important?"

"We Five Spirits will decide. We work closely with The First Spirit, the One who has created everything."

Mr. Marchand wants to know more.

"When will we meet the First Spirit?"

Mr. Steerforth answers him with his usual clarity, while allowing his glance to make a fleeting contact with all of us.

"You will meet the First Spirit when you enter The First Heaven," he says. "While you are here in Sojourn, we five members of the committee shall speak for the First Spirit. He has given us that responsibility. That is his way of testing us."

Once again, his words take us by surprise.

Jayden blurts out his amazement.

"He is testing *all of you*?"

"He often does," he answers directly. "He will be testing all of you, too. He will give you a chance to judge the life you led while you lived on Earth. He will be waiting for those of you whom the committee interviews to perceive whether you made appropriate moral choices."

Mr. Steerforth reminds us that there is much that the blemished characters among us must accomplish before the committee decides whether our group should make the journey to The First Heaven or return to Earth so that we can relive the last year of our lives there and possibly change things for the better. Those of us whom the committee of Five Spirits is interviewing and testing need, first of all, to examine our past. We have to acknowledge what we have done and what we should have done while we were alive on earth. We have to be brave enough to look back without weeping at all the wonderful little episodes and the larger occasions that we have lost.

So we begin, uncertain of our bearings and uncertain of whether we are among those persons whom the Five Spirits will interview. We are even less certain about the outcome of our testimonies. Will the Five Spirits who are questioning us see something of value in our lives? Will our testimonies persuade them to give us back the lives that Boyd Henderson destroyed when he killed us with his AR-15? Will Captain Johnson, whom we have not yet met, become our compassionate advocate or our adversary?

I perceive new layers of tension touching my classmates and influencing, too, the rigid composure of Ms. Patel and Mr. Marchand. Ms. Patel's Asian Indian heritage and her experience as a machine gunner with the first battalion of the Marine Corps in the Iraq War have honed her stoicism. It is a rare occasion when she allows her emotions to disarrange her composure. Mr. Marchand is equally tough-minded when confronting danger or disappointment. A Major in the Marine Corps, he fought bravely in our war in Afghanistan. Ms. Patel and Mr. Marchand learned very early to tamp down their fears and their misgivings. But today a frown touches their brows as the committee closes in on all of us with their questions and their accusations.

Once again, I begin devising a narrative that might convince the committee that I am innocent of grievous wrongdoing. I choose words that point to the extenuating circumstances that would surely excuse the wrongs that I have committed. Mr. Steerforth told the group that the committee already knows what we have done. But are the other interrogating Spirits and Mr. Steerforth aware of the motives that pushed some of us into behavior that they deem reprehensible? I start wondering how many of my classmates are guilty of small or even larger crimes that go unpunished. I already know some of their misdeeds. I haven't any way of knowing the crimes they are hiding.

I ferret out words that might transform my larger wrongdoings into minor infractions. I search for the plausible language that will conceal my malice and my willfulness from the probing eyes of the Five Spirits. But I cannot find the words that obscure or falsify my motives or that exonerate me from the consequences of my deeds.

I steel myself against the punishment that may be coming for me. Only the afternoon and the evening of this day separate me from the grueling interrogation of the Five Spirits. My intuition tells me that each of them is relentless in the pursuit of the truth. I dread the experience of confronting them.

Once more, I hide me from myself.

CHAPTER THREE

PRELIMINARY RULES

The interrogations begin promptly at nine o'clock on the following morning. Mr. Steerforth and his colleagues keep referring to these sessions as "interviews" or as "hearings." They avoid the word "interrogations," with its harsh implications and its promise of grueling cross-questioning. Perhaps, they want to subdue our apprehensions. Possibly, they mean to disarm us. They prefer to question us while our defenses are down. They try to win our trust, so that we shall tell more about ourselves than we had intended to tell. They use soft words and kind manners to trap us.

Whether my classmates or Ms. Patel and Mr. Marchand view the committee exactly as I do, I cannot say. I speak for myself. My experience of wily do-gooders and of self-righteous moralists prevents me from accepting the committee at face value.

I distrust Captain Randall Johnson most of all.

In this courtroom setting, he makes a formidable presence. Standing at six foot, six inches as he enters the room and joins his colleagues at the interviewers' table, he is one of the tallest men that I have ever seen. He is also a young man. Despite all the years that have passed since his earthly death, he has remained twenty-two, the age he was when his plane was shot down during an aerial battle over Berlin in July 1943. His brown-haired handsomeness still wears traces of battle fatigue and wartime bitterness. He rarely smiles. Beneath his no-nonsense demeanor, I detect a harnessed rage against the criminality, potential or activated, of most human beings. He is no ordinary interviewer. As I observe him addressing the group, I silently call him by his rightful name. He is a prosecuting attorney. He is the fully embodied Spirit who may prevent me from returning to Earth. He well may be my executioner.

He takes his place at the head of the long mahogany table where all of us are seated. Miss Dickinson, who is his fiancée, and Mrs. Adams are sitting opposite each other and nearest the Captain. Mr. Steerforth, who is seated at the other end of the table, observes his entrance with keen-sighted attention to all of the Captain's words and to his smallest gestures. Mrs. Steerforth sits on the left side of her husband. The rest of us are seated randomly. All of us might be attending a business conference in a corporate New York tower concerning the latest market shares and the most thriving hedge funds. We might be involved in some university seminar about the villainous Claudius in Shakespeare's *Hamlet* or about the equally villainous Cersei Lannister in George Martin's *A Game of Thrones*. We might even regard this meeting as a mock trial that illuminates the workings of the criminal justice system. The Captain and Mr. Steerforth, as well as their female colleagues, have designed the setting so that we might think so.

But I do not.

They intend to win my trust. They want to defuse my tension. But I refuse to let down my guard. I see them for who they are. They are here to trap me. They know my story. They want me to admit that I failed myself and failed so many other people. They want to declare me guilty of hidden crimes. They want to brand me as the villainous catalyst of the tragedy that has overtaken us, the devious girl who incited Boyd Henderson to commit his murderous deeds.

I sink back into my chair. I hide myself within studious gestures as I direct my attention to Captain Johnson and whenever I pore over the direction sheets before me if he advises the group to do so.

In the very instant that I turn to give him my attention, there flashes within me the thought that others in the group may also be guilty of some wrongdoing. I hold onto that thought and breathe more easily.

The Captain speaks to us. His brisk manner and the hint of an ambiguous smile spark a hope in my classmates that he may be on the level. Perhaps he is on our side. Maybe he wants us to speak truthfully about the lives that we lived and lost on Earth, so that we'll have a chance to return there. If we are allowed to replay our last days on Earth, we might change what happened. We might win back our lives.

This is the hope that fuels the attention of Miss Patel and of Mr. Marchand, as well.

But I withhold my trust. I keep my hope harnessed and waiting.

"All of you know why you are here," the Captain says. "You are going to tell us about yourselves. You may be among those persons whom the committee will interview at length. You may be among those who are called to make incidental remarks about yourselves and about your classmates. We are counting on your speaking the truth at all times. We know your lives. We know you. But we want to find out whether you know yourselves. Do you really understand the positive effects and the troubled consequences of all that you have done while you were alive on

Earth? Are you aware of the grief that you brought others when you failed to do what you should have done?"

He pauses. He observes each of our faces.

My classmates and our teachers visibly stiffen. Vague frowns touch their brows. A few boys (Jayden, Alessandro, Dion, and Shiloh) tightly clench their jaws, as though they are determined to suppress every revealing word that they might utter. Four of the girls (Chloe, Abigail, Brenda, and Sonia) hold themselves ramrod-straight. They are not likely to give way to tears or to wallow in self-recrimination. In some ways, they are like me. They disdain any show of weakness, and they refuse to make any appeal for sympathy.

I do not know everything about these girls. But what I do know convinces me that, if their lives were compared to mine, they would be judged innocent. They have not committed my wrongdoing. They are not accessories to a crime.

Maintaining always his brisk manner, anchored as it is to his military bearing, the Captain sets forth the rules that we must follow.

"Some of you may regard this meeting as a conference of students, teachers, and advisors not unlike your meetings with secondary school counselors and university admissions officers. It is that. But it is also more than that. It is an interview for admission to a stay here in Sojourn and for a permanent place in The First Heaven. It is a forum or symposium or panel discussion where some of you will share your stories and where some of you will offer different points of view about those stories. It is a town hall meeting, too, in which you may assert your opinions about the rules that guide you in your new life here. It is an assembly. It is a convocation. It is a seminar where you may lodge your protests against the committee's probing questions or a classmate's rebuttal of your testimony. It is also a place of confession that may recall for you your meetings with a rabbi or a priest or a minister. It is all of these things. Ideally, your gathering here will become a meeting of minds. Whether we interview you at length or incidentally, each of you will be telling us the truth of your life as far as you understand that truth. All of you will also be listening to each other and judging the accuracy of what you are hearing. You are obligated to challenge the remarks of your classmates if what they are saying seems false or incomplete or misleading."

The Captain's words increase the tension in the room. Not only are the Five Spirits on the committee our potential accusers. Our classmates may turn against one another, as well.

Brenda Flynn is the first to lodge a protest. Her words instantly draw the attention of everyone in the room. Her titian-haired prettiness has not yet faded, nor has her hourglass figure. All of us know that on Earth she was a good student from a troubled home. She did everything that she could do to help her alcoholic mother and her war-traumatized father. She became a substitute mother for her younger siblings, a sister and two brothers.

As usual, her words are temperate, and self-control is her stock in trade. Nevertheless, she takes issue with the rule that will allow classmates to judge each other's behavior in a public gathering.

"How could my classmates know anything important about the motives that compelled me to behave in a particular way? How could they know about my fears and my anguish?"

Without hesitation, the Captain answers her.

"Your classmates will tell everything that they see and understand," the Captain explains. "They will have to support their statements with solid reasoning and with clear-cut evidence. They will risk punishment if they make false accusations or foolish conjectures."

Brenda is not satisfied.

"What if they tell what they believe is the truth? What if their reports are merely subjective and not the truth at all?"

The Captain answers her more curtly now. He resents the suggestion that he and his colleagues might not be able to determine what was true and what was inaccurate or false.

"The committee knows your stories," he says. "We know who you are. We know what you have done. We are waiting for you to declare yourselves to us."

"Each of us may have more than one self to declare," Brenda says. "Each one of us may have identified ourselves in different ways to the people who were part of our lives. Those persons may have known only one of the selves that defined who we were. How could any of our friends or even our acquaintances know everything there was to know about us? How could they possibly give an authentic testimony of who we were, while we were alive on Earth?"

The Captain is not to be put off the course that he intends to navigate.

"The committee knows everything about all of you," he says once again. "We are waiting for you and your classmates to tell us all of it. We'll prod you with questions. We'll nudge you toward retractions when you tell us something false. We'll praise you for your honesty. We'll invoke penalties if you refuse to tell the truth. Your lies might even imperil the group's chances of going back to Earth."

Shiloh Jackson throws out an uneasy question. Often congenial when he was alive on Earth, he is in this moment both guarded and brooding—characteristics he acquired whenever he found himself in the presence of adversaries who sought to give him a hard time because he is a Native American.

"I can't speak for the others," he says. "I speak for myself. I never knew for certain who I was when I was alive, back there on Earth. I couldn't decide which person I should be. There were so many voices around me, telling me who I should be. I never really decided for myself. I didn't live long enough for that."

"You made some important choices even during the brief time that you were allotted," the Captain says. "There's enough to go on to figure out who you were. The choices that you made tell us a great deal about who Shiloh Jackson was."

The Captain's words fail to ease Shiloh's tension. The Captain's last remark, especially, stirs Shiloh's displeasure.

"The choices that you made tell us a great deal about who Shiloh Jackson was."

Shiloh's troubled brow tells me that he distrusts the committee. Despite their courteous manner and their low-keyed presentation of themselves, each member of the committee might be setting a trap for him and, possibly, for all of us. I am not surprised when Shiloh nods politely to the Captain, his sign that he has nothing more to say at this time. Nor am I taken aback when Shiloh almost imperceptibly withdraws to a secret place inside himself. He, too, is hiding. At least, that is my guess. But I cannot imagine that his desire for concealment harbors wrongdoing equal to my own.

Now Miss Dickinson, the Captain's fiancée, tells us something important.

"Eventually, the committee will be questioning Boyd Henderson, the student who killed all of you. You will have a chance to question him, too. But that questioning will come later."

I watch the faces of my classmates. I imagine what my face must look like. Even after death, we cannot restrain the looks of anger, surprise, and despair that alter our expressions. There are no bitter words that we care to utter. Nor do we care to shed any new tears. There will be time to endure more profound levels of our sorrow. But now is not the time. Hearing Miss Dickinson's announcement about Boyd Henderson, our group stays very calm as we enclose ourselves inside a cautious silence. Even as we do so, we keep our attention fixed upon Miss Dickinson. She is making still another announcement.

"The Evaluation Committee is especially interested in three persons who were involved in the school shooting. One of those persons is Boyd Henderson. Our security guards have brought him to our Detention Center for Killers thousands of miles away from us, on the northern tip of Sojourn. The other two persons whom the committee intends to question are right here in your group. They are Ari Bachman and Cassandra Winslow."

At first, Ari freezes. He cannot bring himself to move or even to speak. In this silence that falls around all of us, I notice each member of the group eyeing him with new tension and probably with the recollection of the part he played in the tragedy. Ari's excellence as a boxer and as a swimmer and as a goalkeeper for the soccer team means nothing here. Nor does the fact that in Green Hills, Maine, his father is an eminent cardiologist and his mother a respected pediatrician persuade the group that Ari is trustworthy.

The group also studies me, Cassandra Winslow. No memory of my work as a political activist or as a defender of equal rights for women in the business world can soften their view of me. Nor does my privileged life as the daughter of a patent attorney impress them. Because they now recall the role that I played in the tragedy that overtook all of us, their hatred of me is fired anew. I stare back at them with nothing different to say. I already filed my regrets a few days before the shooting. It's too late to say anything more.

But Ari has something to say. He breaks away from the silence, in search of an answer.

"Why me?" he asks. "Why is the committee especially interested in me? Or in Cassandra? We are not the ones who did the shooting."

Mrs. Adams breaks in here. Once again, her voice is unfriendly and even abrasive.

"We have our reasons for being interested in the two of you," she says. "We have just cause for being interested."

Not for the first time, Miss Dickinson becomes a mediator. You might think of her as a peacemaker or a conciliator. She tries to put Ari and me at ease.

"The committee is especially interested in the two of you because you were directly implicated in the tragedy. There was a time when both of you were close friends of Boyd Henderson. We want to examine the ways in which you influenced his happiness and his despair."

Ari protests this special interest in him and me.

"We didn't pull the trigger of that AR-15," he says, blunt in his defense of our innocence.

Mrs. Adams takes another swipe at our reputations.

"No," she says. "You didn't pull the trigger. But sometimes you can kill a person without pulling a trigger or wielding a knife or feeding him poison."

I fire back at her.

"Boyd Henderson was not a saint! He belonged to the Devil's party!"

Mrs. Adams scoffs.

"You and Ari belonged to that party, too."

Brenda Flynn bursts out with her own denunciation of Ari and me. Crying is against her grain. Her hard life has given her the courage and strength that a girl her age seldom possesses. Yet today she starts crying. The memory of the good days that she spent with Boyd Henderson come back to haunt her.

"It's true!" she declares through her weeping. "Cassandra and Ari didn't have to use a high-powered rifle or a snub-nosed revolver. They had their own ways to destroy Boyd Henderson."

Miss Dickinson tries to smooth things over.

"There is no need to hurl accusations at one another," she says. "We shall find out the truth. But we must maintain a civil manner. Permit me to remind my colleagues on the committee and the newly arrived dead people that we must work in harmony with each other. Our goals are the same. We want to set the record straight. That is why we are placing the spotlight on Ari and Cassandra. There was a time when they were among Boyd Henderson's closest friends. We shall continue to review their relationships with him. That review may be a way to discover the things that pushed young Mr. Henderson into madness and murder."

Miss Dickinson pauses. Her studious glance takes in all of us. She waits for her colleagues on the committee and every member of our group to express further displeasure. The stillness with its discreet influences overtakes the room. She is pleased that no voices rise in enmity or rebuttal. She chooses the next moment to clarify the rules that will dominate the inquiry.

"The committee is, as I have already mentioned, especially interested in Ari and Cassandra. But we may want to hear from other members of the group. We may invite some of you to speak of yourselves, always briefly and always following the guidelines that Mr. Steerforth will be explaining to you in a few minutes. If we call upon you, you must also tell us how your lives connected to Ari, Cassandra, and Boyd Henderson. In this way, we may find the answers to several questions. What kind of human being were you creating from the materials that the First Spirit, your parents, and your environment gave you? Was this human being that you were creating a source of comfort for Boyd or an agent of his unhappiness? Could any of you have saved Boyd from himself? Was there any one of you who pushed him over the edge? What were the good things that you did for him? Why weren't they enough?"

At once, upon hearing what Miss Dickinson says, everyone in our group withdraws into the privacies of self-appraisal. We sift through those portions of our memories that allow the hours and days that we spent with Boyd to unfold inside our solitary seeing. But there is not enough time to consider the weight of their influence upon the human beings we were while we were alive.

Nor is their time to evaluate the merit or the flaw in our relationships with Boyd.

The Captain wants to get on with the hearings. He addresses all of us.

"Let's begin," he tells us. "We'll begin with Ari Bachman."

Before the committee starts questioning Ari, Mr. Steerforth has something more to tell us.

"Please listen carefully," he advises us. "I'll review the most important requirements of the interview, including the guidelines that Miss Dickinson summarized. I'll remind you of the ways that you can fulfill those requirements."

The group is on tenterhooks. Tension holds our breathing tight. Our bodies are bound to stillness as if they were enclosed in a vise. Only Mr. Steerforth's carefully chosen words breaks through the silence.

"These are the rules," he declares. *"First, if we call on you, you must explain why your life on Earth counted for something."*

I observe the sullen faces of my classmates and the anxious faces of Miss Patel and Mr. Marchand. Are their thoughts similar to mine? What words can we offer that prove we led worthwhile lives? What can we say that will convince the committee that the world was a better place because we lived in it? How can we praise our deeds without appearing to be self-deceiving or arrogant or boastful? Perhaps, my thoughts are not the group's thoughts. Possibly, only I am afraid of testifying before the committee. Once more, I scan the faces of my peers and the lived-in demeanors of our two teachers. This time, their faces tell me nothing. This time, they have closed themselves off from even the most casual glance.

I turn my gaze upon Mr. Steerforth. I watch him with a disguised openness, my studious eyes both respectful and attentive. After a momentary pause, he has resumed speaking of the guidelines that we must follow if we are called to testify before the committee and in the company of our classmates and teachers, too.

"The second rule also requires you to support your claims with strong evidence," he says. *"You must explain how your counting for something influenced Boyd Henderson's life. Was it one of the good things that you accomplished during your last year on Earth?"*

Mr. Steerforth pauses, so that we can process the challenges that he is placing before us.

Nobody asks a question or lodges a complaint. We listen quietly, keeping our thoughts to ourselves.

Mr. Steerforth begins speaking again. His deep voice hurries forward with matter-of-fact demands.

"When you describe your relationship with Boyd Henderson," he says, "you may draw upon the witness of a classmate or a teacher who is seated here in the room. Again, I'll remind you that you must be honest in everything that you tell us. If you are not, if you intend merely to mislead us, or if you have a friend here who is willing to lie for you, the committee will know. You will be caught, and both you and your friend will be shamed. You will jeopardize your group's chance to return to Earth."

I refuse to lose hope. I intend to remain wily and elusive. I tell myself that the committee may be bluffing. How can they possibly see into the minds and hearts of all the dead persons who are assigned to their jurisdiction? How can we take credit for befriending Boyd or excuse ourselves because we turned away from him? I'll keep telling myself that I am innocent of every wrongdoing and all the crimes that I've committed. I'll memorize my part. I'll convince even the most jaded of these would-be prosecutors that I've never brought harm to anyone.

Mr. Steerforth rattles on about still another rule.

"The third rule requires more complicated reflection," he says. *"Those of you who are invited to speak must talk about one of the important things that you did not do and should have done for Boyd Henderson. You must explain how your failure to act carried with it bitter and irrevocable consequences."*

His words are painful to hear. They are like the lashes of a whip striking against my still-visible body. They scald my Spirit, whose light glows with tentative vitality. But never do I allow the look of innocence to leave my face. Never will I capitulate to this committee's bullying tactics.

With a calm that has grown eerie because of its suggestion of self-discipline that is both rigorous and supernatural, Mr. Steerforth moves on to the remaining rule.

"The fourth and final rule will test in a different way those of you whom we interview," he says. *"Each of you must recall a mistake you made that hurt someone who trusted you.* That someone need not be Boyd Henderson. The persons who suffered because of your mistakes are here among you. They may be called to testify against you. They may be put to the test, too. They will be asked whether they have forgiven you or whether they still hate you."

The committee is playing with us. They have made us believe that we have a chance to go back to Earth. They have told us that we can relive the last days we spent there. We can change them for the better. We can possess once again the lives that we lost far too early. I don't believe them. They merely want to torment us. From the little that I know about my classmates and my two teachers, I can say without hesitation that all of them are better than I am. But I am guessing that not one of them is perfect. Everyone in our group is a fallible human being. The chances of our getting our lives back are small.

Nevertheless, I keep my face innocent. I hide myself within a studious demeanor.

CHAPTER FOUR

ARI BACHMAN

Even before the Captain begins his questioning, I imagine that the committee and our group will begin peeling away the outermost layers of Ari's self-definition and his stubborn defense of himself. You may be surprised at what I am already anticipating. The committee and at least a few members of our group will show him no pity. The committee will spurn Ari's attempts to appear wholly innocent. Their caustic accusations and trouble-haunted intimations will burn through his soul to its socket. The classmates who have always regarded him as overly competitive will trip him up with their own versions of the human being that he was while he was alive on Earth.

I know that this will happen, though I do not expect you to believe me. My parents named me Cassandra for a reason. I have already told you that my father is a patent attorney. I'll mention now that my mother is an executive secretary in Maine's Supreme Judicial Court. They are business professionals. But they are also literary. They are avid readers of the ancient Greek myths. They were particularly drawn to the story of Cassandra, the beautiful daughter of King Priam and Queen Hecuba. Cassandra had a privileged life. She also had many suitors whom she enjoyed keeping at bay or at least on a long leash. Her young girl's innocence enhanced her playfulness. It put a different spin on her light-heartedness. Her suitors came to understand her. They began to enjoy the game that she was playing with them. And there was always the chance that she might one day grant one of them her favor.

But the god Apollo was a different kind of suitor. He was more powerful than any of the other young men that sought to woo and seduce her. He was the god of light and of the sun and the god of healing. He was the god of magic. Eventually, Cassandra served him as a priestess, meticulous in her chastity and in her exemplary behavior. To win her favor, Apollo gave her the gift of prophecy on the condition that she would sleep with him. She accepted the gift. She could now perceive events before they happened. But, as soon as she accepted his gift, she revoked her promise to him. She would not allow him to seduce her.

Apollo then set a curse upon Cassandra. She could foretell tragic events, but no one would believe her.

My parents chose Cassandra as my namesake first of all because I have brown hair and brown eyes, just as Cassandra had. They also convinced themselves that I was blessed with intuition. A few random incidents that occurred when I was an infant persuaded them that I had a sixth sense or second sight. One time, while lying in my cradle, I awoke in the middle of the night and burst into ear-piercing cries. Hearing me from an adjoining bedroom, my parents took fright and hurried into my room. I kept on crying until they lifted me from my cradle and moved toward the living room. Only then did my parents notice that the room was on fire. A log had spilled out of the fireplace and had ignited the carpet and the sofa and was snaking its way across the wide space before it. A team of firefighters snuffed out the conflagration, but nobody could snuff out my mother's conviction that I was gifted with psychic powers. There was no other possible explanation. My infant's bedroom was located too far away for any ordinary human being to know that the living room was on fire.

A second incident intensified her belief. It occurred shortly after the first one. I was still an infant and my mother was holding me in her arms as we headed toward an elevator in a large department store. But, as we approached the elevator, into which four or five shoppers were entering, I began screeching and, with my tiny hands, started tugging at the collar of my mother's coat. I turned and twisted so vehemently that my mother nearly dropped me. She decided to move back to the infant's wear department that we had just left. No sooner did she turn away from the elevator and find the path that would bring us to infant's wear, than a horrific crash shook the space around us. A cable had snapped, and the elevator had plummeted a hundred feet before crashing. All five persons in that elevator were crushed upon impact and instantly killed.

Still another incident served to convince my mother and my father, too, that I had been born clairvoyant. By that time, they had already named me Cassandra. This latest incident merely fortified their belief in my powers. I was six years old then. My brother Luke, who is ten years older than I, had been saddled with babysitting me for the afternoon, while my parents were at work and while our grandmother Iris, who usually cared for me when I had returned from a day at school, was in her own home, recovering from a bout with the flu. My older sister, Lorna, was busy at her after-school job, stacking books at the public library. On this afternoon, Luke was supposed to be completing his geometry assignment in his room on the second floor of our home in Green Hills. I was in my room on the first floor, at work on a watercolor inspired by a miniature Winslow Homer seascape that was one of the illustrations in my elementary school art book.

Great was my surprise when I heard the chug-chug-chugging of a hotrod hurrying into our driveway. I glanced out of my window and saw who was making the racket. Andy Sanford, the only one of Luke's many friends who was reckless and wild, kept the motor running while he blasted the horn. He was a string bean of a teenager with unkempt red hair and freckled boyishness. Not even his well-worn denims, polo shirt, and windbreaker made him appear conventional. There was something odd about his looks. Looking back now, as an eighteen-year-old young woman, I see that he carried that oddity with what the French describe as *panache* and we Americans call *cool* or *funky*. I knew that he was very popular with the in-crowd at his school that thought of themselves as rebels. To my six-year-old eyes, though, Andy was tall and a bit gawky. I also thought that he was a little crazy. Two other boys whose names I do not recall were with him.

The honking of the horn did not stop until Luke peered out the window. Seeing his friends, he quickly yelled out that he would join them. I might have allowed my brother to hasten away with his friends. I was not afraid of being alone in the house, at least not during an October afternoon when an autumn glow touched everything that surrounded me and made me feel very safe. But on that afternoon there flashed before my eyes the crash of Andy Sanford's hotrod on a distant highway. I also saw the hood of the vehicle and shards of window glass, as well as its rear passenger doors and its rear tires, strewn along the blood-smeared asphalt.

Without pausing, I ran from my room screaming. Already, I was crying and begging my brother not to go with those boys. Breathless and flushed, I told him what I had seen, there in that momentary flash that made me a witness of the battered bodies of the three boys inside the car and the fractured body of the vehicle strewn across the highway.

So urgent was I in my appeal that my brother stood absolutely still, stopped in his tracks by my woeful screaming. He had been rushing to open the front door, leave the house, and jump into Andy's hotrod. But something, possibly an intuition not unlike my own, influenced him to regard my entreaty with levelheaded practicality or the grown-up wisdom that he usually brought to his actions.

"It's all right, Cassandra," he said while gently wiping my tears away with his clean handkerchief. "I understand."

Then, taking my hand and guiding me to the front door that he opened with a decisiveness that I immediately recognized, he called out to Andy and the other boys.

"I can't join you today. I've got a full slate of assignments. See you in school tomorrow."

"Thus speaks the honor student," Andy called back to him with his usual display of street-smart quips. "See you in church."

My brother wanted to warn Andy and the other boys of the danger into which they might be driving. If he told them that images of the crash had flashed across my eyes, they would have laughed at him. Instead, he chose other words that might set them on a safer course.

"Don't travel on the highway," he said without explaining why they should not do so. "Take the side roads. It's less trafficked. You'll have a smoother ride."

"Yes, daddy," Andy said, his words thick with sarcasm and the punchy hint of a quip.

We were to learn that, in spite of Luke's suggestion, Andy and his two friends chose to take the highway.

Later that evening, when my parents were watching the local news on our television, there flashed upon the screen the stark images of a car crash on a highway only a few miles from our home. The car belonged to Andy. It was completely wrecked. The television anchorman was making much of the photos that showed the wreckage in detail. But he gave bigger points to what he called a miracle. Andy and his two friends had survived the crash. They had suffered concussions and broken arms and legs. After their stay in a hospital and after long weeks of convalescence, they would be all right.

Luke never forgot that afternoon when I stopped him from entering Andy's car. Even later, during our many clashes of temperament, he refrained from holding grudges or treating me roughly. He was the only person who believed my predictions.

"You are my good angel," he used to say.

In Sojourn, the Five Spirits have taken away some of the powers within my foresight. Nevertheless, I can often foresee the future.

I am telling you all these things as my way of explaining why I perceive in advance that the committee and our group will be giving Ari Bachman a hard time. I am aware of Ari's good qualities. I also know his faults. I know them well.

With blunt authority, the Captain begins the interview.

"Tell us about yourself, Ari Bachman" he says. "Tell us why your life on Earth counted for something."

Ari waits before he speaks. With brown eyes that narrow slightly, he peers at the Captain with the ingrained antipathy that he often directed against those persons whom he regarded as intrusive while he was alive on Earth. He is judging him. He does not flinch before the prospect of abrasive questioning. He does not cower. He does not invoke the innocent or vulnerable persona that had often served as his cohort whenever he was caught betraying a friend or lying to his parents or attempting to make somebody else take the blame for his wrongdoing. He's going to tough his way through this session. At least, he is going to try.

Already, I am beginning to respect him. But I do not plan to defend him if the Committee or even some members in our group set a trap for him.

With subdued yet militant authority that rides on the crest of fake fatherliness or, perhaps, the contrived concern of an older brother, the Captain prods Ari forward.

"Just tell us the truth, Ari," he says. "The truth doesn't require hesitation or permit embellishment. Why were you of value while you were alive on Earth? What makes you think that you counted for something worthwhile? Tell us all of it, and tell it quickly."

Ari begins. His voice, with its husky timbres, does not waver. He directs his glance with a well-practiced openness, not only at the Captain, but also at every other being in the room. His manner is matter-of-fact. He might be competing in a cross-country race or a swim meet. He is prepared to do the things that he needs to do if he expects to emerge as a winner.

"I was a good son," Ari says. "I listened to my parents and tried to follow their rules."

At once, the Captain detects a red flag.

"You tried," he says. "But how often did you succeed?"

"Often enough. My parents rarely complained about my behavior."

The Captain pushes further.

"But they did complain. The committee is aware that your parents had good reasons to complain. Tell us about them, all the reasons why they complained."

Ari holds his ground.

"Their reasons were trivial when compared to all the achievements I made. I was enrolled in every advanced placement class that my schedule allowed. Those classes required hours and hours of study. I did all that and more. I trained hard for the cross-country team, and I became a champion. I devoted hours that I couldn't really spare so that I could help out our swimming team. And I did help them. We won all the important medals. My parents had no reason to complain."

Mrs. Steerforth comes into it now. The soft precision of her words subverts her detachment from whatever discomfort or anxiety that Ari is concealing.

"But your parents did complain, Ari. There were times when they were very disappointed in you."

Ari eludes her question. He keeps on talking, curtly overlapping her assertions.

"I did my parents' bidding in so many other ways. In spring, I helped with the gardening. I loamed and mulched the turf. I planted roses, begonias, impatiens, and geraniums. In summer, I mowed the wide lawns in the different wings of our home. In fall, I raked leaves, and in winter I ploughed snow. My parents could well afford to hire a gardening team. But they didn't do so. Instead, they made me their dray horse. My brother and my sister were away at college. That left me with the brunt of the work. I didn't complain."

"Not complaining was in your favor," Miss Dickinson says, in her attempt to boost Ari.

Mrs. Adams bristles. She is not going to accept Miss Dickinson's praise of Ari.

"Why should you complain?" she asks him, though her words are more than a question. They are a challenge and a criticism. "Your parents gave you a safe and privileged life."

Again Ari hurries to defend himself. Again he nearly overlaps the person addressing him.

"I was their robot. They even made me their auto-mechanic. I serviced their cars. I washed them twice every week. I changed the filters and the spark plugs when they needed to be changed. I rotated the tires. I vacuumed the interiors."

"Most good sons pitch in to make the household run more efficiently," Mr. Steerforth says. "Helping out at home was a way to thank your parents. Instead, you resented them for asking you to carry out the ordinary duties of a good son. Don't allow your resentment to spoil the impact of your good deeds. Otherwise, you will cancel the merit of them. In reviewing your case, the committee will perceive your bad feelings and count them as a strike against you."

Ari does not back down. He challenges the fairness of Mr. Steerforth's remark. He defends himself even more assertively.

"Why will the committee take points away from me? The committee should give me a higher score because I obeyed my parents in spite of my feelings. I did all the things that they told me to do. I even asked a girl to the junior prom that I thought of only as a pal, because my parents forbade me from asking the girl that I really liked. They said that she was unsuitable. They said that she belonged to a different religion. They told me I should ask a Jewish girl."

Hearing his testimony, even with its bitter and defensive subtexts, Miss Dickinson stays on Ari's side. Unlike her fiancé, Captain Johnson, or Mrs. Adams and the Steerforths, she has not lost her capacity for pity and for empathy.

"You were an obedient son. By deferring to their will, you showed your respect for them."

"I *was* obedient. But I was not always happy."

About Ari's obedience, the Captain has more to say. He sees things differently. His experience in the war has made him harsh and unforgiving of other people's flaws. The brutal years of piloting bombing missions against Nazis in the Second World War have leached his senses of pity and forgiveness.

"You were not always an obedient son."

He waits for Ari's response. He expects a rancorous denial or a self-serving justification. But Ari plays dumb.

"I don't understand. I don't know what you mean."

The Captain comes at him now with grim-faced determination. He aims to unsettle him. He throws out just the right words.

"You understand," he says. "You know what I mean. You can never forget Boyd Henderson's Ferrari, though you have often tried."

"Of course I remember it. It was a GTC4 Lusso in gleaming metallic blue. It was a perfect vehicle. It rode like a comet, with a top speed of two hundred fourteen miles per hour. It had a powerful V12 engine and six hundred eighty horsepower. It was a four-seat beauty with a seven-speed dual clutch transmission. It also had a three-door shooting brake with all-wheel drivetrain. I'd never before seen such a sleek chassis and a luxury interior or driven a car with such tremendous horsepower."

"You were impressed."

"I sure was. I was even more impressed when Boyd said I could drive it."

"Did you drive it often?"

"I don't remember how often."

"Try to remember."

"I drove it whenever Boyd said I could."

"How often was that?"

"Whenever he didn't want to drive it."

"Why wouldn't he want to drive a splendid car like that one? Most teenagers who own a new Ferrari would want to drive it all the time. They wouldn't be asking a friend to drive it for them."

"I don't know why. I only know that he let me drive the car."

"When didn't he want to drive it? And why didn't he want to drive it?"

"There were times when he didn't feel well."

"What made him sick? There was a time when Boyd played soccer and baseball, among several other sports. He was named the most valuable player for both the soccer and baseball teams in your high school. The committee knows about him. In those days, when he was a sophomore, Boyd was a healthy boy. What happened to change things?"

"Once in a while, he drank a little."

"A little? What do you mean by 'a little'?"

"It's hard for me to remember. The drinking happened more than a year ago, when Boyd and I were juniors. That seems a long time ago."

"Did he always drink only a little?"

Ari says nothing. He cloaks himself in willful stillness.

The Captain closes in. His words are a hardened command.

"Tell us," he says. "We already know the answer. But we want you to tell it. We are giving you a chance that you may not deserve. We are waiting for you to speak the truth."

With brooding reluctance, Ari answers him.

"Sometimes Boyd drank more than a little."

"When he drank too much, did he ever allow you to drive the Ferrari?"

"Of course he did. He didn't want to get himself into an accident. He played it smart. He asked me to drive. Even if we were on a double date, he'd ask me to drive."

Mrs. Steerforth pushes him further. She borrows from his verbal overlapping. He has not completed his remark when she overtakes him.

"Did you drink when you were with him?"

"Maybe once or twice. Liquor wasn't any temptation for me. I don't like scotch, bourbon, or whiskey. Those were Boyd's favorites."

Mrs. Adams, who appears pinch-faced and suspicious, hurries in now. Before he has finished speaking, she topples the sound of his remark. Her voice is abrasive and impatient.

"On what occasions did you drink with him?"

Ari stays in control. He meets her disdain with a piercing gaze.

"Twice, I think. I remember there was one time after we'd left our junior prom. We were with our girlfriends. We were headed for a nightclub in a neighboring town. We had fake IDs. Boyd said the after-dance party should begin before we arrived at the club."

Mrs. Adams was displeased.

"That was a crazy idea—drinking while you were driving. But you went along with it."

"Yes."

This time the Captain overtakes his remark. He slams into him. He's on the attack. His accusation is swift and relentless.

"You drank," he says. "You drank more than a little. Despite your promise to your parents that you would never drink any liquor, not even beer."

Ari stays tough. He keeps the Captain at bay.

"All the guys drank. I didn't see anything wrong in it."

The Captain's eyes glow with eerie radiance. For a moment, flames engulf his entire body. They purify, rather than burn, his militant physique.

The sight of him rouses new apprehension within our group. Everyone is increasingly uncertain of him. Is the Captain on our side, guiding us toward a return to Earth? Or is he our nemesis? Is he here in this room to set traps for all of us? Does he intend to trick us into a confession of our wrongdoings and then exact a harsh retribution? I glance at the worried faces of my classmates and our two teachers.

I mask my apprehension. I busy myself with recording the highlights of this meeting. I appear calm and reflective.

For the moment, Ari also stays calm. But I know him well. I am more than a little familiar with his moods. I imagine that my classmates and our teachers do not see in him what I see. Anger is rising inside him. It is not ordinary anger. It is fury. I wait for him to unleash it. Right now, he holds himself steady. He is going to stand by his statement that he did not see anything wrong with drinking a few beers with his pals.

The Captain bears down on him.

"You did see, and you chose to disobey your parents."

Ari keeps his voice low yet insistent as he hurls new words at the Captain.

"My parents didn't have to live my life, though they tried. They never had to walk through the school corridors as I did and, with clenched fists, stand tall even though some of the guys and a few girls mocked me for being square or a good little Jew boy. My parents never knew about my after-school fights or about the guys I beat up."

The Captain keeps bearing down.

"Those fights were just the beginning. They weren't only about your following all the rules and working hard to stay on the honor roll. They were about something else. What was it? Why did the guys want to pick fights with you?"

Ari keeps the Captain waiting. He does not want to answer the question. Yet he sees no way around it. I sense what is coming. I know what Ari feels. Talking about it is painful. He takes time to compose himself. He's trying to keep a lid on his anger. When he does speak, he stays in firm control. He refuses to pity himself. He is forthright and matter-of-fact.

"I'm a Jew," he says. "Some of my classmates hated me for it. They had no reason to hate me. They were just following their parents' lead. They were keeping alive their parents' irrational hatred of Jewish people. They were also feeding their own desire to harm anyone they thought was different."

"You never told your parents about them."

"No."

"Why not?"

"I was ashamed to tell them that some students in my school were anti-Semitic. There were rumors that some of them were neo-Nazis. Anyway, I didn't want my parents to know about them or to worry about what might happen to me at school."

Miss Dickinson chimes in. She is still on Ari's side, but with reservations.

"Your decision was commendable, though wrong-headed," she tells him. "You showed that you loved your parents and that you did not want to give them reasons to worry about you. But you hid the truth from them. That's never a good path to follow."

Ari senses Miss Dickinson's good will. He tries to keep her on his side.

"I handled the problem in my own way," he explains. "I had always fought well, if I had to. But I wanted to improve my fighting skills. So I persuaded my father to let me train with a retired boxer who coached men and boys at the private club where my father was a member. I told my father that boxing would improve my agility as a runner and a swimmer. It would also give me more confidence in myself."

Mr. Steerforth wants Ari to tell more.

"What happened after you had a few months of training as a boxer?"

"I knocked out two of the tough guys at school who cornered me in an alley and were looking to beat me up because I am Jewish. After that, the word got out. I wasn't going to be their victim. If those guys thought they were going to bring their neo-Nazi gang after me, they changed their minds when they found out that I'd formed my own gang. I'd made plenty of friends with the guys who boxed with me at my father's club. They knew the score. Some of them were Jewish. Some of them were not. It didn't matter. They were on my side. Together, we could beat the crap out of the tough boys from my school."

The Captain eyes Ari with guarded respect. Clearly, he understands and appreciates Ari's courage. Still, Ari's courage carries with it a serious flaw. The Captain bears down again.

CHAPTER FIVE

THE NIGHT OF THE DANCE

"You didn't tell your parents about this problem with the Neo-Nazi gang," the Captain says.

"I didn't want them to get upset."

The Captain presses forward.

"Was that your only reason for concealing this information from them?"

"I wanted to work through my problems in my own way. I didn't want to be the helpless boy who cries out to his parents every time something goes wrong for him. Besides, my father helped me without realizing he was doing so. He made it possible for me to box at his club."

Ari's words are sensible and revealing. Nevertheless, they fail to placate the Captain.

"You hid the problem from your father. You also hid the fact of your drinking. Your parents had warned you against maintaining your friendship with Boyd Henderson. He was always getting into trouble. He was a loose cannon. But you disobeyed them. Even though you had driven your own car to the junior prom, you chose to enter Boyd's car and place yourself in a dangerous situation."

"I thought I was helping him. He had been drinking in secret while we were at the dance. I was surprised that the teachers and the security guards who were monitoring our class didn't notice his erratic behavior. But Boyd was always clowning around.

Maybe they regarded his high spirits as a normal response to the dance and to being with his girlfriend."

Mr. Steerforth bulldozes his way into this tense examination of Ari's behavior. No longer does he impart a "nice guy" persona. To my eyes, at least, he appears case hardened and ruthless.

"You drove the Ferrari at a high speed," he declares. "That night of the dance, you had been drinking heavily. You were less drunk than Boyd. But you were far more intoxicated than you had ever been. Your vision was blurry. Your driving skills were impaired. You lost control of the car and sideswiped a Lincoln Town Car in the opposite lane. All four passengers were seriously injured. Yet you did not stop Boyd's Ferrari. You kept on driving, possibly oblivious to the danger that you were bringing to others.

"Minutes afterward, when you were speeding through a country road that bordered a farm, you lost control of the car. You swerved off the road. You crashed into a tractor that had been left near a huge field of strawberries. The collision lifted the Ferrari high into the air. It somersaulted across that field. When it landed, it made a swathe thirty feet long before it came to rest at the side of a paddock, where horses usually grazed during mid-afternoon. No horses were grazing then. It was midnight, and darkness clothed the area like a shroud. Moments earlier, the farm and its people had been peacefully sleeping. Then the thunderous echo of the crash, the beaming headlights of the Ferrari, and the incessant honking of the car's horn wakened them to the trouble that you and the Ferrari had brought them."

Mr. Steerforth pauses. He studies the effect of his words upon Ari.

The Captain observes Ari, as well.

Their interest in Ari's response does not surprise me. That interest is anchored to their probing of his past and to their prodding him to tell the truth. Nor do the frowns that touch the faces of my classmates surprise me. Their acceptance of Ari has always been ambivalent, despite his excellent grades and his success as an athlete. But the traceries of fear that alter their expressions make me pause as I decipher the implicated meanings of their uneasiness.

Mr. Steerforth doesn't let up. He hammers away. He continues to beat down Ari's reluctance to tell all of the truth.

"Why don't you tell the rest of it?" he asks. "You know what happened right after the crash. You should tell us about it. You should tell us so that you will avoid the consequences of not telling."

Ari resists his threatening manner.

"I don't remember," he says. "I'd had a few drinks. I didn't see things clearly."

Once again Mrs. Steerforth enters the battle. She is her husband's backup. She is the legal expert who double-checks the facts that incriminate a suspect. She finds the clues that corroborate the evidence her husband has uncovered.

"You were thinking clearly enough when you persuaded Boyd's girlfriend to reposition Boyd's unconscious body in the car. With her help, you moved Boyd into the driver's seat so that the police would believe that it was he who had been driving recklessly. "

Ari's anger is reaching the boiling point. Nevertheless, he stays in control.

"I don't remember doing that," he says. "I would never double-cross a friend. Besides, his girlfriend would never have helped me carry out such a plan."

Mr. Steerforth hurries to support his wife's accusations.

"Boyd and his girlfriend had been arguing all that evening. He was going to drop her. He'd grown weary of her neurotic problems and her self-centeredness. The girl that he was dumping was looking to avenge herself against Boyd. Your plan to blame him for the car crash pleased her."

Ari answers these charges with low-keyed conviction.

"I don't believe that any of this happened. You are imagining things."

Mrs. Adams, even more irate than before, repeats and clarifies the serious charges that the committee is lodging against Ari.

"We are not imagining things. We know the facts. You know them, too."

"You don't know all of the facts. Boyd was as much to blame for the crash as I was."

"You were driving the car. You crashed it. Admit your wrongdoing. Take the blame from which you have been running for over a year. Tell us the truth about that wildly racing Ferrari. Tell us what really happened."

Ari stares her down, even though ghostly rays shoot out of her eyes and burn the air in front of her. The laser beams stop in mid-air, hovering mere inches from the place where Ari is sitting. He grimaces, but he does not move back in fear. I read his mind. I know him well. I imagine every detail of his thinking. He is telling himself that death has robbed him of his parents and his brother and sister. Death has stolen, too, the friends who enhanced his life as a young man with a bright future. He has nothing more to lose except, possibly, the chance that the committee will allow our group to go back to our lives on Earth. He ponders the value of that chance. He makes a wily choice. Instead of lashing out at Mrs. Adams with anger equal to hers, he encloses himself in silence. He lets her do the talking.

He will not remain silent long. Part of the story is missing, and he and I are the only ones from our group who can tell it. Since Ari's in the hot spot, he will eventually do the talking. There flashes in my private seeing the fiercer confrontation that is about to unfold.

In this moment, though, Mrs. Adams intensifies her role as a prosecutor. She is upset that Ari conceals his guilt within a show of silence. She lashes out at him, spewing through her teeth the facts that have attached themselves to his crime.

"You wanted the police to believe that Boyd Henderson caused the crash and the serious injuries not only to those four people in the Lincoln Town Car, but also to himself and to your girlfriend. You also wanted them to believe that it was not you, but Boyd who had wrought serious damage to a farmer's crop of strawberries and to his tractor."

Confronted by the stark reality of these charges, Ari decides to fight back. For the first time, he raises his voice while defending himself, though he is not ready to tell everything that went wrong that night. He begins again, this time with what he regards as his strongest defense.

"I saved Boyd's life—and my girlfriend's life, too. If he'd been driving the car, he would have got himself and my girlfriend killed."

The Captain blasts his way into it again. His anger reaches a new pitch. It transforms his appearance. The human body that he inhabits vanishes not gradually, but instantly amidst a swirl of billowing flames. A death's head and the bleached bones of a cadaver consume his humanness even as they verify his mortal nature. Yet only for a moment does his body reveal the death that has consumed his Earthly image. Only for that moment do the horrific images overtake the rangy form that has convinced us that the Captain is one like ourselves, a human being who was killed while he was very young. But the Captain is not like us, at least not completely. Though he lived on Earth for a while, he has been dead for three quarters of a century.

"You blamed Boyd Henderson for your crime," the Captain says. His voice is harsh and unforgiving. "Boyd lost his driver's license. He was charged with leaving the scene of an accident. His insurance company had to pay plenty to the injured parties. It cost Boyd's father sixty thousand dollars to get him out of prison after he'd served ninety days. It cost him even more to place his son in a private facility for young drug addicts."

Again, Ari fires back an abrasive reply, his anger uncoiling with an even fiercer energy.

"Boyd ruined his reputation before the crash. Only a few months earlier, his parents had checked him into a rehab center because of his addiction to hard liquor, cocaine, and marijuana. He was always getting into trouble and pulling friends down to his level. He was a powder keg. Even his closest friends didn't know what he would do from one minute to the next. He was never innocent. The people who knew him branded him guilty for life."

Ari's rancorous defense of himself goads new levels of the Captain's fury. The Captain blasts him with another volley of accusations.

"You concealed the truth. You were the driver. You caused the crash. You refused to take the blame for your crime. You let the blame fall upon him. You failed to be a friend to a youth who was actually crying out for help. You didn't listen. You didn't care."

Ari still does not back down. His words are even more blunt. He makes no pretense at hiding his hostile feelings.

"I did care, at least in the beginning. Boyd's wildness awed me. I thought he was *the* anti-hero. I envied him because he was a rebel."

Miss Dickinson comes into it again. She wants to defuse this acrimonious exchange between the Captain and Ari. She does so by gently asking a question.

"What changed your opinion of Boyd?"

Ari calms down. For a moment, he ponders her question and then offers her an even-tempered answer.

"Boyd wasn't smart. He didn't care whether he got caught when he did something crazy. In school, I had a solid reputation. I had a stellar record. I made all the right moves. I didn't want to lose what it had taken me years to build. I soon grew weary of Boyd and his perverse need to make trouble."

As gently as she can, Miss Dickinson reminds Ari of a fact that he cannot plausibly deny. Her words sound maternal yet insistent.

"You didn't help him."

Her gentle manner wins Ari's trust, at least a little. He is willing to tell more about the night of the dance. He directs his words to her alone, even though the other members of the committee, as adversarial as they are relentless, are giving him their complete attention.

"I never knew that Boyd was asking me for help," Ari explains. "Besides, I stayed friends with him. We just didn't see one another very often."

"You were with him on the night of the crash."

Ari hesitates before the painful truth of Miss Dickinson's gentle remark. Now he decides to tell her so much more about the night of the prom.

"All during the dinner dance, Boyd was not only wild. He was also strange—even surreal. It felt good to be in his company again. That night, I was looking for adventure. With our girlfriends beside us, Boyd and I could find an adventure. It didn't matter that Boyd and his girlfriend were breaking up. She was game. She was looking for adventure, too.

"At first, my date was afraid of the trouble we might be making for ourselves. But a few shots of vodka gave her confidence. We headed northwest, to our favorite beach in Owls Head, thirteen miles away. We were going to swim in the nude on that unusually warm April night. We intended to enjoy some romancing right there on the moonlit beach. Afterward, if we were lucky, we'd find a couple of stray kayaks that had been left on the beach, probably by drunken partygoers. We'd borrow them and battle our way across rough ocean waters."

"You never arrived at the beach," Miss Dickinson reminds him.

"We might have. But, weaving in and out of his drunken stupor, Boyd got it into his head that he was the one who should be driving. Every so often he'd push himself against me and try to take the wheel. I'd gently nudge him back to his place in the front passenger seat, and he'd nod off, losing himself again inside his stupor."

"Something went terribly wrong, though."

"Yes."

"Tell us about it."

"We were making our way on a country road that was surrounded by huge farm fields. Even at night, I could calculate that the property held a hundred acres. I was beginning to enjoy the drive again. I felt that we were on our way to a few beach thrills and maybe an adventurous episode on the ocean. I was driving smoothly now, because Boyd was in a deep sleep. Or at least I thought he was. Our girlfriends were seated comfortably in the back, sharing their stories about the dance. We were passing through that peaceful farm road, and I was imagining that everyone and everything that lived on that farm were at peace. Then, without any warning, the whole night went haywire."

Ari pauses. I sense his anguish. It is painful for him to recall the violence of the crash and its wretched aftermath.

Once again, Miss Dickinson draws upon her Big Sister persona and her soft words to coax Ari to tell all of us about the violence that destroyed whatever happiness he and his friends had experienced that evening.

"Please go on," she urges him. "I know it's not easy for you. But you must tell all of it. Otherwise, you'll jeopardize your chance to return to your life on Earth. You'll deprive your classmates and your teachers of their chances, too."

"The night went haywire the moment that Boyd awoke and began punching me in the face and in my right shoulder. He wanted to drive his car, and I wouldn't let him. While my left hand was clasping the wheel, I used my right hand to fend him off. But he kept coming back at me with a hard punch to my gut and rapid-fire jabs to the side of my face and my ear. With my one hand, I fought back and for a couple of minutes managed to keep him at bay. But when he landed a hard jab at my ear, my senses started reeling. I thought I was going to pass out. I returned my right hand to the wheel and was going to bring our speeding car to a halt. But Boyd slammed against me with brutal force. He placed his hands on the wheel, covering my hands with wrenching pressure as each of us fought for control of the car. Already, the car was zigzagging across both sides of the road. I remember that our girlfriends started screaming. They knew how dangerous Boyd could be.

"'Stop fooling around!' I yelled. 'You'll get all of us killed.'

"'That's what I'm here for,' he said. 'I'm Mister Death.'

"No sooner had he said so than he pressed his foot upon mine and accelerated the speed of the car. That's when we sideswiped the Lincoln Town Car. Before my left foot could touch the brake, the car careened off the road, shot through the strawberry fields, flipped, and flipped again. I must have passed out for a few minutes. I don't remember the car coming to rest in one of the fields. When I came back into the scene, I noticed that Boyd had been knocked unconscious by the impact of the crash. He was slumped beside me, smelling of whiskey and cocaine. His face was bruised and his left arm was bleeding.

"My date, Sonia Janowski, was also unconscious. In this period, we were friends rather than romantic partners. She is here with us in this room. All of you can see that she is a very pretty girl, with blonde hair, blue eyes, and a radiant smile. The history of her family prodded my interest in her. She is a Polish Jew whose relatives died in the Nazi concentration camps in Dachau during The Second World War. I was drawn to her first of all because of her beauty and, after that, because of her excellence in math and science that convinced me we shared the same interests.

"Though on the evening of the dance she was wearing a seat belt, Sonia had hit her head against the door when the car flipped over. Boyd's date was all right. She'd been lucky. She didn't have a scratch on her.

"The windows were smashed, and the front passenger door and one of the rear doors had been sheared off when the Ferrari collided with the Lincoln. The horn was blaring, and sparks of fire were snaking their way out of the hood of the car. I turned off the ignition to stop the fire. I tried to open the door, but it wouldn't budge. With all the force I had in me, I heaved myself against the door. It opened. I stepped out of the car. Though I was hazy and wobbly, I looked cautiously around me, while surveying the scene. I wanted to get help. I didn't know how seriously Boyd and my date were injured. My cell phone had been wrecked in the crash. So had Boyd's.

"I was hoping that at least one of the girls had carried her cell phone inside her purse and that it still worked. I peered into the back seat of the wreckage. But only my date was there. What had happened to Boyd's girlfriend? Had she been thrown from the car? Was she lying dead on the road that had hurled our car into the farm fields? My heart sank. If she had died, then everyone would blame me for her death. Nearly frantic now and still wobbly, I turned from the Ferrari and was about to find my way back onto the road in search of her. Then suddenly, without my expecting her, Boyd's girlfriend was standing beside me. She had climbed out of the car when I was unconscious.

"'We're in a mess,' she said. 'There's going to be plenty of trouble for all of us and especially for you.'"

"'It wasn't my fault,' I told her. 'You saw what happened.'

"'I know that it wasn't your fault. But Boyd will be glad for you to take the blame. He enjoys dragging people down to his common level.'

"'It's unfair,' I said, dazed and confused by the way that the night had spun out of control. I thought about my parents and the scandal and the lawsuits that would be pinned on them. I thought about the scholarships that would no longer be available to me the following year, after I was graduated from high school. I thought about the Ivy League universities that would close themselves off from me. I thought of all the years I'd studied hard and done the right things. My life was ruined, and I was only sixteen.

"In the faraway distance, I saw lights glimmering from the main house on the farm. The people who lived there were awake now. They had heard the crash of the Ferrari that had flipped over and over before it bounced thirty feet and landed against the cedar fence of a paddock. I imagined that the owner of the place and maybe his sons or a few field hands were dressing hastily and, after jumping inside a pickup truck, would be driving across the long path that bordered the field and the paddock where the speeding Ferrari had landed.

"I felt trapped. I felt that all the people who could harm me were closing in. They'd be relentless. They'd make certain I was punished for driving a car so wildly and for causing my classmates grievous injury and maybe even death.

"I prepared myself for the worst. Within the next half hour, the police would arrive. They were going to arrest me. I'd be sent to a reformatory for wayward youth.

"I was dazed. I couldn't think straight. I cannot say with certainty whether the shock of the crash left me confused or whether it was the fear of being caught and branded a criminal. I only know that Boyd's girlfriend seemed like an answer to whatever prayer could save me. I felt that I was awake in a cursed dream that was unfolding. I felt that my body was not my own. I felt separated from myself and from the life that I'd been living. Then I heard a girl's voice speaking to me. The voice belonged to Boyd's girlfriend. She was saying all over again what I should do. When she told me that I should move Boyd's body into the driver's seat, I didn't hesitate. It was Boyd who got us into the accident. He was the one who caused the Ferrari to spin out of control."

The committee has been listening with keen-sighted awareness of Ari's past. Their stern faces, with their mysterious melding of ghostly and human, are scrutinizing even the smallest details of Ari's demeanor and the nearly imperceptible evidence of his rebellious nature. To their rheumy eyes, Ari isn't sufficiently contrite. He doesn't want to admit his moral failing. He wants Boyd Henderson to be the fall guy. He wants the committee and every member of our group to regard him as an unwitting victim caught in the web of Boyd's renegade behavior. Compared to Boyd, he is an innocent.

The committee is prepared to condemn Boyd for his horrendous crimes. Only a year after the night of the junior dance, he killed thirteen people. That is an altogether different matter. It is not difficult to believe that they regard Boyd as an abomination. Ari does not belong to that bestial league. Nevertheless, they cannot bring themselves to trust him. They want him to reveal more about what happened on the night of the dance.

Once again the Captain pummels him with a probing question. He wants to drive Ari into a narrow corner from which there is no escape. He is waiting for him to face himself. He will keep on pressuring him with questions. He will wait for as long as it takes Ari to tell all of his secrets.

The Captain has uncovered one of Ari's darker secrets. He knows that the reality behind that secret ignited the massacre that took place at our school a few days ago.

"Who was Boyd's girlfriend?" he asks, well aware that the girlfriend was a catalyst in the shooting at our school. "Is she here with us now?"

Ari fakes a pensive stance. He summons a reflective look. He appears to be sorting through his memories. He's a good actor.

"I'm not sure," he says. "The night of the dance happened a year ago. So many things happened since then."

The Captain sees through him. Ari wants to protect that girl, even though she is guilty of more insidious crimes than his own.

"You know that she's here. I think you had better tell us who she is."

Now I come into it.

CHAPTER SIX

BOYD HENDERSON'S GIRLFRIEND

"Ari doesn't need to say anything," I say. "I can speak for myself. I was one of the girls who were riding in that Ferrari when Ari was driving it. I was Boyd's date."

Mrs. Adams calls out my name, as if she means to remind the committee of who I am exactly. My classmates and my teachers need no reminder. They are well acquainted with who I am.

"You are Cassandra Winslow, the girl who incited the massacre that occurred more than a week ago."

"I am."

The Captain breaks in.

"We'll hear more about your involvement in that crime soon enough. Right now, you can explain what else happened on the night of the crash, a year before the massacre. You can tell us in detail how your lies about the crash goaded Boyd Henderson's fury."

"Boyd had it coming," I tell them, brazen and unrepentant. "He always gave me a hard time. He'd rough me up if I voiced an opinion that didn't fit in with his rotten view of the world. On the night of the junior dance, he told me that we were through. He'd found another girl."

Miss Dickinson urges me to tell more.

"You loved Boyd. You felt betrayed. In spite of the conflicts that marred your relationship with him, you loved him. You shared your body with him. You'd allowed him to touch your soul."

"I don't know what love is. Looking back, I see that I admired Boyd's recklessness. There was danger in him. He was waging a battle against society's narrow-minded conventions and against the oppressive rules that tamped down our freedom. I liked all those things about him. But I never loved him."

Mrs. Steerforth comes into it now, as mean-spirited and scornful as ever.

"Then it wasn't difficult for you to betray Boyd."

"I didn't betray him. Neither did Ari. We passed sentence on him. He'd caused the crash. He was guilty. He deserved the punishment that the law meted out to him."

"You and Ari lied. You moved Boyd's body into the driver's seat. You told the police that he was driving wildly because he wanted to kill himself and to kill all of you."

Ari rushes in to defend me.

"I'm the one who told the police that story. I'm to blame."

"At last, you admit your guilt."

"I *am* guilty of lying. But I didn't anticipate all the bad things that happened afterward because of my lie. I didn't understand."

The Captain comes back. He does not accept what he hears. He fires back his objection.

"You and Cassandra Winslow set in motion all the punishing episodes that weighed Boyd down. After his ninety-day detention in a reformatory and another ninety days in rehab, the town regarded him as an outlaw. Though your high school readmitted him as a student on probation, you and your classmates treated him as if he were a pariah.

"Some teachers identified him as a dangerous troublemaker. They didn't give him a chance. They expected him to make trouble. His very presence made them uneasy. He was unorthodox not only in the way that he dressed, but also in the many ways that he questioned and often challenged the prevailing rules in the school and in the community.

"The administrators closed in. So did the police. They decided not to like anything about him—not his clothes or opinions or his driving. They devised punishing episodes that harnessed his freedom. They never forgot that he had served time in a reformatory."

Ari goes on fighting hard. He is under tremendous pressure. He strains to maintain self-control. But a fury is still churning inside him. I imagine what he is feeling. The Captain is focusing on the things that our classmates and teachers did wrong. But he is not giving sufficient attention to the many ways that they helped Boyd.

"All that negative stuff happened at the beginning of our senior year," Ari says. "Then Ms. Patel and Mr. Marchand stepped in. They became his counselors. They drew him into advanced placement courses in biology, physics, French and Spanish. He had a facility with languages and with science. They also persuaded him to return to the soccer and baseball teams and to join the swim team. He won a prize for his history project about America's commitment to the wars in Iraq and Afghanistan. Everyone at the school started looking at him in a more positive way. They saw that he was walking tall on a new path. For the first time in years, he felt good about himself."

The Captain has more to say. He does not accept the significance of these "feel good" episodes in Boyd's life. They can never outrank the murderous deeds in his dark history.

"Those feelings didn't last long," he says. "Something bad happened. Someone spread a rumor about him that reawakened suspicion and even fear."

Ari turns very still. He knows the identity of the person who spread the rumor. But he is waiting for that person to come forward and accept responsibility for the wrongdoing.

Impatient and badgering, Mrs. Steerforth tries to push Ari into revealing the name of the troublemaker and the lie that stole Boyd's newly earned happiness.

"Tell us about it," she demands. "Tell us about the rumor. Tell us who spread it."

Ari resists her impatience and her badgering.

"I don't want to talk about it," he says. "I wasn't the bearer of tales at that time. I don't want to be one now."

The Captain doesn't let up. His angry words once again lash out at Ari.

"You know who spread the rumor. If you want the committee to consider sending your group back to Earth, you had better cooperate with us. Tell the name of the person who set Boyd up for a fall. Tell us about the rumor that nearly drove him mad."

Ari still keeps the lid on the fury that is churning within him. His face turns pale, as though he is vanishing more swiftly than he or anyone in this room anticipated. His voice is husky and weighed down by his grief.

"I can't tell," he says. "I can't. It's unbearable even to think about it. I couldn't begin to choose the words that would make sense of it."

I come into it again. I meet the Captain's abrasive manner with the cutting edge of belligerence. I tell him what he is waiting to hear.

"*I* spread the rumor."

A hush overtakes the room. My admission surprises nobody. The committee is well aware of my devious behavior. My classmates and my teachers also remember.

The Captain detects my belligerence and my unrepentant manner. He is not pleased.

"Why?" he asks. "Why did you deliberately harm Boyd Henderson's already damaged reputation?"

I turn on him now and on the committee.

"How many questions do you need to ask? What good are they? Answering them won't change things. What's done is done. It can't be undone."

Miss Dickinson intervenes. There is a genuine urgency in her words. She wants me to say the right things. She wants our group to win the committee's favor. She would like us to win the privilege of returning to Earth so that we can relive the days that led to our tragedy. She wants us to find out whether we can alter the horrific things that happened.

"Perhaps the events of that day can be undone," she says. "Everything depends upon your answers to our questions. Everything depends upon how much you are willing to tell us about what happened."

I hesitate. I'm pleased that she is on our side. I tell her what she wants to know.

"I set Boyd up for a fall. I wanted to pay him back for humiliating me. We'd been going steady for more than a year. Then, on the night of the junior prom and without a valid reason, he told me that we were through. We should enjoy prom night and then make a clean break of each other. I pretended not to care. I told him that plenty of other guys wanted to go out with me. What I didn't tell him was that I'd already heard that he wanted to start dating a Latina named Adriana Montalban. I'd also heard that he told his closest friends that she was terrific. He told our crowd that I'd grown unexciting. I was predictable. I was a phony. I pretended to be a rebel, but in my heart I was a frightened girl who didn't want to stray too far from safe conventions and lock-step rules."

Mr. Steerforth wants to know more.

"How did you set him up for a fall?"

"I lied about him. I told my school counselor and, afterwards, the principal that Boyd planned to come to school some day soon and shoot as many students and teachers as he could. He had an arsenal of guns and rifles in his home. The weapons belonged to his father. They were locked in a gun vault, but Boyd had easy access to them. He had a duplicate key that his father had given him because he trusted him. He knew that Boyd was a sharpshooter who always handled those weapons with responsible expertise. What he did not know was that Boyd was messed up. His reformation was a sham.

"I made up as many lies about Boyd as I could. I said that he was following all the rules because he wanted to fool people into believing that he had changed for the better. The night of the car crash was far behind him. He wanted everyone to believe that the time he'd spent in a reformatory and later in a rehab center had saved him. He was pretending that the psychologists who treated him when he was in rehab had opened a different view of the world. He made people believe that he didn't need to do battle with the world. He could learn to negotiate with it and still be his own man.

"All these lies I told my school counselor and the principal.

"I also told the classmates who were popular and who influenced the thinking of all the students vying for their friendship. The news spread quickly. Boyd Henderson was planning to become a school shooter. He wanted to die in a blaze of bullets, and before he died, he wanted to kill as many people as he could."

Mrs. Adams, as acerbic as ever, probes further.

"Did everyone believe your story? They knew that Boyd had dropped you as his girlfriend. You might be making up a story to get back at him."

Hers is a street-wise question. I respect its realism, but I dislike this Spirit/Lady who is asking the question. However, I fire back a brisk answer.

"My classmates remembered what Boyd had said during his rebellious season. More than once, he told his crowd of followers that he planned to bring his AR-15 to school some day and kill a hundred people within fifteen minutes. They remembered what he'd said. That made my story very plausible. Besides, most of those students had been programmed a year earlier to believe that Boyd was no good. They wanted to believe the worst of him."

Miss Dickinson, with her gentle manner, comes back into it again.

"Surely, the principal must have doubted your words. Boyd was making a tremendous recovery from his past errors. He'd made the honor roll, and he'd helped his soccer, baseball, and swim teams to win medals and the praise of the mayor."

"It's true that the principal did not want to believe my words. He did not accuse me of lying. He simply thought that I was needlessly concerned about the threat that Boyd had made more than a year ago. Time had defused that threat. Boyd's good deeds were proving that he was a responsible citizen."

The Captain joins in again. He has been carefully listening to my words. Now he offers his appraisal.

"The principal was on Boyd's side, after all."

"Not completely. I sensed that he was uneasy. I saw the small trace of doubt in his eyes and on his face. I played on that doubt. I told him that the school was no longer a safe place because Boyd was a student there."

Mrs. Adams pushes me to say more.

"The principal did not believe you."

"He did not want to believe me. That's an altogether different thing."

"What exactly did he tell you?"

"'Boyd has no motive,' he said. 'He's a student in good standing, and he's making all the right moves. He's a walking success story. You need not fear his becoming a school assassin. Things have changed for him. He's popular for the right reasons. He has no motive for killing anyone.'"

The Captain knows me well. He is aware of how wily and vindictive I was.

"You wouldn't give in. You pleaded with the principal. You begged him to regard Boyd as a potential killer."

"Yes. I did plead with him. But he kept saying that Boyd had no motive."

Miss Dickinson asks another question. A frown touches her brow. Her memory of my behavior dismays her. She knows what's coming, but, rueful and solicitous, she asks her question anyway.

"What made the principal change his mind?"

"I told him other things that Boyd had said a year earlier about committing the perfect crime. He wanted to find out whether he was one of the supermen about whom the nineteenth-century German philosopher Friedrich Nietzsche had written. If he could devise the perfect crime and carry it out, he would prove that he was one of those transcendent individuals whose extraordinary capabilities allowed them to rise above the laws and the rules that bound ordinary people."

Mrs. Steerforth tries to sort out the meaning of everything that I've been saying. She wonders aloud.

"But Boyd planned to kill himself right after the massacre. What good would that do for him?'

"There would be a purity in his acts of murder. He would kill at least a dozen of his classmates and maybe a few teachers. Maybe he would even kill a hundred. He would show that a teenager could be very powerful, if he chose to be. He could do amazing things. He'd work out a complicated murder plan, and he would carry it out for all of posterity to ponder. The real kicker would be his murder of himself."

I pause. I am surprised that I am unhappy as I tell the committee and the group what happened.

Miss Dickinson, in her quiet way, urges me to explain more of it.

"Boyd Henderson hated life. He hated himself. Where did that hate begin—and when?"

"He came from a privileged background that was actually very rough on him. His father gave him many possessions and didn't pay too much attention to him. When he wasn't focusing on his career as a television anchor and a documentary filmmaker, he'd penalize Boyd harshly for any trouble that he'd made for himself and for the family. He'd bring Boyd to the boxing ring within the gym of his private club. Boyd was a vigorous boxer. But his father would box with him so fiercely that he often knocked him out. Boyd's scars would heal. But not all of them. Not the ones that burned into his mind."

"Many teenagers have been kicked around by their families," Miss Dickinson says. "But very few of them become mass murderers."

"I told the principal that I didn't know very much about Boyd, even though we'd gone together for more than a year. Most of the time, he closed me away from his thoughts. But this much Boyd did tell me: He used to dream of the people he was going to kill. He dreamed of their dead faces."

"Did the principal believe you?"

"Yes. A little. Enough. He called a meeting that involved Boyd's parents, teachers, coaches, and counselors. Boyd was there, too. So was I."

Unsmiling, Mrs. Adams pries and pushes.

"Why were you there?"

"The principal wanted me to tell them what I feared in Boyd and why."

Though he knows every detail of what happened, Mr. Steerforth acts as if he is hearing it for the first time. About my fear of Boyd, he is skeptical. He wants to know how those persons at the meeting felt.

"Did anyone there believe you?"

"No. But they let me down easy. They gave me points for good intentions. They said that I wanted to protect my classmates and my teachers. I wanted to protect Boyd from himself. But there wasn't any need to be afraid. Boyd had become a reliable citizen. He was doing all the right things. Everyone at the meeting said so. They had photos of him on their iPhones that showed him on a soccer field, at a swim meet, and in the school play. They showed him playing the saxophone during a school concert. They showed him with his celebrity parents and his best friends on a cruise ship heading for Hawaii. He looked happy in every one of the photos. He had recovered his best self."

Miss Dickinson is glad to hear what I am saying.

"So the meeting went in Boyd's favor."

"It did. But that didn't seem to matter to him. The meeting and all the personal questions humiliated him. Worse than that, he was never free of the rumors about his earlier plan to become a school assassin."

Mrs. Adams comes into it again, with one of her taunts.

"You saw to that."

"Yes. I still hated Boyd. I hated him for breaking up with me. I hated him for dating Adriana Montalban after he dropped me. I hated him for having the strength to choose a better path. I hated him for all these things. But most of all I hated him for messing me up and making me feel that I wasn't worth anything."

Mrs. Steerforth has a question.

"Why did your breakup matter so much? You've told us that you didn't love him."

"He told the friends whose good opinion was important to me that I wasn't anyone special. He was glad to be rid of me."

The Captain bears down heavily.

"Your lies wrecked his life when he was most vulnerable. His defenses were down. He'd begun believing that life was really good. Then, little by little, because of their renewed doubts of him, your classmates turned away from him. Even his soccer, baseball, and swim mates kept him at a subtle distance. Suspicion shadowed him like a storm cloud. His anger festered. The bitterness that had always plagued him came back to haunt him, day and night."

I fall silent. I am beyond bitterness and despair. I cannot even petition for forgiveness.

Ari comes back into it.

"But Boyd didn't give into the bitterness—at least, not right away. I'd heard those rumors about his plan to become a school shooter, but I didn't believe them. In spite of the car crash and all the grief it caused him, he was willing to begin a new chapter with me. He never knew that in those hours right after the junior prom I'd been driving his car. He was so drunk that night that he didn't remember anything that happened after he'd left the dance. When he returned to school from rehab, we weren't close friends. But we were teammates who'd learned to tolerate, if not like, each other. There were times when I wanted to tell him the truth about the crash. But I didn't."

The Captain wants Ari to tell more.

"Why not?"

"I didn't want my parents to find out. I didn't want to get myself arrested if Boyd went to the police or to his lawyer. I didn't want to lose my scholarship to Yale or the reputation I'd built for myself through years of doing all the right things. Besides, nothing could undo the crash. And, despite his time in the reformatory and in rehab, Boyd had done all right. He beat all the odds. He was winning his race."

Mr. Steerforth ponders all that he has heard. He holds Ari in a steady gaze. With stern face and matter-of-fact words that are tinged with melancholy, he asks another question.

"If you could have the chance to relive that year, would you do anything differently?"

A sob leaps out of Ari's throat. He clenches his fists. Perhaps, that is his way of stopping himself from completely breaking down and crying. He struggles to keep his sorrow at bay. He has been taught that a man never cries, and he holds himself to that credo. Nevertheless, his voice cracks as he answers Mr. Steerforth's question about whether he would live the last year of his life on Earth differently if he were given the chance to do so.

"I'd try to. Oh, God, how I would try."

CHAPTER SEVEN
BRENDA FLYNN

The Evaluation Committee carefully observes Ari as he struggles to keep his grief at bay. The Captain respects Ari's manly struggle to keep his feelings tightly harnessed. Mr. Steerforth regards Ari as a complicated specimen with a brooding, self-centered nature that is often at odds with his makeshift attempts to help other people. Mrs. Steerforth finds it hard to forgive Ari for placing blame for the car crash upon the already disreputable Boyd Henderson. Mrs. Adams does not think any better of Ari because he allows his remorse to overcome him while he is seated in the company of his peers and of the committee members whom he regards as strangers. Her no-nonsense character and rough-hewn disposition disdain any emotional display even when it is anchored to genuine feelings. Perhaps, her years as a nurse have solidified and deepened the detachment that is her signature response to human frailty of any sort.

I understand these Spirit/bodies. Even before I died, I saw who they are. In some vague way that I could not completely explain to myself, I knew that I would be meeting them in Sojourn sooner than I wanted. While I was alive on Earth, I dared not tell anyone else that, from time to time, they visited me. They hovered about my dreams. They lurked in shadowy corners whenever I betrayed the trust of friends or derided acquaintances who followed all the rules. Each time that I saw them, their appearances underwent various transformations. In the first moments of my sighting them, they were full-bodied human beings—or so they seemed. When I tried to turn away from them or to close my eyes to their presence, they prevented me from doing so. I could not move. I could not stir in any way. Their powers held me firmly in place. In this manner, they compelled me to study the rapid changes of their appearances.

Spellbound, I watched the flesh of their human bodies ripped away from their frames. I saw the gleaming bones of their skeletons. I witnessed the grim expressions of their death's heads. I saw bodies and bones vanish in an instant and then swiftly reassemble. Once again, their bodies were whole and intact, but before my eyes they were vanishing into nebulous Spirit/lives. No longer were they palpable or corporeal. They were impervious to touch and to proximity. For a few moments, they floated or lurked in the distance. They observed me with clinical detachment and then teleported toward me. Only then did I clearly behold their ghosts—clouded Apparitions, eerie Shadows, and disquieting Phantoms. I felt their cold breathing upon my face, so close to me were they hovering. I heard them whisper to me. Sometimes they spoke in unison, as though they were chanting a warning to me. On other occasions, only one of them spoke to me. Always, though, their message was the same.

"Beware of yourself."

I did not at that time know their names. Years were to pass before they greeted me as members of the Evaluation Committee. But I remembered my quickened sight of them as their human bodies rose before me momentarily and then flared into eerie transformations. Those bodies belonged to Mr. and Mrs. Steerforth, Captain Johnson and Miss Dickinson, and Mrs. Adams.

Now, eight days after I have died, I do not imagine that my relationship with most of them will be a happy one. Here in Sojourn, the Five Spirits have increased my supernatural powers even as they have diminished my power to predict the future. Far away from Earth, I can see you clearly. But I cannot always foresee what is going to happen to my friends. Nor can I perceive what is going to happen finally to me.

But I see Ari Bachman's future, at least in its general outlines. I am not yet certain whether his future will keep him in Sojourn and eventually bring him to The First Heaven. Possibly, though far less likely, he will return to Earth. No matter what happens to him, his future will be happier than my own.

In the late hours of this morning, without even trying, he has made a friend of Miss Dickinson. He has impressed her. His capacity for genuine anguish instantly becomes a bond between them. She, too, has experienced heartbreak. But her heartbreak derived not from anything she had done wrong. On the contrary, she had led an exemplary life. The Fates sent her a different kind of grief. As a young woman in her early twenties, she lost the only man that she could ever love. He died as a war hero, but that honorable death did not allay her suffering. For the next seven decades, she endured the loneliness of being without him. Now, together in death, they will never be divided.

I imagine that she is an ideal partner for Captain Randall Johnson. Her quiet manner and her love of people tempers his blunt militarism and his ingrained cynicism about the nature of most human beings and, for that matter, of some equally fallible ghosts.

At the moment, the Captain is not concerned with fallible ghosts. He has come here to this conference room that subtly simulates a courtroom so that he can wrest the truth from reluctant or frightened defendants. You probably think of a defendant as a person who has been accused of a crime. You are right. But you may be limiting the application of the legal term. You regard a thief, a traitor, or a killer as defendants. Again, you are right. But you and I are also defendants. We have committed the crime of being born. We are fallible creatures. Even when we follow most of the rules, we may from time to time find ourselves in messy and wayward situations of our own making. Nobody is flawless. We all make mistakes. We count ourselves lucky when others tolerate our errors or never become aware of our wrongdoing.

I understand the Captain. I have often maintained a similar view of human beings. The world is a rough place, and we who move so vulnerably through it often learn to be hardhearted. Hardness of heart is our strategy for survival. The Captain learned that strategy while he was piloting bomb missions over Nazi Germany during World War II. I learned that strategy in my day-to-day encounters with overly competitive high school peers and in my dealings with arbitrary and repressive adults. I learned how to fight back. I learned the art of being wily. I waged my battles while undercover and almost always went undetected. Of course, nothing comes free. Hardheartedness is costly. It robbed me of my capacity for truly loving anyone.

I imagine that the Captain would applaud my strategy for overcoming my adversaries or, at least, of keeping them at bay. But he and I are not really alike. There is purity in his hardheartedness. He applies moral principles to his blunt or harsh treatment of others. He seeks the truth. He wrenches confessions from even the most sinister wrongdoers. Unlike him,

I thrive in concealment. I falsely accuse my enemies and my rivals. I lie to other people. But I try not to lie to myself. I know who I was when I was alive on Earth. I have accomplished little of which I can be proud. Nevertheless, I'll tough it out. There will be no sad songs for me. Nor do I crave them.

The Captain takes over once more.

I know that he has not finished questioning me. But my foresight reveals that he will not be calling me into the spotlight at this time. Except for Miss Dickinson, the members of the committee are probably too angry to continue questioning me. They need to step back. They require a break from my duplicity. Right now, the Captain and the other members on the Evaluation Committee want to question a girl who tried to help Boyd Henderson.

"Let's get on with it," he tells his colleagues on the committee as well as the thirteen of us who make up the group. "Let's get to the bottom of things. Let's find out the whole truth."

Before he calls out the name of the girl that the committee intends to interview, he surveys the faces of my classmates and my teachers peering at him from their seats at this long table. But I refrain from peering. I barely glance at him. I am adamant in my decision to conceal my thoughts from him. What better place for him to discover my thoughts than through my facial expression? Our faces reveal so much of who we are. A laugh, a frown, a tear, or a hint of fear—they are a language unto themselves, with no need of words to validate their meanings.

Whether the Captain perceives my efforts to conceal myself, I cannot say. He takes no special note of me. Instead, he calls out the name of the girl who will now be testifying before the committee. She will also be answerable to any member of our group who wants her to explain herself more clearly or who requires more evidence to support her assertions.

"The committee wants to hear next from Brenda Flynn."

All of us study Brenda with guarded interest. The committee already possesses their own ideas of her merits and her failings. They are aware of most, if not all, of the accomplishments, disappointments, and errors that defined who she was while she was alive on Earth. With few exceptions among us, we ten students who were her peers at that time and who continue to be so in this first stage of our Afterlife were able to discern only the surface meanings of her life. Miss Patel and Mr. Marchand probably knew even less about her. Like all of us, she was never exactly the same person to the friends and acquaintances who were a part of her earthly existence. Without dissimulation or disguise of any kind, she expressed different facets of her personhood to each of us who passed through her life in profound or superficial ways.

How could it be otherwise? We are always vanishing from one another. Too often, we hide our authentic selves out of fear that our friends or newfound strangers will adversely judge us. Even when we do not intend to withhold ourselves from our friends, we rarely show them ourselves unaltered and accurate. We are always changing. Sometimes we change with nearly imperceptible subtleties. Occasionally, we change in more emphatic ways. We leave behind the human beings that we had, for a time, so clearly represented. That part of who we have been vanishes. Perhaps, we enter a new cycle in our lives. Possibly, we become devious or altruistic. Or maybe the vanishing derives from our growing up or growing older.

Our lives on Earth are a trial run. As we make our varied journeys on Earth, we experience a succession of vanishings. We vanish by degrees. We store inside our memories the images of who we have been. Only at the last, as new experiences and old age overtake us, do we lose those images. On Earth, we create the templates for the vanishing of our bodies that will occur when we enter Sojourn, the temporary haven that we are compelled to inhabit before we begin our passage to The First Heaven.

You know the experience of vanishing as well as I do. A friend that you think you have made for life moves away. Years later, you see her and do not recognize her. Only after she introduces herself can you begin to place her. She is not the same person. Time has wrought upon her its irrevocable alterations. She is thinner or heavier. She is staid and predictable, rather than lighthearted and adventurous.

You may have experienced the vanishing within a close friend when he betrays your trust. After the betrayal, he can never be the same person. The goodness that emanated from the purity of his soul or from the power of his will has vanished. That vanishing may have occurred over time by degrees or in the flash of a punishing instant.

The person that our group knew as wild and generous and self-centered and original Boyd Henderson did not change overnight. He vanished from himself little by little. The episodes that broke his life apart and eventually made him a monster happened over the years. Those episodes cannot exonerate him from his crimes. But they serve to illustrate my point. We carry our ghosts inside ourselves long before we die. We separate ourselves from the various forms that our bodies have taken while we are alive on Earth. When we enter Sojourn, the first stop in our passage to The First Heaven, our Earthly death gradually separates us from our bodies. In a word, we become disembodied. But that vanishing of our bodies need not be final. Our bodies may become palpable once more, fused though they are with our redefined Spirit/lives. You may recall that Mr. Steerforth and his colleagues explained this process to our group.

I tell you all these things for a reason. You should not expect to discover everything there is to know about any of us here in the group that the Evaluation Committee chooses to interrogate. Each of us is made of so many selves. Some of those selves have vanished and will not be revealed even under the most militant questioning. What you take away from the testimonies of my classmates and from me may reveal only a portion of the truth of who we were when we were alive and were making our journeys on Earth.

If any one of us in the group makes honesty a personal code, that individual is Brenda Flynn. With her, what you see is what you get. Concealment is alien to her forthright nature. On more than one occasion, she has made it clear that she dislikes me. Only a few minutes ago, she lodged a protest against me, here in this conference room. She believes that I was a catalyst in the downfall of Boyd Henderson. She discovered the plots that I devised against him. She tried to thwart those plots. She worked hard to save Boyd from his enemies and from himself, the most violent of his enemies. I might be inclined to call her Goody Two Shoes because of her temperate manner and her self-effacing acts of kindness. But she is no softie. Her demure personality is made of pure steel.

Brenda is far too virtuous for my taste. There is a part of me that respects her for her steadfast character and her generous disposition. There is a part of me that dislikes her. She is the girl that, without even trying, won the affection of Boyd Henderson. That affection might have become romantic love. But Brenda resisted that emotion. She became his "adopted" sister instead. Of course, he was not worthy of her. But that is a story that the Captain and his colleagues will be drawing out of her. I already sense the tension. The Captain does not really understand Brenda's relationship with Boyd. He will challenge her remarks about him. But Brenda Flynn is a girl who refuses to be browbeaten. I perceive the clash of wills. I know. I see it coming.

The Captain proceeds with his usual brusque authority. Brenda's reserved femininity does not constrain his suspicious nature or the driving force of his questions and commands.

"Brenda Flynn, tell us why your life on Earth counted for something."

Brenda is sitting between her friends Chloe Bradbury and Alessandro Bianchi. I imagine that she finds solace in being near them. On Earth, they shared the same values. They believed it was their responsibility to help their relatives and their friends who had hit a rough patch in their lives. Their good deeds often went unsung because they were kept private. Being unnoticed or taken for granted did not deter them from their good deeds or diminish the fervor they brought to their rescue of the needy and the downtrodden. They needed no applause from a doting audience. That kind of adulation they often received from their extracurricular activities. Alessandro, with his olive-skin handsomeness and his Italian self-assurance, was one of our school's top-notch boxers. Chloe, a radiant brunette, found early success in television commercials. Brenda, unpretentious and keen-minded, had won national prizes for her cabinet making.

Each of them was paving a smooth path to whatever future they cared to own.

The Captain and his colleagues know all these things. They regard Brenda's friendship with Chloe and Alessandro as a mark in her favor.

Her association with Boyd Henderson is an altogether different matter. For most members of the Evaluation Committee, the friendship casts a dark shadow upon her.

I know the way they think. Already, the roiling scenes that are about to occur flash their enmity upon my seeing. Yet my anger and apprehension do not prevent me from viewing the outcome. Here in Sojourn, I can do nothing to change what is about to happen, even though my foresight often gives me knowledge of it. You probably remember what I told you. At the moment I was born, the Five Spirits cast a spell upon me. They have allowed no one except my brother Luke to believe my predictions. Throughout the court trial that is beginning, I shall have to wait for the turbulent scenes to play themselves out.

You already know that I do not care for Brenda. But I like four of the Spirits even less. Despite the negative statements that her honesty may compel her to make about me, I am expecting Brenda to put up a good fight. She can be feisty. She can be strong-minded and daring in her defense of the truth.

I hold myself very still. In this confrontation between Brenda and Captain Johnson, I know what is going to happen. The scene will not be pleasant.

The Captain's blunt manner has once again anchored his opening command to hostility and distrust. He should be *requesting* Brenda to tell us about her life. Instead, he has issued a militant order.

Brenda takes a moment to summon her thoughts. I imagine that she is selecting the appropriate words that will push her forward.

The Captain interprets her hesitation as an unwillingness to tell the committee and the group about her life. He charges in, willful and accusatory.

"Come, come, Miss Flynn," he says. "Don't hold back. Don't try to hide from us. We know your story. We want to hear you take responsibility for it. Why was it important for you to be born? In what way did your life count for something?"

Brenda begins speaking. Her voice clearly expresses who she is. It is a confident voice. It is a voice that carefully chooses her words. Once she speaks those words, she will have no cause to call them back. They impart her candor, openness, and integrity.

"I was born to help those human beings who needed me."

"Who were they?" the Captain wants to know. "Who were these persons for whom your life made a difference?"

"My sister Mary Ann and my two brothers, Craig and James. They were much younger than I and could not do for themselves. They had not yet learned how to fend for themselves. I was caring for them. I was teaching them how to be self-reliant."

Mrs. Adams comes into it now.

"What did you teach them?"

"I taught them how to dress themselves. I taught them how to bathe properly and how to brush their teeth twice a day. I showed them how to use an iPhone and how to complete school assignments on their iPads. From me, they learned how to swim, play tennis and soccer, paddle a canoe, and fish for bass. I taught them to have hope and to believe that they could make things better for themselves."

Miss Dickinson joins in. Intuitive and admiring, she offers Brenda words of praise.

"You were more than a good sister," she says. "You were both mother and father to your brothers and your sister."

"I had to be," Brenda answers her. "There were no other favorable options for them. There was only the prospect of institutional care, lockstep charity centers, and well-intentioned foster homes that would keep my sister and my brothers apart from their real family."

Mrs. Adams wants to know more. As usual, she is pushy and bad-tempered.

"Where were your parents? What were they doing for you and for your siblings?"

"Very little, I'm sorry to say. They were ill and unavailable to us."

Mrs. Adams pushes further. She glares at Brenda.

"That doesn't tell us much. What was their illness? Why weren't they available to you?"

Brenda stares her down. Then, as though she is dismissing Mrs. Adams from her thoughts, she allows her glance to scan the other members of the committee and every one of us in the group. It is to the other members of the committee and to all of us in the group that she addresses her remarks.

"My father suffered from post-traumatic stress disorder. He had been a Major in one of the combat units stationed in the Parwan Province of Afghanistan. He had killed many enemies. He had seen many of his friends being killed. He was a good leader. He saved as many lives as he could. He was there in the thick of things for three years. Witnessing all that carnage takes its toll upon a man. It burns out his soul. It makes him carry always an inescapable feeling of guilt. His friends have died, but he has survived. He feels unworthy. He believes that he should not be alive. He finds ways to kill himself. Some veterans kill themselves with a revolver. Even though he found some success as a civil engineer in Green Hills after his Army service, my father spent much of his time killing himself with scotch, whiskey and bourbon."

Mr. Steerforth asks a pertinent question. He knows the answer, but he would like the group to know the score.

"Did your father spend any time with you and your siblings? How did he treat you?"

"I think that he wanted to love us. There were days when, with the counseling of other combat veterans giving him a boost, he convinced himself that he was turning a new page in his life. On those days, he sailed or kayaked with us. He brought us to Disney World in Florida. He taught us how to make woodcarvings of birds, squirrels, and ponies. He could be very loving. He could also be frightening, descending into wild rages and his private hell right before our eyes when he was drinking at home rather than at his club or in a local bar."

Mrs. Steerforth gets into it now. Her voice is grating, and her manner is cold and harsh.

"What about your mother? Wasn't she there for you and your siblings?"

"She tried to be. She tried very hard."

Mrs. Steerforth is not pleased. She is looking for a reply that is clear-cut and precise.

"Maybe she didn't try hard enough. Why else would you have to take her place?"

Brenda does not cower in fear before Mrs. Steerforth's displeasure. Hearing her mother disparaged, she makes wariness her sentry. Her anger flares up. She fires back at Mrs. Steerforth.

"My mother tried very hard. When my father returned from his war, he was a stranger to her. There was no haven of peace inside him. There was no way that she could connect to him or solace him. He wouldn't let her in. He didn't know how to love anymore. For him, love counted for nothing. Knowing how to kill and how to guard himself against enemies counted for everything. The war destroyed their marriage. It destroyed both of them. My parents had meant the world to one other. In their happy years, they had brought light into each other's darkness. They had made each day together seem extraordinary. In a special sense, the war killed both of them. It put out their light. It drove both of them to heavy drinking."

Mrs. Steerforth doesn't let up.

"Your mother and your father turned their backs on you and your siblings."

Brenda flinches, as though Mrs. Steerforth has slapped her. Worse than that, Mrs. Steerforth has once again derided Brenda's mother and father. Brenda is not about to let her get away with it.

"My parents loved us," she declares, her voice raised clearly in defense of her parents. "My siblings and I accepted them with all their faults. That's what love is. It means total acceptance, with no excuses for backing away when the person who is loved has fallen into trouble."

Mrs. Steerforth tightens her jaws and presses her lips. She wants to take another jab at Brenda. But the Captain comes back into it. I imagine that he has a muted respect for Brenda's father, who is a tried-and-true war hero. He is probably less sympathetic to the chink in that man's armor, the fault line in his toughness, the rift in his granite surface. The Captain cuts to the chase. He does not object to Brenda's defense of her parents or to the guardian care that she gave her two brothers and her sister. But he does object to her relationship with Boyd Henderson, the monster that killed thirteen innocent people.

He begins with a temperate assessment.

"Good work, Brenda. You earned high marks for your work on the home front. Your life on Earth counted for something. You taught and protected your siblings. You eased the burden for your troubled parents. That is to your credit."

He pauses. His features stiffen. Shadows fall around him, momentarily consume him, and just as swiftly lift away. He appears to ponder Brenda's situation, as though her life on Earth were a problem that was insufficiently resolved. A new frown creases his brow. Then he takes up that part of her Earthly life that disturbs him.

"How did your counting for something influence Boyd Henderson's life? Did you make your friendship with him a good thing?"

If tension is churning within her, Brenda gives no evidence of it in this moment. Instead, she answers the Captain's inquiry with a smooth competence.

"I tried to make our friendship a good thing," she says. "In that period of his life, you had to work at being Boyd Henderson's friend. He was all messed up."

"Tell us about it," the Captain says, the curtness of his words playing a game with her composure.

Brenda doesn't skip a beat. Neither a frown nor fear touches her pretty oval face. For the time being at least, she keeps her retrieved composure intact.

"When I first met Boyd, he had just been released from a reformatory and from rehab. He was trying to find his way back. I thought that his returning to the school that had made so much trouble for him was a mistake. I told him so during our first meeting. He sat with me in the cafeteria during lunch in the second week of his return. He'd noticed me because I had praised a painting that he had worked on in our Art class. Mr. Carter, our teacher, had placed Boyd's painting, as well as the paintings of every other student there, on the walls that encircled that spacious room.

"Boyd's painting showed a young man who was drowning in stormy ocean waters. The captain of a fishing trawler was throwing him a life raft. But there was no certainty that the youth would take hold of the raft or that he had the strength to wage battle with those punishing waters. I admired the blending of the boat's shining rescue beams with the blackness of the waters and the churning storm-grayness of the sky.

"I saw in the painting a statement about Boyd's own life, though I didn't say so. I suppose you could call it an allegory of his life. He was that drowning youth in need of rescue. But the painting did not tell whether he could rescue himself or whether others might rescue him. The painter left his fate indeterminate.

"When it was my turn to comment on his work, I gave the painting my unconditional praise. The other students held back their praise. They could not overcome the ambivalence they felt toward Boyd because of his former wildness, his past drug addiction, and the aftermath of the car crash. They were advanced placement students who had never broken the rules and had done all the right things. They were ambitious. They were aiming for careers on Wall Street, in government, and with giant corporations. Boyd had brought bad publicity to the school. A scandal of that sort jeopardized their chances for being accepted at the top universities. That afternoon in Art class, some students said the painting was depressing. Others wanted to know how the youth had fallen into the water. They refused to enter the dramatic moment that the painting depicted.

"I was pleased when Mr. Carter, our Art teacher, agreed with me. He told Boyd that he had done everything for the painting that a good artist should do. I saw Boyd's face brighten, though he was careful to keep his elation in check. He glanced at Mr. Carter with respectful appreciation. Then, he turned to look at me, with a hint of a smile and a slight nod that I told myself was his way of saluting me for the words of praise that his painting had sparked from me.

"It was there, in the school cafeteria, a few days later, that I told Boyd that he had made a mistake returning to the school. He needed a new place. He needed new schoolmates, instead of the ones who kept branding him a rebel or a criminal.

"I liked the way he responded to my remark. I detected in him a strength of character that he might not have shown to many people."

"'I don't want to run away from these people,' he said. 'I'm going to stand up to them, and I'm going to stand tall. There doesn't have to be any confrontations. I can turn the other cheek, up to a point. I don't want to make trouble. I just want to do the right things. Maybe I'll be lucky enough to find a few people who are willing to help a drowning man.'"

"'I'll help you,' I said. 'I'll be one of your rescuers.'"

In her soft-spoken, lady-like manner, Miss Dickinson asks a pertinent question.

"Did the painting inspire you to be his rescuer?"

"Perhaps it did. I'd like to believe, though, that I would have tried to rescue Boyd even without the painting. Of course, I wasn't the only one who was working to rescue him. Some of my classmates here were also pitching in."

Miss Dickinson beams. She is pleased to hear about these good deeds.

"Please tell us some of the things that you and your friends did to save Boyd from his adversaries and from himself."

"Alessandro, Shiloh, and Dion welcomed him back to the soccer, baseball, and swim teams. They developed an easy-going camaraderie with him. Their friendship with Boyd and his excellence as an athlete inspired the loyalty of his teammates and a willingness to shed the prejudices that they'd built against him."

Miss Dickinson wants to hear more.

"Please tell us what you did. How were you a positive influence upon Boyd Henderson?"

"I listened to his problems. I told him not to worry about the people who wouldn't let him forget about the mistakes he'd made. Those people were probably unhappy about their own lives or guarding their plans for big-time careers. Besides, the past persists into the present. It haunts every one of us. We can't get rid of it. Saint Paul once wrote that we carry our past with us. It is the body of death that we carry on our backs. Paul knew how it is with us. He would agree, I think, that while we are alive we are more than our past. We keep revising the scenarios that are our lives.

"'You are already revising,' I told Boyd. 'You are no longer an outsider or a malcontent. You've become a team player.'"

"What did Boyd say?" Miss Dickinson asks. "Was he viewing his return to school in the same way?"

"At that time he was learning to view it in that way. His friendship with his teammates and with me gave him confidence that he could make his life work for him, after all. That confidence didn't happen right away. He had to prove himself to his teammates, to me, and most of all to himself. When he first returned to our school, he no longer knew where he stood in society. He was uncertain about who he was. He was struggling to redefine himself in relation to our school and to the wider Green Hills community. He was starting all over again. He was going right back to the beginning. He was trying to be reborn."

Miss Dickinson offers more praise.

"You were helpful to him in many ways. I know. Even before you and I met, I saw your life flashing before my eyes as though it were a dream flashing upon these video walls that surround us. My colleagues on the committee saw those scenes, too. Your classmates here did not need that video. They actually witnessed your living through those days. Nevertheless, I am asking you to tell us about one other way in which you influenced Boyd's life for the better."

Brenda reflects upon a proper answer to the question.

"I persuaded Boyd to try out for a leading part in our school's production of Thornton Wilder's play, *Our Town*. At first, he didn't want to do it. I told him that trying out for the part would be a realistic test of his confidence. It would also be a statement that he was a valued member in our school community. He was used to appearing in public. His fine showings on the soccer, baseball, and swim teams had boosted his reputation. He was also earning some impressive merit badges. He was one of us. Even if he didn't get the part, he would look good. He wanted to help the drama club. He wanted to help the school."

Miss Dickinson offers another of her beaming smiles.

"He did get the part," she says, "and he was very good in it."

"He was wonderful," Brenda agrees. "Playing the lead was, I think, his happiest experience at school. It felt even better than winning soccer and baseball games or coming in first place during a swim competition."

"Tell us more," Miss Dickinson says. "We all want to know why the play brought him such happiness."

"People saw him in an altogether different way. He was playing George Gibbs, a youth from a small town in New Hampshire called Grover's Corners. In *Our Town*, George is what we like to think of as all-American. He is athletic. He is respectful to adults and loyal to his friends. He falls in love with Emily Webb, who is absolutely the ideal girl for him. George represents a wholesome youth who is growing into a responsible man. He will do all the right things with his life.

"To become George, Boyd changed his image. He sported a crew cut. He was clean-shaven. He wore clothes that belonged to the early years of the twentieth century. He showed George's strong points and hinted at his vulnerability. He embodied perfectly the image of an all-American youth. Our classmates and their parents liked what they saw. They became convinced that Boyd wasn't such a bad fellow after all. Boyd had grown up. He had changed for the better."

Miss Dickinson comes in again with an insightful remark.

"Boyd tried so hard. He *did* change for the better, at least for a while."

"Just for a while," Brenda says, her voice melancholic and bitter. "At the end, though, he was his own worst enemy."

The Captain comes back in. He is not pleased to hear so much praise and sympathy being accorded a killer. His anger pushes him into attack mode. Once more, he is a stern prosecutor confronting this girl named Brenda Flynn, whom he refuses to trust or even to pity.

"How else did you count for someone special in Boyd Henderson's life?" he asks her. "Did you sleep with him?"

This second of the Captain's questions startles my classmates. There are no prudes among us. Yet the Captain seems to be crossing a line that he should not even be approaching. His question surprises his colleagues on the committee, too, though Mrs. Steerforth and Mrs. Adams merely raise their eyebrows and gash their lip lines with smirks. They like to think the worst of everybody.

The Captain's question about whether she slept with Boyd does not take Brenda aback. She meets his caustic tone with a matter-of-fact answer.

"We never mentioned the subject," she says. "Besides, we were looking for a relationship without the complications of sex. Anyway, Boyd was dating someone else."

The Captain presses harder. He mentions my name.

"We know that girl is with us now. She is Cassandra Winslow. We also know that Boyd dropped Cassandra and started seeing you."

I wince at the sound of my name. Once again, my humiliation goes public. I notice the committee's and my classmates' ambivalent glances directed toward me. Those glances take me in for just a moment, and then they move back to Brenda Flynn. She is responding to the Captain's remark about Boyd's choosing her as his steady date.

"Boyd and I were never romantic."

"I know that," the Captain says. "But I wanted you to say so. I wanted the committee and everyone in your group to hear you say so.'"

"We were pals," Brenda explains. "We were like brother and sister. We'd play tennis with Chloe and Jayden. We sometimes went sailing along Penobscot Bay. We'd take in a movie or go to an art gallery. Always, there were other friends with us. When we were sitting alone together in a local restaurant or when we were hiking along a scenic trail, we'd chat about our future plans and about our current problems. Our friendship was very helpful for both of us. It made us feel that we had someone to count on if we fell into real trouble.

"Then Boyd met Adriana Montalban and fell in love with her. She was a beautiful Latina. They began dating after his relationship with Cassandra was over. I was very happy for both of them. In our occasional private talks and always when I saw Adriana and him together, I felt that Boyd had recovered from his damaging past. He was making a new and happier life for himself."

At the mention of Adriana's name, new sorrow and dismay take hold of my classmates and teachers. That same melancholy touches the brows of Miss Dickinson, the Steerforths, and even the parched nature of Mrs. Adams.

Only Captain Johnson refrains from any show of emotion. Instead, he probes further. He is waiting for Brenda to tell him everything.

"Do you regret your friendship with Boyd Henderson?"

Brenda resents the question. She has a vague contempt for the Captain because he asked it. But she doesn't skip a beat. She keeps her wits about her.

"How do you expect me to answer that question? Boyd Henderson killed me."

"Will you ever forgive him?"

"Maybe one day I'll be able to forgive him for what he did to me. But I can never forgive him for what he did to himself."

The Captain isn't finished with her yet. He zooms in for the kill.

"Tell us the mistake you made that hurt Boyd Henderson and hurt your classmates."

"I did what I had to," Brenda says. "I turned away from Boyd when, despite my encouragement and the counseling of some of our classmates and a psychologist, he began smashing himself up again after a gang of racists raped and killed Adriana. I discovered that he was snorting cocaine again and threatening revenge against all the people in the school that were bringing him down. I lashed out at him for making a friend of Kurt Drexler, a political radical in our school who was preaching neo-Nazi and White Supremacist propaganda. I became uneasy when I found out that he and Boyd were making more than a few visits to the local gun club. They'd bought AR-15 rifles and were becoming sharpshooters while firing them."

Hearing these words, Ari blasts his anger at her.

"You turned away from him when he needed you most of all. If you'd stood by him, you might have saved him from himself. You might have saved all of us."

"I did what I thought was best. I no longer felt comfortable being around his anger and his depression. I was increasingly fearful that his friendship with Kurt Drexler was going to get him into trouble."

Chloe Bradbury, the girl who was Boyd's leading lady in *Our Town*, chimes in. She is tearful and sincere. Her grief wells up, though she is trying hard to contain it. It is grief for herself first of all. But her sorrow is large enough to include all of her classmates and her two teachers who died because Boyd Henderson killed them.

"You should have alerted his parents or a school official. That might have changed everything for us."

Brenda recognizes the genuine nature of Chloe's grief. If Chloe's words have roused her anger, Brenda does not show it. Instead, she meets those words with a quiet restraint.

"I alerted his psychologist," Brenda says. "Dr. Miller is a compassionate man. I believed that he was the one person who could really help Boyd. I know that he tried to help. During the time Boyd spent in rehab, he learned to trust Dr. Miller. In those last days before the school shooting, though, Boyd resisted even this good doctor."

Chloe nods in affirmation. She knows that Brenda has spoken the truth. But truth brings her no comfort. She bows her head, defeated. What's done is done. Boyd's crimes cannot be undone. The killings are irrevocable. What is even more daunting, the committee's allowing us to relive those last days seems more unlikely with each passing hour.

The Captain does not share Chloe's acceptance of Brenda's version of what happened. Now he drives his antipathy forward with new accusations.

"You turned away from Boyd when he was most vulnerable," he says. "You thought more of your own comfort than of his wellbeing."

"I had to live my life!" she shouts. "I had to back away from Boyd so that I could nurture and protect my two brothers and my sister. I had to keep my father and my mother away from gin and whiskey and bourbon. I had to maintain good grades, and I had to stay involved with tennis, swimming, and soccer. I believed that, if Boyd didn't have me to lean on, he'd get used to relying on himself. Anyway, Dr. Miller was there for him. And I never completely lost touch with Boyd. He knew that I still had love in my heart for him. But I needed to be away from his troubles. I was carrying the problems of my family. I couldn't handle any more."

It's Mrs. Adams turn to snap at Brenda.

"You pretend to be a good person," she says. "But where is your compassion? What pity or mercy did you show Boyd when you broke away from him?"

Once again, the floodgates of Brenda's anger open. She shouts out her protest.

"I don't have to pretend! My actions speak for themselves!"

Mrs. Adams goes on ranting at her.

"Where is your mercy? Boyd Henderson was drowning, and you didn't reach out to him. When you were alive on Earth, you were a churchgoer. You were a believer. I know all about your life. You used to sing hymns in your church. One of those hymns was Maurice Bevans's 'There's a Wideness in God's Mercy.' You should have remembered the words of that hymn before you turned away from Boyd."

"Maybe there is a wideness in God's mercy," Brenda tells her. "But there has to be a point where even God withholds mercy. He waits for us to take responsibility for our own lives. Boyd was doing that. I was helping him a little. Others, including his athletic coaches and some of his teammates and a few loyal classmates, were doing even more to bring him out of the trauma of Adriana's death.

"Then, Boyd started to pay attention to what his enemies were saying. They spread lies about him because of their malice and envy and their willingness to bring harm to anyone who appears vulnerable. They revived those rumors about his wanting to be a school shooter. They spoke of the car crash as though it had happened only the day before. They talked about his previous drug addiction and about the time that he spent in a reformatory and in rehab. They mentioned the beating that his father had given him in the boxing ring within an exclusive men's club. Boyd caved in to these enemies. They drove him into madness. He came to believe that everybody in our school was his enemy. I'm not certain he even knew that he was shooting at us, the persons who were trying to help him. At any rate, God did not show mercy to him that day or to us."

The committee and our classmates quietly listen to Brenda's recollection of her friendship with Boyd. Hearing her words that suggest God has abandoned us and left us to our own resources, we withdraw into a contemplative mood. We say nothing. We wait for Brenda to say more. After a minute or so, she does.

"But God is always aware of what He is doing," she says. "I believe that there is a reason why He did not show us mercy on the day of the shooting. Maybe one day, here in Sojourn or in The First Heaven, He will tell us why He allowed the killings."

Brenda's words stir me in ways that make me uneasy. I perceive her goodness. I feel shame that I could never measure up to her moral level. I never even approached it.

I can imagine that God may one day show mercy to my classmates. But, earthbound in my disposition even when I am separated from Earth, I stay realistic. I cannot imagine that He will ever forgive me for my wrongdoing.

I wait.

Later today, each member of the committee will question me again. I shall no longer be able to hide from them. Nor will I be able to hide the alliance I made with the fiendish neo-Nazi and White Supremacist, Kurt Drexler. In secret, we worked together to ruin Boyd's life.

You, as well as they, already know about my first crime against Boyd Henderson. It was a crime of false reporting. In an hour or two, you, as well as the committee, will hear me tell of the ways that my false reporting and my evil pact with Kurt Drexler reaped new and more terrible consequences for Boyd and for me. I was the catalyst of the tragedy. Though Boyd's evil was larger than my own, his crimes would not have existed without my wrongdoing. Every one of you will understand why God will withhold His mercy from me—for all eternity.

Am I the one who will prevent my classmates and my two teachers from returning to Earth?

I think so.

I go on waiting. I still try to hide.

CHAPTER EIGHT

KURT DREXLER'S PLOT

Early that afternoon, before he begins interrogating me again, Captain Johnson glares at me with contempt. In his eyes, I am a traitor to the friends who trusted me. I am the weaver of evil plots that conjoined my will with the murderous impulses of a neo-Nazi and of other racists. I am a rabble-rouser, having incited the fear and anger of schoolmates and teachers as I branded Boyd Henderson a potential assassin. In this hour, it is my association with Kurt Drexler that stirs the Captain's interest and rouses his scorn and his loathing.

The Captain has his reasons for despising Kurt Drexler. In this moment when I am confronting the Captain's new flare of anger, I calculate the merits and the liabilities of Kurt's character. I quickly scan my bitter memory of him. I try once more to comprehend his influence upon what happened in the days that preceded the school shooting. Kurt is not among our dead. But his presence hovers over the school tragedy.

Kurt is eighteen years old. He is of German-Austrian descent. Tall—6 feet, one inch—he is exceptionally good-looking and subtly narcissistic. At Green Hills High school, he was a creditable swimmer and soccer and baseball player. He was one of the top five students in Green Hills High School. He was also multi-lingual, having attained fluency in German, French, Italian, Spanish, and English. Before Green Hills High School, he lived in Europe for six years and went to school there when his father, a renowned oncologist, was on the research staff of a Swiss clinic. His mother is a successful playwright with a global following. Kurt earned early acceptance to Yale, Brown, and Harvard. He chose Yale. He is headed for pre-law undergraduate studies and, afterward, a major law school. His future includes the corporate world and eventually government posts. Duplicity and cold-heartedness are his secret weapons. He is incapable of genuine feelings for anyone. His scientific detachment closes him off from strong relationships with his peers and with everyone else. He has occasionally expressed neo-Nazi sympathies and racist hatreds to friends who are as amoral and unscrupulous as he is. To the friends who think like him he calls himself a White Supremacist.

If the committee of the Five Spirits allows my group to return to Earth, you will meet Kurt there, in episodes unraveling in perhaps a different way. Right now, though, our chances of returning to Earth appear very slim. In this very moment, as if to remind me of my precarious situation, I hear once again the Captain's rancorous voice.

His hatred of Kurt and me looses upon me a spate of questions.

"What made you take up with Kurt Drexler? What motive drove you into a friendship with him? Hadn't your friends warned you against him? Why did you ignore their advice?"

I do not allow the Captain's stern voice to frighten me. I meet him on the battlefield that he has chosen for us. I answer him with words that are confident and determined.

"When I was alive on Earth, I rarely listened to warnings," I tell him. "Friends and teachers were well-meaning, but they did not have to live my life. I ignored their advice because I wanted to live my life my way. I did not care to become a puppet whose every move was determined by their conservative politics and their worn-down conventions."

My insolence does not please the Captain. He manages to keep his anger harnessed. He pushes forward. He knows my deviousness. He knows my guilt. But he wants to draw out of me my reluctant confession. He wants me to speak the words that publicly condemn me. He will take pleasure from watching me tell each member of the committee and every one of my classmates, over and over again if necessary, how I ignited Boyd Henderson's fury and drove him into madness. Deliberately, I have answered only two of the Captain's questions. I ignore the militant impetus of the other two questions. I know that I shall have to answer those questions. I'll have to explain why I teamed up with Kurt and why we plotted against Boyd.

I let the Captain wait before I answer those questions. I feel his anger simmering. He observes my contrived self-possession and my more authentic obstinacy, propped up as they are by arrogance. I am learning to loathe him. I understand who he is. He is the prosecutor whose probing questions will trap me. Because of my crimes, he may punish everyone in my group. He may raise his voice against our returning to Earth. I don't know what he will do. In Sojourn, my foresight fails to show me what will finally happen.

With words that are more abrasive now, the Captain sends my silence scattering.

"You haven't answered the most important of my questions, Miss Winslow," he tells me. "You are holding back. You are hiding. You are jeopardizing the group's chances of going back to Earth."

My classmates freeze up. They want me to do the right thing. They are hoping that I can appease the Captain. They think that I should confess.

Shiloh Jackson hurries into it.

"Tell the Captain what he wants to know," he says, his emotion-charged words more of an appeal than a command. "Don't ruin our chances to get our lives back."

I am surprised that Shiloh's words do not anger me. For an instant, pangs of sorrow leave me breathless. I feel pity for him. His forlornness sits upon him awkwardly. He is not used to being wretched and vulnerable. While he was alive on Earth, his brawny physique and his well-earned stoicism usually subverted even the smallest signs of wretchedness and vulnerability.

In my silence, I fight back. I do not want to feel pity. I want to feel nothing. I'm waiting for the free fall into oblivion and forgetfulness.

I close down. I cancel out even the smallest drop of pity for Shiloh and for myself. In that way alone will I protect the only self that I am willing to tolerate. I do not care to break down or to beg for anybody's forgiveness. As genuine as it is, my remorse cannot bring back the dead. Nor does it make me worthy of forgiveness. Even here, in Sojourn, I am the same human being that I always was, way back there in Green Hills, Maine, on the planet Earth. I am fallible. I am incorrigible. I am beyond reformation.

So I tell myself, withdrawing as it has sometimes been my habit to inscrutable stillness and wily disguises.

Shiloh has more to say. His words are blunt this time, and they are more attuned to the tough-mindedness that he represented while he was alive and finding his way in Green

Hills. But, his bluntness notwithstanding, his words are no less urgent.

"Don't screw up," he says. "Don't make things worse for us than they already are."

I'm inclined to ease his anxiety. My first impulse is to tell him that I have no intention of screwing up. But once again my perverse willfulness holds me back. I say nothing. I stay hidden inside the secret recesses of my silence.

Now the Captain lunges at me with another of his caustic directives.

"Quit stalling," he says. "I already know your motive for teaming up with Kurt Drexler. So do my colleagues who are here in this room observing your every move and listening to all your words. But most of your classmates do not know your motive. Miss Patel and Mr. Marchand do not know it. This committee is calling on you to tell the truth. Explain your motive for linking up with so problematic a young man as Kurt Drexler."

I tell myself that I have nothing to lose. I have already lost what matters most to me. I have lost the better self that I once cultivated, during the brief years of my innocence when I enjoyed following all the rules and when I imagined that I would be of some use to the world.

So I begin to answer the Captain's question.

"It wasn't a motive that first drew me to Kurt," I tell him. "It was merely chance. I sat next to Kurt in a Film Studies course that was part of our advanced placement program. We were exploring the ways that a real-life event can influence the writing of a play or a book as well as the making of a film."

Miss Dickinson smiles. I imagine that the premise of the course intrigues her. She is eager to know more.

"What real-life event became the focus of your study?" she asks.

"The Leopold and Loeb case."

Mrs. Adams quickly expresses her displeasure.

"That was a gruesome case," she complains. "It makes a nasty statement about the human capacity for evil. Why in Heaven's name did your school bring it into the curriculum?"

"It's part of our country's history," I say. "It actually happened. My classmates and I thought the course was very special. It clearly illustrated how books, plays, and films draw upon the real world to make their art."

Mrs. Adams doesn't let up.

"Nathan Leopold and Richard Loeb were foul murderers," she says. "Years ago, after they died and came to Sojourn, a higher committee than ours came close to condemning them to an eternal vanishing."

Jason Teng, with his scholarly interest in criminal justice, asks a pertinent question.

"What saved them from that punishment?"

Mrs. Adams abruptly answers him. Her skepticism and disillusionment are in full force.

"The sentimentality of one of the judges saved them. He called the killers tragic young men who had ruined their lives even though they'd had everything to live for."

"They *were* tragic," I tell her. "They killed an innocent boy and spent the rest of their lives suffering for it."

"They were killers," Mrs. Adams says. "They deserved what they got."

Mr. Steerforth makes a suggestion. He directs his words to me.

"Miss Winslow, some of my colleagues and I have forgotten the particulars of that case. Perhaps, you can explain what it was all about."

I tell him and his colleagues what they want to know.

"In 1924, Nathan Leopold and Richard Loeb committed what newspapers of that time referred to as the crime of the century. The fact that they came from two of the wealthiest families in Chicago made their crime even more horrific. By the most rigorous academic standards, they were deemed extraordinary. Even before they were eighteen or nineteen, they had established themselves as brilliant students in science, math, and foreign languages. They were also drawn to the German philosopher Friedrich Nietzsche's concept of supermen whose superior intellects exempted them from following the rules and ethics that bound ordinary people. They decided to put Nietzsche's philosophy into practice and to prove to themselves that they personified the supermen about whom Nietzsche had written.

"They killed a fourteen-year-old boy named Robert Franks. They killed him not because they needed money or because they regarded him as an enemy. Robert Franks was, in fact, Richard Loeb's second cousin. The two killers persuaded the boy to hop a ride in their automobile so that they could discuss a new tennis racquet that might help him to improve his game. During the ride, Loeb bashed the boy's head in with a chisel. Later, they hid the body and sent a ransom note to his parents. They concealed the body in a culvert by some railroad tracks.

"At that time, Leopold dropped his eyeglasses. Eventually, when the police discovered the body, they also found the eyeglasses that had a special hinge mechanism. Only three persons in the Chicago area had bought eyeglasses with that type of frame. That discovery led the police to Leopold. Right after that, Loeb confessed to the murder, and Leopold admitted that he had been an accomplice. At their trial, the famous defense attorney Clarence Darrow pleaded for their lives. He persuaded the jurors to connect justice to mercy when they were passing sentence upon the killers. Darrow reminded them that the legal system should do more than execute or imprison wrongdoers. It should rehabilitate them. The jurors heeded his petition. The majority voted against execution. Instead, they sentenced the two youths to life in prison."

"Those blackguards should have been executed," Mrs. Adams fumes. "A life for a life. That's the kind of justice they deserved."

I lodge a rebuttal.

"Leopold and Loeb were not monsters. They were human beings who made a terrible mistake. They killed an innocent boy, and they spent the rest of their lives making amends for it. In prison, they worked to educate their fellow inmates. They reorganized the library. They created courses of study that helped prisoners to attain middle school and high school equivalency. They taught those prisoners. They also worked as volunteers in the prison hospital."

Mrs. Adams is seething.

"They led soft lives there."

"They suffered," I tell her. "When he was thirty, Loeb was killed by an inmate who attacked him with a razor and inflicted multiple wounds over much of his body. His friend Leopold spent most of his life in prison. He was an old man when he was released and spent his last days in Puerto Rico, away from the lurid headlines and the bleak memories that had haunted him while he lived in the United States."

As I finish my summary, I observe the effect of my words upon my classmates and teachers and upon each member of the committee. All of them are observing me with new interest. They are not used to my defense of the erring and the defeated. They do not associate me with altruistic gestures and compassionate responses. Nor do I. Once again, I surprise myself. My pity of others has not died, after all. I don't mind. But I do not plan to pity myself. That is the way toward despair and madness.

Miss Dickinson wants to know more.

"Please tell us how your study of the Leopold and Loeb case brought Kurt Drexler into your life."

I cannot help myself. Even against my self-serving impulse to conceal as much of the truth as I can, a spark inside me pushes me to say more than I'd planned.

"Kurt was mesmerized by the case," I explain. "So was I. Leopold and Loeb tried to commit the perfect crime. They were careless. They left clues behind them."

Mrs. Adams sniffs and hisses. She starts to complain again.

"Leopold and Loeb failed," she says. "Their case proves that there are seldom any perfect crimes."

"That didn't stop Kurt and me from using their case as a template for what not to do if somebody ever decided to commit a crime. We studied the case from every angle. In our Film Studies class, we read and discussed Gilbert Geis's and Leigh Bienen's analysis of the case in their book *Crimes of the Century*. We learned other details about the case from Hal Higdon's *Leopold & Loeb: The Crime of the Century* and from Simon Batz's *For the Thrill of It*. We studied Meyer Levin's novel *Compulsion*, as well as the play that he wrote about the case. Levin changed the names of the killers, but he was writing about Loeb and Leopold.

He knew them well. He had been their classmate and friend at The University of Chicago."

Mr. Steerforth asks a new question.

"You say that you and Kurt Drexler involved yourselves in group discussions about the Leopold and Loeb case. Did you and Kurt ever discuss the case when you were alone together?"

"We did and very often. In fact, the case became something of an obsession for both of us, especially when we watched two films that dramatized the tragedy."

Miss Dickinson comes in again, ethereal and soft-spoken.

"Please tell us the names of the films, Cassandra. Even those of us here who know about the Leopold and Loeb tragedy may have forgotten the films that the tragedy inspired."

"The earlier of the films was Alfred Hitchcock's *Rope*. It had been released in 1948. We watched the DVD in our classroom. We watched it several times, so that we could analyze the motives of the two killers and the mistakes they made when they carried out their crime. The film was an adaptation of a stage play by Patrick Hamilton. He changed the names of the characters, but they were stand-ins for Richard Loeb and Nathan Leopold. Arthur Laurents drew upon the play when he wrote the screenplay for Hitchcock's film. In that film, the two young men do not kill a boy. They kill a friend who is their age. Nor do they bash in his head. They strangle him with a rope. Even today, movie buffs praise the virtuosity of Alfred Hitchcock's direction with his long, uninterrupted takes that intensify the suspense.

"The second film that deepened our understanding of Leopold's and Loeb's killing of an innocent boy was *Compulsion*. Meyer Levin's novel and play were the basis of this riveting film. Richard Murphy wrote the screenplay, and Richard Fleischer directed it. The film was released in 1959. We saw it on DVD a few months ago. Those were the last months that we lived."

The Captain pushes his way in again.

"You say that you and Kurt Drexler studied the Leopold and Loeb case as a template for what not to do if *somebody* wanted to commit a murder. Was that *somebody* Kurt? Was it you? Was it both of you together?

I fall back to silence. Because my foresight does not show me everything that is going to happen here in this courtroom setting, I resist speaking the words that will expose my malice, duplicity, and monstrousness. I cannot bear facing the truth all the time. Even now, when I am dead, the truth assails me with its whip-lashing facts and its memory of my irrevocable deeds.

I plan to sidestep the Captain's questions. I intend to equivocate. I am going to lie.

But the Captain's next words tighten their chains around me.

"I know what happened," he declares. "Everyone on the committee knows. You need to confess. Sooner or later, you will have to face the truth. You and Kurt plotted out a high school shooting and persuaded Boyd Henderson to team up with you. Admit it. You and Kurt are the monsters who planned all of it."

I protest his accusation.

"It was only a plan. I didn't intend for it to go as far as it did. I tried to back out of it."

The Captain rams into me again, with his contemptuous dismissal of my excuses and his harsh branding of me.

"You are a murderous accomplice," he declares. His voice seethes with furious righteousness.

"I didn't mean for it to happen," I answer him.

I feel a grimace warping the facial expression that I carefully cultivate for others to see. Yet I hold my senses tight. I retrieve my calm. I keep back the angry tears that might otherwise well up to disarrange my fake composure. I harden my features. I bring my usual tough-mindedness to the moment. I do not want to rouse my classmates' pity. Nor do I want to explain in grim detail everything that happened in the days before the shooting. Even now, most of my classmates are unaware of how deeply implicated I am in the horrifying plan that spawned the school massacre. If they knew the full story, they would call me their killer. I remember the words that Mrs. Adams used as she excoriated Ari and me for blaming Boyd for the car crash on the night of the junior prom. I also remember the unspoken words that were yoked to that rebuke.

"You don't need an Ar-15 rifle or poison or a dagger to kill someone. Spreading false information about the person you mean to bring down will be enough."

Kurt Drexler and I devised a plan that destroyed Boyd and drove him into madness. The Captain waits for me to tell my classmates about that plan.

I fall back to silence once more. Adamant and uncooperative, I refuse to tell the story.

The Captain insists.

"Get it over with," he commands me. "Make your confession. You teamed up with that undercover neo-Nazi and secret racist Kurt Drexler. The two of you were playing with Boyd Henderson's mind. You pushed him into his murders."

Once again, dry-eyed and rebellious, I protest.

"I didn't pull the trigger of that AR-15. I didn't shoot anybody."

The Captain's anger is relentless.

"You didn't need to pull that trigger," he shouts. "You didn't need that rifle. You used Boyd as your weapon."

Seething with rage and at the edge of despair, I fire back at him.

"I don't want to talk about it!" I exclaim. "I didn't pull the trigger. There is nothing more that I need to tell."

Every one of my classmates and my two teachers cast their questioning glances upon me. Their fates hang in the balance. If I refuse to tell what happened or if I fail to tell the truth, they will lose the chance to return to Earth.

Miss Patel comes into it now. With her steadfast empathy, her inherent elegance, and her calm self-possession, she chooses words that seek to awaken the better side of my nature.

"Tell us what really happened, Cassandra," she begins. "You can do it. You can be that generous and good-hearted human being you were when I first taught you during your freshman year. Give yourself, your classmates, Mr. Marchand, and me a chance to go back to Earth and relive those days before the shooting."

With no warning at all, my fear rises up to disturb my equilibrium. Before this good woman whom I have always respected and whose opinion has always mattered to me, I find myself speaking the words that I was determined to hold back. They are part of the burden that I have carried ever since we arrived in Sojourn. They have drained me of my hope. They have tied me to their doubts. They have tormented me with their punishing implications.

"I would like to help all of you," I say. "But I'm not certain that going back to those days before the shooting is a good thing.

It will be painful for every one of us to live once again for a few days with those persons who counted for something, only to lose them once more because we failed to change things for the better. What if I'm the one who can't change so that things will be better? What if I can't find my way back to that better person who was the Cassandra Winslow you first knew and taught during that freshman year when I was innocent of wrongdoing and I believed that I was going to be someone who helped the world?"

Miss Patel prods me with her gentle words. She wants me to revive my hope. She wants me to keep my despair at bay.

"You won't know the answers to those questions unless you go back to Earth," she says. "Don't squander this chance to go back—not only your chance, but also our chances, as well."

Miss Dickinson joins in, her temperate words and her gracious manner rendering her a sister in spirit to Miss Patel.

"Tell your story, Cassandra. Tell us what really happened on those days before the shooting. Tell us about the pact that you made with Kurt Drexler. I can't promise that the committee will decide in favor of your group's returning to Earth. But you will not imperil your chances if you tell all the truth about you and Kurt and those final days before the killings. In fact, you will enhance the possibility that the committee will allow you to return to Earth."

For an instant, I reflect upon her careful words. Then, I begin to tell what happened.

"All of you know part of the story. It involved Ari's crashing up Boyd's car on the night of our junior prom last year and, with my prodding, casting the blame upon Boyd. I couldn't forgive Boyd for having turned away from me, after we'd been dating for a year. It gave me pleasure to plot against him. Ari and I have told you about that night. I also told you what happened after the crash. Boyd spent three months in a reformatory and three more months in rehab. But I felt that punishment wasn't enough. I vowed that, if I ever had the chance, I was going to avenge myself against him in even more destructive ways.

"When he returned to school as a senior, Boyd worked hard to be a different person. With the help of school counselors, teachers, athletic coaches, and a few school friends, he made a tremendous comeback. Those were his lucky days, when everything seemed to go right for him. He even began his romance with the girl of his dreams. She was Adriana Montalban, a popular student who was also enrolled in many of his classes."

The very mention of Adriana's name rouses the interest of the Five Spirits. They know the important part that she played in the Green Hills tragedy. But in this moment they say nothing. Adriana's name also brings looks both pensive and melancholic to the faces of my classmates and my teachers. A hush falls upon them. They lower their heads, as if they are in mourning and as if they want to conceal their faces in shadows.

I hurry to remind them of the importance of Adriana in Boyd Henderson's life.

"All of you here knew Adriana, and you know what eventually happened to her. But her story needs to be told again if you want to understand why Boyd Henderson became a killer.

"Adriana Montalban was a Latina. A dark-haired, life-loving beauty, she was drawn to the arts. She achieved superb performances with the school's Modern Dance Group. She also regarded math and science as her favorite subjects. She planned to become a pediatrician. Her keen mind, supple body, and inherent discipline helped her to become a proficient JROTC cadet. All these accomplishments made her parents very proud of her. Her father had served as a Special Forces captain in the United States Army during the war in Afghanistan. He is now a pharmacist. Her mother is an elementary school teacher in a Latinx ghetto. Adriana had three younger siblings: two brothers and a sister.

"During her senior year, she began a romance with Boyd Henderson. He became the love of her life.

"Boyd regarded Adriana as a special gift that his good angel had sent him. She was the reward he'd earned because he'd put his life back on the proper track. But his well-earned success lasted only a short time. Kurt Drexler and I saw to that. The Film Studies course about Leopold and Loeb gave us the idea for a plot against Boyd that would not merely injure his reputation. It would destroy him. Adriana Montalban was going to be the linchpin of our plot. We knew that Boyd's love for Adriana had rescued him from hopelessness and despair. Cutting Adriana out of his life would be a quick way to destroy him.

"The idea that we could destroy Boyd pushed us forward. We hadn't yet decided how Adriana would fit into our plot. That would come later. Before we used Adriana, we decided to set another plot in motion. I wasn't the only one who hated Boyd. Kurt hated him, too. But he concealed his hatred from him. They didn't think alike. Boyd regarded his teammates as loyal friends and even spiritual brothers. Kurt *acted* as if he were a brother to every one of his swimming, soccer, and baseball teammates. But he was nothing of the sort. He was their secret rival. More often than not and because of his ingrained wiliness, he stole the spotlight from everybody except Boyd. When he did not earn the spotlight, he watched with envious eyes the praise that his teammates received. Yet none of Kurt's teammates saw through him. Perhaps, their disciplined solidarity and the positive effects of their brotherhood blinded them to his self-centeredness.

"But I saw through him. Within the first hour of our meeting and in all our meetings after that, I recognized him as a kindred soul. We were both lost inside our devious ways. We shared a disguised contempt for humanity and an inordinate pleasure in subverting rules and laws and conventions. We also enjoyed plotting against competitors and against friends who had disappointed or betrayed us. We believed that nothing could thwart us. No one could stop us from carrying through whatever plot we devised.

"We made the Film Studies course our launch-pad for committing the perfect crime. Kurt and I agreed that our target was going to be Boyd Henderson. Over and over, we reviewed our reasons for hating him. Boyd was the golden boy of the swim and soccer teams. Kurt's excellence on those teams seemed to pale when they were compared to Boyd's achievements. In Kurt's eyes, Boyd's victories made him untouchable, despite the scandal of the car crash and his well-known addiction to drugs that had brought him low the previous year. I hated Boyd for walking out on me and making it clear to his teammates that I was a neurotic problem they should avoid.

"Kurt and I wanted to destroy Boyd, but not too quickly. We wanted to watch him disgraced and suffering. After searching for a way to trap him, we decided to draw upon my earlier plot against him. In fact, this new plot we devised turned out to be a rerun with variations of that scheme. Once again, while using fake IDs, we posted photos of Boyd on Facebook, Instagram, and Twitter. Those photos showed him wearing a combat camouflage uniform and pointing an AR-15 at the observer. Other photos placed him against an arsenal of weapons that included not only the Ar-15, but also the AGM-1 Carbine, the Beretta BM59, the Browning Semi-Auto 22, the Remington 750, the Smith & Wesson M & P 15-22, the Ruger SR-556, and the Mauser M1916. A banner spread across the wall behind him carried these words: SCHOOL SHOOTER.

"Another photo showed Boyd on the night of the car crash. He was handcuffed and lying on a gurney. His head and face were smeared with blood. He had just regained consciousness. Aware that the police had handcuffed him and were standing by as sentries, he was barking profanities at them. His grimace gave him the look of a hardened criminal.

"There were other incriminating photos. Kurt and I posted a pair of them juxtaposed to each other. The first of these photos showed Boyd as he appeared on stage as George, the wholesome and athletic protagonist of *Our Town*. He was wearing a crew cut and cotton shirt and trousers that recalled the look of a youth's appearance in the early part of the twentieth century. Next to that photo we placed the picture of him wearing the combat camouflage uniform and wielding an AR-15. We placed a banner beneath this pair of photos that offered some advice to the viewer: DON'T BE FOOLED. THE REAL BOYD IS NO CLEAN-CUT GUY. THE REAL BOYD HAS KILLER INSTINCTS & CARRIES A RIFLE.

"The photos went viral. More than two million people clicked on them. Most of these viewers lodged protests against Boyd and notified the police and the National Guardsmen in their areas. Television news programs around the country showed the photos, and TV anchors interviewed apprehensive parents, as well as irate government and school officials. Within twenty-four hours, Boyd Henderson was branded as a former drug addict and a potential serial killer. It didn't help Boyd's case that a fifteen-year-old student had recently killed ten people in a school in Virginia. The police closed in on Boyd. They arrested him as a person of suspicious character with dangerous and possibly murderous impulses.

"Then Boyd's self-involved parents stepped in. They hurried back from career assignments that had placed them in Berlin and Hong Kong. The news of their son's trouble cast a dark shadow upon them. There might be a backlash that would condemn their parenting and imperil their careers. To prevent that from happening, they acted swiftly. They hired a top-notch lawyer for the hearing that took place in Green Hill's Family Court. They brought in a renowned psychiatrist. They called upon Boyd's teachers and coaches to defend him and to verify his honorable status at our high school. They sought out the identities of the persons who had first posted the photos. Boyd's parents never discovered who had posted the photos. But the team of lawyers and the psychiatrist they hired to exonerate their son were successful in their efforts. Boyd's coaches and teachers provided a credible validation of his honorable character.

"Nevertheless, the damage was done. From that time forward, the public distrusted Boyd. The parents of his teammates pressured their sons and daughters to steer clear of him except for the teams' practice sessions and their soccer and baseball games and swim competitions. Several of the colleges and universities to which he had applied for admission turned him down despite the impressive academic showing he had made in his senior year. The admissions officers of those schools did not care to forgive him for his past transgressions and for the unfavorable publicity that he had more recently drawn to himself.

"The police also gave him a hard time. When a masked youth appeared in the corridors of a neighboring school and killed nine students with his M89 Sniper Rifle, state troopers brought Boyd into the Green Hills police station for questioning. Enraged that the daughter of a fellow trooper had been killed in the attack, they roughed Boyd up and tried to coerce him into a confession. A news photographer took some pictures of the questioning, there in a drab, isolated room within the police station that looked like a prison cell. Once again, photos of Boyd that carried negative connotations went viral.

"Boyd's lawyers lodged a protest. His parents sued the newspaper and some online news outlets for disseminating scandalous images of their son and for treating him as though he were the school assassin. Eventually, they won their case. But it didn't matter. Even when the police apprehended the sixteen-year-old youth who was the assassin, the rumors that branded Boyd as a brooding individual with killer instincts refused to go away.

"Boyd lost hope. Fake news had nullified all the hard work of his reformation after the crash. It didn't seem to matter that excellent universities in Germany, England, and France had accepted him into their programs. He felt that he was being cast out of his own country. He was being written off as a frequent troublemaker and a potential killer.

"Nevertheless, he worked even harder to restore his image. At the end of March, as his high school senior year was swiftly moving forward, he won a top prize in a statewide boxing tournament, and he earned A's for his term projects in biology, physics, calculus, Spanish literature, and the English Renaissance. Lately, his parents were making a special effort to stay involved in the day-to-day challenges that his busy and controversial life generated. They could not, of course, always be available. His father's career as a television anchor and a documentary filmmaker and his mother's career as a fashion designer often required them to be away. But Boyd's grandmother was available. She provided meticulous guardian care, and she entrusted her grandson to the additional watchful counseling of his coaches, teachers, and the psychiatrist with whom he continued to confer.

"Miss Patel and Mr. Marchand helped him to find his hope once more.

"'Go to Europe,' Mr. Marchand advised him. 'You can make your life exactly as you want it to be.'

"Born in Marseilles to American parents, Mr. Marchand had studied at the Sorbonne in Paris and at Cambridge University in England. His studies focused upon French, German, and Italian literature and also included mathematics and music.

"Ms. Patel also encouraged Boyd. She had earned degrees in biology and physics at Oxford University.

"Their years of study in Europe had been auspicious. They did not hesitate to point Boyd in the same direction.

"'You have been invited to join an extraordinary academic program,' Miss Patel reminded him. 'Within a trimester schedule that offers England as your home base, you will be able to study not only at Cambridge University, but also at the Sorbonne in Paris and at The Technical University of Berlin. Turn away from the injustice that has befallen you here. Choose a better life outside this country.'

"Boyd listened to these teachers who had always been on his side.

"'I'll go to Europe,' he said. 'Maybe, that's the place where I can make things turn around for me.'

"A few days later, in early April, when he and Kurt were on their way to swim practice in the grand new pool that was located inside the east wing of their school, Boyd happened to mention his plan to study abroad.

"'That's a terrific idea," Kurt told him. 'You will meet the best people who can put you on the path to a successful career.'

"'I'll do all right,' Boyd said. 'Having famous teachers on my side will be a big plus. But my greatest boost will come from Adriana. She'll be studying in Europe with me. She's been accepted into the same university program.'

"'I didn't skip a beat when I heard that news,' Kurt told me later that afternoon, while he recounted this friendly exchange with Boyd. 'I brought a beam to my face. I patted Boyd on his right shoulder. I chose words that convinced him that I was happy to hear his news.'

"'You're a lucky guy,' Kurt told him. You'll have famous teachers, three first-rate countries, and Adriana. You are in for a fabulous year.'

"Boyd grinned, even though he was not yet comfortable with the pleasure that his new-found happiness was bringing him.

"Kurt described that moment to me a few hours later, in the privacy of his bedroom after we'd enjoyed an hour of sex when nobody else was in his grandparents' home. As he reviewed what had occurred in that brief conversation with Boyd, a look both wretched and menacing held his features tight.

"'I hated Boyd even more because of that grin,' he said. 'I hated him for winning Adriana's love. I hated him for lining up a bright future. I felt angry. I was desperate. I wanted to steal Boyd's happiness from him. I wanted to ruin his life and run free of all consequences. All through our practice, I kept thinking of ways to commit a crime against him and get away with it. But that would be only the beginning. I wanted my anonymous crime to push Boyd into a greater crime that would completely destroy him.

"'The right idea hasn't come to me yet. But I do know this much. Our plot has to involve a crime so horrible that nobody will ever forgive Boyd Henderson or forget his name. Without revealing our real motives, you and I will set up Boyd to become a school shooter.'

"'How can we do that?' I asked him. 'Right now, Boyd's too happy to shoot anybody. He's primed for some great years in Europe with his girlfriend.'

"'I'll find a way,' Kurt answered me. 'Or maybe you will. Maybe you'll come up with a plan that will work.'

"It took me less than a minute to discover the plan that I'd been hiding even from myself ever since Boyd fell in love with Adriana Montalban.

"'What if something bad happens to his Adriana?' I asked Kurt. 'What if some of your neo-Nazi and White Supremacist friends rough her up? What if they rape her and then kill her?'

"'Kill her? No. That's going too far. My friends have done some bad things. But, as far as I know, they've never killed anybody.'

"'There's always a first time,' I said. 'They would take pleasure in killing a Latina.'

"'No. No,' he said. 'The idea is too horrible even to contemplate. If anybody should get killed, that person should be Boyd. Let my friends kill him.'

"'Not a chance. I'm not interested in making him a martyr. You and I have to push him into becoming a school shooter. He'll come to a bad end. Then you and I will have succeeded in constructing the perfect crime. We'll watch Boyd carry it through and take the blame for it.'

"Observing my enthusiasm for murder and mayhem, Kurt grinned with wily interest.

"'You are quite a girl,' he said. 'You have the heart of a killer. You and the world will get along just fine.'"

My classmates and teachers and the Five Spirits have been listening to me with a mixture of anger, disappointment, and bitterness.

I fall silent again.

I do not want to reawaken the memory of what happened to Adriana Montalban. That memory is unbearable. It exposes Kurt and his gang as savage beasts and racists. It brands me as their accomplice, a devious malcontent with murderous impulses and an equally savage disposition. I do not lie to myself. I know who I am. I'm no good. But I have no interest in begging forgiveness from you or from my classmates and teachers or from the five judgmental Spirits who sit in this courtroom deciphering the subtle and unsubtle layers of my guilt.

I close up. I tell myself that the Spirits will condemn me for my part in the crime against Adriana. There is no way that they will allow my classmates and teachers to return to Earth. My guilt casts a dark shadow upon the group. Though my ten peers and my two teachers are fallible human beings, they are innocent of my crimes. Yet my guilt has stained the group's essential goodness. How can we ever go back? How can we win the chance to alter the outcome of our tragic day?

My classmates and my teachers are waiting for me to go on with the telling of the pact that I made with Kurt. They know a few important things about me. But, while we lived on Earth, not one of them knew about my involvement in the killing of Adriana Montalban. Nor did they guess that it was I who first contrived the makeshift plot against Adriana and that it was Kurt who helped me to perfect it.

Still I remain silent. Adamant and unrepentant, I expect the harshest punishment. I am wondering whether my guilt will draw upon me eternal extinction. That is the punishment that the First Spirit and these Five Spirits usually mete out to the most fiendish criminals—the hardened abominations who have corrupted their humanity beyond the perimeters of forgiveness. Instead of vanishing by degrees and becoming an acceptable Spirit, I shall vanish forever. This temporary haven that calls itself Sojourn and the two Heavens will no longer know me.

This bleak prospect does not unnerve me. My actions warrant no less a punishment. There is a part of me that welcomes it. I'll be getting what I deserve.

In this very instant, while I pass sentence upon myself, I notice Miss Patel observing me with tears misting her eyes. But she is not weeping for herself. She is crying for me. She comprehends the hidden nature of my anguish. She knows my pain. If she were seated next to me, she would reach out to me with a consoling touch of her hand upon my shoulder or a murmuring counsel that tells me not to lose hope or to surrender to bitterness and despair.

Now I recall the words that Miss Patel offered me on this very day, about an hour or so into this session. They are words not unlike the ones that Ari and Shiloh and Miss Dickinson also spoke to me as they made appeals to my better nature that were either urgent or angry or heartfelt.

"Tell the truth," they said. "That's the only way you will save yourself and save us."

In a flash, with the impact of a crash of thunder, my hope revives. I am ready to go on with my confession. I want to tell the truth about my involvement in the killing of Adriana.

But I have waited too long. Captain Johnson hurries back into it now. Once again, his words are rancorous and accusatory.

"Those neo-Nazis and White Supremacists did not act alone. Without lifting a hand against Adriana or firing a Beretta BM59 or a Colt snub-nosed revolver at her, you also killed her. You plotted the crime with Kurt and his henchmen. You even suggested the place where they eventually killed her. It was an isolated country road, only a couple of miles from her parents' home. She was on her bicycle, riding along a forest path to see her grandparents. She travelled that route every Saturday morning around nine o'clock. Her grandparents loved hearing her tell of all the good things that had happened to her during the preceding week. She felt like a grown-up young lady as she sat with them at their breakfast table, sharing orange juice, blueberry muffins, fresh fruit, and tea. They enjoyed listening to her as she told them about her work for her school's Student Council and about her latest tennis match. They asked her about her Science Fair project, for which she was using the Polymerase Chain

Reaction to 'copy' DNA. They also asked her about her study of Shakespeare's *Twelfth Night* and *A Winter's Tale* in her Advanced Placement English class and about her progress with German, Chinese, and Spanish. They wanted to know whether she had played Brahms and Rachmaninoff on her piano at her private music lessons and whether her teacher was pleased.

"Adriana's grandparents looked forward to her Saturday visits. On the morning that she was murdered, they wondered why she had not arrived at her usual time. What could have detained her?"

The Captain pauses in his telling the group about the tragedy that overtook Adriana Montalban. I begin wondering whether he, too, is grieving because of Adriana's death. He was neither a friend, nor an acquaintance. He died long before she was born. Yet his new awareness of her horrific death is a scalding wound upon his senses. Even as a Spirit, he feels anguish. He still rages at the injustice that blemishes the characters of most human beings. In this very moment, he begins once again to rage at me. Instantly, his face and his eyes glow with fire. His skin shoots away from his angry demeanor. His flesh burns to its socket, and I gaze upon the grim reality of the Captain's death's head and the whole skeletal form of him. Then, just as swiftly, the awful imagery of the death's head and the skeleton scatter away, and Captain Johnson stands before me in his military uniform. His grim-faced ruggedness is a formidable presence, his disposition is volatile, and his words are threatening.

"You know what kept Adriana from reaching the home of her grandparents," he shouts. "You and your White Supremacist friends planned all of it."

I feel beaten. I am trapped by the ugliness of what I have done. I can tell myself the truth. I have never lied to myself. While I was on Earth, I learned to live with my crimes. But hearing someone else speak about them is an altogether different experience. I don't like it. I prefer to condemn myself. I dislike second-hand appraisals of my conduct. I was there.

I speak out. I intend to set the record straight.

"Yes," I confess. "Kurt and I mapped out the whole thing— where it would take place and how many of his friends would be there to do away with her."

"To kill her!" the Captain shouts. "Don't soften it by saying your friends were going to do away with her. They killed her! You and Kurt helped them! That's the truth of it."

I throw an answer to him.

"Kurt's gang of racists killed her. He wasn't there. Neither was I."

Miss Dickinson asks a question.

"What are the names of the boys who killed Adriana?"

"I wasn't often in their company," I answer her, gently and low-keyed. "I was never in the same classes with them, even though they were seniors. They travelled in different circles. There were four of them. They were Gregor Neumann, Stefan Mayer, Bram Ziegler, and Werner Schreiber."

Miss Dickinson asks another question.

"Who were they? What kind of students were they?"

"They were in the top ten percent of their class," I answer her. "Bram and Werner were headed for careers in the Air Force and the Marines. Stefan wanted a life on Wall Street. Gregor was going to study international law."

Miss Dickinson wants to know more.

"They sound ambitious. They were preparing to be responsible adults. What made them want to kill an innocent girl? How could they possibly live with themselves afterward?"

Mrs. Steerforth rushes in with new, hostile words.

"Those racists don't deserve to go on living," she says. "They are wretched creatures, completely without conscience. If, by chance, they remember the dreadful murder they committed, they will tell themselves that the killing was only an experiment. They wanted to commit the perfect crime and get away with it. They succeeded in their mission. They are reveling in that fact. They will tell themselves that there are far too many people alive on Earth. One girl less doesn't matter."

Her caustic remarks fire up the Captain. He lashes out at me again.

"You knew that they were going to rape Adriana and then kill her. Yet you did nothing to stop it."

"I did try to stop it!

"Take a look at the murder your plot spawned."

No sooner does the Captain speak these words than the video wall surrounding us flashes its eternal memory of the murder.

We who have been sitting in this courtroom find ourselves suddenly in the forest with its flourishing greenery, its chirping birds, and its scampering squirrels. The early morning April sun casts its rays upon trees, bird, and squirrels, as well as upon the lithe form of Adriana. She is riding her bike with easy precision along the smooth path that is leading her to the home of her grandparents. A dainty basket of early-blooming red, pink, and yellow impatiens and begonias is perched upon the handlebars of her bike. There is blitheness in her appearance and a supple grace in her movements. Her radiant smile expresses the joy that she is experiencing by living so completely in this moment.

We stand close enough to touch Adriana, but she cannot see or touch us. Her world, with its already-lived pastness, is trapped in its own time. Yet its trouble-haunted incident unfolds before us as if for the first time. To Adriana's eyes, we are not visible, even though we have not yet shed our bodies.

In these first minutes of our watching her, the entire scene conveys a halcyon mood. We might be inside a forest of Eden. Adriana imparts that kind of innocence.

Then, suddenly and without warning, the mood changes. Dark shadows invade the scene. They are not the natural shadows that the canopy of trees casts upon the bike path, filtered as those shadows are with the sunlight streaming down through the canopy. Human figures cast these shadows. The figures and their shadows belong to Gregor, Stefan, Bram, and Werner. On their bikes, they rush toward Adriana, blocking her escape as they surround her. Gregor rams his bike into hers with terrific force. She falls away from her bike as it topples across the path. Then, Bram is the first of the young men upon her. She screams and kicks and twists her body, trying to free herself from his brute handling of her. With her fingernails, she claws at his face. She sinks her teeth into his arm. He spews profanities at her as he knocks her out with a fierce punch to her jaw.

Bram rips away her clothes and, after tossing off his own clothes, carries her away from the bike path and into a darker region of the forest. He is the first to rape her. Stefan, Gregor, and Werner, now also naked, quickly take their turns. They look like hulking beasts battering some delicate prey. Their eyes gleam with the ambivalence of hatred and desire. A hellish redness flushes across their lascivious faces. Erotic groans and grunting drive their breathlessness.

After they have finished and just as Adriana begins to regain consciousness, the four men bash in her head with the hammers they have carried inside their windbreakers. Blood and brain tissue shoot out of her head, speckle the air, and spill across the path. Her once-lovely face has folded into itself, crumpled and distorted. Her soft brown eyes have dropped out of their sockets, and her mouth that had always displayed a glistening smile has drooped open, toothless and blood-laden.

The four murderers quickly put their clothes back on. They leave Adriana's body inside the dark of the forest and her overturned bike with its colorful array of flowers at the side of the road. Without looking back, they hurry away on their bikes.

In the next instant, the wall video heaves up the scene and sends it scattering. The green forest, the blood-smeared corpse, and the four foul murderers disperse, float away, and disappear.

Here, in this courtroom within the natural satellite of Earth called Sojourn, the Five Spirits, my classmates, and our two teachers once again fall silent. The horror of what we have just watched leaves us speechless. Even Captain Johnson falls silent, though only for a moment. His battle experience during The Second World War has earned him a higher tolerance for the massacre of human beings. He is the first to find words that condemn me.

"Now do you understand what your plot has wrought?" he asks me rhetorically. "Because of the plan that you made with Kurt Drexler, an innocent girl was savagely murdered, and four young men became killers."

Before I can answer him, Abigail Emerson, our school's champion swimmer, comes into it now, weeping and screaming.

"Monsters! That's what Werner and Bram and Gregor and Stefan are. Monsters! So is Kurt Drexler! And so are you! All of you killed an innocent girl!"

Chloe Bradbury, one of our school's great beauties as well as an actress in television commercials and a volunteer at a local soup kitchen, also lashes out at me. She, too, is weeping, and her voice carries forward the tremulous sounds of deep-seated grief.

"You also destroyed Boyd Henderson when he'd been following all the rules, doing all the right things, and learning to be a good man."

I fire bitter words back at her. I, too, am angry and screaming.

"I didn't kill anyone! I did everything I could to stop Kurt and his gang!"

Miss Dickinson returns to the conversation. Her calm voice, tinged with melancholy, coaxes me to explain myself.

"Tell us what you did to prevent the murder of Adriana Montalban."

I pause before I speak. Everyone's eyes hold me in their gaze. There are tearful eyes. There are disdainful eyes. There are angry eyes. There are accusatory eyes. I do not resent their pity or their distrust or their rancor. I do not flinch from their gaze. The White Supremacists' murder of Adriana that I have just witnessed in its surreal replay of the actual event and my memory of Boyd Henderson's killing of my friends, teachers, and me have drained me of the sorrow, alarm, and vindictiveness that my friends' disdain might once have caused me. My character is blighted with wrongdoing. My soul is scarred beyond repair. Yet, hardened and willful, I want to help rescue my friends and my teachers. I do not care to be the obstacle that prevents them from returning to Earth. I need to rescue myself, as well, if that is possible. I'd like to find out whether all of us, friends and teachers working together, can change the events that happened on the day that Boyd Henderson shot us dead.

I am ready to tell all of the truth.

CHAPTER NINE

THREE DEATHS

My words come rapidly now. I want to tell the group what really happened. I want to confess. I do not wait for hesitation to trammel my words. I do not allow my usual deceptions to overtake my will.

My classmates hang on my every word. The Five Spirits also watch me and listen to everything I say. They know my story, but my telling it here and now will test my honesty and the faint heartbeat of my possible reformation.

As I begin, my gaze upon my classmates and teachers and upon the Five Spirits is steady and earnest. My voice sounds vibrant and determined.

"Even before Kurt's gang murdered Adriana, I smelled disaster in the air. I knew I had to stop it from happening. The murder of Adriana would be so gruesome that we would never be free of it, even if the police never discovered that we were the plotters and the killers.

"A week before the murder was to take place, I met Kurt at his grandparents' home. As usual, his grandparents were traveling. So were his parents, though they were expected to return from Europe on the following day.

"Kurt had given me a key to the house, so I let myself in without ringing the doorbell. I'd already phoned Kurt, telling him with muted urgency that I needed to see him. He was in the midst of a workout in his grandparents' home gym. That

Saturday morning, he'd been lifting weights, riding a stationary bike, running on a treadmill, and hitting an eighty-pound punching bag. Bare-chested and terrifically muscular, he was wearing black boxer shorts, black socks, and black sneakers. His ruddy skin glistened with perspiration.

"He was ready to take a swim in the pool that was located in the spacious room adjoining the gym. But, understanding my urgency, he wiped his face and his chest with a towel and, after planting a light kiss on my cheek, waited for me to speak. He nudged me forward with quickened words that were anchored to his ingrained guardedness and his well-honed cynicism.

"'You've had second thoughts,' he said. 'You're getting the jitters. You are afraid to take the leap. Plotting a murder and seeing our gang carry it through is too big a deal for you to comprehend. Your small-town conventions hold you back. You are reluctant to admit that you can get away with murder without being punished.'

"'What we are planning to do is wrong,' I told him. 'I should have recognized that from the moment we began plotting the murder. We'd be killing an innocent girl who has never wronged us in any way. We have no motive for killing her, unless you are still holding a grudge against her for politely turning away from your advances.'

"Kurt stared at me for a long moment. There was derision in that look and the vague outline of a sneer on his lips.

"'We have a better motive,' he said. 'We want to commit the perfect murder and get away with it.'

"'I can't do it,' I told him. 'It's cold-blooded and inhuman. I don't know how I let you talk me into making the plan. I can't even understand why you would want to do such a thing. You lead a privileged life. You have a good future ahead of you.'

"'I know why I want to do such a thing. I also know why I could talk you into this plan for a murder. You know, too, though you don't want to admit it.'

"'I don't know.'

"'You and I are both wretched. Beneath the trappings of upscale middle-class life, we feel powerless. I can't stand my tyrannical father, and you can barely tolerate your conservative parents. They push us around. We are puppets dangling awkwardly on their strings. High school is another tyranny. That place with all its lock-step rules makes me feel suffocated and imprisoned. Not even sports give me the freedom I want. They are just another form of tyranny, with coaches, parents, and classmates relentlessly pressuring us to win and throwing their unforgiving responses at us if we lose.'

"'We'll be free of the pressure. We'll run free of high school, too, in a few months. Let's not ruin things for ourselves.'

"'We won't be ruining things for ourselves,' Kurt answered me. 'We'll simply be proving that we have power and that we can make our own rules.'

"'Don't do it,' I tell him once more. 'Don't persuade your gang to commit this awful crime.'

"'You really don't want to be a part of it.'

"'No.'

"'Then stay out of it.'

"'I will. But what about you?'

"'That's my business now,' he told me. 'You are not involved in it anymore.'

"He turned away from me and, without inviting me to join him, hurried on to the swimming pool. His face wore a stern expression, and his lips were pressed tightly together, suggesting the adamant will that would be goading the four students in his gang to murder Adriana Montalban, the girl he had secretly desired who had politely turned him down.

"I knew that I had to act quickly if I was to save Adriana. I couldn't alert the police or the school officials because they wouldn't believe me. They already regarded me as an overly emotional girl who allows my imagination to fill my mind with melodramatic problems and violent plots. Besides, I didn't want to implicate myself in a murder plot.

"Instead, I went to Kurt's parents two days after I backed out of the murder plot. They had just flown in from Europe and planned to return there in a few weeks to fulfill career obligations. His father was conducting cancer research in a Lausanne clinic, and his mother's new play was opening in a Paris theater. They believed my story, and they acted swiftly to prevent their son from making a mess of his life. They brought him to Europe, returning there earlier than they had anticipated. Once he arrived in Berlin, Kurt was going to have a private tutor help him complete the closing requirements for his senior year. His parents thought only of *his* safety. They did not alert the police or Adriana's parents. They wanted to protect their son's reputation. They told themselves that they were doing the right thing. After all, Kurt assured them that he had talked his friends out of committing the murder.

"But Kurt lied to his parents. He did not try to talk his racist friends out of killing Adriana. I know. My foresight showed me the truth. Kurt urged his friends to go ahead with the murder. He played upon their hatred of Adriana because she was a Latina. He goaded them into the killing. They really didn't need much prodding. Even if Kurt had tried to talk them out of the killing, his friends would have followed their own will.

"After Stefan, Bram, Gregor, and Werner killed Adriana, Boyd Henderson began to lose his mind.

"At first, he closed down. Whenever I passed him in the school corridors or that one time I stopped at his table during lunchtime in the school cafeteria to tell him how sorry I was about what happened to Adriana, I saw how changed he was. No longer was he buoyant or flippant or open. A sickly pallor was overtaking his ruddy complexion. His eyes were bloodshot from lack of sleep. His heart was broken. He had lost the love of his life. He was willing himself not to feel anything.

"Even when the police questioned him about his relationship with Adriana, he held himself tight. I know, because my uncle was one of the detectives who questioned him. If he felt humiliated at being treated like a murder suspect, Boyd showed no resentment. He mumbled through his honest narrative concerning his love of Adriana and the happiness that their compatibility had brought both of them.

"'I never thought that I'd pity a suspect,' my Uncle Ben told my father. 'But I pitied Boyd Henderson. He reminded me of the shell-shocked guys that I'd sometimes see when I was a medic assigned to combat duty in Iraq.'

"The police didn't detain Boyd for long. On the morning that Adriana was murdered, Boyd was at an airport in Boston, meeting his parents when they arrived from the West Coast, where they had attended a five-day celebration of *Time Magazine*'s one hundred most influential people. Boyd's father was setting the bar high for documentary filmmaking, and his mother was redefining high fashion for women. News photos had captured vivid images of Boyd greeting his parents as they entered the VIP section of the airport terminal. There was further proof of his innocence. The lab report from the forensic pathologist proved that the semen found inside and on Adriana's body was not Boyd's.

"Only at Adriana's funeral did Boyd break apart, though not right away and not all at once. At the wake, there were signs that all was not well with him. He insisted on standing sentry at the side of the closed coffin that held Adriana's body. He did not want to leave her alone as crowds of relatives and friends took their turns to pay their final respects to the young girl that had already disappeared from their seeing. The loveliness that she had once worn so naturally lived now only in their memories. On the next day, Boyd once again stood or sat tall, ramrod straight, and tearless, this time during the funeral Mass at Saint Mary's Catholic Church where Adriana had served as an acolyte and had sung in the choir. But, at the gravesite an hour later, the fury and the despair that he had suppressed rose up to overwhelm him. No sooner had the funeral attendants lowered the coffin containing Adriana's body into the grave, than Boyd rushed by the funeral cortège, the hundreds of mourners, and four security guards and jumped into the grave.

"'Bury me with her!' he yelled. 'Bury me with her!'

"Two rugged pallbearers jumped into the grave after him. Punching their faces and their chests and nearly blinded by his tears, Boyd nearly overcame them. But they also were trained boxers and excellent fullbacks on the school's football team. Together, they managed to knock Boyd down, stunning him with their jab-hook-cross punches. Then, they lifted him out of the grave as two security guards pulled him forward and into their custody.

"Nobody arrested him. But everyone was shocked as they witnessed the grief that was tearing him apart. They wondered whether he would eventually do away with himself. To protect themselves from public criticism, Mr. and Mrs. Henderson placed their son in a clinic, where a team of psychiatrists and grief counselors treated him for his severe depression and his mumbling threats of suicide.

"He stayed in their care for three weeks. Then, because he appeared to brighten at the prospect of returning to his program at school and to the friendships he had started to build with fellow athletes, his doctors allowed him to resume his day-to-day schedule as an honors student who was completing his senior year.

"He acquitted himself well in all his courses and in every swimming and tennis competition in which he participated. On the surface, he appeared to be adjusting to the death of the girl he loved. But those students who were closest to him saw that the extraordinary spark that had animated his spirit had left him. His life-loving exuberance had died, and so had his belief that he would always find a way to make a friend of happiness. The memory of Adriana still haunted him. It always would. Even the most cynical of his friends were moved by the change that was destroying him.

"I was one of those cynical people. There was a time when I would have enjoyed seeing Boyd suffer. But not then. Not during the last days that I lived on Earth. Not when my involvement in Adriana's murder haunted me day and night. I was the one who told Ari Bachman that when Adriana Montalban died Boyd Henderson died with her. I died, too. I had wandered too far away from the remnants of goodness that lay dormant within me. I could never retrieve the innocence that I had so carelessly squandered. I felt that I could no longer call myself human. I belonged to some earlier and savage form of our species. I had made my pact not only with those savages of old, but also with savages from my everyday world who lumbered toward one crime after another. Bram, Stefan, Werner, Gregor, and Kurt were those savages.

"I wasn't the only one who suffered because of the harm that I'd brought upon Boyd. Ari also suffered. He did not know about my involvement in Adriana's murder. But he could not forget the dirty trick we played on Boyd. That trick tarnished Boyd's reputation and threatened his future.

"You have to believe me when I tell you that, as self-protective and dishonest as we had often been in our friendship with him, Ari and I were heartsick and guilt-ridden because of the blame we'd cast upon Boyd during the car crash of the preceding year. We did not enjoy seeing him suffer. We never expected that a young man as bright and adventurous as he once was could slowly break apart before our eyes with incremental flashes of despair and without ever calling out for help.

"Even without that cry for help, Ari and I decided that we were going to try to rescue him. We met privately with his teachers and coaches and with his swimming, soccer, and baseball teammates. Every one of them made certain to keep Boyd busy with his academic studies, with his swim meets, and with his baseball games. In his free time, they drew him into other activities that challenged him and that he enjoyed.

"Ari, Dion, Shiloh, and I went skydiving with him in Lebanon, Maine, which is about eighty miles from Green Hills. We wondered whether skydiving was a realistic option for Boyd, since he had given signs of being suicidal. But, after checking with the owners of the skydiving school, we learned that a computerized automatic activation device called a cybernetic parachute release system was designed to activate the parachute in the event that the skydiver failed to deploy it. We needn't have worried. On that afternoon, Boyd gave himself completely to this new experience. It gave him an adrenalin rush. It made him feel like an altogether different person. He had a blast. So did Ari, Dion, Shiloh, and I.

"From a Cessna 206 that was flying at fourteen thousand feet at a speed of one hundred twenty miles per hour, the five of us jumped into what we thought was an amazing adventure. After a sixty-second free fall, we parachuted for five minutes into the vastness of space that received us as temporary floating specimens that had dared to test ourselves in what we regarded as an altogether different dimension.

"After we made our soft landings, we saw elation touching Boyd's face. From our own experience of this skydiving, we imagined that he had forgotten his grief for all those minutes that we were floating in space. Even after we landed, his elation stayed with him for an hour or two.

"But when we arrived back in Green Hills his face grew pensive, his mood turned somber, and his eyes looked haunted once more.

"In the weekend that followed, Jayden, Sonia, Ari, Brenda, and I persuaded Boyd to join us for some whitewater kayaking on Ogunquit's Tidal River. During the weekend after that, Boyd accompanied Miss Patel, Mr. Marchand, Dion, Chloe, Ari, and me to New York, where we saw two upbeat shows: *Hamilton* and *School of Rock—The Musical*. We also found time during another weekend to go horse riding on a farm in Casco, Maine. On every one of these excursions, Boyd appeared to regain his zest for life. We believed that he was recovering from the tragedy of losing the girl he loved. We sensed that, because of the murder of Adriana, he would never again be the really young Boyd. He had not merely grown up. He had grown old, even though he had just turned eighteen. But he would make do with the cards that The Fates had dealt him. He would survive.

"Then, just a few weeks before we were to be graduated, the gang that called themselves The White Supremacists got drunk at a party and began bragging about having committed the perfect murder. They said that Kurt Drexler and I had made the plan and that they had the guts to carry it out. Stefan and Bram did most of the bragging. But Werner and Gregor, who were far less drunk, grew alarmed when they saw that a hush had fallen upon their peers who only minutes earlier had fired up the party with rapper music, lively dancing, sensual overtures, and casual profanities. The White Supremacists had not mentioned Adriana. But suddenly her ghostly spirit had entered the room.

"Aware that Stefan and Bram had revealed themselves as killers, Werner and Gregor began laughing at their crowd of friends who were now observing the four of them with astonishment and suspicion. Still laughing, Werner and Gregor took out their iPhones and began snapping pictures of the group.

"Chloe Bradbury was the first to speak. A frown revealed her doubt of them and the displeasure that these rough fellows often roused in her.

"'Why are you taking pictures of us?'

"'Werner and I want to show you how startled you look,' Gregor said, with a fake lightheartedness. 'Stefan and Bram have been joking around, and all of you have believed every word of their nonsense.'

"Chloe was not happy. Nor had Gregor's too-casual words allayed her doubts of him and his cohorts. But she made no reply to his remark. Instead, her gaze upon these White Supremacists became even more searching.

"Shiloh was the one who replied to Gregor's words. He, too, was not happy. His language was blunt and pertinent.

"'Stefan and Bram are way out of line,' he said. 'Joking about murder doesn't make them look good in any way.'

"'You are absolutely right,' Gregor said. 'We'll just change the subject. Let this party resume. We are here to have a good time.'

"The party did resume. The band began a new set. Guests danced as exuberantly as ever. They ate hamburgers and steaks and sipped soft drinks. They spoke of swimming, tennis, and horse riding, as well as of the latest flicks and the new Audis and Alfa Romeos that the parents of three or four in the group were giving them as graduation presents.

"The atmosphere retrieved its normalcy, but only on the surface.

"On the days that followed that party, a rumor spread around our school that Kurt Drexler's parents had brought him to Europe because he was mixed up in Adriana's murder. Chloe Bradbury, who had kept silent about Bram's and Stefan's remarks about devising the perfect murder, heard the rumor that was spreading and told the chief of police in Green Hills. Immediately, he called Werner, Bram, Stefan, and Gregor into the station for questioning.

Their fathers accompanied them and made up a story about their sons being on a weekend camping trip with them on the Saturday of Adriana's murder. They had the witnesses to prove it. The fathers also refused to have their sons provide the forensic lab with samples of their blood, semen, skin cells, and hair. They claimed that acceding to that request would cast undue suspicion upon the boys. Adriana's parents were navigating all the legal channels that might compel the boys to provide the samples.

"The battle for the samples was still going on when another rumor circulated about Boyd Henderson. This rumor claimed that Boyd believed that Werner, Bram, Stefan, and Gregor had killed Adriana. He was planning to kill them. Once again, the police questioned Boyd. He remained composed throughout their grueling interrogation.

"'Of course I want Adriana's killers brought to justice,' he told the chief of police and the district attorney. 'They deserve to be executed. But I'll leave that job to all of you.'

"The police and the district attorney respected his direct manner and his understated presentation of himself. They saw in him a young man who had nothing to hide. They recognized, too, the militant self-control he had attained through the harsh experiences that his fate had dealt out to him.

"'I don't think that Henderson will give us any problems,' the police chief told my uncle over dinner and a few drinks at the private club where both of them were members. 'He won't make any wrong moves. He's too smart to do that. He has a good life ahead of him.'

"Nevertheless, as though he wanted to make certainty more certain, the chief mentioned that he and his team were going to keep an eye on Boyd.

"Two days later, another rumor spread across our high school campus. The rumor sprang from a seedling of truth. The police chief and a local detective came into the school's administrative wing to do a further check on Boyd's conduct. There, they conferred not only with the principal and with Miss Patel and Mr. Marchand. They also questioned Ari, Dion, Shiloh, Jayden, Jason, Alessandro, Abigail, Sonia, Chloe, Brenda, and me. Each of us had been in close contact with Boyd. He regarded most, if not all, of us as his loyal friends. He was more likely to express his true feelings to us rather than to inquiring detectives and policemen who were strangers to him.

"The chief and the detective wanted to know whether Boyd had ever expressed a desire to kill the four students who had bragged about their murder of Adriana Montalban. They also wanted to know whether he was recovering from the tragedy of having lost the girl he loved or whether he was harboring a murderous hatred toward the four suspects. From time to time, he might have inadvertently revealed this hatred of the four White Supremacists to us. We were, after all, the friends and teachers who were helping him to rally from his trouble. That was the reason we had been called to this private conference. We were the ones who could prevent Boyd from carrying through any plan of revenge that he might be devising against Adriana's killers.

"Without any hesitation whatever, our group assured the chief and the detective that Boyd was making a more than adequate recovery from the tragedy that had overtaken his life. His studies and his athletic competitions kept him busy. The recent excursions we had shared with him horse riding, skydiving, and theatergoing in Casco, Lebanon, and New York had brought him once again into the wider world. Those excursions had awakened his adventurous spirit. They reminded him that Adriana would want him to reclaim his happiness. She would not want him to condemn himself to a life of grieving and isolation.

"The police chief and the detective left that meeting convinced that Boyd was going to be all right. He had friends and teachers who were helping him. He also had a school psychologist, famous and congenial parents, and an affectionate grandmother and her assistants, Mr. and Mrs. Courtney, guiding him into a complete recovery.

"Boyd might have recovered. But another vicious rumor brought him low again. It blasted the trust he had placed in his friends and favorite teachers. It destroyed his emerging conviction that he could shed his past and make a better life for himself.

"This new rumor asserted that the classmates and teachers that he regarded as friends were not friends at all. They were sentries assigned to monitor his conduct. They were working in the service of the police and school officials. They were conspiring against him. Maybe they even believed that he was the one who had killed Adriana after he and other young men had raped her.

"He closed himself from all of them. When he was in their company, he was courteous. He was involved. He was buoyant. But he was playing a role. He was impersonating a healthy individual who had learned to focus on realistic goals and who had no interest in quarreling with the world. But there festered in the secret corner of his awareness a hatred of these friends that he could no longer trust and a disdain of a world that allowed murderers to run free.

"During these final weeks before graduation, he held himself steady. He was waiting for the forensic lab to obtain samples of the four White Supremacists' blood, semen, skin cells, and hair. Each day he expected to hear that the police had arrested Werner, Stefan, Gregor, and Bram for the murder of his girlfriend. But the lawyers representing the four killers still refused to provide the samples. Instead, they advised their clients to relocate outside the country, right after their high school graduation.

"Boyd feared that the four killers would run free of the consequences of their killing. He also became convinced that the classmates and teachers whom he had regarded as friends were collaborating with the police to frame him for the murder of his girlfriend. For three rigorously controlled days and three sleepless nights, he thought of nothing else. The police would convict him for a murder that he had not committed. Everyone else would believe that he had killed the one person in the world whom he had tenderly loved and even worshipped.

"Then, on an early June afternoon at school, he went mad and shot everyone in our group that he believed had turned against him—the thirteen people who had not killed Adriana. He ran away right after that, in search of the four neo-Nazis who had killed Adriana "

I pause. I wait for the Five Spirits and my group to question me further or to challenge my testimony. I do not have to wait long. No sooner have I finished telling my version of what happened than Mrs. Steerforth flings another of her accusations at me.

"Only twelve of those persons whom Boyd Henderson killed were innocent of Adriana's murder," she says. "You are not innocent. You were an accessory to that murder. You were the one who planned it. You and Kurt Drexler. Then Stefan, Gregor, Bram, and Werner did the killing. But it was your plan that initiated everything. What you did was unforgivable. You are rotten. You shouldn't be allowed to exist even as a Spirit. You should be expelled from all existence. You should be made to disappear forever."

I am not surprised that her words condemn me for all eternity. In the bitter privacy of my own soul-searching, I have already condemned myself. I've told you how it is with me. I'm no good. I am beyond salvation. Yet there stirs within my burnt-out soul the dying embers of pity, mercy, and charity toward others. I want to help the group. I'd like them to have their chance to go back to Earth and relive those last days before the shooting. If we go back, I shall foresee what is going to happen to my classmates and my teachers. But the Five Spirits will not allow me to warn them. Nor would my classmates or my teachers believe me. I am, after all, well named. I am Cassandra, the girl nobody believes, even though I can see into the future.

Rather than meet Mrs. Steerforth's denunciation of me with an anger equal to her own, I suppress my hatred of her. Politic and cautious, I defend myself within the safe perimeters of temperate speech and judicious self-assessment.

"I tried to prevent Adriana's murder," I say. "I've explained all the steps I took to stop Gregor and the others from killing her. If anyone should bear the blame for the murder besides those four thugs, it's Kurt Drexler. He didn't do anything to prevent them from going ahead with the plan that he and I devised. As for me, I admit my wrongdoing. Kurt Drexel and I initiated the plan for the murder. It was our plan that pushed those boys into killing Adriana."

Mrs. Steerforth continues to rebuke me.

"At last you admit the truth, when it's too late to make amends for your crimes and your errors. You've contaminated your group. You've imperiled their chance of returning to Earth."

Miss Dickinson comes into it now, with a gentle cautionary remark that she directs toward Mrs. Steerforth.

"It's too early to make that kind of judgment, Amelia," she says. "The committee will have to decide together whether this group will be going back to Earth."

"Cassandra is an ugly blemish upon this group's identity. She has told one lie after another. She has never told anyone the truth. She has devised plot after plot that has betrayed her loyal friends and brought harm to the innocent. It is better that she prepare for a bleak reckoning."

I stay temperate. I keep in mind my classmates and my teachers. Nevertheless, I allow my words to hurry forth, challenging Mrs. Steerforth to reconsider her judgment of me.

"I've always told the truth, but only to myself. Deviousness, not fear, has often persuaded me to hide the truth from everyone else. You say that you want the truth. That request is neither unusual, nor formidable. But what do you do when someone tells you the truth? Are you and your Spirit colleagues like most human beings? Many people who ask for the truth want to hear it for the wrong reasons. When they have the truth, they use it as a weapon against the persons who believed that their honesty would save them or, at the least, diminish the punishment awaiting them."

My well-reasoned words do not allay Mrs. Steerforth's anger. On the contrary, my words draw new fire from her.

"Whether or not you tell the truth about your plots and your deceptions, Time has recorded them. You can never alter or erase them unless the committee grants you that privilege. But you have not earned that right."

I become myself again. No longer do I repress the raw nature of my feelings or yoke my remarks to matter-of-fact statements that I regard as temperate. Insolent no less in ruin than in strength, I challenge Mrs. Steerforth to reconsider her harsh judgment.

"I may not have earned the right to go back to Earth," I tell her. "But the others have. The committee should not hold my wrongdoing against my classmates or against Miss Patel and Mr. Marchand. They've done nothing so grievously wrong that it should prevent them from going back to Earth."

Captain Johnson frowns at my insolence. But he also notices my concern for my peers and my teachers.

"You mean well, Miss Winslow," he tells me. "I'll give you that. You want to help your group. You express a loyalty to them that is commendable. But you are in no position to advise the committee about its decisions."

Mr. Steerforth, who has been listening to all of our words and observing and interpreting our gestures and our expressions, returns to this courtroom exchange. His self-control remains exemplary. His emotional detachment makes him appear as parched as ever and a bit stodgy.

"It's too early to make decisions or to file pleas or to enter judgments," he says. "We've heard in brief or extended testimonies from every member of the Green Hills group. We have gathered a great deal of information. But we need to know more. There is one person whom we have not questioned. He may be the most essential person of all in our quest to discover the motives behind the tragedy that took so many lives."

Mr. Steerforth's announcement takes firm hold of our attention. I imagine that all my peers and my teachers have guessed who this essential person is. But Abigail Emerson has not guessed. Mr. Steerforth's words leave her puzzled and even somewhat apprehensive.

"Who is this person?" she asks.

At the moment, Abigail Emerson, our school's swimming champion, seems confused and disoriented, as though she has just awakened from a deep sleep and yet finds herself still caught in a dream.

Mr. Steerforth pauses before he answers her. He takes a moment to study her face and mine and the faces of my other classmates and my two teachers.

We, in turn, stay tense and alert as he chooses the words that identify this most essential person. I know who he is, even before Mr. Steerforth announces his name.

"He is the classmate who killed all of you," Mr. Steerforth tells us. "He is Boyd Henderson. Look straight ahead as the doors slide open. You will see him. Accompanied by two sentries, he is now entering this courtroom. He is walking briskly toward us. Perhaps, he is ready to tell his part of the story."

CHAPTER TEN

BOYD HENDERSON

No sooner does Boyd approach the round table where all of us are gathered than a skirmish breaks out.

Mrs. Adams lets out a shriek and points an accusatory finger at Boyd.

"Fiend!" she screams. "Fiend! Beast!"

She starts to rise from her chair, her gray hair suddenly turned electric and aflame. It flows and ripples about her, as if it were wind-blown, though no soft breeze or quickened wind has entered anywhere else in the room except the place from which her ample body rises to its full height. Her face, eyes, and body glow with fire. Her grimace gives her the look of a mad witch, and her fingernails that have sprouted talons intensify her threatening manner.

"Murderer!" she shouts. "Cold-blooded murderer!"

She starts to spring from her chair. She means to attack Boyd, who is flanked by sentries while he stands a few feet away from Captain Johnson, who is seated at the head of the long table. But Mrs. Steerforth and Miss Dickinson hurry from their places and, with a press of their hands upon her shoulders, send small electric shocks through Mrs. Adams' entire body and quickly subdue her.

Instantly, Mrs. Adams' face and body change back to the more subdued appearance of a trouble-haunted matron.

"There, there, Maggie," Mrs. Steerforth says with a soft, sympathetic voice that surprises me. "Don't take on so. He's not the person you think he is."

"But he looks just like him," Mrs. Adams whimpers. "He looks like the boy at the ski resort in Aspen, Colorado, who killed my Howard and our three children."

Miss Dickinson gently pats Mrs. Adams' shoulder. Her voice is filled with pity.

"He is not that boy," she says. "You remember what happened to that boy. One of the Spirit committees in the northern zone condemned him to eternal disappearance."

Mrs. Adams feels embarrassed.

"I'm a foolish woman, I know," she says. "I should have grown used to what happened so long ago. But this boy's face brought it all back."

Mrs. Steerforth comforts her further.

"That is only natural," she tells her. "We never lose our important memories. Sometimes, they flare their signals when we least expect them."

Miss Dickinson offers Mrs. Adams a few more encouraging words.

"You needn't get upset. Your Howard and your three children are Spirits now. They are on their own assigned missions to help the living and the newly dead. But you will be seeing them soon enough. You'll feel better again."

During this commotion, Boyd has remained standing near the Captain, who is seated in his judge's chair. Neither Boyd nor the Captain seems to be perturbed. Both men, in fact, look battle-hardened and impassive. Though he has never served in the armed forces, Boyd could easily pass for a gunnery sergeant from the Marine Corps who has been trained to kill enemies with machine guns, rockets, and anti-tank missiles. Dressed in combat camouflage, he looks war-weary and bitter. But Boyd is not a Marine, and the war he has waged was of his own making. For the most part, he killed friends, not enemies.

I know Boyd well. I imagine what he is feeling. Beneath his stoic exterior, he is wretched and lost. He stands condemned by himself first of all. If the Virginia state trooper had not gunned him down, he would eventually have killed himself. His guilt is like a combat stiletto ripping his insides apart. The horror of his crimes lives, lacerating and implacable, within his always-present memory. Yet, despite his private torment, his rugged features remain impassive. He will not ask us for our pity. He will not ask us for our forgiveness. What he has done is done forever. His foul crimes have branded him eternally as a coldblooded killer, a ruthless avenger, and a crazed assassin.

In these quickened minutes since his appearance here in this expansive room that serves as a courtroom, a conference hall, and a public chamber for an inquest, Boyd has not spoken even one word. The skirmish involving Mrs. Adams, Mrs. Steerforth, and Miss Dickinson has prevented him from speaking, even if he wanted to do so. But, with his militant and penetrating gaze, he has observed everyone in the room. He has accorded the Five Spirits only scanning glances. Instead, he has fixed his gaze upon the thirteen of us—his classmates and his teachers—whom he killed a week ago.

All of us are watching him with furtive and tightly harnessed antipathy.

There is a moment when I detect his nearly imperceptible frown and the slightest tremor at the corner of his mouth. In this instant, he looks as if he might break apart. He might not be able to keep at bay the surging power of his anguish and the churning guilt that wants to rise out of him in a torrent of self-accusing words and horrified yelling. Quickly, this moment passes. His lips tighten and conceal the tremor, and the clenching of his fists overrides his need to yell out his pain.

Now the Captain is about to address him, killer to killer. But the Captain has killed to protect his country and the territories of his allies from enemies that wanted to despoil and overrun them with tyranny and oppression. He has killed because of his sense of duty and because of his abiding honor, as hard-grained and as pitiless as that kind of honor is capable of becoming. In contrast to him, Boyd has killed without honor, without sufficient cause, and without any justification. He wreaked havoc upon the innocent and upon his murderous self. In the moment that he killed my group and me, he lost his soul. He died before the state trooper killed him, though that was not the first time he died. I am the one who killed him first of all. I am the one who killed him before he lost his soul and before the state trooper shot him down. I lied about the car crash. I spread false rumors about him. I branded him a drug addict and a potential school shooter. I prodded Kurt and his gang to kill the girl that Boyd truly loved.

Boyd is still dying and will die for all eternity unless the committee determines that he should disappear forever.

Right now, while he is waiting for Captain Johnson to address him, these thoughts are afflicting him with brutal and unremitting emphases. I notice that he is observing me with cold reserve. He shows no inclination to rush upon me and, with a karate blow to my neck or my chest, to kill me once again. There will be time enough for new methods of violence in ghostlier demarcations that, paradoxically, are timeless. In this very moment, Boyd stands tall and soldierly. He waits for the Captain to issue a directive, a request, or an order.

Captain Johnson proceeds with his usual cold-hearted authority.

"We know who you are," he says. "But the rules require you to provide information about yourself, and to tell us why you have come here."

Boyd quickly answers him. He is as articulate as ever. His words express a keen mind and a trenchant realism. How swiftly the memory of our happier times together comes back to me. In those days, his cutting-edge intelligence enhanced rather than subverted his shrewdly calibrated rebelliousness. My group and I, and the Five Spirits, too, give him our complete attention.

"I am Boyd Henderson. I am eighteen years old. I have come here to explain myself to you, even though I no longer know exactly who I am. I'll tell you the bare facts, and you can draw your own conclusions.

"I was born in Green Hills, Maine, but I lived there only from the time I turned fourteen. That was the year my parents divorced. Until then, I traveled the globe with my parents. My father, Rodney Henderson, is a television news reporter and a respected filmmaker. Some people in the business call him the most famous of all the news anchors and documentary film directors. He has written twenty-one best-selling books and filmed prize-winning documentaries about the various global crises. He has covered the ongoing wars in Iraq, Afghanistan, and Syria, and the aftermath of natural disasters, including a hurricane in the Dominican Republic, an earthquake in Mexico, and a mudslide in Colombia. His father was a stockbroker who made millions of dollars on Wall Street. When he died, my father became an even wealthier man. He married into British royalty after he divorced my mother, and, except for a generous financial settlement to my mother and an impressive trust fund and frequent gifts for me, he turned his back on us.

"My mother didn't mind. She quickly remarried, this time to Ricardo Fernández, a Grand Prix auto-racing champion from Chile whose high-speed career included competitions in Argentina, Australia, Belgium, Chile, Russia, Spain, Sweden, Italy, and the United States. My mother put her career as a fashion designer on hold, because she wanted to make the marriage work. At first, she enjoyed being Sandra Henderson Fernández. But her second husband's philandering, his gambling, and his association with mafia dons wrecked the marriage. After the divorce, she resumed her career in New York and was often away from my life.

"I lived with my grandmother, a widow whose name is Catherine Phillips. I had lived with her all through the years of my mother's second marriage. I was still living with her at the time of my death. She was a congenial, though inattentive, guardian. She often traveled outside the country and left me to my own resources. In many respects, she was the template for the woman my mother became. Even at sixty, she looked glamorous and marriageable. Cosmetic surgeons had carefully contrived her glamour. She often socialized with single and married men younger than she was by twenty or so years. They became temporary lovers. They were the badges that she wore as proof of her still persuasive sensuality. But she had no interest in marrying any of her lovers. After the constraints that her marriage to my grandfather had imposed upon her, she decided that she wanted to live life her way, unencumbered by a husband.

"When she was traveling, she left me in the care of the housekeeper and her husband, who was the general manager of my grandmother's palatial home that overlooked Atlantic waters. Their names were Martin and Deborah Courtney. They were a middle-aged couple whose three children had grown up and gone forward to successful careers in other New England states. When she appointed them as my unofficial guardians, my grandmother advised them to invoke sensible rules that would not inhibit my self-reliance or suppress my independent spirit.

"To me, she offered a similar worldly philosophy.

"'You are smart enough to cultivate your independence in a reliable way,' she told me. 'You don't need a babysitter. You will probably make a few mistakes as you move forward to your manhood. Learn from them. Let those life-bruises toughen you.'

"I respected my grandmother. She and I understood each other. In many ways, we were alike. We were self-centered and adventurous. We resented anyone and any creed that wanted to diminish our one-of-a-kind individuality and our personal freedom. At any rate, I took her advice. I cultivated my independence, though not always in positive and life-enhancing ways. Many times, I did do the right things. I earned honor grades. I learned to be a good team player, collaborating with my soccer, swimming, baseball, and boxing mates. But I also drank too much—bourbon, scotch, and whiskey. I learned to crave all of them. I also experimented with marijuana and cocaine. And I drove my Maserati and later my Alfa Romeo and my Ferrari along lonely roads at a hundred-twenty miles an hour. I never crashed a car, though since arriving here in Sojourn I have been told that I was wrongly accused and wrongly convicted of doing so. But the car crash and the reformatory came later, after some mistakes I made ricocheted and brought me low.

"Before that happened, I lived life to the hilt. In summers, I partied on the French Riviera. In winters, I skied on the Swiss Alps. In spring, I kayaked in Finland, and in autumn I hunted red tail stags in Patagonia. In those seasons, I enjoyed being with my father and with my loyal teammates. I felt like a wild god. I believed that no one and nothing could ever harm me. I reveled in my amazing luck. And always, whether I was in Green Hills or Paris or St. Moritz, I slept with many girls and enjoyed all of them. But I never loved any of them until I met one girl whose name is so sacred to me that I am reluctant to speak it. I am not worthy to speak it. But speak it I must. I am an assassin now, and I am branded forever. I cannot change that. What I have done is irrevocable. It cannot be undone. What I can tell you, though, is that this girl, Adriana Montalban, once saved my life. But I could not save hers."

Boyd pauses now. The memory of the girl that he loved so much and that he could not save takes hold of his tough-minded view of himself. The rawness of his grief halts the impetus of his words. That grief scalds his still-vibrant senses. He falls into silence despite his need to make his confession.

Miss Dickinson helps him. Her manner is temperate and gentle. But her words are matter-of-fact and incisive.

"Please go on," she urges him. "It is important that you declare who you are and why you have committed such horrible crimes. The committee can see into your soul. But we cannot discern what you keep lodged in its secret corners. You must tell us everything. You must explain yourself, as well, to your classmates and your teachers."

Miss Dickinson's words push Boyd forward. Now his words come even more rapidly, and his steadfast gaze once again takes in every one of us.

"Adriana, the girl that I loved, first came into my life as a friend at the end of my junior year and, later, when we began dating during my senior year in Green Hills High School. Before that time, on the night of the junior prom, I lost control of my life. The police blamed me for crashing my Ferrari into a Lincoln town car and causing serious injuries to the driver and three other occupants, and to Sonia Janowski and myself. I served time in rehab and in a reform school. I made the experience of reform school even more difficult than it might have been. I gave the guards a hard time, and they retaliated by beating me. While I was in rehab, I got into fights with other druggies. One time, I knocked two of them out. The officials wanted to send me back to reform school. But my father's lawyers stepped in with plenty of money for the rehab's board of directors. When I was released from rehab, I was determined to make a new start. I knew that, in the really important ways, I had become my worst enemy. I wanted to save myself, but I wasn't certain that I could do it alone.

"My father wanted to enroll me into an exclusive private school in upstate New York. But my earlier experiences with private schools were unhappy. I hated the lock-step formality, the rigid codes, and the class snobbery. So I returned to Green Hills High. I bonded with a few old friends, such as Shiloh, Dion, and Jayden. I made some new friends, including two very supportive teachers—Miss Patel and Mr. Marchand. I was aware of the fake news that adversaries were spreading about me in and outside school. But, for the most part, I closed all of that out of my attention. Instead, I concentrated on winning soccer and baseball games, swim meets, and boxing matches. I worked hard to maintain an A average in all my classes. I was making a comeback. I had turned things around for myself. For the first time in years, I believed that I was going to lead a happy and successful life.

"Adriana Montalban inspired me to do all the right things. She taught me to believe in myself and in my innate goodness. It was through her influence that I learned to turn away from spiteful naysayers and pernicious adversaries. Adriana was my lifeline. She was the girl whose very existence completed my own.

"'You have so much to give to the world,' Adriana told me one afternoon when we were making plans for our future. 'I'll always be there with you. Together, we can do our part to make the world better.'

"I believed her. I believed that she and I were going to make the world better.

"Then the world that we were counting on crashed down upon us. There was no other world for me, except the world of death that Adriana had entered.

"When Stefan, Bram, Werner, and Gregor killed her, I could no longer think straight. There was only one reason for me to go on living. I had to destroy her killers. But I didn't get the chance. Bram, Stefan, Gregor, and Werner ran off to different hiding places. Even now I would like to gun them down. I would like to kill them again and again through all eternity."

Miss Dickinson comes into it once more, this time with a pair of compelling questions.

"But why did you kill the classmates who are seated here in this room? Why did you kill Mr. Marchand and Miss Patel? They did not kill Adriana."

"No, they did not. But some of them, like Cassandra Winslow and Ari Bachman, were my secret adversaries. I believed that all the others were conspiring against me with school officials, grief counselors, and the state police. I had convinced myself that they were trying to stop me from killing Adriana's murderers. They were even casting doubt upon my innocence. They were saying that I might have killed Adriana."

Jayden jumps out of his chair, vehemently protesting Boyd's remarks.

"We never said that!" he shouts. "We always tried to help you!"

Dion rises out of his chair just as swiftly. He, too, is raging.

"You killed us!" he yells. "You killed us even though we are innocent!"

Shiloh joins the two protesters. His fury is even more rancorous.

"Killer!" he screams. "Cold-blooded killer! You stole my life from me. It will never come again. Never! Never!"

Jayden, Dion, and Shiloh rush upon Boyd, who stands near the Captain and makes no attempt to defend himself. I imagine that he wants to be punished. He stands tall and stalwart as if he were a statue made out of granite. Jayden, Dion, and Shiloh take turns pummeling him. Each of them jabs him first of all, setting up a rapid series of punches. They batter him with bruising right crosses. They come at him from the side, using their hips and legs for power. Their hooks travel out from their shoulders and turn in toward their target halfway through their punches. They use different combinations: jab-jab-cross, jab-hook-cross, cross-hook-cross, and jab-cross-jab-cross-hook-hook.

Blood sprays out of Boyd's eyes, nose, ears, and mouth. His muscular body wavers and totters and nearly keels over from the force of the vigorous punches. But he does not fall. Nor does he ever raise his fists to defend himself. He wants to die again. He is hoping that these three youths will land blows so lethal that he will die for all eternity.

Blood keeps spilling from his face and his forehead. It seeps through his camouflage war suit. It stains his jaws and his hands. His three adversaries keep assaulting him with their barrage of punches. They never tire. They never let their guard down. Like vicious automatons or hostile robots, they go on fighting.

Abruptly, Captain Johnson waves his hand with a gesture that is as brusque as it is commanding. He has a military appreciation of the boxing skills of these three angry young men. The unceasing power of their punches and their tenacious need to destroy their enemy appeal to the Captain's killer streak and to his well-honed sadism. But he wants to get on with this interrogation. He wants to achieve some closure in this tragedy that has taken so many lives.

"No more," he tells Dion, Shiloh, and Jayden. "You've made your point. You hate your killer. If I gave you the chance, you would tear him apart limb from limb. But I'm not giving you that chance. We have another end planned for Boyd Henderson."

No sooner does he wave his hand in his autocratic manner than Jayden, Dion, and Shiloh withdraw to their assigned places.

Surly and melancholic, they enclose themselves inside the privacies of their unrelenting anguish.

More startling to my eyes is what happens next. With another wave of his hand, the Captain transforms Boyd's appearance. Instantly, the wounds to his eyes, ears, face, and mouth disappear. His combat camouflage suit carries no bloodstains. His body bears no pain from the brutal attack it has just endured. But as supernatural as the Captain's powers seem, he cannot alter the guilt that scalds Boyd's soul or the memories that haunt and scourge Boyd's mind.

Nor does he attempt to silence Chloe Bradbury's tearful outburst or Sonia Janowski's heartrending complaint.

"You've never said that you are sorry," Chloe cries out through her bitter tears. "You've killed us, but you've never even apologized."

"We were your friends," Sonia reminds Boyd, without tears and with the leadership mystique that always defines her blonde and extraordinary presence. "We wanted to help you. Look at what you've done to us. We'll never be on Earth again. We'll never see our loved ones there. We no longer possess the future toward which we were working. You've killed us, and you haven't asked us to forgive you."

Boyd quietly observes the two girls. There are no tears in his eyes, either. He does not try to escape from the melancholy that oppresses him. I told you that I know him well. He will not throw himself upon the mercy of our group or upon the clemency of the committee. He is not looking for mercy or compassion. I expect him to explain himself to Chloe and Sonia and to all of us as well.

He does.

"I *am* sorry that I killed all of you," he says. "But what's the good of that? My being sorry isn't enough. My sorrow cannot bring you back to your life on Earth. It's too late to be sorry. It's too easy. Remorse is overrated, at least in my case, when it can't undo my horrible crimes."

He pauses. He looks around the room and waits for all of us to challenge his remarks with new angry words and with threatening gestures. But we have nothing to say. We stay subdued and watchful as he continues to explain himself.

"I have told you that I am sorry for what I have done. I meant what I said. I hope that you believe me. But I cannot ask for your forgiveness. My crimes are so horrible that they are beyond forgiveness. I deserve to be punished. I deserve to be condemned. I deserve to disappear eternally."

Miss Dickinson hastens to warn him about the gravity of his assertions.

"Do you realize what you are saying? You are passing sentence upon yourself. You are telling us that you don't want to go on living, here in Sojourn or in The First Heaven or back on the Earth that has been your home. You are condemning yourself to eternal death."

"I deserve no less a punishment," Boyd answers her. "The truth is that I would regard eternal death as a gift. I would no longer *feel*. I would be finished with anguish, guilt, and despair. Being kept alive as a Spirit is a punishment that would be too hard to bear. I am no longer human. I lost my humanity when I killed my classmates and my teachers. I am a foul beast that acts without reason or compassion. Because I have killed like a savage, I have lost Adriana forever. Even as a Spirit, I would not be allowed to be with her. She is everything that I am not. She is innocence. She is compassion. She is goodness. Once not so long ago, when we first met, she was teaching me how to be all those things. But she is dead now. She is with the good Spirits. Never again will she stand by my side."

Mrs. Steerforth has something more to say.

"You *are* loathsome, Henderson, but you do have a realistic sense of yourself. You are right not to ask for forgiveness. I for one will never grant that to you. I detest the bleeding hearts among us whose sentimentality will push stern justice aside and grant you a pardon. Some crimes can never be forgiven. Your school shooting is at the top of the list."

Boyd listens to her repudiation of him and says nothing. His face is once again impassive. His inscrutable eyes pierce her surfaces. Her words draw neither his anger, nor his resentment. His standing at attention enhances his militant appearance.

Captain Johnson comes into it again.

"You are one of a kind, Henderson—at least in my experience," he says. "You really want to die forever. Your saying so is not mere swagger. I can tell. I can see into your soul. You have guts. You would have been a good killing machine for the Army or the Marines. Anyway, you are not the one to decide whether you will die forever or live here as a Spirit or try your luck once again on Earth. The committee and the teachers that you killed will decide that soon enough in a trial that is similar to, though different from, the traditional jury trial in the United States. We shall be casting our votes and striving to reach the right verdicts about the lives of each of the persons who were killed at Green Hills High School, whether they were victims or murderers. Six of us will become jurors. But, as the Captain of the committee, I shall make the final judgments."

This news neither surprises, nor alarms Boyd. His face remains inscrutable. But the Five Spirits know what he is thinking. So do I. His grief is genuine. His death wish is as adamant as it is irrevocable.

But good-natured Miss Dickinson does surprise him. Her words stir into tentative life the hope that had died in him.

"Don't rob yourself of the chance to go back to Earth," she tells him. "You may be able to undo the horrible murders that you have committed."

For an instant, his eyes gleam, and amazement touches his face.

"I'll do anything the committee asks of me, if I can undo the murders."

"You have already done what we've asked of you," Miss Dickinson explains. "You have told us the truth."

"There is something else you need to know," Boyd tells her.

"What is that?"

"The best reason for my going back is to save the people that I killed. But I do not care to stay on Earth. If I can die, clean and guiltless, I'll be an acceptable Spirit. Maybe then I'll be reunited with Adriana. She is the only reason that I would want to go on living as a Spirit, here in Sojourn or in The First Heaven. Without her, I prefer to die eternally."

Miss Dickinson has more to tell Boyd.

"You may not have to die eternally," she says. "Nor will you have to wait much longer before you see Adriana."

"I don't understand."

"You will be seeing Adriana in a few minutes. She'll be helping all of us to reach our verdicts."

Captain Johnson says more.

"You will see Adriana," he says, "but she will not see you—at least not at first. She knows about your crimes, and she has been grieving. Unless she asks to see you, you will remain invisible."

No sooner has he said so, than he waves his right hand with the virile authority that reflects his temperament.

Boyd disappears to our seeing.

On this occasion, Boyd does not vanish by degrees. That will happen only for those recently dead persons whom the committee deems acceptable because they have not committed horrible crimes. There are those individuals in my group who are basically virtuous. Imperfect though they may be, they have generally followed all the important rules of good behavior. Even Ari, with the sting of remorse always plaguing him, may pass muster with the committee.

But the committee will not find me acceptable. Though I have not killed anyone with rifle, dagger, or poison, I am nonetheless evil. I prodded Kurt and his gang of thugs to kill Adriana. I also initiated the plan for the school shooting. I am evil. Once more, I confess it to you. When the Captain makes his final decision about whether my group will go back to Earth and relive those days before the school shooting, I may be the obstacle that keeps my classmates here in Sojourn. Because the Five Spirits diminished my foresight when I arrived in Sojourn, I do not know what will finally happen to us. If my classmates are allowed to move on to the First Heaven, they will vanish by degrees from the bodies they have always called their own. They will become Spirits with some of the personality traits and character flaws that always identified them as human beings who were both unique and unpredictable. Sometimes, for special missions that bring them back to Earth, they will retrieve their flesh-and-blood bodies. Once in a while, they will be sent to Earth as Shape-Shifters. They will appropriate someone else's body as a wily undercover agent to trap a killer, perhaps, or as a benevolent presence to solace a grieving family.

My intuition tells me that every one of these Spirits will be among the Chosen. The committee will judge them as acceptable. But I do not imagine that I shall be among them.

Nor can I imagine that the committee will find Boyd acceptable. He has killed in cold blood and without justification. He has killed thirteen vulnerable people. He is right to condemn himself. Unless the committee gives him the chance to redeem himself by sending him back to Earth, he will disappear forever.

Right now, in the very instant that the Captain waves his hand, he disappears only for the time being.

He is still in the room. But he will be a silent observer until Captain Johnson waves his hand once more and commands him to stand at attention, visible and militant. I know. I can see that part of the future.

In the meantime, we wait for Adriana to appear.

We wait as well, though with far more tension, for our two teachers and four of the Five Spirits to reach a verdict about whether we have earned the right to go back to Earth, as full-bodied and energetic as we had been a week before the school shooting.

In the back of our minds, as far back as we can push it without forgetting that it is there, is the other apprehension that we feel. After the committee reaches a verdict, Captain Johnson will deliver his final judgment.

CHAPTER ELEVEN

CONFESSIONS, DOUBTS, AND PROMISES

Ten minutes later, when Adriana enters this courtroom setting, she looks more beautiful than ever. Her face and body are unblemished. Her head is not smashed. Blood is not spilling out of her forehead, ears, nose, and mouth. Her brown eyes are not torn out of their sockets. Her arms, pelvis, legs, and teeth are not broken. Here, in Sojourn, a little more than two months after her rapists attacked her in an earthbound forest, she has recovered her loveliness. She beams with vitality. Light radiates from her very essence.

My classmates and my teachers are instantly awed by her appearance. She looks not merely human. She looks supernatural. She evokes the images of saints and martyrs that you sometimes see on religious calendars. Yet she is so accessible. She approaches us with the ethereal self-possession that was her trademark when she was alive on Earth.

"It is so good to see all of you," she says as she peers upon our group, seated as we are at this long mahogany table. "Yet it is also very sad. I was not expecting any of you for a long time. I believed that you were going to enjoy happy lives."

Our group calls out various greetings to her, in clear-throated friendliness.

"We've missed you, Adriana."

"You look wonderful."

"You're the best, Adriana. You always have been."

"We've missed you so much."

She smiles her gleaming smile. Our words please her. "I've missed you, too," she tells us. "I've missed all of you."

Chloe, Abigail, Sonia, and Brenda start to cry. Adriana's melancholic words about expecting us to lead happy lives have stirred anew our awareness of all the years that our deaths scooped away from us. Those of us who do not cry remain very still. With the taut strategies that we acquired from our vulnerable childhoods and our more cynical adolescence, we hold our senses in.

Miss Dickinson leaves her place and hurries over to Adriana. She embraces her in a sisterly manner. In terms of their youth, they could be sisters. Only four years separate their ages, though Miss Dickinson's life on earth began many decades before Adriana's and spanned more than ninety years. You probably remember what I told you several days ago. Here, in her Afterlife, Miss Dickinson chose to be twenty-two again. That was her age when her fiancé, Captain Johnson, was killed during the Second World War.

"I'm glad that you are here, Adriana," Miss Dickinson says. "When the committee summoned you, we made a request, not a command. After all the terror and grief that you have endured at the hands of your killers, we did not want to cause you any new pain. We wondered whether it was too early for you to see the classmates who had always been your friends on Earth. We thought that a reunion like this one might intensify your awareness of all that you have lost."

"It's all right," Adriana says, while she directs her words not only to Miss Dickinson, but also to everyone else in the room. "*I'm* all right. Besides, I'm not the one who needs encouragement right now. I've made peace with death. I've come here to help my friends. I want them to understand that, even in death, we can make a difference. It is just as Mr. Steerforth and other members on the committee have explained. After the proper training, we may be allowed to return to earth as brave and friendly Spirits.

"Sometimes we shall be visible. Sometimes we shall assume human bodies not unlike the ones we possessed while we were alive on Earth. Whether we are seen or whether we are ghostly presences, we can rescue good people from being murdered. We can dissuade troubled individuals from deceiving or betraying others. We can persuade them not to kill themselves and not to kill others. We can inspire them to believe in themselves and to believe in other good people, no matter the color of their skin, their religious persuasion, their gender and sexual preferences, or their economic class."

Adriana pauses. She does not want to appear overbearing. Yet she would like to inspire our courage. She would like to defuse whatever prejudices we have carried from Earth with us. Only in that way can we shed our bodies of death and become rescuing Spirits. I know what she is thinking. With steady eyes, I look into her mind and into her soul. In this moment, she hopes to do all of these things. She hopes to do even more than these things.

I wait for her to tell us her other reason for appearing to us, in this hall of justice that resembles a courtroom and is known by other names, including a council chamber and a tribunal.

I do not have to wait long.

"I've come here not only to help you," she says. "I've come so that you can help me."

Her gaze continues to cast its influence upon us for the moments that it takes her to speak these words. Before anyone in my group can ask how we can be of help to her, she turns her gaze first upon the Steerforths and Mrs. Adams, who sit in their places watching her; then upon Captain Johnson, who is facing her; and right after that upon Miss Dickinson, who is standing next to her.

"I'm asking all of the Spirits to help me, too."

"What would you like us to do?" Miss Dickinson inquires.

"First, I would like my classmates to tell me everything that happened to Boyd Henderson after I died. What caused him to commit such horrible crimes? Surely, it was not my death alone. People die every day, and they leave their loved ones behind them to grieve publicly and, after the funeral, to deal with their grief privately. That is what happens almost all of the time. The ones who are left behind do not become killers.

"Something more than his grieving for me pushed Boyd down into madness. What was it? What or who broke him apart?"

I am on the brink of confessing my guilt to her. Yet the enormity of my wrongdoing holds me back. I have not lied to myself or to you. I told you how it is with me. I planned Adriana's death. But, when I drew back from the horror of my plan, I could not prevent the murder. Now I cannot find the words to ask her forgiveness. Even my hardened nature cannot summon the petition that asks Adriana for her pity or declares my repentance.

I shroud myself in silence. The stillness wraps me in its folds. I am the newly dead who will not spring back to Earthly life or revive herself as a benevolent Spirit. My fate is sealed.

Nor do any of my classmates answer Adriana's questions. Their memories of Boyd's descent into madness are too harrowing to revisit. Their suppression of that time negates any inclination to speak.

It is Miss Patel who answers Adriana's questions.

"Boyd broke apart for many reasons," she says. "You know some of his story. You were alive when his downward spiral began. Two of his friends betrayed him. They blamed him for a car crash. He had to serve time in a reformatory and in a rehabilitation center. He lost his status in our community. People regarded him as a rebel and a criminal."

"Who were these friends?" Adriana asks while a frown with delicate traceries touches her brow. "He never told me."

"Boyd never knew who they were until after he was killed. They are here in this room with us. Maybe they will tell you who they are. Maybe they will explain themselves."

Once again I enclose myself within the ambiguities of silence. I am not ready to make another public confession.

Ari speaks up instead. His words come slowly and carry the burden of his guilt and the heft of his sorrow.

"I was the one who lied about the crash," he says. "I told the police that Boyd was driving the car. But I was the driver. I was the fake friend who didn't care whether the lie that I told would ruin Boyd's life."

Surprise and dismay bring another frown to Adriana's forehead.

"Why did you do such a bad thing?" she asks, her voice more excited now. "Boyd trusted you. He liked you. What made you turn against him?"

"Boyd didn't want friends. He wanted worshippers. He also wanted to stand alone in the limelight. I had wearied of being his follower. Besides, he did cause the crash. When he pressed his foot on the accelerator, the car spun out of control and crashed into an oncoming Lincoln Town Car. I wasn't about to take the blame for his carelessness."

"But you lied," Adriana says, her voice filled with more sorrow than anger. "You harmed Boyd far more than you imagined that you could."

"I did," Ari replies. His intonation quivers with regret. "I did harm him."

Adriana notices his regret and goes on observing him. She has not yet decided whether she will forgive or condemn him.

It is Brenda who fires out an accusation.

"You were envious of him!" she declares. "You wanted to bring him down. You wanted to see him break apart."

Ari fires back. This time he keeps his voice steady. Brooding and self-hating as he is, he stays in control.

"I wasn't the only one who wanted to get back at him," he says. "There were many others who were tired of his pushing us around. He was due for a comeuppance. The lies that I told about the car crash were only the beginning."

Adriana, with her sorrowful voice, needs to know more.

"Who were the others?" she asks. "Who else wanted to get back at him?"

"At least one of them is in this room," Ari answers her. "That person will have to speak for herself. Maybe she will also tell you the names of the other students who betrayed Boyd."

Is it because I am a lost soul that I refuse to confess my crimes to Adriana? Reluctant though I am, there is a fury within me that compelled me not more than an hour ago to confess my wrongdoing to the committee and to my classmates and teachers. But this moment at which I now arrive makes everything different. Is it because the sight of Adriana's innocent face stirs within me so anguished a shame? Whatever it is, my conscience stays tethered to silence. I dare not speak. I have already caused Adriana's death. I have also been the instrument of her boyfriend's madness and disgrace. My telling her even briefly about my complicity in Boyd's violent end will draw her into a second dying. Or so it will seem to her inconsolable awareness.

With her gentle nature still prevailing, Miss Dickinson prods me.

"It's time, Cassandra," she says. "It's time for you to make your public confession once again."

I surprise myself. I make no protest. I accept the inevitable. What must be will be.

I direct my words to Adriana. Everybody else in the room knows most of my story. She knows only part of it. I begin with brisk clarity. I avoid ambiguity and equivocation. I leave no room for doubt. I choose words for their matter-of-factness.

"Before you met Boyd Henderson," I tell Adriana, "I convinced myself that I loved him. I became obsessed with him. I told myself that he was the only guy that I could ever love. But what I felt for him wasn't love at all. It was merely the quickened passion that feeds upon its own desire and offers to its honest partner fraudulent pledges of love in return.

"Boyd discovered that I didn't love him, and he turned away from me. When that happened, I vowed that I would bring him down. On Facebook, Twitter, and Instagram, I posted photos of him dressed in Army combat camouflage and wielding an Ar-15 rifle. The message that accompanied those photos said that Boyd wanted to be a school shooter. The police and school officials became involved. They gave Boyd a hard time. They kept files on him. For a time, they even had private detectives trailing him.

"Possibly, you knew about the photos and the police. But you did not know that I initiated the scandal."

Adriana has something to say.

"It's hard for me to understand why you would do such a thing," she tells me. "I've never hated anyone, not even when they disappointed me."

"I've hated plenty of people," I answer her, "especially when they disappointed me."

"I feel sorry for you," she says.

"You haven't heard all the wrong things that I've done," I tell her, brazen yet truthful. "When you do, you may at last know how it feels to hate somebody."

Adriana stiffens. She is dreading the bleak words that I am about to utter. She guesses that those words involve Boyd and even herself.

"Say what you need to say, but say it quickly. I do not care to linger over the horrors that have happened."

I do not hesitate. I hurl the thunderbolt.

"I planned your murder," I tell her.

Adriana tightens her lips. She presses her hands together, as though this prayerful gesture might help her withstand the shock of what I am confessing to her. Even in death, she feels anguish. Even here in Sojourn she can cry out her pain or shed tears. But she does not cry out. Nor does she weep. Instead, she meets my gaze directly and, with her stoical capacities intact, waits for me to tell her more.

"I planned your murder with Kurt Drexler. Kurt thought that the plan was an experiment. We were testing our power. We'd find out whether we could devise the perfect murder and get away with it. But it was more than that with me. It was more than an experiment. For me, it was an act of revenge. I would be a primary instrument in killing the only girl that Boyd could ever love.

"It wasn't hard for Kurt to persuade four of his friends to kill you. Stefan, Bram, Gregor, and Werner already had conflicted feelings about you. Each of them had tried to date you, and with your gentle manner you had turned them down. Your being a Latina excited them. But it also made them uneasy. They wanted to sleep with you, but they would never marry you. 'White Supremacist studs never marry Latina girls,' they used to tell their teammates in high school locker rooms, in private gyms, and in underground beer halls. 'It's against the Constitution or should be.' Their raping you was my idea, though Kurt and those four savages did not object. It made the murder more complicated. Getting away with it would make us feel even more powerful."

Adriana hangs on. She stays in control. Her forbearance does not surprise me, nor does her strength of character. At school, she had always been a leader and a defender of justice. Always, in her personal relationships, she had been a loyal friend and an advocate of the needy and the mistreated. I hated her for her merit. Maybe I still do. At any rate, I hasten to tell the rest of my story to her.

"Shortly before the day on which Kurt's four thugs were supposed to commit the murder, though, I backed out of the plan. I warned Kurt not to go through with it. He promised that he would talk his four friends out of murdering you. But he didn't even try to talk them out of it. They carried my plan through. They murdered you.

"After that happened, Boyd went crazy. He spent time in a sanitarium. His stay there helped him only a little. But, when he returned to school, all of us made an effort to revive his hope and his will to live—his determination to go forward with his life. For a while, our friendship worked for him. Then he found out the names of the four classmates who had killed you. He discovered my complicity in the murder. He lost his trust in all the good people who had been helping him recover from his grief. In his mind, even those good people became mixed up with the enemies who had planned your murder and carried it out.

"He wasn't thinking straight. He was out of his mind with grief and despair. He went on a rampage. He came to school hunting down the four thugs who murdered you. But they weren't there. They'd heard a rumor that Boyd was looking for them, and he was carrying an Ar-15 rifle. They ran off to their relatives in Virginia, North Carolina, Texas, and Arizona.

"By the time that he entered our school with his rifle, Boyd believed that Ari, Brenda, Chloe, Jayden, and all the others in our group had planned your murder with Kurt and his gang and with me. In his mind, everyone in our group was equally guilty. So he killed us all.

"He was hunting down your murderers when a state trooper caught up with him in Virginia and killed him.

"So there you have it," I told her when I had said all that needed saying. "It's not a happy story. In fact, it's very tragic."

Adriana looks spent. She too is fighting despair, even though she has come to us with encouraging words and with reasons for making the best of our future, whether we are to make our lives as Spirits here in Sojourn and the First Heaven or to return to Earth as full-bodied human beings. She has not yet processed completely the terrible news about Boyd. On Earth, he was her ardent lover. He was an Honors student, an excellent athlete and team player, a life-loving adventurer, and a sensitive guy who wrote poetry in his spare time and who kept a vividly detailed journal about his extensive travels. He personified all of that goodness. Willful and rebellious in his earlier high school years, he was learning to be a reliable human being who was setting realistic goals for a life that would be worth living. He was planning, as well, to share his life with her. He was also thinking beyond himself. He was finding ways to help the downtrodden and the neglected.

Adriana is about to respond to my story. I know what she is going to say. I can see into her heart, just as these Five Spirits see. I know the suffering that is still afflicting her. I perceive just as clearly the hard road that lies ahead for her and for all of us.

"Your story *is* tragic," she says. "Yet it feels unfinished. I was taught that the innocent and the brave sometimes rise up and vanquish their enemies. I was also taught to believe in second chances. Everyone here deserves a second chance."

"What about me?" I ask her. "Why should I have a second chance?"

"To find out whether you have learned from your mistakes," she says. "To find out whether you are willing to help rather than harm people."

The Captain has something to say now. Until this moment, he and the other Spirits have shrouded themselves in silence. Cautious and meticulous, they have been observing the faces of everyone in our group and listening to every word that passes through our lips.

"What about Boyd Henderson?" he asks Adriana. "Do you think that he is worth saving?"

"I want to believe in him," she says, "despite the horrible crime that he has committed. If I could see him and if I could talk to him, I would know for certain whether he deserves a second chance. Besides, it's not just a matter of his deserving that chance. It's not merely a question of whether he should go back to Earth or be condemned to disappear forever. He has to go back to relive his last days on Earth. He needs to be tested. He needs to make different choices. Only in that way will some of us or all of us be saved."

I observe Miss Dickinson and Mr. Steerforth nod their approval. Even Mrs. Steerforth and Mrs. Adams offer this sign of approval, but only with stern reluctance and only after Mrs. Adams imparts words that make this muted show of approval conditional, dependent as it is on the verdicts that the committee will reach within the next hour. It is not only Boyd who must attain the final approval of these Spirits. Our entire group needs their approval.

For now, the matter of Boyd's reappearance is essential. The Captain reads the faces of these four Spirits and then, without any hesitation at all, waves his hand.

Instantly, Boyd reappears. The two sentries who have stood a few feet behind the Captain while they waited for Boyd to return now move beside him, flanking him once again.

Accompanied by Miss Dickinson, Adriana walks toward him. She is overjoyed as she arrives at the place where he stands and reaches out to touch his right hand.

"You are here," she cries out. "You are really here. You are not a mirage or a hallucination. I touch your hand, and I feel the warm blood flowing through it. In that way, you are like me. Our blood is still warm. We have not died completely. We have not yet turned into ghostly Spirits, though we have already begun to vanish. Oh, it's wonderful to stand here with you. It's wonderful to feel that you and I belong together."

Boyd's face comes truly alive as he listens to her excited words. At once, his ghostly pallor leaves him. His features grow ruddy, and a broad smile returns his lost handsomeness to his face. But only for a moment does his face spark with the pleasure of seeing her, the only girl he could ever love. The sorrow that has haunted him quickly returns. The memory of the killings that have befouled him will not leave him. That memory burns through his mind and his heart. It has not left him even in death. It will not leave him unless he is allowed to return to Earth for a new testing of his character or unless the Spirits determine that he should disappear forever.

In this moment, when he is being reunited with the girl that he loves, Boyd finds it difficult to speak about any of these things. Only when Adriana speaks of their belonging together does he find his own words that tell her how he feels. Before he speaks these words, though, she repeats the words that have solaced him, as though these words are an echo rising from her soul.

"You and I *do* belong together," she says, while expressing elation as profound as the joy she experienced a minute ago when she told him those words for the first time.

"Do you really believe that?" Boyd asks her. "Do you really believe that we belong together, even after I've made a mess of my life?"

"Even after," she tells him.

There is sadness in his joy. Regret folds its tentacles around his conscience.

"You are so good," he says. "You have never done anything wrong. You have never harmed anyone. But I have harmed other human beings. I've killed them without sufficient cause. I've forfeited all the qualities that made me human. I'm no better than a predatory savage."

"That isn't you," Adriana protests. "I refuse to believe that it is you. You made the wrong choices. The real savages—the students who killed me—goaded your fury. They pushed you into the killings."

She plants a kiss on his lips. He returns the kiss with a press of his lips upon her lips. I sense the melancholy that enfolds her mind and her soul. I perceive with equal clarity the guilt and bitterness and despair that will not let go of Boyd's awareness. There is new moral acuity in his understanding of who he was and who he has become. When he and Adriana break away from their kisses, he delivers the verdict about himself that only a half hour ago he reported to the Five Spirits and to the classmates and teachers that he killed.

"The blame belongs to me," he says. "I have a will of my own. I made my choice. It was the wrong one. I deserve all the punishments that are coming to me."

"Of course you were wrong," Adriana says. "You committed a horrible crime. You are right to consider it unforgivable. But the Five Spirits may give you the second chance that you feel you don't deserve. You have to go back to Earth if they will let you."

"I'll go back, if the committee allows it," Boyd promises her. "I'll do my best to change those last school days for the better. But where is the good in that for you? If I stay true to what is right and just, I'll bring no harm to our classmates and teachers. There is no way that I can help you. I'll be reliving only those few weeks after your death. You will already have died. I won't be able to save you."

Adriana hurries to correct his expectations. Nearly breathless with excitement yet perfectly in control, she explains the way things will be.

"I *will* be alive," she says. "You will be reliving the last year and, more importantly, those last days *before* my death and before the school shooting. It will be my mission to stop those four thugs from murdering me. You will have to work with JROTC cadets to stop Werner, Bram, Stefan, Gregor, and the rest of their gang from killing our classmates and our teachers."

Her words surprise Boyd.

"How do you know all these things?" he asks her. "How do you know what my mission will be?"

Adriana does not hesitate to answer him.

"Miss Dickinson explained all of it to me. The other Spirits filled in some additional details."

Mrs. Steerforth adds a remark that brings a caustic edge to her displeasure. Her remark surprises my classmates and my teachers.

"One other individual among us also knows some of the things that will happen to each of you if you get the chance to go back to Earth. But she does not know how the mission will end."

My classmates and my teachers murmur among themselves. They look at each other and at me. They whisper questions to one another. "Is it you?" "Are you the one who knows what will happen to us?" "Can you see into the future?"

Now Alessandro speaks up. He states his question with brisk efficiency, girded as it is to an understated urgency.

"Who among us knows about the enemies that we may have to fight if we go back to Earth? Who is this person who knows the future?"

Captain Johnson steps in.

"My colleagues on the committee and I know the future," he says. "But the person among you who has also been born with the gift of foresight should come forward now. You owe it to your classmates to identify yourself. They may feel more hopeful knowing that the First Spirit granted you that gift even before you were born, because you come from a line of brave defenders of the truth."

The Captain does not tell them that the First Spirit set limits on that power when my ancestors became arrogant and thought themselves equal to the most powerful Spirits. They still had foresight, but no one would believe their predictions. I share their punishment. I, too, am arrogant. Though I have foresight, almost nobody has ever believed my predictions.

But this time is different. This time my classmates and teachers would believe me if I could tell them what I know. Right now, they are waiting to know who among them can predict the future. I do not speak. I enclose myself within the silence that has overtaken the courtroom.

My classmates, as well as Miss Patel and Mr. Marchand, are caught up in the suspense of this moment.

I let them wait for a long minute. Then I speak out.

"I am the one who knows some of the things that will happen if we get the chance to go back to Earth. But I do not know how the mission will end if we go back. I could not tell you even if I wanted to. The Five Spirits have cast a spell on me. Always, when I was alive on Earth, I did tell my friends and my family about the good things coming their way. I warned them about the disappointments and the emotional and physical smashups that were in store for them. But only my brother Luke listened to me. The First Spirit has favored him. He did not want Luke to suffer death or injuries from a car wreck. Nobody else listened to me. Nor did they remember my predictions after each accident and success changed their lives. Now the Five Spirits have set limits on my foresight. Even though I want to tell you what I do know, I cannot. The Spirits will seal my lips whenever I speak of the mission and its probable outcome."

Shiloh serves up a pertinent question. He directs it to the Five Spirits.

"Why are you doing this to us? Why are you preventing us from knowing whether our mission will be successful if we get a chance to go back to Earth?"

The Captain answers him with clear-headed authority.

"Your mission will be a test for all of you. It will test your courage, your conscience, and your loyalty to one another. If you knew the outcome before you entered the mission, there wouldn't be much of a test for any one of you."

Chloe submits another pertinent question. Her words carry a trace of resentment.

"What kind of test will there be for Cassandra?" she asks. "She already knows what is going to happen to us if we go back to earth."

The Captain is quick to answer her.

"Cassandra does know what is going to happen to most of you. But she doesn't know what is going to happen to herself. She, too, is going to be tested."

The Captain's answer satisfies Chloe and everyone else in my group. There will be no favorites on the battleground that we will be entering if we go back to our homes on Earth.

Adriana shifts our attention from this concern about the way our return to Earth might end. There is an issue that is even more pressing.

"We mustn't worry about the way things might end for our mission," she says. "The important thing right now is to win the privilege of going back to earth. Our going back is essential if we want to reclaim our lives."

Miss Dickinson agrees.

"You are wise to say so, Adriana," she says. "Getting permission to go back should be the top priority of your group."

Miss Dickinson's remark and the exchange of words involving the Captain, Mrs. Steerforth, Alessandro, Chloe, and Sonia rouse the self-hatred and remorse that Boyd has tried to suppress during these last minutes. I know what he is thinking. I understand the cause of his apprehension. He is pondering his future with Adriana. It is to her that he directs his next words.

"Even if I get the chance to go back," he says, "I may not find the way to a happy reunion with you. Maybe I can save our classmates and our teachers. Maybe you can save yourself. But I don't expect to come out of this alive. I don't deserve to go on living, not in Sojourn or on Earth. I'm not worthy to be with you, not after the terrible murders that I've committed."

Miss Dickinson has something to say.

"If the committee allows you to return to Earth, accept that as a priceless gift. It will give you the chance to make amends for your wrongdoing. If you do everything well, you will redeem yourself to yourself. You will be able to live with yourself once again, without the doubts or recriminations and without the self-hating."

Adriana comes back into it.

"You and I belong together," she tells Boyd, "whether we live on Earth as human beings or in the First Heaven as acceptable Spirits."

Boyd tries to be optimistic. He wants to believe what Adriana is telling him.

"I'll work hard to become worthy of you," he promises. "Let's see what happens."

CHAPTER TWELVE

VERDICTS

The trial continues.

I'll take a moment to review the procedure that the Spirits have been imposing upon this legal scene. So much has been happening in this room. You may want to refresh your understanding of the assignments that each of us must carry out while we are in this environment.

We keep our seats in this courtroom that carries the precise formality of a judicial chamber most of the time and that imparts at other times the volatile atmosphere of a police station interrogation and the hardened cynicism of a prosecutor's conference room. Captain Johnson still serves as the presiding judge. He sits, alert and formidable, at the head of the long table. The other four Spirits are the jurors who, having listened to our testimonies, will now reach the verdicts that exonerate or condemn each of us. They will base their verdicts not only upon these testimonies. These four jurors will also base their verdicts upon information that they knew about our lives even before we died and that we had no time to reveal in these hearings. Their Spirit powers have granted them that knowing.

Miss Patel and Mr. Marchand will also serve as jurors. Because of their courage on battlefields in Iraq and Afghanistan and their integrity in all the other areas of their lives, Captain Johnson has asked them to join the team of jurors. This news surprises and pleases my classmates. They regard it as a favorable sign. They expect Miss Patel and Mr. Marchand to vote in their favor. But I harbor no such expectations. I know Miss Patel and Mr. Marchand better than they do. These teachers will never stray from the truth or betray an ethical code. Steadfast and honorable, they have pledged themselves to remain both objective and accurate in their assessment of each of the eleven students who became the victims of the school shooting.

Together with the four Spirits, Miss Patel and Mr. Marchand complete the *petit jury* that will assist Captain Johnson in deciding our fates. The French adjective *petit*, which means "small," indicates that this jury will include six members, rather than the twelve that make up a grand jury.

My classmates and I are the defendants.

The six jurors will not retire to a private room to discuss their findings. They will impart whatever conclusions they reach right here, in this meticulously appointed room where my classmates and I are sitting within the privacies of our own compunctions and tensions.

The six jurors and the judge will also decide Boyd Henderson's fate.

Captain Johnson moves swiftly to begin this final cycle of our trial. With his familiar militant bearing, he addresses himself to Miss Patel.

"The ball is in your court, Miss Kavya Patel," he says. "You are first up. We want you to tell us the verdict you've reached now that you've heard your students and my colleagues offer their insights and their questions about the persons involved in the shooting that took place in Green Hills High School."

Miss Patel does not hesitate. With the leaderly composure and quick-witted conviction that have always defined her behavior, she declares her verdict.

"I am in favor of the group's returning to Earth," she says.

"What is the basis for your verdict?"

"The majority of students whom the school shooter killed are essentially decent human beings. They are not without flaws. But they have many merits that outweigh those flaws. For instance, Dion, Shiloh, Sonia, and Jason have bravely combatted the slurs and conflicts generated by their racist peers. They never stopped believing in the essential goodness of most human beings. They never accepted the roles of victims into which their adversaries wanted to push them. They always showed a loving respect toward their parents. They helped the needy and the downtrodden in their community. They gave the best of themselves in the classroom and in athletic competitions.

"I can give similar praise to many of the other students here. But I shall allow Mr. Marchand and some of the Spirits to make specific remarks about those students.

"Some of my fellow jurors may pause before Cassandra's diabolical scheme to bring harm to her former boyfriend and to the innocent girl caught in the aftermath of that stormy relationship. Cassandra's deviousness and her murderous scheme are black marks against the group. But she, by herself, is not the group. She is an anomaly. She is an aberration, a departure from what is normal or usual or expected. Most adolescents do not behave in the appalling way that she has made her trademark.

"Nor should Ari's deceptions keep the group from returning to Earth. Ari has done many things well. He has most often been an obedient son. Always, he has excelled as a student and as an athlete. Another strong point in his favor is the courage he showed as he confronted the peers who were persecuting him because he is a Jew. If he returns to Earth, he will be tested in new ways. He deserves a second chance. He should have the opportunity to atone for whatever wrongs he committed while he was on Earth.

"There you have all of it," Miss Patel says. "It's my verdict, with my reasons for reaching it."

If the Captain is displeased by her presentation, he does not show it. As the presiding judge in this court, he keeps himself inscrutable. In this moment, his rugged features are unreadable. His thoughts are impenetrable.

I, too, conceal myself behind a calm and pensive demeanor. I do not protest Miss Patel's lacerating appraisal of me. There is a part of me that respects her honesty and her tough-mindedness. Her words should not surprise you. I've already told you that I am no good. I am the chief liability in this group. Miss Patel has the guts to say so. My crimes tarnish my peers because of their association with me. Only time will tell whether I'll bring them down with me.

Ari is less clever than I in hiding his feelings. Miss Patel's mixed review of his character has not dispelled his sullenness. But vague traces of relief bring a flush to his face. At least one juror has cast a vote in his favor, as conditional as that vote may be. Perhaps other jurors will do the same, forgiving him his errors and, at the same time, granting him a chance to redeem himself.

Jason, Dion, Sonia, and Shiloh sit quietly at attention. Miss Patel's praise of their good conduct pleases them. But her praise has not dispelled their fears that the wrongdoers in the group may prevent them from going back to Earth. Only for an instant do they allow themselves to glance my way. They pity and they hate me. I imagine that their hatred unsettles them. They are not used to hating anyone. As though they are thinking in unison, they turn away from me and focus on a different kind of tension—the court proceedings that continue to unfold around them.

In this very moment, Captain Johnson is inviting Mrs. Adams to speak her mind.

"Let this court hear your verdict," he says. "If you know any reasons why this group from Green Hills, Maine, should not be allowed to return to Earth, you must state them now."

Mrs. Adams has been waiting for this opportunity to damn all of us. With her hard-edged temperament and her inveterate ruthlessness, she delivers a blistering tirade that seals our fate.

"Cassandra Winslow has a criminal's mind," she begins. "She is a dangerous plotter, an habitual liar, and a promiscuous girl. She has a murderous character. She has conspired with rapists and killers. She has scandalized and tarnished this group. She has robbed them of their chance to go back to Earth."

Captain Johnson wants to know more.

"Your verdict is insufficient, Mrs. Adams. It doesn't consider the moral characters of other members in the group. You need to tell us how you judge at least some of these other members. In your opinion, are there any students among them who are worth saving?"

Mrs. Adams ponders his question at the same time that she resents it. Nevertheless, she has no choice. She is bound by the rule that requires her to provide an impartial verdict, one that is free of the bitterness that she carries from her own tragic past.

"Brenda Flynn is a bright spark in the group," she admits. "She kept her family going when her parents fell into trouble. She cared for them and for her siblings. She devoted many hours to community service, and she maintained an honorable standing in her school. She also tried to help Boyd Henderson before he decided to become a killer. Her failure in this regard cannot be held against her. Through no fault of hers, Henderson became a monster.

"Brenda wasn't the only bright spark among her peers," Mrs. Adams says. "Miss Patel has already remarked favorably about Sonia, Jason, Dion, and Shiloh. They deserve praise. They bravely combatted the racism that was infecting their school. Alessandro saved two children from drowning, and Jayden helped a war-torn Marine to walk and to swim again and to have hope.

"Their virtuous actions increase the merit of their group. But Cassandra Winslow's criminal behavior has robbed them of the privilege of returning to Earth. She doesn't deserve a second chance. She should disappear eternally. The other students in the group will be better off staying here in Sojourn. They can be useful as Spirits and Shadows who will be allowed to return to Earth only after some proper training. Eventually, they can save lives and prevent crimes.

"Now you have all of them," she tells Captain Johnson. "The reasons behind my verdict. I'll not change any of them. I'm not interested in allowing cheap sentiments and eleventh hour conversions to sway me. I want Cassandra Winslow to stay dead. If I allowed the other students in her group to go back to Earth, she would have to join them. There is no way that they could relive those last days without her."

Angry words leap out of me.

"You are punishing innocent people because of my crimes," I tell her. "Where is the justice in that? There is none. Your verdict is willful and wrongheaded. It steals from the victims. It deprives them of their chance to make the Earth a better place. It takes away from them their right to create lives of happiness for themselves."

Mrs. Adams rages back at me.

"Don't talk to me about justice! Was it justice that refused to allow my husband and my children to come back to me while I was alive on Earth? What kind of justice looked upon my grief and brought me no solace after they and ten other people were shot down in a ski resort shooting? The judges said that my husband had led a dissolute life. He was a drunkard and a gambler, and he slept with much younger women whom he often treated roughly. I forgave him his mistakes. But the committee of Spirits that reviewed his case did not forgive him. They prevented everybody who was in his group, including our three children, from returning to Earth.

"My husband had not committed a murder. Nor had he plotted a crime. Yet those Spirits condemned him and destroyed my happiness. Today, I'm invoking their kind of wild justice that makes no provisions for the fallible natures of most human beings or for the forgiving heart."

Her words rouse my pity, but they cannot completely deflect the anger and contempt that I feel for her. Despite my ambivalence, I find my niche in understatement. No longer do I rage at her. Instead, I carefully modulate the timbre of my voice. I choose words that are matter-of-fact and temperate.

"I feel sorry for you," I tell her. "Those Spirits not only deprived you of your innocent children and your errant husband.

They also destroyed your empathy. They turned the love and the sympathy that were in your heart to hatred and malice. They ruined you. They turned the life-loving woman you used to be into a bitter and unforgiving Spirit."

Mrs. Adams detects my pity and resents it. Adamant and ill-natured, she once again announces her verdict.

"You are a blight upon your group. It is you who have stolen their chance to go back and relive the last days before the shooting. You have made it impossible for me to consent to their returning to Earth. That is my verdict, and I'll never change it."

I withdraw to the raw edges of silence and to the bleak caverns of my own bitterness.

Captain Johnson nods to Mrs. Adams. He is satisfied that she has clearly expressed her viewpoint, abrasive and punitive as that viewpoint remains.

But I am not satisfied. Nor are my classmates, who sit reflective and disheartened after hearing Mrs. Adams' negative verdict. They may be reluctant to fire out their protests at her hard-hearted assessment. I am not.

"What's the point of going on with this trial?" I ask. "Mrs. Adams has cancelled all our chances for returning to Earth. Now it doesn't matter what the other jurors say. Without a unanimous decision from the jury, we've lost our best chance to go back to Earth."

Captain Johnson stays patient and low-keyed.

"Every juror must declare a verdict," he explains. "Otherwise, this trial would not be valid."

He waits for me to lodge another complaint or to counter his remark with a more incisive analysis than his own of our group's imperiled situation. I do neither. Instead, I retreat to silence. I allow a fake calm to touch my face. I glance at the troubled faces of my classmates.

The Captain studies me for a moment and then turns his attention to more pressing matters.

With the efficiency of a judge who is overseeing these courtroom proceedings by means of carefully calibrated authority, he addresses Mrs. Steerforth.

"The court wants to hear your verdict, Mrs. Steerforth. Be as brief as you can. Provide evidence for the decision you have made."

Mrs. Steerforth surprises me. A frown troubles her brow. A stammer takes hold of her speech. Her hesitancy suggests that her thoughts have been navigating the turmoil of doubt and indecision.

"It has been very difficult for me to reach a verdict," she admits. "I've had to take care not to league Boyd Henderson with this group, though he killed every one of its members. I've had to keep telling myself that his crime did not infect the character of this group. The one person who did infect the group with her murderous plots and her prevailing narcissism is Cassandra Winslow. Except for her, every person in the group made the Earth a better place because they were a part of it.

"Miss Patel and Mrs. Adams rightly praised many of the students who enhanced the merits of their school because of their team spirit and their knack for giving the best of themselves while they met all the challenges confronting them. They brought honor to their parents by doing all the right things. They brought food and clothing to the needy and the downtrodden. They combatted racial prejudice, sexual predators, and the abuse of women in the work place. They cheered up friends who were feeling low. They encouraged shy friends to believe in themselves. They forgave the friends who sometimes disappointed them. They did all these good things and more.

"Abigail and Chloe were among these students who made life better for those persons who were around them. It is true that both girls were, at times, self-centered and manipulative. They used their beauty and their femininity to win the top spots on their school's Student Council that should have gone to peers who had created a more realistic plan for improving the computer and biology labs and the lunch menus. But Chloe and Abigail did see to it that those gifted peers joined the Council. They made those plans for improving their school a major part of the Council's new prestige, and they gave those peers full credit for their achievement.

"They also helped Boyd Henderson make a successful comeback after he returned to school from his six months in a reformatory and in a clinic for drug addicts. They were in no way responsible for the bad choices that Boyd made after that.

"I'm less certain about Ari Bachman. His lies against Boyd Henderson became the catalyst for Boyd's first downward spiraling and for the loss of his standing at his school and in his community. Ari's refusal to confess his crime and thereby take responsibility for his wrongdoing is a very black mark against him. But his volunteer work in his community, his diligence as a student, his brave stand against racists, and his dutiful relationship with his parents count as marks in his favor.

"Despite these reservations, I am casting a verdict in favor of the group's returning to Earth. Like Miss Patel, I believe that the students in this group deserve a chance to remake those days before the shooting. They'll be tested. They'll need a great deal of courage. Their going back is a Janus-faced gift. One side of the gift appears comforting and rewarding. The other side conceals the danger and the terror that await them.

"I'll be happy if the group gets their chance to relive that tragic day. I'll also be troubled. Nothing on Earth or here in Sojourn or even in The First Heaven comes easy. I can't reveal the names of the students in this group who will succeed in their mission and who will perish. But I know who they are. I believe that each of them must go back to meet the fate for which they were intended."

Hearing her ominous words, my classmates appear even more troubled. Because they have been vanishing by degrees that are almost imperceptible, I can easily discern the emotions that alter their facial expressions. Their courage struggles to dispel the fear that is rising within them. They do not cringe. They do not smile. They do not cry out. They remain very still. They sit with soldierly discipline and at complete attention. Mrs. Steerforth's verdict has pleased them. But her concluding remarks, delivered as extemporaneous warnings, have disconcerted them. They are like travelers in boats that are unmoored from safe harbors on stormy waters. They are human beings untethered from all the places that knew them when they were alive on Earth. They are emerging Spirits who have not yet found their new homes in the Afterlife. Carefully observing them, I discover within myself an even more intense respect for the tough manner with which they are resisting their vulnerability.

The Spirits notice their stoic responses with muted approval.

Captain Johnson is especially pleased by my classmates' ability to override their fears and to prepare themselves for all the battles that might be hastening toward them.

He is also pleased with Mrs. Steerforth's realistic assessment of the group's precarious situation.

Once again, he nods to a juror who has fulfilled her task. Then he turns to Mr. Marchand.

"The Court wants to hear your verdict, Mr. Jean-Pierre Marchand. How do you judge these students whom you taught when all of you were alive and not anticipating your deaths in Green Hills, Maine?"

Mr. Marchand readily complies with the Captain's request that, because of its militant subtext, has the ring of a command.

"I am pleased that Miss Patel and Mrs. Steerforth have offered positive verdicts about the Green Hills students. I am especially interested in Miss Patel's judgment. Like me, she was there, at Green Hills High School. We taught these students. We shared their hopes and their apprehensions. We witnessed their diligent approach to challenging academic programs and their commitment to extracurricular activities that included athletic teams, science competitions, music and theater, the Student Council, and the JROTC program. We came to know the various levels of their giftedness. Most of them were team players. They were ambitious. They were life-loving. They believed that they were going to make the world a better place.

"I need not repeat the praise that Miss Patel and Mrs. Steerforth accorded so many of these students. But I do want to say a few words of praise on behalf of those students who devoted their time and their talents to helping other human beings.

"In his sophomore year, Jayden McDonald applied CPR to a senior citizen who collapsed in a shopping mall. He kept that aged gentleman alive while a crowd of murmuring shoppers looked on with self-protective detachment or hard-edged indifference or genuine empathy. When the emergency medics arrived in the ambulance that would bring the ailing man to a nearby hospital, they saw at once that Jayden had done all the right things. Because he recognized that the man was suffering from cardiac arrest, Jayden had applied hands-only CPR, without rescue breaths. He understood that this procedure was more likely to bring the man back to consciousness.

"A woman who stood nearby later remarked to the television news people that Jayden had brought a professional medic's skill to his CPR maneuvers. He had knelt beside the man and placed the heel of his own hand on the center of the man's chest. He kept his arms straight, covered the first hand with the heel of the other hand and interlocked the fingers of both hands together. He kept his fingers raised so that they did not touch the patient's chest or rib cage. He leaned forward so that his shoulders were directly over the old man's chest and pressed down on the chest about two inches. He released the pressure, but not his hands and let the chest come back up. He repeated these compressions until the man revived.

"The ambulance crew saluted Jayden as a well-trained rescuer. They saw that his quick and precise action had saved the man's life.

"Jayden is only one of the students in this group whose actions helped others.

"In his junior year, Alessandro Bianchi took time from his busy schedule to tutor Dion Williams, a soccer teammate, in calculus and trigonometry. He helped Dion to maintain the honor grades that made his acceptance into an excellent university more likely.

"In his senior year, Alessandro helped his friend Shiloh Jackson, who was worried that he would not be accepted into any university's ROTC programs because he was not as buffed up as he needed to be. He was doing well in our school's JROTC program. I know, I was his instructor. But Shiloh wanted to do more. Alessandro persuaded him to enter a rigorous fitness program at the private club where his father was a member. The first-rate instructor there monitored the program. To boost Shiloh's morale, Alessandro signed up for the program, too, even though he had already passed through the program with flying colors. The extra physical training made all the difference for Shiloh. He was accepted into the ROTC program at the University of Pennsylvania.

"These two friends whom Alessandro had helped passed it forward. Shiloh and Dion defended a gay student, Malcolm Grayson, when he came out during his senior year. With some of their athletic buddies, they fought off a neo-Nazi mob that wanted to attack Malcolm at a football stadium. During the halftime of a decisive game, Malcolm, a swift and rugged quarterback, had scored two touchdowns. In the melee that followed the first half of the game, Malcolm was no pushover. He fought well and knocked down four or five adversaries. When a gang of ten boys rushed upon him, he drew out a Colt revolver and fired three shots in the air. The shooting sent the attackers scattering. The security guards and the police gave no trouble to Malcolm. They didn't like gays. But they liked neo-Nazis and rampaging mobs even less. Though they offered no words of praise to Malcolm, in their hearts they respected him for defending himself against a pack of losers.

"After that violent episode, Dion and Shiloh, as well as Ari Bachman, convinced Malcolm that he should rely on his fists rather than a revolver. They talked him into honing his fighting skills by taking up boxing. They worked out with him at the private gym within the club where Ari's father was a member. Once the word got around that Malcolm and his straight friends were well-trained boxers, the neo-Nazi gang left all of them alone.

"There are other students here who have made this group something special. Miss Patel and Mrs. Steerforth have named some of them. I could name even more, if the time permitted. Having made these few remarks, I want to state with clarity and without reservation that I endorse almost all of the students in this group. My verdict favors them. They should have the opportunity to return to Earth. I am confident that they will make those days before the school shooting play out in an altogether different way and all for the better.

"I see the group as a miniature world. In so many ways, it mirrors the larger world we inhabited while we were alive on Earth. Some of the persons that make up the group are virtuous and law-abiding. Some are wayward and devious. The group should not be punished because of the wrongdoing of one or two of its members. Let all of these students go forth, I say. Let them relive their last terrifying day on Earth.

"Miss Patel and I will be with them. Like these students, we understand the tremendous opportunity we may be granted. We are also aware of the new and unfamiliar disappointments, perils and tragedies that may await us. Nothing about this return journey is certain. No bleak omens or beatific signs influence our expectations. We have only our courage to guide us, and our hope, and the conviction that, in spite of all the dangers, we may be able to change things for the better.

"I'll say it again. Give us permission to go forth. Allow us to do battle against blind chance and against the evil of our adversaries."

Once again, both hope and fear touch the faces of my classmates. Once more, they harness their emotions to straight-back postures and disciplined attention. They sit in silence, speechless and unmoved, as though a spell has been cast upon them. But no magic spell binds them. No monstrous adversary hovers near them to stifle their words and to steal their courage. The fear that the jury and Captain Johnson in his capacity as judge may not allow them to return to Earth stymies their hope and their confidence. But an even greater fear possesses my classmates. If they return to Earth, their fates may plunge them into horrifying scenes in which they will be helpless to save themselves or to rescue anyone else.

With an official nod that is no less militant than the ones that he offered to the other jurors, Captain Johnson seals his approval of Mr. Marchand's presentation.

Now he turns to the fifth juror.

"This court wants to hear from Mr. Steerforth. What kind of verdict have you reached in this intricate case that we have before us?"

Mr. Steerforth looks dour. He is altogether too stern and gloomy. He has lost or abandoned the good-humored manner that he conveyed in his first meeting with our group. Perhaps, the burdens of his duties as a juror have worn down his affability and his optimism.

I do not envy him his assignment. He knows where our fates are leading us. He may not care to send us back to Earth into a battle that we cannot possibly win.

He speaks at a fast clip. He is terse, spot-on, and no-nonsense.

"I am in favor of this group's going back to Earth. I approve their going not because these students are perfect human beings. They are not. No human being has ever been perfect. But in many ways these Green Hills students have represented valuable ideals. Students such as Shiloh, Dion, Alessandro, Sonia, and Brenda have shown the love they have for their country. They, as well as Jayden, Jason, and Abigail, have defended honorable principles and protected besieged minorities. They have loved their parents, and they have forgiven them for their faults. They have set realistic goals for themselves, and they have worked hard to achieve those goals.

"There are liabilities in the group, none more egregious than Cassandra Winslow. Being allowed to return to Earth will test her character in new and sometimes terrible ways. Like her classmates, she must strive to make a new ending for herself.

"The First Spirit has always given every human being a chance to make their lives morally acceptable. In this rare case, He is willing to give these students and their two teachers a second chance. If the final judgment of this court proves to be in their favor, they will return to Earth. They will do battle with their adversaries, and most of them will strive to be the best human beings that they can be.

"I'll echo Mr. Marchand's favorable words. Go forth, be brave, and conquer your enemies as well as yourselves. Become new."

Captain Johnson offers Mr. Steerforth his official nod and then turns to his fiancée, Miss Dickinson. He modulates his militant manner. He softens the timbres of his voice. He allows the hint of an affectionate smile to touch his lips.

"The Court would like to hear from you, Miss Dickinson. Your insight has always proved reliable. Your point of view has never failed to be judicious. Let us hear what you have to say about this group from Green Hills."

Miss Dickinson meets his gaze with the decorum and self-possession that have always identified her to herself and to everyone else. She proceeds with brisk assurance and total conviction.

"My verdict is an affirmative one. This Green Hills group has earned the privilege to go back to Earth. Most of them are brave enough to combat all the enemies who will be attacking them. Those students in the group who have not yet activated their courage will be compelled to do so now. They need not be afraid. All of life is a battlefield. The few who have not been tested should count themselves among the most fortunate of human beings. Nevertheless, even these fortunate students have been traveling on fields where battles sometimes flare their horror when they are least expected. If this court allows them to go back to Earth, they will witness the horror close-up, as they did on their last day when a crazed classmate killed all of them. Now they will work to change the outcome of that wretched scene. Now they will be fighting alongside their more worldly classmates, who have already fought wily opponents and perverse wrongdoers.

"Going back to Earth will give everyone in this group the chance to fight for what is right. The brave who have been tested will be tested once again. Those who have remained innocent of the world's follies will have to stand tall and be counted among the brave.

"I wish I were going with you. I wish I could change the minds of savage killers and sadistic plotters. I wish I could make them understand that the strongest weapons they can wield do not include an AR-15 assault rifle or a Colt Cobra revolver or a Beretta pistol. Their strongest forces live within their ability to love their fellow human beings. Those forces include their willingness to rescue the imperiled, to care for the downtrodden, and to defend the innocent. One of their greatest forces derives from their capacity to get up fighting after the world's injustice has knocked them down.

"I say all these things not knowing whether the Green Hills students and their teachers will be allowed to return to their homes in Maine. I cannot speak for my fellow jurors and for the equally honorable judge who is presiding over this case. I speak for myself. Without any hesitation and with prayers that they can win their future battles, I cast on behalf of all these students and their teachers a very positive verdict. To the question of whether they should be allowed to go back to Earth, I state for the official records an unconditional 'Yes.'"

The trial is over.

Five jurors have issued verdicts that favor our group's returning to Earth despite my devious and sometimes murderous plotting and Ari's criminal lies against Boyd Henderson.

Here in Sojourn, Mrs. Adams' negative verdict does not create a problem for the court. Captain Johnson, as the presiding judge, does not require unanimous agreement among the jurors. The majority vote counts for a great deal. Only the Captain could cancel the influence of the jury's majority decision. He alone has the legal right to agree with the jury's decision that our group should go back to Earth to alter the terrible outcome of the day of the shooting. He also has the right to reject the jury's decision and to keep the group from returning to Earth.

All my classmates and our two teachers are aware of Captain Johnson's legal powers. His harsh view of most human beings and his unsentimental interpretation of their behavior rouse our doubts of him. It is unlikely that he will make a decision in our favor.

Nobody among us speaks. Tight-lipped and fatalistic, we hold ourselves very still.

As I observe him, Captain Johnson might be a hangman at a county crossroad and I the condemned awaiting the opening of a trap door, the swift falling through, and the rapid and fatal breaking of my neck.

He might be an executioner in a revolutionary country standing on the scaffold of a guillotine and releasing the weighted and angled blade from the top of the tall, upright frame. The blade swiftly falls and cuts my head away, flinging it into a convenient pit below the scaffold and leaving my inert and headless body safely secured with stocks at the bottom of the frame.

So I imagine, not believing in last-minute rescues or in the probability that men as war-hardened as the Captain could discover in their character either compassion or mercy.

Now, with this new tension that hovers around each of us and with an unremitting dismay that burns through our souls, we wait for Captain Johnson to deliver his judgment.

His husky voice carries the conviction that he has drawn from his knowledge of our troubled lives. His manner is forthright and even-tempered. His presentation is as terse as it is scrupulous.

"After listening to the opinions of these six jurors, I find myself in agreement with the viewpoints of the majority. I believe that the Green Hills students and their teachers should go back to Earth to redress the grievous injustice to which a killer's bullets condemned them. Most of these students led decent lives. Their teachers also followed all the appropriate rules. It isn't often that the victims of wrongdoing can work to revive the justice that died when they did. But they are being given the opportunity to do so."

The Captain pauses. A frown furrows his brow. Now he addresses my classmates and me with even more personal assertions. He has the look of a field-grade officer briefing a squadron before they go forth to a new battle.

"Some jurors have already indicated the liabilities of your returning to Earth. They have acquainted you with the precarious reality of your situation. You will be combatting new and old enemies. You will have to make decisions that require quick thinking and accurate responses. You will be tested again and again. You must strive to save your lives without losing your souls. That is your mission. That is why you are being allowed to return to your homes in Maine. Your challenge is to alter the injustice of that day when you were shot down. As Mr. Steerforth told you, nothing on Earth or in Sojourn or in The First Heaven comes easy. Fight hard. Fight well. Come out clean and conquering."

Mrs. Adams is not pleased with the Captain's decision, but she is smart enough not to challenge him.

Everyone else breathes more easily. The five jurors who are in favor of our returning to Green Hills wait for Captain Johnson to adjourn this meeting. Their benevolent glances suggest that they want to rise from their places and hurry to congratulate us.

Before the Captain can close this trial, though, Brenda Flynn calls out a spate of questions.

"What is going to happen to Adriana Montalban and Boyd Henderson?" she asks.

The Captain quickly answers her.

"They will be going back to Green Hills," he says. "They, too, will be embattled. Whether they are fighting for good or for evil, they will meet the fates that they deserve. They will bring Justice back from the dead."

Having said so, he closes the trial with his usual competence.

All my classmates leave their seats and begin hugging each other. Some of my peers cry out elated hurrahs, careful to keep the sound of them cautious and hushed. Four girls and two of the boys softly cry as their anxieties hurry away from them, at least for these minutes. They cry in astonishment, as well, while happiness, a familiar stranger, nearly overwhelms them.

I do not cry out elation that I cannot feel. I do not weep. I have gone past elation and weeping. But I have not gone past fear. I know what is coming. I get ready for the danger. This time I have no choice. I shall have to confront it. There will be no place for me to hide.

CHAPTER THIRTEEN
THE FIRST TEST

Instantly, after Captain Johnson waves his hand, we find ourselves back on Earth. But we do not return to the day of the school shooting or the days before that, when we were completing our senior year. Instead, we enter once again the night a full year earlier when we were caught inside the glamour, merriment, and danger of the school's junior prom. We are reliving the surprise and waywardness of the evening that incited our rebellious aptitudes and precipitated all manner of complications a full year before we died in the massacre that overtook our school.

I remember every detail of what happened the first time we lived through this night. But Boyd, Ari, and his girlfriend Sonia Janowski have merely a vague recollection of having navigated the perilous velocity of this scene, all of its punishing momentum and its out-of-control rapidity. They have entered this evening with the eerie feeling that they have already seen and heard the events that are now unfolding around them as if for the first time. Yet they are not certain. The ambivalent newness of the scene is part of the first test. This night is going to challenge all of us to make the right moral choices and to explore the unknown regions of our courage.

I do not know how this night will end. Nor do I know the outcome of the other tests awaiting us. My foresight has enabled me to glimpse some of their terrors that flash upon my seeing and just as quickly vanish. The flaring horror of the blood-drenched corpse of a rugged African American; a fearful image of a mutilated face that is no longer a face but only shards of raw flesh that belonged to an even younger Asian girl; the protruding bones of an Hispanic boy's teenage body and the gaping hollow of his smashed face and toothless mouth—all these murdered corpses acquaint me with the turbulent and ghastly scenes that my classmates and I shall soon be entering as we struggle through the three tests that will determine our fates. My classmates are hurrying toward these scenes without knowing that they are waiting there as the backdrop for savagery and rebellion inside the sun-flecked light of a school or the shadowy alcove of a forest path or the murky darkness of a country road.

I alone shall recognize them. But in these new trials or tests that the Five Spirits have set before us, I am powerless to anticipate the moment when these terrors will reveal themselves and just as powerless to keep them at bay or to alter the moment when they rise up to destroy us. Nor have I the power to warn my classmates about them. If I tried to warn them, the Five Spirits would stop my tongue, seal my lips, and render even vague allusions to these dangers as meaningless doggerel.

Even without my warning of the terrors that lie in wait for us, my classmates and our two teachers understand that we are being called to the three tests before us to prove that we have courage and virtue on our side. We need to defeat our adversaries. We need to thwart school shooters. We need to elude the temptation of joining the savage predators such as racists and neo-Nazis with their promises of making our country supremely white again and of deporting or imprisoning or killing innocent non-whites and other foreigners. We need to fight on the side of justice.

Don't get me wrong. I'm no eleventh-hour convert to goodness and charity. On the other hand, I'm not interested in leaguing myself with racists, killers, and rapists. I'm just your usual ambitious citizen. I'll take my chances on the team with a genuine capacity for heroism. I don't see myself as one of the heroes. I'm no Alessandro, Brenda, Adriana, Shiloh, or Dion. But I want to rub shoulders with them. Maybe, from them, I'll learn the value of being virtuous for its own sake. I'd like to pass every one of these tests with flying colors. I'd like to get out alive from the conflagrations that we are facing.

Suddenly, as soon as we land in Maine, the night of the junior prom unfolds around us. We are living once again in that warm springtime a year before the school shooting.

Our first test begins.

Boyd's Ferrari speeds along a lonely country road that is surrounded by a hundred acres of farm fields. Acres and acres of these farm fields hasten past us as the Ferrari shoots its way into the mysteries of this night with torpedo-like velocity and with the tautness of a sprung arrow. We are heading toward the beach at Owl's Head. Ari is driving recklessly, having made a bond with danger and adventure a few hours earlier as he allowed himself to be caught up inside the revelry sparking our school's junior prom. The dance has ended. But for the four of us, the excitement of these hours after the dance is just beginning.

Leaning beside Ari, Boyd Henderson slumps in his seat, woozy with vodka and marijuana and, from time to time, pushes himself out of his daze to peer at Ari, whom he fails at first to recognize. Once or twice, he lurches forward and tries to grab hold of the wheel. With a wild laugh, Ari brushes him aside and keeps on driving.

In the rear seats, Sonia and I have been chatting about the glamorous gowns that the most popular girls were wearing and the tuxes and suits that gave the star athletes a bit of dash. But the speed of Ari's driving and Boyd's vague attempts to take control of the wheel are making us nervous. I should be impervious to unhappy endings. I usually am when my foresight gives me knowledge of them. But I don't know how this night will end. I only know that we are headed for trouble.

"Take it easy," I tell Ari. "The beach will be waiting for us, no matter how long it takes us to get to it."

"I know what I'm doing," Ari tells me. "I'm giving us a good time. Sit back and enjoy it."

"Of course I'm enjoying it," I tell him, flippant and willful despite my pledge to myself that I am going to choose a different way to relive these days that the Five Spirits have granted us. "I'm planning to become the mistress of Death."

Ari breaks into a laugh that sounds as careless as it is hard-hearted. He pushes his foot down on the accelerator, and the car zigzags across the road.

Sonia screams with laughter that ripples across the edge of her fear.

"You are driving like a madman!"

Ari lobs a brash retort her way.

"I'm glad you like it."

Sonia and I laugh in spite of our misgiving. Tonight, Ari has surprised both of us. He has rarely befriended wildness or brashness. His adventurous spirit pleases us at the same time that it incites our fears.

Hearing our laughter, Boyd laughs as well. His is a husky laugh that travels across the circuitous route of his drunken stupor. Once again, he rises out of his slouching posture and reaches for the wheel. At first, Ari nudges him away, but to no avail. Boyd persists. He wants to drive. Now, Ari's nudge becomes a shove that throws Boyd back into his slumping position and more deeply into his sleepy haze.

In this eerily familiar hour when I alone am completely aware that we are reliving the night of our junior prom that occurred more than a year earlier, Boyd also surprises me. He does not waken from his stupor to punch Ari in his face and at the top of his right shoulder. Nor does he land rapid-fire jabs to Ari's ear or slam against him with brutal force or cover his hand with wrenching pressure as the two of them fight for control of the car. Tonight he does not press his left foot upon Ari's right foot and send the car careening off the road. Instead, Boyd drifts more deeply into sleep. It is as though this sleep, like a caul or an amniotic sac, is protecting him from a fatal ending in this very hour when he is being reborn.

So I imagine, while understanding how imperiled the four of us are as Ari drives us into dangers that I remember and toward dangers that will be new to all of us.

The car goes on racing with arrow-like trajectory into the darkness of the road. On and on it races, a solitary car hurtling and weaving and bolting through the darkness that suddenly, before our startled eyes, turns spectral and ominous when the moon peers down upon us as though it is a primitive and wily hunter that has sighted its prey and is pursuing us.

Just as suddenly, a different flare of lights leaps onto our path. A Lincoln Town Car, traveling at an acceptable fifty miles an hour, is nearly upon us. Ari tightens his grip on the wheel and swerves. But it is too late. The Ferrari in which we are riding sideswipes the Lincoln with tremendous force. The echoing thuds and smashes of the collision splinter the air with shards of glass and with furious and metallic explosions. I catch sight of the Lincoln catapulting into a thicker darkness that has eluded the stalking moon. For just an instant, my quickened glance shows me the astonished face of a rugged and silver-haired, middle-aged man bearing down on the steering wheel and struggling to bring his car under control. A blonde, screaming woman who is probably his much younger wife covers her face with her hands while her slim, fragile body, bound as it is to a seat belt, lurches forward and instantly recoils, her right shoulder just grazing the passenger door. Inside the rear interior of the car, the impact of the crash lifts the shadowy, belted figures of the other couple away from the cushiony backs of their bucket seats and even more quickly, with a fierce push, returns them to an upright position. Out of control, the Lincoln zooms beyond my seeing. But the screeching of its tires and the explosive bursts afterwards tell me that the accident has flung the Lincoln and its four bleeding occupants into prolonged misery and unrelenting pain.

Perhaps it is my special sight that makes these fleeting images so vivid. No ordinary eyes can instantly discern so many specific details. At any rate, my sighting of the catapulting Lincoln flashes with swift, surreal emphasis for a moment or two and then disappears. Or, rather, my awareness of what is happening to the Ferrari in which I am a passenger displaces the battered reality of the Lincoln.

Our car is leaping away from the road. Everything whirls away from me, spiraling and swiveling into a confusion of upturned bodies and loose, scattering objects that might be purses, cigarette cases, a flask of whiskey, and two tightly rolled travel blankets. The windows smash apart, the front passenger door and the rear door near my seat shear away, the horn is blaring, and sparks are snaking their way out of the hood of the car. The car flips and flips again, barreling and somersaulting and burrowing into the murkier darkness of strawberry fields. It flips again, bounces thirty feet, and lands against the cedar fence of a paddock.

Even at rest, I am caught inside the whirling motion. I close my eyes and try to retrieve my equilibrium. After a few minutes, the spinning stops, and I am myself once more, wary and alert and able to survey the wreckage. I am surprised that I have survived the crash without any injury. I wonder whether the Five Spirits have spellbound me to a fate far worse than the spun velocity of this crash.

In the faraway distance, I see lights glimmering from the main house on the farm. The people who live there are probably awake now. I wonder whether the owner of the place and perhaps his sons or a foreman, after dressing hastily and after jumping inside a pickup truck, are driving across the long path that borders the field and the paddock where our Ferrari landed.

I quickly climb out of the car. There is no door to hinder my exit. At once, I notice that Sonia is unconscious and bleeding. Her limp body is leaning away from the seat belt, and her head has grazed the wrecked door. I imagine that, even though she is wearing a seat belt, she hit her head against the door when the car flipped over and disengaged the seat belt. I rummage through the lopsided remnants of the rear interior and scoop out the plastic bottle of water that I'd carried in my purse. I pour some of the water into a handkerchief and lightly dab Sonia's forehead and face. Her lips are bleeding, and jagged gashes imprint themselves, blood-smeared and abrasive, above her left eye and upon her right arm.

Her blue eyes flicker for an instant. She peers at me quizzically, without at first recognizing who I am. She strains to see more clearly and, seeing, to connect me to the known and the comprehensible. Then, while struggling past her confusion, she remembers. She opens her mouth because she wants to tell me something. But she cannot yet find the appropriate words.

"It's all right," I tell her. "I'm going to get people to help you."

Now she finds the few words that let me know that she understands.

"Thank you," she whispers, just before she sighs with raspy weariness and passes out.

As cautiously as though I am moving a brittle figure that at any moment might break apart, I move her body slightly until it is leaning against the cushioned back of the seat. I am careful not to move her body any more than that. She may be suffering from internal injuries and, for the time being, is safer by remaining in the reclining position, her face upward and her body leaning into the back of the cushioned seat. Taking hold of her right hand and using my first and second fingertips, I check her pulse. I press firmly but gently on the arteries of her wrist. I use my watch to calculate the beats per minute, counting the pulse when the second hand of my watch is on the twelve. After counting for sixty seconds, I am relieved to find that Sonia's pulse is beating seventy beats per minute. I leave the coolness of the handkerchief upon her forehead, and I grab hold of a lightweight blanket and cover her body that, though still warm, has begun to tremble.

I climb out of the rear of the car and look with searching gaze through the window on the driver's side. Ari and Boyd are unconscious, but their breathing is regular. I try to open the door on the driver's side, but without any success. Most of the window's glass has burst asunder, but the jagged edges prevent me from reaching inside the car and pressing on the mechanism that might open the door. Ari is slumped across the steering wheel, with a small lump protruding from the left side of his head and blood-darkened contusions on his chin and his left hand. His steady breathing gives me hope that he is not in immediate danger.

I hurry to the front passenger side of the car, where the door has been sheared away. I wedge myself into a place beside Boyd and, taking gentle hold of the wrist of his right hand, I discover that his pulse is beating faster than Sonia's. Boyd is a different case from both Sonia and Ari. Like them, he has been knocked unconscious by the impact of the crash. But he is moaning as though he is in pain. His body slumps against Ari, and he reeks of whiskey and cocaine. His face is bruised and swollen, and his left arm is dangling. I guess that it is broken. Once again, I take a handkerchief from my purse and pour spring water into it. I make a compress of it and place it upon Boyd's forehead. With firm and steady hands, I raise his head and move him away from Ari. I guide his body into a more comfortable position as he leans into the soft, cushiony back of the bucket seat. I grab a second blanket from the rear interior of the car and fold it about Boyd to bring warmth to his body. But I need to do more. What I need to do is to get help as quickly as I can.

The car horn is still blaring. At any other time, if the honking of the car horn became a problem, I would simply take a pair of needle-nose pliers from the trunk of the car and disconnect the car horn's fuse. But on this night I am grateful for the incessant honking of the horn. It is an alarm that may alert the occupants of the farmhouse about our trouble.

The sound of the horn does not bother me. Rather, the sparks of fire snaking their way out of the hood send a ripple of fear through me. Inching my way around Boyd, I stretch out my right arm past him and past Ari, but I cannot manage to make contact with the ignition key. I reach out again and fail, stymied by my fear that I may jostle the injured bodies of Boyd and Ari. The sparks snake higher and crackle with a more intense energy. I wonder if the engine is about to explode. I stretch my arm as tautly as I can. The tips of my fingers touch the key without grasping it. I try again and fail again. Then, with my upper body pushing forward, my outstretched hand does touch the key and turn off the ignition. After a moment, the sparks subside and then disappear.

I push back the panic that is rising within me. What if Ari or Sonia or Boyd is suffering from life-threatening injuries? Once again, the thought takes hold of me that I need to move fast. I need to push danger out of their way. I have to phone 911. I notice Ari's smashed cellphone tottering at the edge of the dashboard. I remember that Sonia and Boyd had left the dance without their phones. That leaves only my phone as a potential agent of our rescue. Quickly, I search for my purse, find it on the floor of the rear interior of the car and sight as well, lying next to it, the smashed remnants of my phone. But the purse still holds the Beretta pistol that in this moment seems useless when compared to my need for a phone. Nevertheless, I hang on to the purse that contains the loaded Beretta. It takes me a moment to remember that I carried the Beretta to protect all of us from the highway robberies that have been occurring across most of Maine.

I open the glove compartment, relieved to find that it is intact and workable. From one of its corners, I grab a flashlight, test it, and am pleased to see the gleaming rays that it sends forth. I leave the car and, with the assistance of the flashlight, begin to survey the area.

At once, I see light beaming from the farmhouse that stands in the faraway distance. I am surprised that the blaring car horn has not alerted the occupants to our presence. I debate whether I should wait for these people to come to our car or whether I should hurry to the house to tell them about the accident and about our need for emergency rescuers. I decide to hurry forward, with the beam of the flashlight keeping me on the cleared path that is leading me to the farmhouse. But no sooner have I begun the trek, than I hear Ari's troubled voice calling out to me.

"Wait for me," he says.

I turn around and notice how tense and battered he looks. Because he is limping slightly, I imagine that the crash has left him with a sprained ankle or a bruised kneecap.

"Stay with Sonia and Boyd," I tell him. "You're in no condition to take a long walk."

"I got us into this mess," he answers me. "With your help, I have to get us out of it."

In this instant, he does not seem to be the Ari that I thought I knew so well. Gone are the undertones of arrogance and the suggestion of a sneer at the right corner of his mouth. Instead, he is navigating perhaps for the first time his fallible nature and his suppressed vulnerability. Yet he does not appear to be weak. On the contrary, there is strength in his determined manner and in his matter-of-fact admission that he has brought serious trouble upon himself.

"We have to get to a phone," he says. "Sonia and Boyd need medical attention. So do the people who are trapped in that Lincoln."

Without another word and with the flashlight revealing the path that lies before us, we make our way to the main house that stands as if waiting for us. Illumined by my flashlight and by the intermittent rays of the moon, the farmland spreads its abundance across the wide span of this property that we can see only as random fragments, so blanket-like is the darkness covering almost everything around us.

Ari is limping with the pain of each step. But I refrain from asking him if he prefers that I hurry ahead to get help for the injured persons in the Ferrari and in the Lincoln and to ask the farm family to drive one of their trucks to the spot where Ari is now standing at rest, until the waves of pain that are traveling through his ankle and foot subside. His tight-lipped expression that resembles the grimace of a soldier going into combat suggests that he wants neither my pity nor my coddling.

From a distance, we hear a dog wailing vehemently, its cries not unlike the keening of a grieving and fear-laden human being. Closer than that, a red fox scampers across the path that lies twenty feet in front of us. The moon, rather than my flashlight, casts its sheen upon this fox's auburn pelt and its bushy tail that is flecked with white. The light of the moon also reveals a small rabbit caught as in a vise and still squirming and squealing between the sharp teeth of the fox. When it reaches the middle of the path, the fox pauses to observe us more closely just for an instant before it hurries away into the darkness, never easing its crushing hold of the rabbit.

We trudge onward. We are making headway. The farmhouse looms larger now and closer.

Thunder cracks the silence, winds howl, and lightning flashes its jagged signs across the suddenly moonless sky, the moon having momentarily concealed itself behind an array of clouds that presage rain.

We increase our pace. Compelled by the stoic discipline that he has often made his friend, Ari takes longer strides, apparently heedless of the pain that I imagine is cutting through his ankle and his foot. We do not speak. Now is not the time for words. This hour requires our courageous and quick-thinking action.

When we are only a few paces from the farmhouse, more wind and thunder and lightning overtake the sky. The moon keeps on glowing in the midst of scattering clouds. To my eyes, the scene looks eerie and nightmarish. There is no beauty in it. There is only the menace of the storm, its windswept fury pushing out of the sky the swirl of battering winds and a stinging flood of rain.

Drenched with rain yet relieved that we have at last arrived at our destination, we climb the six brick stairs that lead us to the door of a large Georgian Colonial house. I notice the muted yellow of the shingle siding, the gabled dormers, the white rectangular columns, and the symmetric windows. I notice, too, the deep redness of the door and its solidity. In my quickened glance, the house creates the impression of an immaculately kept possession.

Even at this late hour, every window in the house is lighted. The house radiates an effulgence of light, a dazzle so bright that it transforms the darkness of night into the sun-misted illusion of day. The effect seems supernatural. The driving rain, the clap of thunder, and the jagged streaks of lightning intensify the eeriness of the scene.

I am surprised to find the door open. Upon hearing the crash of our car, did the people who live here light up their house as a signal that would draw us to it? Why didn't anyone jump into a farm truck or a four-door sedan and drive directly to our Ferrari, smashed and immobilized against the paddock fence? Why isn't anyone standing at the door to greet us with a friendly smile or with wary concern? These questions goad my curiosity. But they do not prevent me from crossing the threshold and calling out to whoever might be waiting for us.

"Is anyone here?" I cry out, my voice pushing through the silence and leaving the hint of an echo at the end of the long entrance hall, with its cathedral ceiling and its highly polished floor.

No one answers.

I peer at Ari, who leans against the inside of the sturdy door.

"We'd better wait here," he says. "I'll ring the bell. That ought to bring someone to us."

He moves back, beyond the threshold, and rings the bell at the side of the door. The bell makes musical sounds. I recognize the first bars of a Chopin nocturne. But even these sounds bring nobody to us.

I raise my voice and once again call out the words that alert whoever is in the house about our presence.

"Is anyone here? We need your help."

The sounds of my words ride through the long, gleaming hall and push their echoing refrain toward the high wall at the hall's end.

Nobody answers my call.

"There's no use just standing here," I tell Ari. "You wait here. I'll move down the hall and try to find a telephone. We need to alert the police and a hospital."

Ari's frown tells me that he does not approve of my suggestion.

"We should stay together," he says. "I'm coming with you."

"All right," I answer him, "if you think you're up to it."

"I'm up to it," he says.

I nod my assent and make certain that I do not speak any words that coddle him. I admire his toughness and his willingness to keep on walking, despite the pain that he is enduring.

I move ahead of Ari, impatient to meet the person or persons who can help us or, at the least, allow me to borrow a cell phone or to use their landline phone. I approach the first door at my right. Its whiteness gleams with a purity that seems inviting, even though it is closed. Undeterred, I knock as loudly as I can.

No one opens the door or calls out a greeting.

By this time, Ari is standing behind me. He makes no protest when I turn the gold handle of the door and open it.

Instantly, the room comes alive with its flawlessly crafted contemporary look. I take note of this room's relaxed persona: its pale walls, amply upholstered sofas and chairs, and antique rugs in soft, woodsy tones. I notice, too, the long, well-lighted windows and the pristine wool curtains in a soft muted plaid.

Prints and watercolors are another brightness touching the walls and influencing the warmth of the spacious room.

Without any words to validate my favorable impression, I begin to believe that this room is calling me to step into it.

No sooner do I enter it, than I see what I had not previously noticed. In the far left corner of the room that I could not see when I was standing at the gleaming white door, a lamp has been overturned, a beige sofa has been splattered with the redness of blood, and there are bullet holes in the lower panes of a long window, the cracks in the glass spreading with spider traceries. Beneath the window, the headless bodies of a man and a woman lie sprawling on the carefully polished floor. Their gory heads lie near their naked bodies.

The man's body, bleeding and bullet-riddled, is young and muscular. His face, caving into itself, may have been handsome. His eyes are half-closed and blood trickles from his mouth. His head wears a brown-haired crew cut that I associate with military personnel and with beefed-up athletes.

The woman's body is also bullet-riddled and bleeding. She, too, is young. Sensuality has not yet abandoned her curvaceous body, but it has made a temporary pact with the horrific underpinnings of bullet holes and blood. Her blonde head that has been sliced away from her body shows her right profile, having tumbled into that nearly casual position near her feet. Her right eye bulges out of its socket, her right cheek is bloodstained and sunken, and her mouth, swollen with blood, gapes in surprise. The beheading has drained away the beauty she may have possessed.

Next to her body lies a French Infantry short sword. It has a solid brass hilt and its blade, smeared with gouts of blood, measures approximately twenty-four inches. I recognize the sword. It is similar to the one that my brother Luke used with success in a fencing competition.

So shocked am I by the sight of the corpses, I cannot push the scream out of my throat. Just for an instant, I gag and choke up as though I am going to vomit. Quickly, I turn away from the two corpses and reclaim my proper balance.

I turn around to face Ari, who has been leaning against an amply upholstered wing chair a few feet behind me. He looks grim-faced and startled, but he stays in perfect control of himself.

"What have we got ourselves into?" he asks.

"Let's get out of here," I tell him.

With no other words to impel us forward, we move as fast as we can toward the doorway through which we had entered. Or, rather, I move fast. Ari, with his injured foot and ankle, maintains a trudging pace that is serving him with moderate effectiveness.

When I reach the door and move back into the hall, though, I am taken by surprise. A tall white-haired man with a jagged scar traversing the left side of his face and with bloodshot, killer eyes glazed in fear and anger is slapping me so hard that I fall down, dizzy while moving in and out of consciousness. The long, wide hall is spinning around me, and my grizzled assailant is hovering by me. He is wearing a black shirt, black trousers, and black suede shoes. Vague-minded and knocked down, I imagine that he is Mister Death coming to scoop me away. I see him reaching into the pocket of his trousers. I see his hands taking hold of the pistol grip of a revolver that I recognize as a Colt Anaconda.

But, before he can slide the revolver from his trouser pocket, the man keels over and falls to the floor, surprised by the series of jabbing punches that Ari has smashed into the side of his grizzled face.

Still woozy, I notice the revolver dropping out of his pocket.

Ari notices, too, and hampered though he is by his fractured ankle he moves swiftly and reaches down for the revolver. The pain of his ankle pushes him into a kneeling position as he reaches for the gun.

I try to get up. I want to help Ari. But once again the room begins spinning around me.

Ari takes hold of the revolver. He is struggling to stand up and comes close to retrieving his tall, muscular stature. But our assailant has already risen from the floor and lands a solid punch to the back of Ari's head. Ari falls to the floor, but his hand never lets go of the revolver. The man with killer eyes jumps on him.

With his broad shoulders having lost none of their strength and with his boxer cleverness, Ari flips him over to the side, always holding steady the revolver in his hand.

The man who wants to kill us leaps up, falls upon Ari's back, and grabs a tight hold of Ari's right arm that is holding the revolver. Ari throws himself into a somersaulting motion, and the scar-faced man rolls off him. Ari lets rip with a solid left to the killer's jaw. Because his opponent is momentarily stunned, Ari pushes himself into a standing position. Once more, the killer jumps upon him. Ari falls. The killer pins him down. They struggle for the revolver. Two bullets shoot out of the revolver. One of them hits Ari. The second hits our assailant. Ari's wound is serious. Blood is spilling from his chest. He loses consciousness. The assailant is also wounded. But the bullet has merely grazed his left temple.

I see all that is happening, even as I strain to find my proper balance. While the combat between Ari and the killer is ongoing, I get up from the floor and fumble about for my purse. It takes me less than a minute to locate it about twenty feet from the doorway beyond which I crossed three minutes ago. I open it and grab hold of my Beretta pistol. I turn around to the menacing sight of the scar-faced man aiming the Colt Anaconda at Ari's head. Instantly, I fire the Beretta at the killer. The bullet explodes through his forehead as the revolver falls away from his hand and hits the floor with a dull thud. Even as his body topples over, I fire again and again. Blood swooshes out of his eyes and mouth and chest.

In this moment, I am not sorry that I have killed him. Already, I am grieving because I believe that he has murdered Ari.

I hurry over to Ari and am elated to find that he is alive and coming back into consciousness.

"Don't worry about me," Ari whispers. "Phone the police and a hospital. Boyd and Sonia and the people in that Lincoln need looking after."

"I'll do that," I tell him, without mentioning that he, too, needs a physician.

I hurry on to a room other than the one where the beheaded corpses lay. This time I open a door that brings me into a sitting room, with its plaster and painted wood molding, pale peach walls, and the curved legs, carved claw feet and elegant lines of Chippendale, Queen Anne, and Hepplewhite furniture. The beauty of the room, which is the emblem of civilized living, becomes my stay against confusion. After a quick search, I find a landline phone tucked into a corner of a secretary desk.

I dial 911.

With matter-of-fact precision, the operator connects me to the nearest hospital and to the police.

It will take a few days before the police and a group of detectives have sorted out the sordid details of the owner of the farmhouse into which Ari and I had stumbled. The owner's name was Max Rowley. He was an eccentric millionaire who enjoyed living in the modest style that mirrored his early days as a hardworking farmer who was also a canny investor in New England real estate and in blue-chip stocks on Wall Street. He married when he was sixty. His wife was twenty-five. One of their farmhands became her lover. On the night of the killing, Rowley had returned from a New York business trip earlier than his wife expected. He found her in bed with her lover. He chased them from the bedroom and shot and beheaded them in the living room.

Boyd and Sonia are going to be all right. From the car crash, Sonia suffered a concussion. She is going to stay in the hospital for three days, and she will learn to cope with occasional headaches for a month or two.

Boyd's injuries are more serious. He is suffering from a concussion, a broken arm, a broken leg, and internal injuries. He is going to be hospitalized for three weeks. After that, he will convalesce in a rehab center.

A few hours after Rowley shot Ari, the surgeon tells Ari's parents and me that Ari is a very lucky young man. He was only a couple of inches away from a fatal wound. But he is doing very nicely after an hour's surgery. After an extended recovery, he can still look forward to a long life, one that includes soccer, boxing, swimming, and sailing.

The newspapers and television make much of my shooting a murderer. They also praise Ari for bravely confronting the killer. In fact, his brave attempt to subdue the killer brings him the sympathy of the public. Even the judge who presides over the court hearing that involved Ari's reckless and drunken driving and the ensuing car crash is more sympathetic than he might otherwise have been. Nevertheless, the judge has to uphold the law. The injuries that the car crash has wrought upon Boyd and Sonia, as well as upon the four people in The Lincoln Town Car, cannot be treated lightly. Ari loses his driver's license for a year and has to pay a stiff fine for speeding. His auto insurance increases after the company insuring him pays a hefty sum for all the damages that the crash has inflicted upon six human beings and upon personal property.

The outcome of the trial does not displease Ari. He sees the rightness of it. More than that, he sees that he and I have passed this first test that the Five Spirits have prepared for us. We do not speak of the next test that the Five Spirits have devised for us. Nor do we mention the new dangers that will imperil our lives.

CHAPTER FOURTEEN
THE SECOND TEST

I have no time to be haunted by the memory of the gruesome corpses that lay, bullet-riddled and beheaded, on the carefully polished floor of that Georgian Colonial farmhouse. Nor is there time to recall the scar-faced and sinister killer who attacked Ari and me. I am not even allowed to keep for a few hours the solace of the favorable aftermath of that blood-smeared scene. The public's approving glances and their kinder words cannot allay the foreboding that goads my apprehension. Those soft glances and gentle words cannot keep back the new dangers that are overtaking me and threatening with new intensities all of my classmates.

Some of those dangers involve my relationship with Kurt Drexler. Suddenly, as if overnight, an entire year after the night of the car crash has vanished away. I awake to find myself in bed with Kurt. We are in his bedroom within the second floor of his traveling grandparents' home. A black suede headboard; a custom-made European oak bed with its royal blue pillows, sheets, and coverlets; and a white cowhide rug intensify the clean, minimalist design of the room. Three-drawer night tables, oval-bent and mirrored, flank the bed and enhance the metallic implications of the room with generous beveled edges, dark silver leaf finish, and round bun feet. Lamps with bold rectangular lines and black nickel finish stand on the night tables and serve as sentries to the oversized bed. Vivid canvases with hunting, mountain climbing, and fishing scenes lend color and texture to the pale gray walls. Sunlight, April-radiant and shimmering, passes through the floor-length panoramic window, its cobalt blue drapes pulled aside and deferring to the potent influence of the sun.

That same light suffuses Kurt's rugged nakedness and washes over the soft flesh of my body as we lay love-sated and musing in this quarter of an hour after our vigorous copulation.

I am reliving the scene, though I am not quite certain where it is leading me.

Once again, as if from an uneasy and familiar dream, Kurt and I are leaning into a galaxy of pillows. We are smoking cigarettes imported from Patagonia. They are not the marijuana cigarettes that Kurt and I have occasionally enjoyed because they allow us to drift away from all the school rules and social codes that tightly bind us to lock-step responses and subdued impulses. On this sun-misted afternoon, Kurt wants to keep his mind clear and incisive. He is unwilling to let go of the murderous plot into which he is trying to draw me.

In this very instant, he has grown impatient with me. I have been resisting his cunning words about freeing ourselves from the artificial constraints that ordinary folk have imposed upon us.

"The constraints make them feel safe and even empowered," he says as he takes a drag on his cigarette and leaves the bed. "Those are the same people who set all the rules. They call a world safe as long as it abides by their creeds and their prejudices. Most of them are nickel-and-dime tyrants. They're nobodies, but they can be dangerous. With a crowd to back them, they lash their whips and fire their revolvers against anyone that they perceive as a rebel."

I watch his muscular physique, naked and predominant, swaggering across the room toward the panoramic window. He peers out at a scene that I can easily imagine even as I remain here, leaning into the comforting pillows of his bed. In my previous visits to his bedroom, I too have observed, below and beyond the window, the vivid greenness and the wide expanse of the lawn that stretches outward toward the lake. I have noticed within the center of that lawn the garden of early-blooming tulips, roses, and begonias. I have studied and savored the placid waters of the lake, and the surprise of a seabird poised upon the blue-green delicate ripples. I know what Kurt is watching. I also know what he is thinking, because of the disquieting words that he has spoken only minutes ago as well as on other days. I know because of my intuition and instinct and foresight.

"You and I aren't like those nickel-plated tyrants or like the conventional people they control with their hampering codes and narrow ethics," he says, as he turns back to study my reaction to his words. "We can break free of their rules and their codes. We belong to the superior race that Friedrich Nietzsche wrote about in *The Will to Power* and *Beyond Good and Evil*."

"What's on your mind?" I ask him.

He remains standing by the window, stalwart and predominant as he imparts new words that are made edgy with his arrogance and bitterness. In no way does his exposed nakedness render him vulnerable. Nor does even the slightest dram of modesty inhibit his assurance. Instead, he uses his words with the poise and thrust that he has often brought to his fencing competitions, and from time to time he takes a drag on his cigarette.

"We can make our own rules," he says. "We can prove to ourselves that we are not bound by repressive moral codes or by any prohibitions meant for ordinary people."

I know what is coming. I hear each word of his murderous plot even before he utters it. But he still has to say the words. That is our fate. That is our punishment.

"How do we do that?" I ask him. "How do we prove that we are more than ordinary?"

With no hesitation to hinder his thought, Kurt discloses his plan or at least its blunt preface.

"We commit murder and get away with it."

I fall silent, searching for the words that might dissuade him from his plan. I find the words and speak them with careful understatement and with a tight suppression of the fear that his ruthless nature stirs within me.

"Very few people get away with murder," I tell him. "Eventually, their crimes catch up with them. Maybe the police don't discover who they are. But the memories of the killings stay with the murderers. They have to live with the killings for the rest of their lives."

To my cautious words, Kurt listens with sober attention. Then a cynical smile touches his lips and twists into a sneer.

"You surprise me," he says. "You talk like a moralist. Yet you haven't lived like one. There's nothing of the prude about you—in bed or in any other place."

I don't dispute his words. I know who I am. I can be as cynical as he is. But I do not want to be a murderer. Nor do I care to be a pawn in this game of murder that he wants to play.

"You won't get away with it," I tell him once more. "Besides, you don't have a reason to kill anyone."

"Oh, but I do," he says. "In fact, I have two very good reasons."

He walks toward me now. The cigarette hanging from the right corner of his mouth gives him the look of the street-wise toughs he has often ridiculed. But that connection flares only for a moment. Kurt is as jaded as those toughs, but he is far more cosmopolitan. His privileged background has given him many opportunities for advancing himself as an exemplary human being. His schooling—much of it in Europe—has been first-rate. He has a wide-ranging knowledge of subjects as varied as foreign languages, world history and world literature, chemistry, physics, mathematics, geology, astronomy, and oceanography. He is a superb athlete, having excelled in soccer, swimming, boxing, and tennis. At eighteen, he has already travelled around the globe.

Yet he is a failure. He disdains the mission that fate has handed him. With his gifts intact, he should be on his way to becoming a man who will make our world a better place for all good people. In these quickened weeks since we have been going steady, I have sometimes wanted to tell him how lucky he is to have been born into a wealthy family that has made it possible for him to elude ordinariness. But I do not speak these words to him. I do not feed him this praise. He *is* extraordinary. But he is also no good. I know. I recognize in him the same wayward inclinations that afflict my own character: contempt for most people, a willingness to flout ethical codes, and a hardheartedness that has made betrayal and deviousness friends of more than casual acquaintance.

He walks toward me, intent on telling me his "two good reasons" for committing murder. When he arrives a few feet away from our bed, he does not say anything. He keeps me waiting, stoking my curiosity even as he brings a pensive gravity to his gaze upon my nakedness. It is a gaze that carries no prurient desire. Our fierce and prolonged copulation has eased his desire. His gaze is sizing me up for a different purpose. He is trying to figure out what he has to do to draw me into his plot. Even now he is devising the combination of words, phrases, and sentences that will ensnare me to his will.

Before he speaks, he grabs a burgundy robe from a chair and with casual-seeming self-possession covers his naked muscularity. He takes a drag on his cigarette and holds his steady gaze upon me. Then, as though he knew all along what he was going to say, he speaks the words that, in spite of my tough-minded awareness of the world's evil, startle and dismay and frighten me.

"The two best reasons for our committing murder are Adriana Montalban and Boyd Henderson."

"They may be your reasons," I say. "But they are not mine."

"They should be," he tells me. "Boyd two-timed you. He humiliated you. After dating you for more than a year, he walked out of your life. Adriana stole him from you. Everyone at school knows about them. They talk not only about them, but also about you. They say that Boyd has made a fool of you. He's told his closest friends that you're not so hot. Adriana excites him in a way that you never could."

I hold myself very still. I'm standing at the edge of a precipice. If I speak the wrong words, I may begin the swift plummeting into the darkness from which there is no rescue. That darkness is the bottomless chasm that will swallow me, after Kurt casts me away because I refuse to become a partner in his murderous plot. That same darkness will burst into the hell on Earth to which I condemn myself if I help him to kill Adriana and Boyd. I am not quite ready to turn away from Kurt. It is not love that binds me to him. It is self-hatred. Fallible and vulnerable at the same time, I have a perverse need to be punished. In spite of my realistic awareness of the danger that he is bringing into my life, I cannot will myself to resist him. I am the moth to his flame, the careless bluebird to his hypnotic presence.

Yet resist him I must if I am to save my classmates and our two teachers from Kurt and his gang of killers.

I do not grow angry when Kurt taunts me with the memory of Boyd's walking away from me. Nor do I vow to avenge myself against Adriana. Instead, I choose temperate words that could save Kurt from himself and that could keep my friends and my teachers out of harm's way. I make a speech. I give Kurt a pep talk. In this room where we have reveled in our carnality, I am at once his lover, his counselor, and a seer.

"I bear no grudge against Boyd or Adriana," I say. "I've moved on. I've already begun remaking my life. I have no interest in holding on to the past. Take your cue from me. Break free of hatred and revenge. When you tried to date her, Adriana turned you down. But the world didn't stop because you were disappointed. Nor did it steal anything important from you. Your pride was jounced. So what? Every day, people suffer disappointments and defeats far more grievous than your own. Besides, you are still Kurt Drexler. You're the guy who's headed for the top. Boyd and Adriana are not standing in your way. The only obstacle to your future success is you. Forget this 'perfect murder' scheme. It's not worthy of you. It makes you conventional and run-of-the-mill. Anyone can be a murderer. Only a few men and women can drive their success to the top of the mountain. You can be one of those men. Or you can be a killer. You cannot be both."

Kurt meets this spate of words with a grin. Like his character, his handsomeness is somewhat warped. He is not a pretty boy or a male model. There is something too conflicted and unresolved in his features. His blond crew cut is its own force field, bonding his animal magnetism with a militant persona and a subtly callous disposition. Thick eyebrows, a sardonic fold in the eyelids, a cleft chin, and the hint of a sneer in the left corner of his mouth also subvert the popular notions of handsomeness. His grin has made a pact with the sneer. I perceive at once that he is going to treat my pep talk with light-hearted disdain. My temperate words have roused his contempt and his anger. The grin partially conceals the contempt and the anger. But the sneer and the disdain complicate the light-heartedness. Wily and disingenuous, he closes himself off from me. He knows for certain now that I am not going to be his accomplice in murder. I have refused to be his gun moll or the kewpie-doll puppet whose every move he controls as though I am tied to his wires and strings.

"You're good, Cassie," he says. "You're really good. You've memorized all the correct words. You speak them with absolute conviction. Maybe your saying those words so often has convinced you that they are true. But you know as well as I do that men at the top have the fiercest killer instincts. They ride roughshod over anyone that they regard as a rival or an adversary."

"Not every man at the top is evil," I say in rebuttal of his cynicism. "Many of our leaders uphold the law. They're the ones who count. They change the world for the better. You can be one of those good guys."

He laughs. He makes it clear that he is humoring me.

"Maybe I will be a good guy," he tells me. "Or maybe I'll become a good killer. I'll send you an email in ten years and let you know what side of the law I've chosen as my inspiration."

He turns away from me now and heads for the bathroom, where he'll take a shower and then hurry on to swimming practice. Clearly, he does not want to discuss his violent scheme to murder Adriana and Boyd.

No sooner does he turn from me, than I call out the warning that he needs to heed if he wants to save himself.

"Forget about killing anybody," I say, urgent and apprehensive. "You're better than that. Leave the killing to scoundrels."

"Yes, Snow White," he answers me. "If you wave your magic wand, maybe I'll even turn into Prince Charming."

He is still laughing. But his laughter is as hollow as his promise. He won't let go of his plan to commit "the perfect crime." Already, he's written me off as his partner. He has changed his murder plans. I know. I foresee. He intends to make Adriana and me his first victims. He'll save Boyd for a big showdown later. In a day or so, he is going to make a pact with the neo-Nazi gang of which he is a secret member. They call themselves White Supremacists. I also foresee the violence that is hastening toward Adriana and me, though I do not know whether I can help either of us escape it.

It is useless to alert the police about Kurt's murderous plot. My ability to see into the future shows me that, if the police question Kurt, he will invoke his inveterate wiliness to convince them that he is playing a joke on me. He'll tell them that he is testing me. He wants to see whether I will take a moral stand and not budge from it. He wants to find out whether I will refuse to go along with his murder plan or whether I will agree to murder two people.

Clairvoyant and realistic, I see that Kurt will phone his parents and urge them to fly home from their latest career assignments in Europe and stand by him while the police continue to barrage him with blunt questions and abrasive insinuations that are calculated to confuse him or, perhaps, to draw from him an unwitting admission that he has, indeed, contemplated killing the girl who has spurned him and framing the boy who has stolen her from him. Assisted by his influential parents and their high-powered lawyers, Kurt will persuade the police that he is on the level. Even the most jaded of the police will become convinced that Kurt is just a bright kid who is making his girlfriend the subject of a scientific experiment.

These tense and duplicitous scenes unfold before my seeing as though they are really happening. By not telling the police about Kurt's sadistic plot, I prevent the scenes from happening.

Nor do I tell my parents or my teachers or the school principal about Kurt's "experiment." My foresight shows me that all of these well-meaning advocates will sound the loudest alarms that will bring state troopers and national guardsmen onto the scene. The troopers and the guardsmen will handle Kurt roughly, and his parents will file a lawsuit against them, as well as against my parents, teachers, and school principal. The newspapers will portray Kurt as an imaginative honors student with a philosophic bent and a scientific mind that is already monitoring a meticulous study of human behavior. These same newspapers will excoriate the troopers and guardsmen and everyone else who has wrongly accused him and brutally mistreated him. Even veteran journalists will assert that police brutality harms the lives not only of poor African Americans and Latinxs, but also of affluent whites.

I see all these scenes with clarified vision. There is no practical reason to enter them. There is only the dangerous certainty that, after his lawyers and the public's opinion exonerate him, Kurt will accelerate his plan to murder Adriana and me. Without the police on his tracks and with the White Supremacist gang of which he is a secret member to carry out the murders, Kurt will stay free of suspicion and of blame.

I have to think fast. I have to move swiftly.

First of all, I alert Adriana about the danger facing us.

I visit her after school on the following Monday, when she is at home alone. Her parents are away at work, and her younger siblings are busy with baseball and swimming practice at the middle school that they attend.

I explain why it is useless to alert the police or to ask our parents to rescue us.

"This is madness," she protests. "You have no proof that Kurt will do these horrible things. Think, Cassie. Think. Be hard on yourself. Admit that you are imagining these things because you want to get even with Kurt. He's dropped you, and you want to imagine the worst of him."

"You have to believe me," I tell her. "Kurt and his thugs plan to murder you and me. I know what we must do to protect ourselves. But I do not know when Kurt's thugs will attack us or whether we can save ourselves."

Adriana ponders my words. She notices the intensity of my belief in what I am telling her. Her common sense and her good-hearted nature dispel whatever doubts are assailing her.

"Let's bring Boyd into this," she says. "He'll know what to do. He's the one who can rescue us."

"We mustn't do that," I exclaim. "If he tried to save us, he would be killed. That much I know. I can see some of the future. We are the only ones who can try to save ourselves."

Adriana looks worried. A frown touches her brow with traces of apprehension. But her suddenly taut jawline and her clenched fists subvert any suggestion that she is helpless or that she is going to die without fighting her assassins. Now she makes direct eye contact with me. She challenges me to tell her more.

"How do we do that?" she asks. "How do we try to save ourselves?"

"We make friends of our Beretta pistols. We pay frequent visits to the rod-and-gun club where my father is a member. We get one of the sharpshooters there to give us a few review lessons in the best ways to handle our pistols and our revolvers. We carry our revolvers at all times when we are away from school. We avoid buildings where there are metal detectors. But, whenever we are alone or with our friends in open spaces, we must carry the Berettas."

"I'll do whatever you think needs to be done," Adriana says. "But are you certain that we have to go into this danger alone? Isn't there a friend or parent or detective who might try to save us?"

"I wish there were," I answer her. "But I have seen what the future holds for us. Anyone else who tries to save us will die. We have to be brave enough to try saving ourselves even if it is our fate to die when an assassin fires his Glock revolver into our brain or plunges his dagger into our hearts."

Adriana grows calm now. She accepts the challenge that looms before us. Like me in this one aspect at least, she is a realist. She believes me when I tell her that only we two females, newly initiated into our womanhood, have the power to save ourselves. Without any evidence to prove that I can see some of the future, she nevertheless finds truth in my words. Her willingness to believe me gives me hope. The First Spirit must have influenced her to believe me, just as He once influenced my brother Luke. Possibly, we can overcome the brutal thugs who want to rape and murder us. We may die while we conquer them. At least, we shall die with our honor unblemished.

Matt Evans, a business-like sharpshooter who manages the rod-and-gun club where my father is a member, efficiently guides us through our review of the Beretta Px4 Storm Sub-Compact handgun. Matt has a thick mane of silver hair even at sixty and a still-rugged body that fought in Lebanon, Grenada, and Panama. He is a precise and matter-of-fact instructor as he explains to us that this Beretta pistol offers minimal muzzle-jump and keeps recoil mild. The tilt-breech system is designed to work with the rest of the frame to dissipate both the kick in the web of the shooting hand and the muzzle rise that happens at every shot. Its stainless steel barrel requires less maintenance and is corrosion-and-sweat-resistant. With interchangeable back-straps, this Beretta pistol adapts to different hand sizes and grip sizes. Most of its controls are either ambidextrous or reversible, making it easy to shoot and train with either hand dominant. It is a perfect choice for concealment in a hip or shoulder holster.

Matt understands that Adriana and I are not newcomers to the skill of firing a semi-automatic handgun or a rifle or a snub-nosed pistol. Both of us are cadets in the JROTC program at Green Hills High School. In addition to our training in the Junior Reserve Officer Training Corps, we have also excelled as members of the school's rifle club. But our experience with firearms does not allay our apprehension about the violent hour that is hurrying toward us. Matt knows nothing of our danger. Nevertheless, his review of the Beretta pistol persuades us that, if the neo-Nazis/White Supremacists attack us, we'll have a fighting chance to save ourselves.

"You girls know the score," Matt tells us as we complete this late afternoon handgun review with him and prepare to return to our homes. "Use the Beretta wisely. Fire it only if there is no other way to save yourselves from a robber or a killer."

"We'll use it well," Adriana tells him. "That's a promise."

He leaves us with another thought.

"It's a sad pass we've come to, when good people like yourselves have to carry a weapon to protect yourselves from assailants. But we live in a world that is more violent today than ever before. To survive in it, you need to be combat-ready."

"We are ready," I tell him, "and we are vigilant. We'll keep our eyes open, and we'll give any killer that crosses our path a hard time. That's another promise."

"Good for you," he says, serious and levelheaded. "No killer will take either of you by surprise. You'll shoot him the second after he draws his revolver or his rifle."

The words of this good man encourage us. So do the next four days encourage us when no killers leap out of the haze of a sun-filled afternoon on the tennis courts of Green Hills High School, where Ari and I are involved in a doubles match with Boyd and Adriana. Nor do Adriana and I sight any of Kurt's neo-Nazi friends when we are alone with our coach and our kayaking team on the wind-rippling waters of a lake about three miles from our school.

On the tennis courts, there are no metal detectors around to reveal that we are carrying our Berettas in our oversized tennis bags. Our pistols are stored in the secret inside pockets of our bags, their presence disguised by our racquets, tennis balls, bottles of water, sunscreen, hats and visors, towels, first aid kits, resistance bands, reels of string, and ice packs. It is unlikely that any killer will approach these courts. They are private. An armed security guard keeps a careful watch over us. If any stranger approaches the courts or if some young tough with a razor cut and a tattooed face manages to get past the security guard, Adriana and I will swiftly move to our tennis bags and to our Beretta Storm pistols.

When we are kayaking with our team, Adriana and I conceal our Berettas in shoulder holsters that we wear beneath our windbreakers. The Berettas do not impede our movements. On the contrary, the feel of them against our shoulders invigorates us. We paddle with stronger rhythms, making certain that our knuckles are in line with the blade of the paddle, that we are holding the paddle twelve inches away from our bodies, and that with each kayaking stroke we allow the paddle to rotate and reposition in our "loose" left hands so that each paddle smoothly enters the water. In this moment, I can imagine Adriana's thoughts. They are like mine. While we are racing across the lake, we are thinking of the Beretta pistol that each of us is carrying. We are anticipating the hour when the killers will show themselves on a lake like this one or along a trail on the horse farm where we ride our Criollos or in the parking lot of a shopping mall.

Adriana and I are not always together. On each of these uncertain days, we immerse ourselves in our separate schedules at school. Many times, we do share the same classroom and participate in the same tennis match or swim meet or JROTC drills. But, despite the unlikely bond that our mutual danger has compelled us to forge with one another, we know that we have to confront fear and hesitation without leaning on each other. We know, too, that we are essentially alone when we face our inner demons or when we confront the all-too-human savages who want to rape and kill us.

I speak for myself now. I awake each morning with a nearly imperceptible tremor in my hands. I am more anxious than afraid. I am more accepting than resistant. Yet, as each new dawn awakens with me, I do not especially want the savagery to happen. But there is nothing I can do to keep it from happening. With every new day rousing my tense anticipation, I go forward to confront the imminent violence. I become my own keen-eyed sentry, capturing in rapid glances every nook and cranny of the rooms and halls I enter. I am never far from my Beretta or from the switchblade that I conceal beneath the waistband of my fashionable denims. I watch for Death to show his gruesome face. I calculate the seconds that it will take me to lift my pistol out of the shoulder holster beneath my jacket. I measure the time I will need to take hold of the switchblade, press the activation button, and watch the blade spring forward. On some days, I convince myself that I'll overcome my adversaries. I'll kill the thugs who want to kill me. I'll kill Death, the ugly specter that haunts me, and live to talk about it. On other days, I imagine that Fate's cards are stacked against me. Death is pursuing me. He is closing in on me. He will surely kill and claim me.

Yet whole weeks pass, and Death does not come to snare me away from my privileged life. The White Supremacists, who are the cadre of assassins that Death will be sending for me, never come near me. So I wait. I begin to believe that my sighting of the future has played me false. Perhaps, Kurt and his gang have backed off. I know that eventually they will attack Green Hills High School. My foresight shows me that, before they attack the school, Kurt's gang will try to kill Adriana and me. But no gang has attacked us. Nor have Gregor and Werner, the two thugs whom my vision revealed as our would-be murderers, come anywhere near us.

I grow confident again. I convince myself that Miss Dickinson has persuaded The First Spirit to push back the date of my death. I tell myself that the White Supremacists will try to kill Adriana and me not when we are alone together. Instead, they will attack us when we are in school with many of our closest friends.

Then, on the thirteenth day of May, in the thirteenth hour that is one o'clock in the afternoon, Adriana and I are ensnared by surprise.

Adriana and I are riding on our electric motor bikes through the woodlands of Green Hills, in the western section of our city. They are Turbo Vado bikes. Each of them is empowered by a 350-watt motor and by a 604-watt-hour lithium-ion battery. They are capable of traveling an impressive eighty miles on a single charge, they maintain a steady twenty miles per hour even on the most daunting of ascents, they can reach speeds of up to twenty-eight miles per hour, and they ride nimbly and quickly down hills, along city streets, and through paved trails.

We are on our way to visit Adriana's grandparents, who live just beyond the woods, in a retirement village that is located three miles from our homes. The baskets perched on the handlebars of each of our bikes are filled with gifts of art books and literary novels that I am bringing, as well as a long-sleeved, azure blue sweater that Adriana has knitted in her spare time for her grandmother. For her grandfather, Adriana is bringing a handmade and hand-painted traveling chess set from Ecuador that she discovered in a quaint shop in Newport, Rhode Island.

Bringing these gifts inspirits Adriana and me with new hope. The world doesn't seem quite so bleak. Eluding the dangers that will inevitably be trailing us once again becomes a reasonable possibility. If the afternoon breeze is chilly and sometimes biting, the wafer-like sun still sends its radiant beams to cheer us, and the green leaves of the tall red maple trees flash and flitter with delicate dancing rhythms that solace our senses.

But the cheerfulness and the solacing do not last for long.

No sooner do we reach the middle of the woods, where the canopies of trees are more abundant and shut out most of the sunlight, than Gregor and Werner make their move. This time Bram and Stefan are not with them. Gregor and Werner are traveling on the cusp of their own murderous fury. Driving their motorcycles with calculated recklessness and armed with stiletto knives and Glock G43 pistols, they rush upon Adriana and me. At first, we maneuver our e-bikes away from them, racing across the forest path and trying in vain to outdistance them. But Gregor and Werner are driving Kawasaki Z125 Pros that are capable of reaching one hundred miles per hour. They overtake us, slamming into our bikes and sending us toppling.

I have no time to lift my Beretta pistol out of the shoulder holster beneath my jacket. Werner has thrown off his helmet, jumped upon me, and pinned me down. I feel his whiskey breath upon my face. I see his prurient gaze upon me. With his big left hand still pinning me down, he frees his right arm and hand to grab the stiletto from the inside of his black leather jacket. I know what he intends to do. He is going to stab me to death and then have sex with my still-warm corpse.

"Girl, I'm going to rape you after I kill you," he says, with a guttural and excited whisper. "You won't even feel a thing."

As quick as a flash of lightning, I use my free right arm and hand as my weapons. With my arm raised and with my fingers held straight and tightly together and slightly bent at the knuckle, I stun him with a karate knife-hand strike to the side of his neck, where both his carotid artery and jugular vein are located. He sways, begins to fall sideways, and then pitches forward upon me. I struggle to release myself from the weight of his body. I try pivoting my body away from his, turning and swiveling and swinging my agile figure as I strain to be separated from his lumbering weight. No sooner do I free myself and begin to grab my Beretta from its holster, than he jumps up with a stiletto in his hand and stabs me in my chest. My senses fail me. I fall into a dark void, hear myself moaning, and leap back into consciousness. Werner is raising his bloodstained right hand again and, with an even more powerful thrust, is about to plunge the stiletto into my chest again.

Before he can cut into my heart, though, Adriana shoots him in the back of his head—once, twice, three times. Blood swooshes out of his forehead, his ears, and his mouth. His left eye flies out of its socket and lands an inch away from my shoulder, his aquiline nose collapses, and his front teeth shatter and drop upon his chin. His body totters, lurches, wobbles, and falls forward. I am too weak to pivot my body once again. I cannot free myself. Werner falls face down upon me. I pass out.

I awake in the post-surgical ward of the Green Hills Hospital. I am in a private room, surrounded by two efficient nurses who are reading my pulse and monitoring the tube that has been inserted into my chest at a line drawn from my right armpit to the lower junction of my chest bone. Heavily medicated, I cannot yet see the room and its people with unimpeded clarity. I drift in and out of awareness, sighting as in a filmed montage my parents' worried faces and the young, kind-hearted surgeon's encouraging expression. I see my brother Luke, with his sober attempt at remaining manly while he stifles the sobs that would reveal his sorrow. I also see my sister, Lorna, who does give way to crying and to telling me how much she loves me. On one of these journeys back into consciousness, I see Miss Patel's sensitive face, but I cannot decipher the words that she is speaking to me or thank her for the warm clasp of her hand upon my hand.

Then, on a day when I am convalescing well, Adriana visits me in this same hospital room.

"You are coming through it all very nicely," she says. "You were badly wounded, and yet you have survived."

Then all of it comes swiftly back to me. Adriana saved me. She saved herself as well.

I search the back of my mind. I peer way, way back into its remotest and most shadowy corners. I call back the afternoon when Gregor and Werner attacked Adriana and me. I observe once again the flare and flicker and burst of action that involved Adriana and Gregor, her gun-wielding enemy. While the action was ongoing, while it was alive and battering and murderous, I glimpsed it from afar in terrifying fragments that rose before my seeing while Werner was trying to kill me.

On that same woodland path that was leading Adriana and me to the home of her grandparents, Gregor is attacking Adriana. From the corner of my eyes, while I am fighting for my own life, I see Adriana confronting Gregor in deadly combat. I see her as she was then and as she remains: a savvy innocent who knows the wicked ways of some men and has learned how to fight back. When Gregor's motorcycle slams into her bike, Adriana is thrown free of the bike. But the force of her fall momentarily stuns her. Luck is on her side, though. The impact of his motorcycle crashing against the bike throws Gregor off his cycle. By the time he recovers his stance, Adriana is taking her Beretta out of her shoulder holster. Gregor, helmeted and agile, leaps upon her. They struggle for the pistol. He aims to take hold of it and then rape and kill her.

She doesn't let go of the pistol. But she needs to break free of the hold he has upon her wrist. Using a Jujitsu technique, she doesn't pull back to get out of his hold upon her. Instead, she squats down into a strong stance, leans forward, and bends her elbow all the way toward his forearm until he can no longer hold onto her wrist.

He does not notice that, for an instant, the Beretta falls out of her hand.

With whirlwind speed, Gregor grabs the Glock revolver from the inside pocket of his jacket. He keeps his hand high up on the handle of the revolver so that his thumb can wrap around to the opposite side. He points it at Adriana.

By this time, Adriana has retrieved her pistol and, while pointing it at Gregor, is about to fire it.

Gregor places his index finger on the outside of the Glock's trigger guard. He touches the trigger and then is about to press down on it.

Two shots ring out, but not from his revolver.

Adriana has fired her Beretta. The bullets crash through Gregor's heart, and he falls backward. He is dead, and she has killed him. His eyes remain staring in panicky surprise. Blood spills out of his chest, trickles down his right arm, and travels across the hand that keeps a tenuous hold upon the Glock revolver.

Without a pause and no hesitation, Adriana sees Werner raising his right hand that carries the stiletto. She sees him bringing it down and plunging it toward my heart. She fires her Beretta into the back of his head that the barrage of bullets turns in profile. She watches the swoosh of blood and brain cells and tissue flying out of his forehead; the blood-soaked, panicky eyes popping away from their sockets; and the startled, open mouth spewing out globs of blood and more blood and a dozen smashed teeth.

The ghastly scene finishes replaying inside my taut awareness. Then I come back to this moment in the hospital when a motherly nurse is checking my pulse and coaxing me to swallow a pill and to drink a Dixie cup of water. I like her motherliness. I swallow the pill and drink the water. She makes a quick exit, but she promises to return very soon.

In the meantime, I am left alone with Adriana, who is standing by my bed arranging the yellow, white, and red roses that her family has sent me. On another of my bed tables, she has also placed new biographies of Ruth Bader Ginsberg, an Associate Justice in the United States Supreme Court, and of the astronaut Mae Carol Jemison, the first African American woman to travel into space. On this same table, Adriana has tucked between the two books a bottle of Kate Spade's *Walk on Air* fragrance. The sight of the bottle cheers me, decorated as it is with a Tiffanyesque blue bow. It is my favorite *eau de parfum*, exuding layers of magnolia, lily of the valley, jasmine, and crinum lily.

"You and your family are spoiling me," I say.

"You've earned a little spoiling," she tells me.

"You're the belle of the ball," I remind her. "You are the hero who has defeated the villains."

"You've done your part, too," she says. "The television anchors and the newspaper journalists say so, and they are right."

She beams a smile at me. At this moment, she couldn't be happier. She has saved my life and her own. Because of her, we have passed the second test. We have battled our enemies and survived.

Without Adriana's noticing, I tremble even as I fake a smile to confirm her belief that I am as happy as she is. Of course I am relieved that Adriana has saved me and that she has overcome Gregor and Werner. Fate has granted us a reprieve from the new horror that awaits us. But Fate is an ambivalent acquaintance. She gives no clue that promises us another victory. She is merely biding time before the third test springs upon us.

CHAPTER FIFTEEN

THE THIRD TEST

I know the horror that lies before us. My foresight, diminished now though it is, shows me flashes of the gory scene that awaits me as well as many other students who will be caught up in it. This horror will explode into our third test. There is no way to escape the horror. My classmates and I will have quite literally to soldier through it.

Kurt Drexler will be the master plotter behind it. He and his platoon of forty killers, who call themselves White Supremacists, will storm Green Hills High School armed with Ar-15 rifles, the AGM-1 Carbine, the Beretta BM59, the Browning Semi-Auto 22, the Remington 750, the Smith & Wesson M & P 15-22, the Ruger SR-556, and the Mauser M1916. They will also carry stilettos, switchblades, and hand grenades.

All of these killers are discontented students currently enrolled in Green Hills High School. Many of them come from privileged backgrounds. The others come from dysfunctional homes with uncaring parents.

Kurt's gang of killers plans to shoot as many African American, Latinx, Asian, and Native American students as they can. They will be hunting down Shiloh, Dion, Jason, and other students from these minority backgrounds. They will search for them in the corridors, the gyms, the study halls, and the cafeteria. These White Supremacists will also be looking to kill Sonia, Abigail, Adriana, Brenda, Chloe, and all the other girls who have supported the #MeToo movement in our school and have worked with school counselors, parents, and the leaders in the Stop Sexual Assaults in the Schools (SSAIS) program. These same girls have worked with Title IX programs to prevent and to combat the prejudice and physical abuse directed against students because of their sexual preference or their gender transformations.

Kurt and the students who belong to his secret murder club will also be tracking down Adriana, Boyd, Ari, and me for personal reasons. He cannot forgive Adriana for spurning him or for killing Gregor and Werner, two of his best and secret friends. Nor can he forgive Boyd for winning Adriana's love when he, self-centered and psychotic Kurt, had planned to possess that love for himself alone. He has a score to settle with Ari, too, for being Jewish and for warning me against his morbid interest in committing the perfect murder. I am not surprised that Kurt wants to avenge himself against me. I refused to do his bidding. I walked away when he expected me to become his murderous puppet.

Thus far, Kurt has run free of any blame for Gregor's and Werner's brutal attack against Adriana and me. The police and two plainclothes detectives have questioned him, just as they questioned all the other senior boys in our school. They have been on the lookout for all the boys who have joined the neo-Nazi gangs and have bonded with the larger group of which the new Nazis are a part, the one that calls itself the White Supremacists. But there is no evidence that Kurt knew Gregor and Werner except from a distance. Even though all of them were seniors, they were never in one another's company in any way that indicated they were close friends or even casual friends except on the most detached or indifferent levels. Besides, Kurt has an unassailable alibi. On the day that Gregor and Werner tried to kill Adriana and me, Kurt was in New York with his parents for a photo shoot contrived by their publicity agents. The Drexlers are being presented to the world as the ideal careerists who also happen to be ideal parents.

The police and the detectives delete Kurt from their list of the youths who may be members of the White Supremacists or of the neo-Nazi gangs. They go on with their search.

I could tell them what I know. I could explain in careful detail that two members of Kurt's gang did try to murder and rape Adriana and me. I could tell these same detectives and policemen what my foresight shows me. A crime even more terrible is going to happen very soon. Kurt and his gang of forty killers will lay siege to our high school. Armed with assault weapons and grenades, they plan to kill at least a hundred students and a dozen or more teachers. I know that this siege is going to happen. I see it in my nightmares. I discover it in my traumatic musings as I traverse the highly polished corridors of my school and make my way with my classmates to my next class. I see its furious savagery and its blood-spewing murders flaring, palpable and relentless, every time that I observe Kurt in our gym or on a tennis court or in the school swimming pool or in our sociology class, where he, two other boys, and three girls are presenting their report about ways that American high schools can work to prevent thefts and murders that often take place on campuses across the country.

But I do not tell the local and state police or any detectives. They will not believe me. I know. My seeing into the future tells me so. I'll be very specific. I'll tell you exactly what I see when the future unfolds itself before my clairvoyant eyes. I see myself pleading with the security guards at my school. I see and hear them scoffing at my words.

"You're imagining things," these aged men say to me after I tell them that forty-one killers are plotting a massacre against my high school. "You're jumpy because you and Adriana have gone through a rough time. But you've come through. You're safe now. We're keeping an eye on this place. So are the police. You have nothing to worry about. "

"I hope that you are right," I say, even though I understand how wrongheaded they are.

I approach the local police with my fears. They are courteous. They are respectful. I'm one of the girls who bravely confronted two neo-Nazis.

"You have what it takes, young lady," the middle-aged captain says. "You have grit. That will always count in your favor."

The captain's assistant, a young lieutenant in his twenties, speaks these words to me.

"It's only natural that you are looking over your shoulder, expecting that other assassins will be there to shoot you down. You'll probably spend the rest of your life being on the alert and making certain that no guy is trying to shoot you down. There's nothing wrong with that. You're being smart not to be too trusting. But loosen up. Our police force and our city's detectives have you covered. There's no need to worry. You and your school are safe from harm"

"Oh, but I do worry," I say to myself. "In spite of what you believe, forty-one students who have formed a murder club *are* plotting a massacre against the school."

I tell my fears to the career-minded principal of our school. He, too, scoffs at my suggestion that rebellious and disaffected students will be storming the school with rifles, knives, and grenades. He has his eye on a future appointment as the superintendent of our school district. His self-regard and his ambitious nature do not allow him to imagine that the world's evil will assault the school that he so carefully administers.

"You are being overemotional," he says, quietly calibrating the even-tempered rhythms of his remark. "Nothing of the sort is going to happen. You have my promise."

His vanity overtakes his common sense. He ignores the violence that is occurring with alarming frequency in our neighboring schools. It is in his best interests to maintain the image of an infallible leader, a well-tested captain who oversees a smooth-running ship. He cares about the students. But he cares more about his career. He anchors his ambitious plans to his collaboration with the School Board. The men and women on that board are chary of allocating more money to our school. They have approved the building of a science wing, an additional gym, and a tennis court. But they have voted against increasing the security in Green Hills High School. They maintain that even a relatively affluent district like ours should not be spending money for protective strategies that may never be used.

Our School Board and our principal are ignoring dangers that are staring them in the face.

Neighboring school districts have more sensible leaders. They are posting armed guards on campus. They are bringing into their schools surveillance cameras that include facial recognition, hand-held metal detectors, buzzer systems, sheriff's deputies and off-duty police officers, protective vests for teachers and students, mandatory ID badges, and bullet shields to fit into students' backpacks. These districts are building chain-link fences that ring the inside of their schools' campuses. They are hiring teachers who carry concealed weapons permits and who have been trained to fire Berettas, Ar-15s, M-4 carbines, and M-9 pistols. Their high schools have life-saving trauma training classes that teach students to stanch the bleeding of classmates who have been wounded during mass casualty events. All their schools have limited points of entry; doors that lock automatically; foldable bulletproof walls, each with a two-panel barrier that comes out of the wall and provides a protective hiding place for students; and first-story windows that slide open and become escape exits from the killers hunting down students and teachers.

Green Hills High School has none of these things.

Now do you understand my dilemma?

I know with supernatural certainty almost everything about the tragedy that is going to happen in my school. I also know, with the same foresight and the same eerie certainty, that nobody will believe me when I sound warnings about the school massacre. So I do not plead with local and state policemen. I do not petition the help of the school security guards or of the principal.

I wait, not knowing when the massacre will occur or how it will end. I live my life, imagining that the sands in the finite hourglass that measures my days have almost run their course, the last of the sand grains allotted to me flowing out of time and sending me into Sojourn or eternal disappearance.

I wait, fulfilling all the tasks and confronting all the challenges that my time here on Earth requires of me. I become more accommodating to my classmates' need for attention or for understanding. I grow more aware of the problems they harbor and more willing to show my compassion through helpful words and deeds. I even regard my parents with new forbearance and with new signs of my emerging affection. They, in turn, arrange their schedules so that they can be at home more often, with guardian eyes and kind words encouraging my hope and spurring me on to new successes at school. More visibly concerned now about my wellbeing, they hire a detective to trail Adriana's and my every move. They fear that the White Supremacists and the neo-Nazis may avenge themselves against us because of the killing of Werner and Gregor.

After a week, though, I persuade my parents to dismiss the detectives. No one has attacked Adriana and me.

"Everything's all right," I tell them with a voice that is both gentle and confident. "The security people at school and the local police have us covered. Adriana and I want to get back to our normal routines. We don't have to spend the rest of our lives expecting that we are going to be assassinated."

"Maybe you are right," my father says. "You were lucky a few weeks ago, when Adriana saved you. Maybe you'll be lucky again. Maybe it's time for you to believe that you are safe."

My mother, whose interest in me still wavers in spite of her good intentions, agrees with my father.

"You're a spunky girl," she says. "There is nothing of the helpless maiden or the clinging and distressed female about you. I'm glad that I have a daughter who is strong-minded and courageous. I wouldn't have you any other way."

I let them talk. I have no desire to hurt my parents. They are who they are. They are ambitious, worldly, self-centered, and self-serving. They have made their pact with a wily world. They know the score. More than a few times they have said, "Get out of my way," to anyone that they perceived as an openly declared adversary or as a witless and too-conservative ally.

I do not tell them what my visionary eyes have shown me. I do not reveal to them the harsh and unremitting truth of my situation.

But I have told you the truth. I'll tell it to you again. These quiet days after Werner and Gregor nearly killed Adriana and me have not dispelled the horror that is moving with calculated velocity toward the students and teachers at Green Hills High School. My classmates and I may die in a few days. I need to find a way that I can save them, even if I cannot save myself.

Here are the facts that you should consider once more.

The White Supremacists have not made a move against us. Kurt and his thugs are too smart for that. They are not interested in avenging themselves only against two girls. They are plotting a mass shooting at my high school. Including Kurt, there will be a platoon of forty-one killers. They will kill at least a hundred students.

I alone cannot save those students. I need to work with a group of brave students. I need to choose one teacher who is savvy and brave enough to lead us into battle when the White Supremacists attack our school.

I choose Mr. Marchand, because of his courageous service as a Marine in our country's war in Afghanistan in 2012. I choose him, too, because he is the leader of our school's JROTC program. He is unlike the retired veterans who lead most JROTC programs. He is young. He is a war hero in the prime of his life. Because of the shortage of veterans who are available for JROTC programs around the country, the Federal government has allowed Mr.

Marchand to lead our program. Every Green Hills cadet respects and trusts him. He is a realist. Battle-tested, he has experienced first-hand the savage nature of human beings. Beneath his even-tempered manner, there lives the combat-ready disposition of a field-grade Marine. More than a few times, he has remarked to Green Hill High's cadets that our school needs to map out a plan for defending itself against any killers who lay siege to the school armed with semi-automatic rifles and hand guns, as well as grenades and tear gas.

I visit Mr. Marchand when he is alone in his office within the south wing of our school. He had locked the door, because he was examining two drill purpose rifles that JROTC cadets will be using in our marching exercises. When he opens the door and allows me to enter, I see his need for privacy. With meticulous care and with ingrained expertise, he is removing the firing pins from an M1903 Springfield rifle and from an M1 Garand. The American walnut wood of the gunstocks gleams across the large desk on which he has placed the rifles. Our school cadets are not allowed to fire loaded rifles. We use the Springfields and the Garands for drills, for public marching demonstrations, and for high-flying, exhibition-style group maneuvers.

I tell Mr. Marchand my fears. I explain how Kurt Drexler and his gang plan to commit "the perfect crime" and get away with it.

Tall as a giant and just as rugged, Mr. Marchand imparts a laser-sharp awareness of everything and everyone around him. With one steady gaze, he can estimate the number of persons seated or standing in a room that he is entering. He can detect the persons most likely carrying a weapon inside the slight bulge of a windbreaker or beneath the pocket of a suit jacket. With that same canny gaze, he can locate the entrances and the exits from a room that is new to him. He can calibrate the speed it would take to race across the room to apprehend a fleeing thief or to leap out of a convenient window or to jump upon a would-be assailant.

In this moment, he is directing his gaze upon me. It is a gaze both gentle and inquiring.

"How do you know?" he asks me. "How do you know for certain that Kurt Drexler and his gang are plotting a massacre?"

I tell him about my frayed relationship with Kurt.

"He wanted me to be his accomplice. When I walked away from him and his plan, he sent Werner and Gregor to kill Adriana and me."

"Have you told the police?"

"I have not. If they did a check on Kurt and the gang that calls themselves White Supremacists, they would find no evidence that could prove Kurt and his secret friends are planning to do anything wrong."

"Yet you still feel certain that these White Supremacists are going ahead with their massacre."

"I do," I answer with no hesitation. "Green Hills needs to prepare for a school shooting. Even if I'm wrong, we won't have lost a thing. If I'm right, we have a chance to survive as long as we are prepared to fight back. We can't afford to do nothing. We need to act now. We need to be ready. We need to arm ourselves with the best weapons."

With quiet gravity, Mr. Marchand listens to my excited remarks. He notices the absolute conviction that I bring to my appeal for his help. He detects the logic in my thinking, the street-wise perception of my comments, and the traceries of desperation and despair in my voice. But only for an instant does he pause to consider the validity of everything that I am telling him. He sees that I am on the level. He accepts as credible and prescient my warning about the horror that is hastening toward our school.

"We do need to prepare ourselves," he says, decisive and commanding. "We'll have to move fast and in secret. We'll enlist our squadron of cadets to help us. There's much that we must do before we can tell ourselves that we are ready. I'll call a meeting of our cadets. Together, we'll make a plan and carry it through."

I feel a cloud lifting. I breathe more easily. Yet I want to hear Mr. Marchand tell me again.

"You're really going to help us?"

"Of course I am. I couldn't live with myself if I didn't heed your warning and come out fighting."

"We don't have much time. Do you think we can do it?"

"Let's find out," he says. "Let's do it and see what happens."

During the late afternoon of the following day, Mr. Marchand holds a secret meeting at his home to devise with twenty JROTC cadets the combat strategies we'll put into action if Kurt's platoon of school shooters attacks our school. Shiloh, Dion, Jayden, Jason, Abigail, Brenda, Sonia, Chloe, Ari, Boyd, Alessandro, Adriana, and I are among the cadets who work together to create a military plan that may save our lives.

The Cooper twins, Daniel and David, are also in our squadron. They are dark-haired and lanky athletes. They also happen to be sharpshooting members of our schools' rifle club. I have not mentioned them previously because my contact with them has been limited to our cadet drills. They are in none of my other classes, and they travel in social groups different from my own. I view their presence in our squadron as a good sign. With their well-honed physicality and their experience as riflemen, they will bring formidable powers to our team. I know. I recognize them in the flashes of the future that rise before my special seeing. But I do not know whether their powers will be enough to save us.

These are the other cadets in our squadron: Miguel Armendáriz, a brown-skinned émigré from Brazil and an excellent goalie on our school's hockey team; Dolores Chavez, an exchange student from Venezuela; Lars Richter, educated mostly in Berlin and now our school's most brilliant student in the sciences and foreign languages; Julieanne Watanabe, one of the great beauties in our school, as well as an excellent student, a peerless gymnast, and a pilot of small aircraft; and Erik Johansen, an accomplished swimmer, an aspiring architect, and the captain of our rowing team. All of them are extraordinary. Every one of them enhances our JROTC program. Though I have only a passing acquaintance with them, I am confident that they would help me and anyone else who might need a kind word or a life-saving rescue. Our squadron is very lucky to have them on our military team.

These seven cadets are lucky, too. They did not die in the school shooting that killed me, along with ten other students and two teachers. Over and over again, I remind myself what has happened to those of us who were shot. We died and briefly found ourselves in Sojourn, a natural satellite orbiting between finite Earth and the eternal First Heaven. Yet, here on Earth again, we who have died are not ghosts. The Five Spirits have granted us a reprieve from death. They have given us back our lives, though for how long I cannot tell. We are here to relive the violent scene that killed us. We are struggling to make certain that the violence of that scene will play out differently. Our JROTC team does not want to be taken by surprise. We do not intend to allow the villains to conquer us. During all of these months of our senior school year and in our freshman, sophomore, and junior years, too, we have trained hard to be a precision team. Now, in these few weeks that fate has granted us, we are becoming battle-ready. Every member of our team is a proficient soldier. Every one of us has made a friend of hair-trigger responses.

Miss Patel is also that kind of team member. As our deputy commander, she, too, attends our meeting that outlines our battle goals. Like her fiancé Mr. Marchand, she is a tried-and-true combat veteran. She served as a machine gunner in the First Battalion of the Marine Corps during our war in Iraq.

Including me, there are twenty cadets in our squadron. There are also two teachers.

As commanders in our corps, Mr. Marchand and Miss Patel have secured the approval of our school superintendent, Mr. Aaron Worthington. A Marine hero who fought alongside Mr. Marchand in Afghanistan, Mr. Worthington disdains the conservative policies of the School Board and of our school principal. Instead of waiting for a tragedy to happen before board members allow our school to fortify itself with armed guards, metal detectors, and a vault of high-powered rifles, he persuades his friends in the National Rifle Association to donate twenty-two rifles to our JROTC plan for protecting Green Hills High School.

Our first order of business is to vote in favor of arming ourselves with semi-automatic assault rifles and pistols. Mr. Marchand's friends in Maine's National Guard agree to lend us additional M-16 A2 assault rifles, M-4 Carbines, M-9 pistols, Remington 750s, Mauser 1916s, and Sig Sauer P229 pistols. Mr. Marchand, our commander, will store our weapons in the floor-to-ceiling gun vault that is located in the arms room that is connected to his office. All of the cadets are familiar with the air gun rifles that we use in our marksmanship competitions. We have also used Beretta pistols and Magnum 44s, because of our training sessions in our local gun club. But during our free hours within the next few days and for several hours on Saturday, we report to the Green Hills shooting range for instruction on the firing of weapons that are new to us. There, Mr. Marchand, Miss Patel, and the Cooper twins put us through our paces as we learn to handle with increasing confidence the high-powered weapons that we'll be using if any school shooters invade Green Hills High School.

Over the next few days, our squadron of cadets grows more hopeful at least some of the time. They believe that we have a fighting chance if Kurt's White Supremacist gang invades our school. But their hope does not dispel their tension. They have no way of knowing what is going to happen when they confront the savages who want to kill at least a hundred students in our school.

We wait, even as we fulfill our academic and extracurricular obligations. Sometimes, we lose hope. We ponder the likelihood of defeat and the swift dying from our killers' bullets. In whispered meetings within our school's corridors, we share each other's nightmares. We try to dispel one another's fears. We try to laugh away the horrific aspects of our situation. At our best, we stay tough. Fatalistic and steadfast, we accept our destiny. Come what may, we'll assume our battle positions. Without a cry of despair or a desperate plea for mercy, we'll confront our enemies. We'll aim our loaded Ar-15s, our M-16s, our Mauser M1916s, and our M-4 Carbines, and we'll shoot our enemies back to the hell that spawned them.

In the meantime, we keep busy.

With the permission of the superintendent, we equip as many classroom doors in our school as we can with lockdown locks that lock a door from the inside. We equip other doors with a Bolo Stick, a barricade device that prevents intruders and killers from opening the door. But there isn't enough time to deploy these devices on every door. Nor is there time to install inflatable escape slides that, with a pull on a lever, spring forward from the space just beneath second-and-third-story school windows. Instead, we show our teachers how to tie a rope or cord around the knob of the door that they want to keep shut. We show them, as well, how to tie the end of the rope or cord to another doorknob in the room. Tying this rope or cord to a similar door that opens away from you gives the first door an anchor. The door becomes a barrier that keeps out gun-wielding assassins.

We work with our school's parent/teacher organization to raise funds for buying bullet shields that fit into students' backpacks. We collect additional funds for protective vests.

We persuade the owner of a fencing company to build at a reduced cost many chain-link fences that will surround the inside of the campus. The superintendent, in turn, convinces the School Board and taxpayers to allocate the payment for the fences that will provide much-needed protection for our school.

We urge a window installation firm to offer us a cost-effective business transaction that will persuade the School Board to pay for floor-to-ceiling, bulletproof windows that slide open as escape exits from a school shooter who has entered the first floor.

We study in new ways and with a keener understanding the entrance and exit points in each wing of our school. We measure our speed whenever we leave a wing and hurry forward to Mr. Marchand's office and the armory that adjoins it. We calculate the time it will take us to run to this JROTC arms room and take hold of our rifles.

We continue to fulfill all our academic obligations and our extracurricular commitments, too.

We go on spending our free hours at the gun firing range, striving to improve the way we handle the AR-15s, the M-16s, and the M-4 Carbines.

We keep a check on Kurt Drexler, on Stefan and Bram, and on the other renegades that we often see with Bram and Stefan, but never with Kurt.

We cadets do all these things while we wait for the horror of those marauding assassins to close in upon us.

Though my foresight does not permit me to know whether I am going to die from an assassin's bullet, I have a premonition that I shall soon die a second death. In my heart, I begin to say goodbye to the classmates that I have known well enough to regard as friends, acquaintances, and adversaries. I say goodbye in my own way, without mentioning the word or allowing eleventh-hour recriminations to sentimentalize my matter-of-fact character. What's done is done. There is no time to revive the dead ends or the missed connections of friendship or to translate my inchoate grief-sounds into words. To find such words might testify to the necessity of language even as those words prove its inadequacy. Instead, I push myself into even more rigorous training for the battle in which I have to save as many of my fellow cadets as I can, though I may not be able to save myself.

The hours at night are the worst for me. At my desk in my room at home, when I am writing a term paper for my sociology class or reading an assigned novel, I am waiting for the inevitable disaster that I do not especially want to happen. I wait alone. In the middle of some nights, I wake up screaming, remembering the burning implosion of the bullets that tore my lungs and heart apart in the school shooting that kicked me out of existence not so long ago.

In the mornings and in the early evenings when I am at home, I am kinder to my parents and more attentive to my brother Luke and my older sister Lorna. I convey my affection for each of them through subtle, almost imperceptible, gestures. I help my mother cook a Sunday pot roast when our housekeeper happens to be away. I join my father for a game of golf when my mother is busy with her classical music club. I tutor my sister in the intricacies of algebra, and I take the time to help my brother Luke paint his room.

If I die in this next school shooting, I shall miss each member of my family. I have no intention of telling you that they are perfect human beings or that I have a need to see them every day. They are like you and me. They are fallible, yet they wear their faults with an inherent ease and with a nearly casual indifference or a lack of awareness. I wouldn't have them any other way. They are not phonies. They've never hidden behind lies. They've never been stymied by fake philosophies or duped by insidious people. Beneath their courteous surfaces, they are street-smart. If I die, they'll grieve about me for a few months or even for a year or two. But then they'll move on. They'll move forward. I respect them for that.

In Sojourn or even in the First Heaven, I know that I shall miss them whenever I happen to think about them. Possibly, the Five Spirits will allow me to come back to Earth to observe or even to interrelate with them as a Spirit or a Shadow or as a Shape-Shifter, a human being with a different identity. My foresight does not tell me all the changes that will happen for me after I die a second time.

Alone in my room, enclosed by the dark and trapped by my apprehension, I grow morbid. I go on waiting for the tragedy to unfold. I imagine once again the massacre that is a blood-gushing, mushrooming cloud swallowing me up as a barrage of bullets rips open my body and burns my insides to the socket.

On the first Monday in June, when our senior class is only two weeks away from graduation, I am at lunch in the school cafeteria with Chloe, Alessandro, Sonia, and Jayden. I notice Kurt Drexler at a distant table, surrounded by a cadre of his swimming, boxing, and tennis teammates. Clearly, he is their leader, though in their young manly ways they calibrate their adulation with understated acknowledgment of his supremacy. He wears their subdued worship of him with an easy informality. At the moment, I hear fragments of their lively conversation. Kurt and his friends are exchanging their views about the errors they could have avoided in a recent tennis match, the vigorous strokes of a first-rate competitor in a swim meet, and the new tires that one of them bought for his top-notch Audi. A lighthearted remark from a rugged red-haired fellow whose name is unknown to me stirs the laughter of the six boys in the group.

Kurt seems very happy. In that instant, I wonder whether he has changed his mind about the school shooting. My heart beats faster. Possibly, the deaths of Werner and Gregor have given him pause. I tell myself that, against all the odds and in spite of his murderous scheming and inherent rottenness, Kurt has abandoned his plot to kill a hundred students. Even as Alessandro and Chloe tell me about a new adventure movie that they saw on the weekend, I keep my attention focused in part upon the surprise of a lighthearted Kurt. I listen politely to their remarks and hear myself promising to catch up with the movie as soon as I can. I hear Sonia and Jayden tell me about their early acceptance to the University of Notre Dame. I also feel the elation that comes over me, I hear the congratulatory words that I offer them, and I watch their beaming faces. There is so much happiness inside them and so much love for each another.

Again my hope rises. Surely, Kurt has come to his senses. He has so much to live for. His is a life filled with privileges. He has changed his mind. He will not go through with his sadistic plan. He has too much to lose.

Then I notice him watching me. With the penetrating gaze of his cold blue eyes, he studies me. No longer does he laugh. His stern features and tight-lipped expression quickly dispel the suggestion of a warm heart and a kind disposition. His gaze upon me is not only cold. It is also murderous.

The friends who are with him take their cue from him. They, too, direct their attention to me. An invisible Spirit, perhaps, or more probably my appearance has weaved a spell upon them and peeled away their disguised civility. No longer do Kurt's cohorts impart a hardy wholesomeness. As they stare at me, their rugged features turn somber and threatening. Though they harness their savage instincts to temperate words and low-keyed responses, I see them for who they are. They are Kurt's henchmen, and they intend to lay siege to Green Hills High School within the next twenty-four hours.

At the close of the school day and before I report for swimming practice, I hurry to Mr. Marchand's office to tell him my impressions of Kurt and his gang. Immediately, he puts our JROTC squad on military standby. He wants to alert the state and city police, as well as our school principal. But I convince him that they will not help us. I remind him of what the police and our principal have said in the past. I tell him what they will say now, if we petition them for help. They will say that our school has its experienced security guards, its lock-down drills, and its bullet-shield backpacks to help students and teachers if any assassin enters our school. They will not redress our concern that no metal detectors or surveillance cameras protect our school. They will insist that there is no need to bring in the police force or state troopers. We'd only be wasting taxpayers' money. I know with bitter certainty that they will say all these things. I see into the future. I hear their adamant rebuttals that undermine our warnings about the danger that is coming toward us. They scoff with contempt or casually dismiss our fears.

Mr. Marchand phones his friend, a battle-proven colonel in the National Guard, to place some guardsmen on our school campus. But the colonel explains why the guardsmen are not available. Many of them have deployed to our continuing war in Afghanistan. Other guardsmen have travelled away from Maine, rescuing the victims of a turbulent hurricane in Mississippi or assisting a search-and-rescue mission in New Hampshire, where six middle school boys and their scoutmaster who were climbing Mount Washington along the Tuckerman Ravine were caught in a violent and unexpected wind storm and have gone missing.

"We're on our own," Mr. Marchand tells me after speaking with the colonel. "Our squadron has to hang tough. Nobody will save our school except ourselves."

"We'll do our best, sir," I tell him while addressing him in a military manner.

"Of course we will," he says as a worried frown touches his brow.

He pauses, considers quietly the thought that gnaws at his certainty, and then finds the words that reveal it.

"If only we knew exactly when the gang of assassins is going to attack us."

"Very soon, sir," I answer him. "Tomorrow is the day. About one o'clock tomorrow afternoon, the White Supremacists will be rushing upon us with their rifles and grenades. I know, sir. I see the killers on the rampage in our school. I see the fleeing students and teachers. I see all of it, as if it were happening right now, though I cannot explain why or how I see."

My voice, tightly controlled, carries no tears or whimpering. Tears cannot help our school now or even a panicky cry for mercy. So positive am I about what I am telling him, so steadfast in my belief that I have witnessed the future before it happens, that Mr. Marchand observes me with new interest. His quickened glance reveals a clarified seeing and a calm acceptance of this clairvoyant gift that makes me special.

"You're a strange girl," he says. "Maybe that's why I want to believe what you are saying. At any rate, we'll be ready. Let come what may tomorrow. We'll keep fighting until we conquer or die."

All that night and into the early hours of day, we wait.

Then, at a quarter to one in the school-busy June afternoon that sends its pre-summer radiance through the panoramic windows and glass walls of our school, Kurt and his White Supremacist gang rush upon us. With AR-15s, M16 A2s, AGM-1 Carbines, M-9 Pistols, and Sig Sauer Pistols, they overtake the school. With M-2 fragmentation grenades, they blow out windows and doors and blocked-off entrances. The grenades kill an aged security guard with no military or police experience who left his post without permission at the main entry point of the school and was on his way to get a cup of coffee in the school cafeteria. They also kill two officials from the mayor's office who had come to the school to lodge a complaint about the petition that the Parents' and Teachers' Association recently submitted for money to pay for sheriff's deputies and off-duty police officers, surveillance cameras mounted high upon school walls, buzzer systems, classrooms with doors that lock automatically, rapid escape slides, and the training of armed teachers.

Instantly, the explosion in the north wing of the main building alerts my JROTC classmates, Miss Patel, and Mr. Marchand that the White Supremacists have begun their siege of our school.

Many of my fellow cadets are in classrooms within different wings of the main building. We race out of these various classrooms and head for the arms room behind Mr. Marchand's office. Without taking time to suit up in our camouflage uniforms, we grab and load our Ar-15s and our Mauser M1916s, dash with lightning speed out of the arms room down through a long, empty corridor, turn left, and burst into the south wing of the school.

By now, sirens are blaring the signals for lockdown. I imagine teachers bolting their doors and students scurrying to hide inside cloakrooms and storerooms and beneath their desks. I am wondering how long it will take the killers to trap students hiding in out-of-the-way stairwells and to break through doors with fragile locks. But I do not wonder for long. Ahead of me, as I rush into the south wing, I enter the field of battle.

There, in the distance that looms its murderous power before us, I see the White Supremacists aiming and firing their weapons at five adult visitors to the school. While he is running forward, Bram mows down a middle-aged building inspector, that gray-haired fellow with a pale complexion and stern features keeling over at once while blood and brain cells spill out of his head and land on the left shoulder of his black windbreaker.

Without breaking the speeding rhythms of his gait, Stefan shoots a young, blonde woman in the heart. I recognize her as Miss Bicknell, a well-regarded professional photographer whom the principal had commissioned to come to our school to take yearbook pictures of students at work in our new science and foreign language labs.

Another White Supremacist, who is short, dark-haired, and rugged, comes face to face with Mr. Grainger, a popular African American who has taught us advanced computer technologies. This killer pauses to study his unarmed victim's reaction. The look of terror and the unspoken cry for mercy freeze upon Mr. Grainger's final awareness. Without any hesitation, the assassin shoots him in the forehead, throat, and chest. Instantly, blood surges out of Mr. Grainger's ears, eyes, throat, and lungs. He falls straight down upon the blood-smeared, polished floor. For an instant, his body stays in a kneeling position. It wavers from side to side and then falls backward. I hear the thud of his head against the floor.

A killer with a buzz cut and light-skinned features speeds across the corridor and fires two bullets from his M-4 Carbine into a wan-looking mother with faded red hair and freckled features, and into her perky five-year-old daughter, whose red hair glows with a natural sheen. The child's freckled face enhances her cuteness. Swiftly, as he passes them, this killer blasts their lives away. His bullets blow away the top of the mother's head and smash through the girl's throbbing heart.

I know. I can see what is happening, as if I were standing next to all of these victims. But I cannot stop it.

My fellow cadets run forward with lightning speed, our weapons now firing their bullets.

The White Supremacists hurry to meet us, returning our gunfire.

I notice eight, ten, twelve, sixteen, twenty of them converging upon us. They race through the long corridor and never cease firing their bullets at us. Their shots are often wild and miss their human targets.

Shiloh, Sonia, and Dion shoot down the first three of the killers who breach the invisible wall that has thus far separated our squadron from them. Shiloh's and Sonia's bullets cut through two of the killers' chests and eyes. Dion's bullet crashes into his enemy's skull, and blood swooshes out of the top of that killer's head and out of his eyes, nose, and ears.

Jayden, Abigail, and Chloe barrage a corps of four killers with Ar-15 bullets. Their enemies fall away in an instant, their eyes glazed with the surprise and furious impact of swift death.

Ari, Jason, and Sonia jump out of an alcove that leads them into the middle of the corridor. They quickly pursue the White Supremacists who have already passed by this alcove without leaving a sentry to shoot down anyone who intends to rush into the corridor and fire away at the backs of the White Supremacists.

Ari, Sonia, Brenda, and Jason do exactly that. They come at their enemies from behind and shoot away four of them, their bullets burning through their lungs and exploding out of their blood-spraying chests.

A bullet from one of these enemies who has turned around to confront us cuts down Ari. He quickly falls way from the relentless charge that our group goes on making against our enemies. Whether Ari is dead, I cannot take time to find out. He falls face down and is very still.

I fire a bullet into the face and mouth of the thug who has shot Ari. He falls backward, his eyes wide-staring and his throat gurgling with the blood spewing out of it and out of his mouth.

I never stop running forward, always aiming my rifle at the next enemy I am going to confront.

Sonia, Brenda, and Jason join our group of cadets. We rush onward, led by Mr. Marchand and Miss Patel. We intercept five of the assassins who are racing toward a corner in the long corridor that will lead them to the locked classrooms that they will probably grenade or attempt to shoot away the locks or fire through the makeshift barricades. One of these enemies is Stefan, the most savage member of Kurt's gang. The bullets from his M-16 burn through Miss Patel's left arm and graze her left shoulder. Her body shudders momentarily, yet she keeps on running forward while she rakes the air with gunfire, taking down not only Stefan, but also two of his cohorts.

With their Ar-15s and a M-4 Carbine, Mr. Marchand, Sonia, Adriana, and Brenda kill off the four remaining assassins who are about to turn the corner and hasten onto the alcove that leads to a galaxy of classrooms.

We keep running onward. Our weapons keep firing at every one of the marauding killers who are racing toward us.

Leaping out of an alcove on the left side of the corridor, Alessandro, Dolores Chavez, and Julieanne Watanabe join us. They are carrying Sig Sauer and M-9 pistols in shoulder holsters. But they are wielding Ar-15 rifles.

Alessandro and Dolores mow down four more of the White Supremacists.

In the same instant, an assassin's bullet wings Julieanne in her left leg, but she keeps on running forward while returning her enemy's fire. Her bullets smash through his chest and through the top of his head as he falls backward, instantly dead.

No other assassins appear before us. We leave this wide and long corridor behind us, covered as it is with the bullet-torn bodies of more than two dozen assassins.

I hear gunshots ringing out from a shadowy corner that leads to a corridor in the east wing. Thirty feet ahead of me, my team does not hear the shots or they make a split-second decision to move ahead to different targets.

Now Erik Johansen, Lars Richter, and Boyd Henderson join me, as we turn on to the embattled corner that will lead us into the east wing. When we round the corner, we see the bullet-riddled bodies of our school principal and of the burly and cantankerous vice-president of the School Board sprawled in awkward postures upon the gleaming floor. Their torsos are splayed face downward and in profile across the pools of blood spilling from their heads, their mouths, and their chests.

We also see the blood-drenched corpse of a rugged African American; a fearful image of a mutilated face that is no longer a face but only shards of raw flesh that belonged to an even younger Asian girl; the protruding bones of an Hispanic boy's teenage body and the gaping hollow of his smashed face and toothless mouth.

No sooner do we sight the five corpses, than five White Supremacists jump out of a shadowy corner firing endless rounds as they catch us in an ambush.

Zigzagging and weaving, we dodge their bullets and then let loose the full range of our firepower.

Lars shoots away the face and skull of the most gruesome of the Supremacists.

Erik takes down an assassin whose rifle has jammed.

Boyd blows away the gaunt assassin whose face is scarred. He also fires upon and kills Bram, the most rugged of these assassins whose left eye is covered with a black patch and gives him the look of a pirate.

My bullets cut through an assassin whose wounded right arm impedes his clasp of his rifle and his aim. For a moment, I hesitate. I want him to throw down his weapon and surrender. But he goes through with the shot and misses. My bullet cuts through his heart, and he falls dead.

We move faster. We speed along this hall and rush into the east wing, where a cluster of portable classrooms looms before us. These rooms are located in an open bay, and their fragile doors and windows render the students and teachers trapped within them especially vulnerable.

No sooner do we burst into the wing, than we come face to face with Kurt Drexler and six of his savage henchmen. Racing forward, all of them are firing Mauser M 98 rifles at us.

We spray the air with our bullets. Erik and Lars cut down three of these assassins who are about to unpin their grenades and heave them toward the doors of the unprotected classrooms. Our bullets rip through the chests and faces of the assassins, and blood rushes out of their bodies as they fall away to death.

As though we are human whirlwinds, Boyd and I confront Kurt and the remaining three assassins.

Boyd barrages the group with bullets from his M-16. His bullets kill the three killers that were serving as backup for Kurt. But their Mauser bullets inflict damage upon Boyd. The rapid fire of these bullets rips through his left shoulder, his chest, and his right leg. Boyd falls down, and I wonder whether he is dead.

The thought touches my awareness only for a moment. I have no time to consider anyone except the enemy that is facing me.

Kurt eyes me with a malevolent stare.

"It's your turn to die, baby," he says. "You and I made this date a long time ago."

He fires his Mauser into me. The bullets rip through my chest, my left shoulder, and my right leg.

Staggering, I fire back again and again.

The bullets from my Ar-15 blast through Kurt's chest and graze the left side of his head.

He also staggers, the impact of the bullets reeling his senses and clipping his aggressive motion.

I fire again, and my bullet rushes through his forehead, blowing away the top of his head, but not before his last bullet smashes into my heart.

In the instant that I die, I become aware that the First Spirit has condemned Kurt and his savage gang to eternal disappearance.

I go out of time and beyond the life I have known here on Earth. I do not look back. There is no need to look back. My foresight shows me that Ari and Boyd have not died. The city of Green Hills is already hailing them, all the other cadets, and our two teachers as heroes who saved hundreds of lives because of their courage and their skill at handling a rifle. The city is also hailing me as a hero who gave her life so that her classmates and teachers could go on living. The friends who understood my troubled soul lament my passing.

Boyd and Adriana will eventually marry each other after they complete their undergraduate studies in Europe. Ari and Sonia will remain friends and go forward to other partners. The tears that these four shed for me are genuine. But my critics pay me left-handed compliments. They say that, although I was an errant creature for almost all of my days, I redeemed myself on my final day through my sacrifice and my heroism.

 My parents keep their sorrow private. In public, they bear up. They busy themselves with their careers and train themselves to think about me only on my birthday and during a few of the national holidays. My brother Luke misses me most of all, and my sister Lorna pays homage to me by writing a *New York Times* article about my self-reliance, my abilities as an athlete, and my interest in bio-chemistry. Once in a while, she weeps for me, though never in public.

I do not weep. Regret and nostalgia are instantly bleached out of me. Once more, I am dead. I am a wandering Spirit in search of a new home. Already, I know that, within this very instant, I am returning to Sojourn, the natural satellite that serves as a temporary haven for those of us who have recently died. The journey is swift and trouble-free.

I arrive. I am here in Sojourn.

I am still full-bodied, yet I am vanishing by nearly imperceptible degrees. By the end of my training in the Afterlife, I shall disappear completely and will be visible only to other Spirits except for those missions that require me to become full-bodied once again.

Miss Dickinson is here to greet me. She is as full-bodied as I am.

"You have done well," she tells me. "You have successfully completed the mission that made your life on earth necessary."

"You knew how all of it would end," I say. "You always knew."

"Not all of it, my dear," she answers me. "The First Spirit gave you the freedom to make your own choices. We five Secondary Spirits watched you and your fellow cadets helping teachers and students prepare for the school shooters. We watched you as you spent hours upon hours at the rifle range, improving your marksmanship and gaining confidence as you handled the Ar-15s, the M-4 Carbines, and other weapons. At the same time, we deprived you from knowing what was going to happen when you confronted the assassins. You stood your ground. You did not flinch. You have grown wise. You understand sacrifice and courage and why they matter."

"Is that the reason you sent me back to Earth? So that I could find out whether I had it in me to sacrifice my life for others and to fight the racists who wanted to kill everyone who looked and thought differently from themselves."

Miss Dickinson ponders my question and then offers me a brisk reply.

"That is one of the reasons," she says. "You must remember that most of your classmates who were innocent victims of your plotting were not supposed to die. That is why they were allowed to go back to Earth and relive the day of the shooting."

"Why did I die?" I ask. "Why did I lose my life a second time?"

"It was your destiny, my dear," she says. "The First Spirit had decreed that you should have a chance to close your life in an admirable way. He was testing you. It's wonderful that you have come through it all. You have passed the test. Now you shall be rewarded."

She is genuinely elated on my behalf. I do not yet share that elation. Nevertheless, there hovers within the secret corner of my soul a finished feeling that influences me to believe that what has happened to me is not only inevitable, but also natural.

Being here in the spacious halls and rooms and countryside of Sojourn teases my curiosity. I see luminous visions and accurate wall videos of the Afterlife that lies before me. At my side as she continues to mentor me, Miss Dickinson sees them, too. She waves her hand, and the image of myself as a Ghost Commando flashes before my awareness. I see myself with other ghostly commandos fighting tyrants and their war-mongering armies from foreign countries. I see my commando unit combatting drug lords, vice rings, child abusers, and crooked politicians.

Miss Dickinson allows me to see more of the Afterlife that has already begun to enfold me. She shows me the video panels that trace my future roles as a relentless Shadow haunting a guilt-ridden criminal on Earth and as a Benevolent Specter bringing solace and hope to a convalescing middle school boy who has broken his leg during a skiing trip. Most exciting of all, she allows me to see myself as an altogether different self, a Shape-Shifter inhabiting the identity of an African American being wrongfully arrested in a Southern ghetto or a young woman in an East Coast city being handled roughly by a prurient employer or by a jaded boyfriend or by a sadistic husband. I fight back, with a stun gun or a court summons or a public exposure of their wrongdoing.

"I like what I see," I tell Miss Dickinson. "There's adventure in it. I feel as though I haven't really died."

"You have died to your first life," she explains. "Now you are beginning a second life. You will be tested in different ways. Your new life will keep challenging you to make the right choices and to maintain your integrity and your courage."

"But I'm still alive!" I cry out, savoring the happiness of this moment. "I'm alive here in Sojourn. I'll be supremely alive if I'm lucky enough to get into The First Heaven. I'll be gloriously and stupendously alive when I return to Earth to watch and protect my parents, brother, and sister, and all the classmates who called me their friend."

Miss Dickinson joins me in my happiness. Her face glows with the pleasure of observing my elation.

"Of course you are alive," she says. "The Spirit world needs you. We need your authentic courage, your steadfast assurance, and your keen mind."

"I'm in it again," I remark. "I exist here in Sojourn and eventually I'll exist in The First Heaven and occasionally in a journey back to Earth. I exist for the good of all these worlds. I'm beginning to understand what a wonderful thing it is to be alive, every single minute, no matter what problems I'm facing and what world I call my own, even temporarily."

Miss Dickinson laughs with the sheer joy of hearing all that I am saying.

"You know!" she exclaims. "You see! You're beginning to understand! You are primed for adventure. Let's get on with the training, so that you can really enjoy your new life."

She beckons me forward. Exhilarated in a way that is both strange and new to me, I follow her. I imagine that she is guiding me into the training area for Commandos, Shadows, and Specters.

Just for an instant, I pause and turn back to you. I remember that it is you to whom I have been telling my story. My supernatural seeing shows me once again not only where you are, but also who you are. I'm not going to say, "Goodbye." I'll be paying you a visit soon enough.

After my training, I may be around you quite often.

If you follow all the rules, I'll protect you. I'll keep you from making that wrong turn on the freeway or from getting trapped by a sexual predator or a devious friend.

I'll guide you. I'll help you to make the right decision about a job or a lover or about leaving home and branching out on your own.

I'll encourage you. I'll remind you of your good qualities and of your achievements, no matter how small or obscure they seem to you.

If you break the rules, I'll haunt you.

I know you. I know where you live.

One of these days, I'll be visiting you. I'll be the Shadow whispering to your blemished conscience. I'll be the Specter weaving a spell that compels you to help a friend or to resist the evil plotting of an adversary. I'll be the Phantom instilling within your soul ordinary fear or stark terror because of your wrongdoing. I'll be the Shape-shifter, borrowing the identity of your friend or of a stranger and helping you to resolve a complicated relationship or to rescue a despairing acquaintance.

I'll be seeing you, even though you may not always see me.

STUDY GUIDE

VANISHING BY DEGREES
A Novel by David Orsini

AUTHOR'S REMARKS: Students are living in an era when teachers in such states as Ohio and Georgia are being trained to bear arms against assassins. Currently, there are five thousand gun club teams in high schools and universities around the country that teach students self-discipline and self-reliance. Programs such as Faster Saves Lives teach students and teachers how to be prepared in the event of a school shooting. High schools have life-saving trauma training classes that teach students to stanch the bleeding of classmates who have been wounded during mass casualty events. Schools have limited points of entry; doors that lock automatically; foldable bulletproof walls, each with a two-panel barrier that comes out of the wall and provides a protective hiding place for students; first-story windows that slide open and become escape exits from the killers hunting down students and teachers; and evacuation slides that spring forth from second-and third-story windows.

Teens and other readers will recognize that the world portrayed in VANISHING BY DEGREES mirrors the world in which they are now living. It is a world filled with joy, sorrow, and danger. It is a world that does not always allow second chances. It is a world tarnished by racism, misogyny, anti-Semitism, neo-Nazis, and white supremacists. It is a world in which the strong-minded work to redress injustice, to protect the innocent, and to guide wrongdoers to a better path.

VANISHING BY DEGREES offers supernatural elements as well as trenchant realism. It also teaches readers how to be self-reliant and how to achieve worthwhile goals.

In the space below, you will find a list of some of the lessons that VANISHING BY DEGREES offers to readers.

WHAT TEENS AND OTHER READERS WILL LEARN
BY READING **VANISHING BY DEGREES**

- The importance of fair play in their relations with peers
- A respect for and an acceptance of multi-racial and multi-national human beings
- The value of quick-witted thinking when faced with a grievous situation
- The need to learn from mistakes and to resolve the complications arising from them
- The courage to defend the downtrodden
- Compassion for the needy and a willingness to extend a helping hand to those peers struggling with home problems
- The advantages of teaming with peers and with teachers to resolve school crises
- An appreciation of responsible parents and an awareness of the factors that cause irresponsible parents to fail
- The necessity for teamwork if parents and siblings are to build a happy home life
- The life-enhancing and sometimes life-saving effects of bonding with law-abiding peers
- The often fatal and irrevocable consequences of violence
- The punishing recoil of bonding with unethical and immoral peers and adults
- The benefits of joining worthwhile groups such as JROTC and athletic teams
- The intrinsic and pragmatic values of telling the truth
- The importance of accepting the penalties of mistakes, wrongdoing, and crimes

BIOGRAPHICAL NOTES ABOUT SOME PEOPLE IN
VANISHING BY DEGREES

ARI BACHMAN. Ari is seventeen years old and the privileged recipient of an Orthodox Jewish heritage. He has dark, curly hair and a ruddy complexion. He is five feet, eleven inches tall. He has a brawny physique. On Earth, he is a cross-country champion, a first-rate boxer and swimmer, and a formidable goalkeeper for the Green Hills High School soccer team. He is a JROTC cadet. Multilingual (English, French, German, Hebrew), Ari is competitive in all things. He is good-natured at times. Sometimes he is surly. He comes from a privileged background. His father is an eminent cardiologist. His mother is an equally respected pediatrician. Ari has two brothers and a sister.

ALESSANDRO BIANCHI. Alessandro is of Italian heritage. A six-footer, he has handsome, sunburned looks. He also has a sunny disposition. He is an excellent student, boxer, and swimmer. A member of JROTC, he speaks fluent Italian, Spanish, and Portuguese. He is a volunteer at a local soup kitchen and at the Veterans' Hospital, where he also plays guitar and sings Italian, Spanish, and Portuguese ballads. He comes from an upper middle-class background. His father is a Family Court judge. His mother is a university professor. He has one brother and one sister.

CHLOE BRADBURY. Chloe is eighteen years old and of English heritage. She is a beautiful brunette. She is tall and slim. On Earth, she is a model in local television commercials. She is a leading lady in high school musicals. She is excellent at math and science. A volunteer at a soup kitchen, she comes from a middle-class background. Her father is a firefighter. Her mother is a social worker. She has a brother and two sisters.

KURT DREXLER: Kurt is eighteen years old and is descended from a

German-Austrian line. He is tall—6 feet, one inch. Exceptionally good-looking, he is subtly narcissistic. He is a creditable swimmer and an adept soccer and baseball player. He is one of the top five students in Green Hills High School. Multi-lingual, he has attained fluency in German, French, Italian, Spanish, and English. He resided and was educated in Europe for six years when his father, a renowned oncologist, was on the research staff of a Swiss clinic. His mother is a successful playwright with a global following. Kurt enjoyed early admission into Yale, Brown, and Harvard. He chose Yale. He is headed for pre-law undergraduate studies and, afterward, a major law school. His future includes the corporate world and eventually government posts. Duplicity and cold-heartedness function as his secret weapons. He is incapable of genuine feelings for anyone. His scientific detachment closes him off from strong relationships with his peers and with everyone else. He has occasionally expressed neo-Nazi sympathies and racist hatreds to friends who are as amoral and unscrupulous as he is. To the friends who think like him, he calls himself a White Supremacist.

ABIGAIL EMERSON. Abigail is seventeen years old and derives from an English heritage. She is blonde. She stands at five feet, eight inches, and she has a curvaceous figure. She is a fashion plate. Her swim suits, dresses, gowns, jerseys and Capri pants set the bar high for all the other girls on campus. She is a prisoner of her parents' ambitious plans for her swimming career. She is fun loving, but a bit self-centered. She prefers athletic males to sensitive, academic types. A JROTC cadet, she comes from a substantial middle-class background. Her ancestors were among the first settlers in Massachusetts in 1620. Her father is a commercial airline pilot. Her mother is a writer of adventure stories for middle-school girls. She has no siblings.

BRENDA FLYNN. Brenda is an eighteen-year-old Irish girl. She enjoys a Titian-haired prettiness. She stands at an average height and has an hourglass figure. She also has a quiet, caring disposition. She is an accomplished swimmer and tennis and soccer player. She is a JROTC cadet. She is also a talented cabinetmaker. An aged woodworking specialist mentored her in the craft of cabinetmaking. Brenda is self-effacing and trustworthy. She is a good student from a troubled home. She has an alcoholic mother and a war-traumatized father. She has to be a substitute mother for three younger siblings: a sister and two brothers.

BOYD HENDERSON: Tall, handsome, and privileged, Boyd is also self-centered and adventurous. He is an eighteen-year-old world traveler with a Scottish-American heritage. He resents anyone and any creed that wants to diminish his one-of-a-kind individuality and his personal freedom. He is set adrift by careless and successful parents. His father is a famous television news anchor and a documentary film director. His mother is a renowned fashion designer. Often on his own, Boyd cultivates his independence, though not always in positive and life-enhancing ways. Many times, he does do the right things. He earns honor grades. He learns to be a good team player, collaborating with his soccer, swimming, baseball, and boxing mates. But he also drinks too much—bourbon, scotch, and whiskey. He learns to crave all of them. He also experiments with marijuana and cocaine. He drives his Maserati and later his Alfa Romeo and his Ferrari along lonely roads at a hundred-twenty miles an hour. He never crashes a car, though he is wrongly accused and wrongly convicted of doing so. But the car crash and the reformatory come later, after some mistakes he makes ricochet and bring him low. Before that happens, he lives life to the hilt. In summers, he parties on the French Riviera. In winters, he skis on the Swiss Alps. In spring, he kayaks in Finland, and in autumn he hunts red tail stags in Patagonia. In those seasons, he enjoys being with his father and with his loyal teammates. He feels like a wild god. He believes that no one and nothing could ever harm him. He revels in his amazing luck. And always, whether he is in Green Hills or Paris or St. Moritz, he enjoys romances with many girls. Later, when good luck turns away from him and he has to serve time in a rehab center and in a reformatory, Boyd stays tough. He returns to Green Hills High School and wins top honors in athletic and academic competitions. But his adversaries spread false rumors about him that cast a dark cloud upon his reputation. Their hostility and a neo-Nazis gang's murder of Adriana Montalban, the love of his life, destroy his hope, pushing him into madness and murder.

SHILOH JACKSON: Shiloh is an eighteen-year-old Native American. He stands at a medium height. He has a slim physique, light brown skin, and black hair. On Earth, he excels at horse riding, swimming, hockey, and boxing. He is also a JROTC cadet and a drummer in the school band. He maintains a congenial manner most of the time. At other times, he is guarded and brooding. His father was a tried-and-true Marine during the wars in Iraq and Afghanistan. He retired from active duty several years ago and began his career as a radiologist. Shiloh's mother is a landscape painter and a maker of Native American pottery. He has no siblings.

SONIA JANOWSKI: Sonia is seventeen years old. She has a Polish and Jewish heritage. Her paternal grandparents emigrated from Poland to the United States shortly before the Second World War. Their relatives who stayed behind died in the Nazi concentration camps in Dachau. Sonja has amber-blonde hair, blue eyes, and a radiant smile. Math and science draw her special interests. She plans to be a pediatrician. She excels in tennis and swimming. She is also a JROTC cadet. Her father is a gemologist and co-owner of a gemological laboratory and appraisal service. Her mother is a certified public account. Sonia has three brothers and a sister.

JEAN-PIERRE MARCHAND: Jean-Pierre is twenty-eight years old. He has a French heritage. Born in Marseille to American parents, he has dark hair and an olive complexion. He stands at six feet, five inches. He has a rangy physique. During student days in France, he played on rugby and polo teams. He won medals for swimming and academic honors at the Sorbonne and at Cambridge University. Later, as a Major in the Marine Corps, he fought bravely in the war in Afghanistan. Afterwards, he became an impassioned teacher of Advanced French classes. On Earth at Green Hills, Maine, he coaches the soccer team and is the commanding officer in the high school's JROTC program. He is serious, but he also has a buoyant manner. He is respected and well liked. He is an outspoken member of The Scholarship Committee for Students Pursuing The Liberal Arts, The Sciences, and The Industrial Arts. He is engaged to Ms. Patel, a teacher of biology and physics. More than once, Jean-Pierre has stood up to the narrow-minded group that opposes his engagement to an Asian Indian.

JAYDEN MCDONALD. Jayden is eighteen years old. He has an Irish heritage. Tall and good-looking, he has brown hair and blue eyes, as well as a sense of humor. On Earth, he is an excellent soccer player and a first-rate captain of the tennis team. He is a saxophonist, a camp counselor, and a JROTC cadet. His family is wealthy. His father is a bank executive. His mother is a lawyer.

ADRIANA MONTALBAN: Adriana is a Latina. A dark-haired, life-loving beauty, she is drawn to the arts. On Earth, she achieves superb performances with the school's Modern Dance Group. She also regards math and science as her favorite subjects. She plans to become a pediatrician. Her keen mind, supple body, and inherent discipline help her to become a proficient JROTC cadet. All these accomplishments make her parents very proud of her. Her father had served as a Special Forces captain in the United States Army during the war in Afghanistan. He is now a pharmacist. Her mother is an elementary school teacher in a Latinx ghetto. Adriana has three younger siblings: two brothers and a sister. During her senior year, she begins a romance with Boyd Henderson. She becomes the love of his life. Boyd regards Adriana as a special gift that his good angel has sent him. She is the reward he has earned because he put his life back on the proper track. When the neo-Nazis kill Adriana, Boyd loses hope, and in a moment of madness he kills thirteen people. In Sojourn, Adriana meets Boyd after he, too, has died. She inspires him to become a new and better person if The Five Spirits allow their group to go back in time so that they can alter the tragedy that has happened to them.

MS. KAVYA PATEL. Ms. Patel is twenty-six, and she is of Asian Indian heritage. She was born in the northwestern Indian state of Gujarat. She has jet-black hair and an oval, brown-skinned face. She has dazzling brown eyes, a turned-up nose, and sensual lips. She is a natural beauty with medium height and a slim figure. She is a gifted teacher of physics and biology. She earned degrees in the sciences and in nursing during her years of study at Oxford University and at Yale University. She served as a machine gunner in the First Battalion of the Marine Corps during the war in Iraq. She is self-assured yet demure. On Earth, she is a defender of women's rights, a JROTC instructor, and a volunteer at Women's & Children's Hospital. She is engaged to Mr. Marchand, an Advanced French teacher. Ms. Patel bravely confronts the prejudice directed at her because of her Asian Indian heritage and because she is engaged to an American.

JASON TENG. Jason is seventeen years old. He is Chinese. He is tall, dark-haired, and lithe. On Earth, he is a brilliant mathematician and an ingenious computer technician. He is an accomplished swimmer and a gifted violinist. He is also a creative writer. A first-rate JROTC cadet, he is self-assured, yet humble. He has always been a loyal friend to his classmates. He comes from a wealthy background. His father is a broker of upscale real estate and the owner of a Boston hotel and six waterfront properties in Camden, Maine. Jason's mother is a homemaker. He has two sisters.

DION WILLIAMS. At age eighteen, Dion is a very tall African-American. He stands at six feet, six inches. On Earth, he is a terrific basketball player and baseball player. He is aiming for a pro basketball career. At school, he forms a jazz group with Jayden McDonald and calls it Swingers. Dion is a JROTC cadet. He is also a savvy auto-mechanic. He owns a 2010 Ferrari. He enjoys the company of several girlfriends. He comes from a middle-class background. His father is a research scientist for a pharmaceutical company. His mother is a medical radiation technologist. He has one sister.

CASSANDRA WINSLOW: Cassandra is eighteen years old for most of the novel. She is of Scottish heritage, and she stands at a medium height. She has caramel-brown hair, blue eyes, and fair skin. She has an impulsive nature. She has the gift of foresight, but few persons believe her predictions. Bitter because so many adults compel her to follow their rules and because her boyfriend has spurned her, she devises plots against her boyfriend and against the adult leaders who impose too many rules upon her. She is a good swimmer and an even better horse rider. In Green Hills, Maine, she is a member of The Governor's Committee for Improving Secondary Schools, a JROTC cadet, and a political activist. She is a defender of equal rights for women in the business world. She supports the #MeToo Movement. Her father is a patent attorney: a founding principal of his firm. He has represented university and corporate clients for over twenty years in intellectual property matters in many fields, including chemistry, chemical engineering, biotechnology, pharmaceuticals and medical devices. Cassandra's mother, a former airline stewardess, is now an executive secretary for a judge in Maine's Supreme Judicial Court. Cassandra has one brother and one sister.

THE FIVE SPIRITS

MRS. HAROLD (MAGGIE) ADAMS: Mrs. Adams is big-bodied, tough-minded, and unsentimental. A sister to Ms. Melanie Dickinson, she spent her Earthly life in Boston, Massachusetts. She died of natural causes when she was in her nineties. In Sojourn, she appears as a woman "nearly forty"—about thirty-eight. On Earth, she was a registered nurse who assisted her husband in his practice of internal medicine. When she was thirty-eight, a teen-age serial killer shot down her husband and their three children at a ski resort in Aspen, Colorado. When she died many years later, she was reunited with them in Sojourn. Yet Mrs. Adams is a bitter and often unforgiving Spirit/woman.

MISS MELANIE DICKINSON: In Sojourn, Miss Dickinson appears as a blue-eyed blonde woman of twenty-two, even though she died when she was ninety-two. The man that she loved saw her on Earth for the last time when she was twenty-two. That was the year when her fiancé, Captain Randall Johnson, was killed in the Second World War. After she dies on Earth, she is reunited with her fiancé, Captain Randall Johnson. On Earth, she was a self-assured woman. She owned a successful dress shop in Boston. She also designed an impressive line of dresses and gowns that became a national brand. In Sojourn, she is a temperate and good-natured mediator.

CAPTAIN RANDALL JOHNSON: In the courtroom setting within Sojourn, Captain Johnson makes a formidable presence, anchored as it is to his brisk manner and his military bearing. Standing at six foot, six inches as he enters the room and joins his colleagues at the interviewers' table, he is a very tall man. He is also a young man. Despite all the years that have passed since his earthly death, he has remained twenty-two, the age he was when his plane was shot down during an aerial battle over Berlin in July 1943. His brown-haired handsomeness still wears traces of battle fatigue and wartime bitterness. He rarely smiles. Beneath his no-nonsense demeanor, there lives a harnessed rage against the criminality, potential or activated, of most human beings. He is a prosecuting attorney. He is the fully embodied Spirit who may prevent wrongdoers from returning to Earth. He well may be their executioner.

Captain Johnson is, nevertheless, an honorable man. Miss Melanie Dickinson is the love of his life, the one bright spark that stirs his ardor for her and influences his hard-won forgiveness of some wrongdoers. Captain Johnson is also an emblem of Stern Justice.

MRS. ROBERT (AMELIA) STEERFORTH: She is the wife of Robert Steerforth, one of the Spirit leaders in Sojourn. She is a well-groomed, sophisticated woman. While she was alive on Earth, she had hosted many grand parties for her husband's business associates and their wives. She also led fund drives for the poor and the disabled and for high school graduates in need of college scholarships. Those are impressive credentials that convince most of the group that she is on their side. But Cassandra recognizes her type. Beneath the decorum, there exists a cynical view of human beings and an unforgiving nature. In Sojourn, Mrs. Steerforth appears as a woman of forty, though she died when she was in her nineties. Her auburn hair is pulled back to make a neat coil at the nape of her neck. If you saw her, you would probably say that her oval face, her hazel eyes and upturned nose, and her sculpted cheekbones make her a lovely woman. But Cassandra, her peers, and their two teachers regard Mrs. Steerforth's occasionally kind manner and her sometimes-heartening words as more important than her attractive appearance.

MR. ROBERT STEERFORTH: On Earth, Mr. Steerforth died of a brain aneurysm when he was forty-two. At that time, he was a vice-president of a steel corporation in Pennsylvania. He died when he was addressing a symposium of business leaders in Brazil. He died suddenly, without a chance to say goodbye to his wife or to their two sons and their daughter. In Sojourn, his lanky body sometimes glows. Its amber sheen moves in and out of brightness that on their first day in Sojourn leaves Cassandra and her group amazed. Cassandra wonders whether he is a god or some holy messenger. Whenever the brightness covering him becomes dim, she and her group see Mr. Steerforth as the man he must have been in the moment that he died. His oblong face, with its forehead, cheekbones, and jawline similar in size; his slightly tousled dark hair; and his well-groomed beard give him the look of a college professor who may be in his mid-thirties or even forty. Mr. Steerforth is honest, reliable, and fair-minded.

QUESTIONS FOR REFLECTION, WRITING, & DISCUSSION

CHAPTER ONE
ARRIVAL

1. The story is told in the first person. Who is speaking? Why does the author, David Orsini, choose a first-person narrator to tell the story rather than tell the story in the third person? What does an author gain by this choice?

2. What happens to the narrator in the moment that her Spirit springs free of her earthbound body?

3. "Right away, we know where we stand with him," the narrator, Cassandra Winslow, says of Mr. Steerforth. What kind of relationship with him does she anticipate? Why does she fear Mr. Steerforth?

4. Describe Ari Bachman in the scene in which he cries out his anguish. What achievements had he made in high school?

5. The Committee of Five Spirits wants to interrogate the eleven students and two teachers who have newly arrived in Sojourn. What is the purpose of their questioning?

6. What happened to Boyd Henderson after the school shooting? What may happen to him when he is brought before the Five Spirits?

7. Miss Dickinson offers more information to the group about their public confessions. What must they tell the committee interrogating them?

8. Near the end of this chapter, why do Mr. Steerforth's words astonish the group?

LOOKING BACK AT THIS CHAPTER

A. Write a summary of this chapter, using not more than six or seven sentences.

B. Write a description of a character who figures importantly in the events that occur in this chapter. Explain why this character is important.

CHAPTER TWO
HIDING AND VANISHING

1. According to Mrs. Adams, how should the eleven students and their two teachers conduct themselves when the Evaluation Committee questions them?
2. What does Cassandra Winslow, the narrator, tell the reader about her speech patterns?
3. Why does Cassandra connect the group to the number thirteen?
4. Describe Dion Williams. What makes him laugh with genuine happiness during the group's meeting with Mr. Steerforth?
5. How do these students learn how to vanish? How do they make themselves reappear?
6. According to this early chapter, who will decide whether the students and their teachers can go back to Earth? What will they expect the students and their teachers to perceive?
7. List the questions that Cassandra raises for the reader in the last pages of this chapter.
8. Why does Cassandra dread the experience of confronting the Five Spirits?

LOOKING BACK AT THIS CHAPTER

A. Write a summary of this chapter, using not more than six or seven sentences.
B. Write a paragraph that reflects Cassandra's definition of herself and that explains the language that she uses.

CHAPTER THREE
PRELIMINARY RULES

1. Describe Captain Randall Johnson.
2. What may happen if the eleven students and their two teachers are allowed to replay their last days on Earth?
3. "We want to find out whether you know yourselves," Captain Johnson tells the group. What two questions does he want them to answer about themselves?
4. To what settings and experiences does Captain Johnson compare the meeting that involves the eleven students, their two teachers, and the Five Spirits?
5. The Five Spirits plan to question Ari Bachman and Cassandra Winslow about the school shooting. What does the reader learn about Ari's activities in his high school? What does the reader learn about his parents?
6. What does the reader learn about Cassandra's relationship with her classmates? What do we learn about her father? In what way does Cassandra react while the group studies her?
7. "We didn't pull the trigger of that AR-15," Ari says about himself and Cassandra. What angry response does Mrs. Adams make after she hears Ari's remark?
8. In the closing pages of this chapter, Mr. Steerforth repeats the rules that the eleven students and two teachers must follow if the committee calls upon them to testify about their lives on Earth. List the rules.

LOOKING BACK AT THIS CHAPTER

A. Write a summary of this chapter, using not more than six or seven sentences.
B. In six or seven sentences, summarize the tensions and the conflicts that flare up in this chapter.

CHAPTER FOUR
ARI BACHMAN

1. What does Cassandra tell the reader about her parents?
2. Summarize the story of the mythical Cassandra, the daughter of King Priam and Queen Hecuba. In what way was the god Apollo involved with the mythical Cassandra?
3. Three incidents convinced Cassandra Winslow's parents that she could see into the future. Summarize those incidents.
4. What does Ari tell the committee about his relationship with his parents and about the tasks he performed at home?
5. Describe Boyd Henderson's GTC4 Lusso.
6. Why does Ari sometimes have to drive Boyd's automobile?
7. Describe Captain Johnson's eerie appearance when he becomes angry as he questions Ari. What questions does his anger rouse in Cassandra's mind and, possibly, in the minds of the other ten students?
8. Explain how Ari resolves the problem with the students who mistreat him because he is Jewish. Do you believe that he handled the problem in a realistic way? What was right about the way he resolved the problem? What was wrong about it?

LOOKING BACK AT THIS CHAPTER

A. Write a summary of this chapter, using no more than six or seven sentences.
B. Write a paragraph that explains the tensions and the conflicts that look back to what has already happened and that look forward to what may happen.

CHAPTER FIVE
THE NIGHT OF THE DANCE

1. Why, according to Ari, did he choose to enter Boyd's car and place himself in a dangerous situation?

2. Describe the accident that occurred when Ari was driving the Ferrari.

3. What deception did Boyd's girlfriend and Ari devise against Boyd Henderson?

4. Describe the transformation that overtakes Captain Johnson as his anger reaches a new pitch.

5. The Captain blasts Ari "with another volley of accusations." What are these accusations?

6. In what way did Boyd Henderson cause the night of the dance to go "haywire"?

7. Drawing upon specific details from the text, summarize what, according to Ari, happened after the car crash.

8. What is the committee's opinion of Ari after he gives his testimony about the night of the dance?

LOOKING BACK AT THIS CHAPTER

A. Write two paragraphs that explore the main themes or dominant ideas of this chapter. Mention specific details that the author uses to develop these themes.

B. Write a paragraph that explains how this chapter contributes to the development of the story that the novel is setting forth.

CHAPTER SIX
BOYD HENDERSON'S GIRLFRIEND

1. When she calls out Cassandra Winslow's name, what words does Mrs. Adams use to describe her?
2. Why did Cassandra turn against Boyd Henderson?
3. In what way did Cassandra and Ari lie about Boyd on the night of the dance?
4. How did Boyd's life deteriorate after Cassandra and Ari lied about him?
5. In what ways did Ms. Patel and Mr. Marchand help Boyd?
6. How did Cassandra "set Boyd up for a fall"? What lies did Cassandra spread about Boyd after his detention in a reformatory and his ninety days in rehab?
7. Describe Boyd Henderson's life at home. Comment upon his relationship with his father.
8. Mr. Steerforth asks Ari whether he would do anything differently if he had the chance to relive the year in which the car crash took place. How does Ari respond to the question?

LOOKING BACK AT THIS CHAPTER

A. Using no more than six or seven sentences, write a paragraph that summarizes the major conflicts in this chapter.
B. Write a paragraph about the important themes in this chapter. Mention specific details that support your answer.

CHAPTER SEVEN
BRENDA FLYNN

1. Which of Cassandra's powers have the Five Spirits diminished? What powers does she possess?
2. Summarize Cassandra's definitions of the noun *defendant*.
3. How did Captain Johnson and Cassandra acquire "a hardness of heart"? How is Cassandra's hardheartedness different from the Captain's?
4. "We are always vanishing from one another," Cassandra tells the reader. Summarize the ways that we "vanish" while we are alive on Earth.
5. What values does Brenda share with Chloe Bradbury and Alessandro Bianchi? Describe the appearances of Chloe and Alessandro. What achievements had they already experienced?
6. Describe the painting that Boyd created for his Art class. Why does Cassandra call it "an allegory of his life"?
7. In what ways did Alessandro, Shiloh, and Dion help Boyd when he returned to Green Hills High School after spending time in a reformatory and in rehab?
8. Summarize the lies that Boyd's enemies spread about him.

LOOKING BACK AT THIS CHAPTER

A. Drawing upon information and specific details that the author provides in this chapter, write two paragraphs in which you compare and contrast the characters of Captain Randall Johnson and Cassandra Winslow.
B. Write a paragraph about the primary themes in this chapter.

CHAPTER EIGHT
KURT DREXLER'S PLOT

1. Summarize the information that Cassandra tells the reader about Kurt Drexler. Mention details about his appearance, his achievements in school, his parents, his career plans, his travels, and his personal beliefs.
2. Summarize the information that Cassandra tells the group about the Leopold-Loeb case. Why were she and Kurt drawn to the philosophy of Friedrich Nietzsche? Whom did Richard Loeb kill? In what ways was Nathan Leopold an accessory to the killing? What led the Chicago police to Nathan Leopold?
3. What does Cassandra say about Leopold and Loeb? What finally happened to them?
4. Describe the pact that Cassandra makes with Boyd.
5. Summarize the information that Cassandra tells the reader about Adriana Montalban.
6. What is the "horrible crime" that Cassandra and Kurt plot against Adriana Montalban?
7. Abigail Emerson and Chloe Bradbury scream their accusations against Cassandra, Kurt, and the four boys who murdered Adriana. What words do Abigail and Chloe use against the wrongdoers?
8. What promise does Cassandra make at the end of the chapter?

LOOKING BACK AT THIS CHAPTER

A. Using no more than seven or eight sentences, write a paragraph that examines the character of Kurt Drexler. Remember to draw upon specific details from the text to support your answer.
B. Write two paragraphs that explore the primary themes or dominant ideas in this chapter.

CHAPTER NINE
THREE DEATHS

1. Summarize the meeting between Kurt and Cassandra. What words does she speak to dissuade him from the plan to kill Adriana Montalban? How does Kurt respond to her urging him to withdraw from the plan? What relationships make him feel powerless?

2. How do Kurt's parents respond to Cassandra's visit? What do they do that is right? What do they do that is wrong?

3. In what ways does Boyd Henderson change after the murder of Adriana? Provide specific details.

4. Cassandra says that, "when Adriana Montalban died, Boyd Henderson died with her. I died, too." What are her reasons for believing that she has "died"?

5. Describe the skydiving episode that involves Cassandra, Ari, Dion, Shiloh, and Boyd. Why did his classmates wonder whether skydiving was a realistic option for Boyd? What do the owners of the skydiving school tell them that dissolves their apprehension? From what plane did they jump? How did Boyd respond to the experience of skydiving?

6. What happens after Stefan and Bram brag about having committed "the perfect murder"? What does Shiloh say as he protests Stefan's and Bram's bad conduct at the party? How do the police become involved in the days that follow the party?

7. Who are the persons that the police chief and a local detective question at Green Hills High school? What does this group tell the police chief and the detective about Boyd?

8. Who, according to Mr. Steerforth, is "the most essential person of all" in the quest to discover the motives behind the tragedy that took so many lives?

LOOKING BACK AT THIS CHAPTER

A. In no more than seven or eight sentences, write a paragraph that explains why a reader may both pity and despise Cassandra. Support your answer with specific details from this chapter.

B. In a paragraph of seven or eight sentences, explain how this chapter further develops the plot line of the novel.

CHAPTER TEN
BOYD HENDERSON

1. Why did Mrs. Adams scream at Boyd and spring from her chair to attack him?

2. According to Cassandra, Boyd looks "battle-hardened and impassive." She compares him to "a gunnery sergeant from the Marine Corps." What other words does she use to describe his military manner? How is Boyd's war different from that fought by a Marine?

3. The Captain addresses Boyd "killer to killer." Contrast situations that have caused the Captain and Boyd to kill. When did Boyd lose his soul? Who killed Boyd first of all? What were the circumstances that led to Boyd's first death?

4. Summarize the information that Boyd tells the group about his background. Mention what the reader learns about his mother and his father.

5. Describe the success Boyd achieved when he returned to Green Hills High School.

6. With a wave of his hand, Captain Johnson "transforms Boyd's appearance." Describe what happens to Boyd's appearance. What is the Captain unable to alter about Boyd?

7. Why does Cassandra believe that the committee will not find her acceptable? Why does she not know what will finally happen to the group and to herself?

8. At the end of this chapter, the group waits for three happenings. What are they?

LOOKING BACK AT THIS CHAPTER

A. In a paragraph of seven or eight sentences, explain the tensions and conflicts that dominate this chapter. Draw upon specific details from the text.

B. Write two paragraphs about the essential themes or major ideas that the author sets forth in this chapter. Use specific details from the text to support your assertions.

CHAPTER ELEVEN
CONFESSIONS, DOUBTS, AND PROMISES

1. Describe Adriana Montalban's appearance.
2. Adriana wants to know what caused Boyd Henderson to break apart. How does Cassandra respond to the question? How does Ms. Patel respond to the same question?
3. Summarize Cassandra's confession. Your answer should refer to her relationships with Boyd and with Kurt Drexler. How does Adriana respond when she learns about the plot that led to her murder?
4. What had Adriana been taught about the innocent and the brave? What had she been taught about second chances?
5. Describe the changes in Boyd's face when he appears to Adriana. What does Cassandra mean when she tells the reader about the "new moral acuity" within Boyd?
6. According to Boyd, who is to blame for the school massacre?
7. If the group is allowed to return to Earth, in what ways will their return be a test for them?
8. At the end of this chapter, how does Adriana describe her relationship with Boyd? What promise does he make to her?

LOOKING BACK AT THIS CHAPTER

1. Using no more than seven or eight sentences, write a summary of this chapter.
2. Write a paragraph that explains how the meeting between Boyd and Adriana is anchored to the theme of transformation.

CHAPTER TWELVE
VERDICTS

1. Summarize Cassandra's review of the procedure that the Spirits have been imposing upon the trial. Who will be the presiding judge? Who are the six Spirits who will serve as jurors? In what room will the jurors set forth their verdicts?

2. Summarize Mrs. Adams's "blistering tirade" against Cassandra. What remarks does Mrs. Adams make about Brenda and Alessandro? Why, in her opinion, do Sonia, Jason, Dion, and Shiloh deserve praise?

3. What does Cassandra mean when she says that the Spirits destroyed Mrs. Adams's empathy when they refused to send her husband and her children back to Earth? What does Mrs. Adams mean when she calls Cassandra "a blight" upon the group?

4. Summarize Mrs. Steerforth's verdict. What praise does she offer the group? What does she say about Abigail and Chloe? What does she say about Ari? Why will the group need "a great deal of courage" if they return to Earth?

5. Summarize Mr. Marchand's verdict. Why is he especially interested in Miss Patel's judgment?

6. Summarize Mr. Steerforth's verdict. Who are the students and what are the facts that influenced his verdict?

7. Summarize Miss Dickinson's verdict. Summarize her advice to the group if they win the chance to return to Earth. What dangers must the group be prepared to meet? According to Miss Dickinson, what are the strongest forces and where do they live?

8. What is Captain Johnson's verdict? What are the liabilities that the group faces when they return to Earth? What is the mission of each person who is returning to Earth?

LOOKING BACK AT THIS CHAPTER

A. Using no more than seven or eight sentences, explain how the author develops the theme of judgment in this chapter.

B. Write two paragraphs that explain how the judgments set forth by the Five Spirits and the two teachers reveal aspects of their personalities.

CHAPTER THIRTEEN
THE FIRST TEST

1. To what night does the group return after they find themselves back on Earth? Do Boyd, Ari, and Sonia recall what happened a year earlier? How will this night challenge the four students who have returned to it?

2. Summarize what happens on the night of the junior prom. How is the evening different from the way it unfolded a year earlier? In what ways is the behavior of Cassandra and Ari different?

3. Describe the eerie sounds and images that Cassandra observes as she and Ari trudge toward the farmhouse.

4. Describe Cassandra's reaction when she sees the bodies of the murdered man and woman.

5. Describe the man who attacks Cassandra.

6. What does Cassandra do to rescue Ari?

7. What does Cassandra tell us about the killer, Max Rowley?

8. Ari accepts full responsibility for the crash. What brings him the sympathy of the public? How does the judge view Ari's case? What are the good qualities that Cassandra and Ari have revealed during this replay of their junior prom night?

LOOKING BACK AT THIS CHAPTER

A. Using no more than seven or eight sentences, explain how the main action of this chapter changes what had occurred a year earlier.

B. Write a paragraph about the courage that Ari and Cassandra reveal in this chapter.

CHAPTER FOURTEEN
THE SECOND TEST

1. Cassandra tells the reader that Kurt Drexler has "the look of the street-wise toughs that he has often ridiculed." She also mentions that Kurt is different from those "toughs." How has Kurt's privileged background made him quite different from those "toughs"? Provide details about his schooling and his athletic training.

2. What are the "temperate words" that Cassandra chooses to save Kurt from himself and to keep her friends and her teachers "out of harm's way"?

3. Describe Kurt as he appears in the paragraph that begins with these words: "Kurt meets this spate of words with a grin."

4. According to Cassandra, Kurt won't let go of his plan to commit "the perfect crime." What does she predict that Kurt will do to carry out his murder plan?

5. Why doesn't Cassandra alert her parents, her teachers, and the school principal about Kurt's murder plot? What troubling episodes does she predict that involve not only state troopers and guardsmen, but also experienced journalists?

6. Summarize the episode in which Cassandra alerts Adriana about the danger facing them. At first, upon hearing Cassandra's warning, how does Adriana respond? With what words does Cassandra answer Adriana's question: "How do we try to save ourselves?"

7. Summarize Gregor's and Werner's vicious attack upon Cassandra and Adriana. How do the girls defend themselves? Provide specific details about Werner's attack upon Cassandra. Tell about Adriana's important part in this episode.

8. Why does Cassandra call Fate "an ambivalent acquaintance"?

LOOKING BACK AT THIS CHAPTER

A. Using no more than seven or eight sentences, write a paragraph that explains the second test that Adriana and Cassandra confront.

B. In a paragraph of seven or eight sentences, compare and contrast Adriana and Cassandra.

CHAPTER FIFTEEN
THE THIRD TEST

1. At the beginning of this chapter, what does Cassandra's foresight show her? How will Kurt Drexler be involved? Develop your answer with specific details.

2. Why will Kurt and his secret murder club be tracking down Adriana, Boyd, Ari, and Cassandra? Provide specific details.

3. Describe with specific details the protective strategies that school districts located near Green Hills High School ("neighboring school districts") are activating against school assassins?

4. In what ways does Cassandra's behavior change toward her classmates and her parents?

5. What does Cassandra tell the reader about Miss Patel's combat service? Describe Mr. Worthington's military experience. In what ways does he contribute to the plan for defending the school against assassins?

6. Describe the protective measures that students and teachers take to defend themselves against assassins. Summarize several paragraphs that begin with these words: "With the permission of the superintendent, we equip some doors in our school with a bolo stick…"

7. Summarize the White Supremacists' and neo-Nazis' attack against the school. What happens to Kurt Drexler and his gang? Who kills Kurt? What happens to Boyd Henderson, Ari Bachman, and Adriana Montalban?

8. What "future roles" will Cassandra fulfill in the Afterlife?

LOOKING BACK AT THIS CHAPTER

A. Using no more than seven or eight sentences, summarize the main action of this chapter.

B. In a paragraph of seven or eight sentences, describe Cassandra's future.

To view further information about books by David Orsini, please visit www.quaternitybooks.com. A TEACHER'S GUIDE is available exclusively to secondary school teachers and administrators. Visit www.quaternitybooks.com.